THE
ASSASSIN'S
PRODIGY

THE ELITE SOCIETY OF CHARACTER ASSASSINS

BETH CIOTTA

BC

PRAISE FOR BETH CIOTTA'S NOVELS

"Freaks, Mods, Vics, Flatliners, cowboys in airships, evil scientists, nefarious flying pirates, and time travel. Victorian England was never so much fun. Ciotta's whimsical steampunk romance, the first in the Glorious Victorious Darcy series, is too good to miss." –Starred review, *Book List* (on *Her Sky Cowboy*)

"Ciotta's delightfully imaginative steampunk historical has just the right mix of adventure and romance." *–Chicago Tribune* (on *Her Sky Cowboy*)

"Ciotta has written another imaginative, whirlwind adventure, featuring a daring hero and a spirited heroine, incredible inventions, and übernefarious villains." *—Booklist*, starred review (on *His Clockwork Canary*)

"Filled with humor, heart and touch of mystery, this is a truly magical book." *–Born to Read Books* (on *Beauty & the Biker*)

"Deep love of family and strong dialogue bolster a refreshing romance that focuses on the emotional rather than the physical." *–Publishers Weekly* (on *In the Mood for Love*)

A genre-bending tale of monster mayhem
and forbidden love…

"Can you enlighten me?" I rasp. "Regarding my situation, that is?"

"Partially. Although I doubt you will believe me. The extent to which you have been sheltered, Miss Albright is both impressive and infuriating."

Tears burn my eyes. "My life feels like one big fat lie."

"Your life, as you know it, is a lie."

The concept sickens me, but instead of curling into a tighter ball, I force myself to unfurl. Propped against the wall, I glare at the self-professed century-old warrior. "Should I be afraid of you?"

"If you're smart, you'll trust me."

The adventure begins...

ONE

One Writer's Nightmare

IT SEEMED LIKE A GOOD IDEA.

Moving out of Aunt Liza's house and renting a place of my own. I'm an adult, after all. The woman who sheltered and raised me for most of my twenty-one years deserves a charmed life with her new husband without a uniquely challenged prodigy underfoot.

I told her that her work was done. She was, I think, relieved. My quirks are exhausting. Coupled with her controlling tendencies, our relationship frayed with the years.

Parting ways was easier than I imagined.

I leased a little cabin nestled in the pines with a majestic view of the mountains. Far enough from the nearest town to be sufficiently isolated, but close enough to have most anything I want or need delivered.

Paradise for a social misfit and reclusive writer.

Sanctuary for a clairaudient freak.

I relished my freedom. Embraced the challenge. Counted my blessings.

I know how to keep the voices at bay. I know how to channel my imagination. I'm happy and self-sufficient.

Or at least I was.

Eight months into my hard-won independence and I, Zoe Albright (prolific author of a kids book series), am floundering. Artistically and financially.

I didn't see it coming. Never thought in a million years my muse would rebel. We've been together forever, Penny and me.

Now we're at odds.

Tonight I'm at my wits' end. Bills are piling up. Walls are closing in. My once cozy cabin is now claustrophobic. I haven't felt this angry or alone in a very long time. I want to call Liza, but I won't.

"I've survived worse things than writer's block."

Determined to invent a suitable proposal before sunrise, I'm jogging on my treadmill and watching cartoons. A runner's high and visual inspiration. Fresh air and a bracing walk would be even better, but it's the middle of the night and there are bears in them thar woods.

"And a vampyric jackalope."

"Shut up, Penny. No! Wait! Keep talking!"

In my stunned excitement, I trip over my feet, lose my grip, and tumble off the treadmill. I spring from an undignified heap, my ankle screaming as I lunge for a pad and pencil. "Give me something! Anything! A title. A concept."

This is the first time I've heard Penny's voice in five days. I'm giddy with relief. It doesn't matter that I don't see her. I *hear* her. Her presence obliterates my suffocating solitude. A friend is a friend—even if she's imaginary.

"Welcome back." Heart pounding, I mute the TV and hunker on the sofa to brainstorm. "I was beginning to think... Never mind. This is awesome. This is great. Let's just do what we do. What we use to do. I'll empty my head and you fill it."

I breathe. I wait. I hope against hope that Penny's back to her silly old self. Any second now she'll prompt, *"What if..."* igniting a creative discussion. Or she'll throw out a one-liner. A title. Like the one that launched my writing career.

I breathe. I wait. I listen. I write.

~~Penelope Pringle and the Vexed Vampire~~
~~Penelope Pringle vs Wolfman~~
The Strange Case of Penelope Pringle and the Sadistic...

"Seriously? For Pete's sake, Penny, throw me a bone! Something warm, wacky, and wonderful!"

She doesn't respond. I assume it's due to her recent obsession with monsters, murder, and mayhem.

"Why can't you get off the gruesome train?"

"Because they're coming."

I'm sweaty from my indoor jog, yet her eerie taunt ices my spine.

I stare at the scribbled titles, anxious and frustrated with the gory scenarios polluting my brain. Mourning the train wreck of our whimsical partnership, I look across my cluttered living room and focus on the framed and pristine publicity poster hanging above my messy desk. A poster that promotes my name and the cover of our debut book:

The Secret Life of Penelope Pringle: Wings of Joy

Under the whimsical font of the title is a vibrant illustration of my imaginary childhood friend turned muse turned protagonist—Penny P.

Bright smile. Piercing blue eyes. Bountiful blond curls. A mischievous free-spirit who dwells in a fictional city in a fantasized version of Victorian, England. Although her 1800s gown is somewhat conventional, her hat is not. Instead of a frou-frou bonnet, she sports a crimson top hat with an exaggerated yellow sash and bow. And goggles. She needs goggles since she often soars through the skies at breakneck speed on her flycycle—a steam propelled bicycle that, upon initiation, sprouts wings.

I smile just thinking about Penelope's delightful shenanigans along with her canine sidekick, Balderdash.

But then my gaze slides to my laptop. My temples throb. Resentment flares.

I curse the multiple dreary proposals stored in my computer files along with pages and pages of handwritten notes now crumpled in the trash bin. "Why did you go dark on me, Penny?"

"Why won't you take me seriously?"

"Because I don't do scary. Because I, we, have a brand."

"We, you, have bigger fish to fry. Like an evil mad scientist intent on global domination!"

"To think I was thrilled to hear from you." I squeeze the pencil I've worn to a nub and jot a plot premise entirely of my own design. Two sentences in, I run dry. I jot another idea and then another, tuning out Penny's ominous influence the way I tune out whispers from the grave.

Scrambling, a unique skill I developed for reducing disembodied voices to a mostly incoherent hum, is effective, but draining, hence my obsession with energy-infused food and drink.

Focusing on a gore-free plot with the requisite happy ending, I race into the kitchen in search of a cupcake.

If I can power through another oppressive night, maybe the sun will shine tomorrow. Maybe I'll be inspired to write about a plucky girl and her talking dog and their latest rip-roaring steampunk adventure. I'm not cut out for creepy who-dunnits and otherworldly crises.

That was my mother's gig.

Victoria Albright had a psychic connection to people who died, but couldn't cross over. Ghosts, spirits, apparitions, specters, phantoms. Unfortunately, I inherited her heightened sixth sense. Or as I've come to think of it: her *Misfortune*.

Bemoaning my supernatural *gift*, I devour a double chocolate brownie in two crazed bites.

Despite the fortifying sugar rush, Penny breaks through my mental wall of white noise. *"You need help, Zoe."*

"I've heard that before."

"I'm not talking about a shrink."

"So what, a diet guru? A collaborator? An optimistic *muse*?"

"An assassin."

"A nefarious sort." *Snort.* "I should have known."

Fed up, panicked, and determined to crank out a plot that will please my editor, I chug a chilled can of Energy X and nab a tin of sugar wafers.

"I don't want to shut you out of my life, Penny," I say as my

Scrambler kicks into high gear, "but if you can't help me, I need to look elsewhere for inspiration."

My livelihood, and life, depend on it.

†

I wake with crumbs on my shirt, a crick in my neck, and an ugly-bad attitude.

I never made it to bed, but I did fall asleep on the couch. Unfortunately, Penny followed me into my dreams along with a mysterious and seductive assassin. A nameless, faceless man who caused me to toss and turn with apprehension and an equal dose of desire. One minute we were fighting side-by-side, kicking *vampyric jackalope* ass. The next we were tangled in sheets doing the nasty and swearing allegiance.

I assume my pulse-pounding delusions are due to sexual frustration and a bone-deep longing for the kind of love I'm convinced I'll never have. I'm pretty sure I'm doomed to be alone. I can't imagine a sane man willing to engage in a long-term partnership with a freak like me.

"Thanks a lot," I say while glaring at Penny's poster. "Like I need something else to obsess on."

She smiles back at me, frozen in time. Better times. Happy times.

Wings of Joy.

I consider ripping her cheery likeness from the wall. It only reminds me of what she once was—what we've accomplished as a team. I'm beginning to wonder if I'll ever produce another uplifting proposal. If I'll ever finish another book. My publisher's been wondering the same thing for weeks.

Stomach churning, I zip into the bathroom, swig chalky

white stuff, pee, and then wash my hands and face without so much as a glance in the mirror. It's not like I have to impress anyone. I'm not going anywhere. I rarely do.

Twisting my long, curly hair into a messy topknot, I hustle toward the kitchen. A shower and fresh clothes can wait. In spite of gorging on sweets a few hours ago, I'm famished. Also, I'm expecting a call.

I toss a frozen breakfast burrito into the microwave, press 'brew' on my coffee maker—preset for eight cups.

As promised, my phone rings at precisely nine-o-clock. I imagine my editor (two hours ahead of me) sitting in her New York office sipping a latte and revising manuscripts—none of them mine.

"How did it go last night?" Julia asks.

"I got nothin'. Unless you're open to a story about a murderous, psychotic freak."

"Yikes."

"Tell me about it."

I don't know what's worse. My shrinking confidence, my editor's disappointment, or the hordes of emails from little kids and their parents begging for Penelope's next tale. There's also the matter of my compromised bank account—a misery of my own making.

"Do you know what the editorial and marketing team discussed this morning?" Julia asks. "The production schedule two years down the pike. And you're not on it. You're shooting your career in the foot, Zoe, not to mention the damage to your finances."

I nibble my spicy egg burrito while peering out my kitchen window—at the vast expanse between my isolated cabin and the Grand Teton Mountains. I soak up the beauty and serenity of Wyoming and brace for a storm. Up until now, Julia has been sympathetic to my dry spell, handling me with kid gloves. Today she sounds all business which only intensifies the gloom that's been dogging me for days. "I've submitted eight different proposals over the last several months."

"Dark, gruesome stories," she needlessly reminds me. "Fine if you're a horror novelist, but you're Zoe Albright. You write whimsical children's adventures starring a Victorian street urchin with an optimistic outlook and enduring spirit."

Not anymore.

"Every author I've ever worked with suffers sporadic creative paralysis, Zoe. It's not uncommon. Just write whatever comes to mind and you'll eventually break through."

Except *whatever comes to mind* these days is ominous.

"I'd suggest a change of scenery," Julia goes on, "but since you're a shut in—"

"I'm not a shut in," I protest. "I get out."

I don't want to be pegged agoraphobic any more than clairaudient. I *want* to be normal. Sadly, that's impossible. Although I suppose it could be worse. The thoughts of the living are closed to me. I'm only sensitive to the thoughts of the dead, which totally stinks in its own special way. Subjecting myself to their misery is a slippery slope, one I avoid at all costs.

I inhale vitamins and protein bars, consume gallons of coffee and *Energy X*, run avidly on a tread mill, and steer clear of crime scenes, car wrecks, morgues, funeral homes, cemeteries... Obvious dead people zones.

It's the not-so-obvious zones that cause me distress. A person can kick the bucket anywhere—by accident, by foul means, by natural causes. Dead people are everywhere. That's why I rarely leave home. Dodging them is exhausting.

"When's the last time you went into town?" Julia asks.

"Two weeks ago," I lie. In truth, it's been a month. Amazing what you can accomplish with the Internet and a rain, snow or shine delivery service. Speaking of... "Someone's knocking on my door, Julia. I'll call you back."

"When?"

"Soon."

I sign off and chuck my half-eaten breakfast. I'd chuck my phone too, but that won't keep Julia from tracking me down. Besides, I don't want to sever our professional relationship, I want to save it. Writing isn't simply a means of generating income, writing keeps me sane.

Frustrated now, I open the door hoping to find Joe, my regular delivery guy, holding the box of assorted sugary snacks I ordered from a wholesaler earlier this week or the interactive fitness program I purchased from an on-line sports store. Anything that affords energy or distraction.

Instead it's a new guy, a cute guy, from one of the express mail services. He stares at me for a minute, an appreciative gaze that brightens my dreary day. "Zoe Albright?"

"Yes?"

"You need to sign for this."

I smile and sign.

He passes me an envelope then leaves. A hint of spicy cologne lingers in his wake.

Nice.

As he walks toward his van, I hear him whistle low, one of those, *man-she's-hot* whistles. I don't think of myself as hot—especially when I'm wearing baggy sweats and a cartoon t-shirt—but a lot of guys are intrigued by my unique coloring. Cherry red hair, apple green eyes, ivory skin (no freckles).

I almost call him back and invite him in for coffee. I don't know *Sam* (I think his badge read), but he looks harmless and I haven't had a face-to-face conversation with anyone since Liza and her husband left for an extended vacation. I'm bored. And lonely. Celibacy isn't a life choice as much as a result of my reclusive lifestyle and social awkwardness. My pulse revs just thinking about an innocent flirtation in a safe zone.

"Your life has reached pathetic proportions, Z."

I'm even talking to myself.

Sighing, I rip into the certified envelope, assuming it's a royalty statement or some such from my publisher.

It's not.

Luckily, I reach my sofa by the time I finish reading the official document. Otherwise I would've conked my head on the hardwood floor when my breath seized and my knees buckled.

Ever had one of those moments where you experience a gamut of emotions in a heartbeat? When time stands still, then rushes by leaving you discombobulated? It's sort of like almost being hit by a semi-truck. Whoosh! Oh, my God!

I feel that way now.

Breathless, I struggle to corral my wits.

I'm not sure how long I've been sitting on this sofa or how many times I've read this document, but at some point I went from stunned to incredulous to freaking furious!

I verify the lawyer's credentials over the Internet. Armed

with a phone number, I call. Given the time difference between the US and the UK, I'm relieved and impressed that he answers. Our greeting is brief, his verbal confirmation life altering.

I breathe. I think. "There must be some mistake—"

"No mistake, Miss Albright. I'm not privy to the details of his passing, but I am confident regarding your father's Last Will & Testament."

Speechless, I listen as the British solicitor recounts my inheritance. He follows with a few kind words about Dominic Sinclair and ends by offering to coordinate my travel arrangements. "Blackmoor Manor must be seen to be believed."

"I appreciate that, Mr. Watson, but... Wait. Yes. Sure. Thank you. And as soon as possible, please."

"Start packing, Miss Albright. I'll be in touch shortly."

On the verge of hyperventilating, I toss my phone and tuck my head between my knees. As Penny would say, I'm gobsmacked!

Learning my father died, not twenty years ago (as sworn by Liza), but less than two weeks ago, is a gut-wrenching shock. The more I think about it, the more I burn.

Part of me wants to call and confront my aunt. Did she knowingly lie to me? Or did my mother lie to her, duping her into believing my father croaked soon after my birth?

Whatever the truth, I can hear Liza now. *"I had your best interest at heart."*

She always has my best interest at heart.

Or so she always says.

It started after my mother died.

I don't remember much about Victoria Albright. I was

only four when she met her suspicious end. But I remember she was always anxious. And I remember her funeral.

The casket was closed, but I heard her loud and clear. She told me to block the voices. No, *"I love you"* or *"I'll miss you"* just... *"Block the voices."*

I asked, *"What voices, Mommy?"* but the funeral director dragged me away before she could answer. He passed me off to Aunt Liza, who, poor thing, got stuck with me for good. It was the first of many times I heard her pet phrase, *"It's your imagination."*

A few days later, on the way to our new home, we drove past a cemetery. That's when I heard them. The voices. All talking at once. All telling me stories. Men, women, girls, boys. I covered my ears. *"Mommy told me not to listen!"*

Still, their woes and pleas stuck in my head. They made me sad. And scared. When I told Liza about the voices, instead of confirming that, like my mother, I'm clairaudient, she hired an analyst to convince me dead people don't talk.

"I have your best interest at heart."

I wanted to believe Dr. Peterson. I pretended I did. I pretended so hard that I fooled him *and* Aunt Liza. Otherwise, I was afraid they'd lock me away.

"That's what they do with crazy people."

I didn't want to land in a padded room or a padded casket. I couldn't block the voices, so instead I coped. Instead, I *Scrambled.*

Pulling my head out of the past and from between my knees, I make a beeline for my bedroom. Dragging a suitcase from my closet, I ring back my editor.

"Well, that was fast," says Julia. "Tell me you're calling to pitch a cheery proposal."

"No, but I do have news. I'm taking a trip."

"You're kidding."

"Packing my bags as we speak." I'm torn between panic and awe.

"Where are you going?"

"England."

"As in New England?"

"As in the United Kingdom."

"But...you haven't been out of your house in weeks," Julia squeaks. "You haven't left your dinky hick town in two years."

"I know."

"Now you're flying out of the country? Why? For how long?"

"My father just died and he left me a house. An estate, actually. It even has a name. *Blackmoor Manor*." I would've preferred something more cheery, but sunshine and lollipops aren't in my current stars.

"I thought your father died eons ago."

"So did I. Anyway, I'm flying over to check it out. According to the solicitor, the house and property are worth a fortune."

"I don't know what to say, Zoe. Sorry for your loss, but congratulations on the windfall?"

"That pretty much covers it." Phone pressed between my ear and shoulder, I cram multi-vitamins and granola bars in a side pocket along with thongs and bras.

"Maybe I should come with you," Julia says. "I could use a vacation."

"You can't afford the time away," I say reasonably. "You're overloaded and backlogged with manuscripts." None of them mine.

"True, but... Let's be blunt, Zoe. You're a little unworldly and a lot eccentric. You're definitely an inexperienced traveler. Do you even own a passport?"

"I do. Listen, Julia, I have to go. Who knows? Maybe a change of scenery will cure what ails me. Maybe I'll come back from England with a completed manuscript. Penelope Pringle's most fantastic adventure yet."

"Nothing would make me happier. Except for you meeting the man of your dreams."

"Let's not go there." Historically, my meet-ups (the few that there've been) ranged from awkward to disastrous. It doesn't help that I'm sometimes distracted by voices. Or Penelope. Oh, how to explain that third wheel to a sane, rational guy.

"At least be open to the possibility," says Julia.

I agree just to end the conversation on a high note.

As soon as I disconnect, Penny screams in my ear. I try to *Scramble*, but that doesn't always work with her. She isn't dead. She's imaginary.

I do what I always do when my muse won't be denied. I open a notepad and nab a pencil.

I document the date and time and Penelope's words, a frantic rant about madmen on the loose.

KILL THE MONSTER BEFORE HE KILLS YOU!

TWO

Braving Trans-Atlantic Dead Zones

THE SIX-HOUR FLIGHT from Wyoming to New York is a blessed blur. Luckily, I'm an expert at diverting negative thoughts. I pass the time with an in-flight movie and the digital music I downloaded to my phone. Losing myself in the creative efforts of other artists is preferable to dwelling on my own lack of inspiration or nurturing the frustration and angst churning in my stomach. Not that I'm a nervous flyer, but I'm definitely an inexperienced one. Plus there's the whole family drama and dead zone thing.

My anxiety doubles when I board my connecting flight to Heathrow Airport. Several more hours in the air. In the black of night. Over the freaking massive, deep and dangerous Atlantic. How many ships and planes have gone down in that ocean over the centuries? How many people have died with unresolved issues?

What's more, let's say I cross *the pond* (as they call it) unscathed. What happens once I set foot on English soil? England's a lot older than America so, logically, more people have died in that country. What if there are double the ghosts? Triple the ghosts? How much caffeine and sugar will I need to effectively *Scramble*? The more I wonder about the spirit population and plethora of dead zones, the more my leg bounces, which earns me an annoyed glance from the passenger seated next to me.

Mouthing an apology, I readjust my ear buds, crank an infectious tune, and lose myself in the singer's sultry voice.

For all of thirty seconds.

I flip through the channels on the teeny screen mounted on the seatback in front of me. Nothing and no one holds my interest.

Oh, man. Things are bad when I can't lose myself in a scene with a hunky actor.

Desperate, I flag down the flight attendant and ask for two mini-bottles of wine. If I can't divert my thoughts, maybe I can numb them. Typically, I'm not one for alcohol. Caffeine is my vice. But if I drink any more coffee I'll be awake all night. Sleep, especially since I'm arriving in England mid-morning, is imperative.

I watch an action hero kick villainous butt and listen to a playlist of 1990s pop. I sip merlot hoping it will serve as a tranquilizer.

Still my wheels turn.

What if the English lawyer (or as he called himself, *solicitor*) turns out to be a scam artist? What if my father's estate is a money pit instead of a money maker? If Blackmoor Manor truly is worth a fortune, why did my father bequeath it to me, a daughter he'd forsaken? Obviously, he knew about me. Why didn't he reach out before? Why did Liza and my mom lie, declaring him dead when he was very much alive? Was Dominic Sinclair a horrible person? Even if he was, didn't I deserve the chance to learn that for myself?

I feel betrayed. By Victoria. By Liza. And, by a lesser degree, Dominic.

I waffle between resentment and twitchy curiosity. I'm desperate to know the parents I never knew. And, truth told, this is a welcome distraction from my awkward parting with Liza and my falling out with Penny.

Flying off on my own, through countless dead zones in search of truth and financial security, marks this recluse as a veritable daredevil. I've never been so reckless or brave. If I wasn't obsessing this moment, I'd be proud.

Get a grip, Z.

While my fellow passengers sleep through the night, I forge a battle plan and seek serenity via complimentary wine.

Midway over the Celtic Sea and halfway through my fourth glass of merlot, I regret not calling Liza before I left the states. My anger and pride clouded my judgment. I didn't give her the chance to explain. Maybe she'll be forthcoming. Maybe she'll prove a treasure trove of information. About my parents. About me. Even though she's been less than forthcoming and more than a little protective over the years, don't I owe her the benefit of the doubt?

What if the plane crashes? I don't want to die with regrets. Regrets often chain a soul to the earth. I don't want to become one of the wretched, miserable ghosts I fight so hard to avoid.

Out of the blue, Penny's voice emerges in my muddled,

wine-soaked brain. *"Stiff upper lip, Z! You're not going to die. You've got big fish to fry. Monsters on the loose and—"*

Scrambling while tipsy is a chore. I devour a cupcake and wash it down with merlot. If I allow my muse free reign, she'll ramble about blood, guts, and gore. I don't want to think about monsters or frying fish. The only fish I can envision are those awaiting me several thousand feet below should this plane crash. Those who would swim around me or nibble at my flesh as I suffer a watery demise.

I don't breathe evenly until the wheels of the jetliner touch down at Heathrow.

As soon as I deplane, I wolf down a protein bar and kick up the *Scrambler*, just in case I walk through a dead zone.

So far, so good. Navigating the terminal, I only hear the voices of the living, albeit in several languages. Even Penny is nowhere to be heard.

I'm simultaneously relieved and anxious.

I'm also a little queasy and a lot impaired. I weave through immigration and miraculously make my way to baggage claim without tripping or getting lost.

Luckily, I breeze through customs. Luggage in hand, I blink away double-vision and focus on the signs held by extended family, hired drivers, and business associates as a way of contacting arriving passengers. I'm looking for E.B Watson, attorney at law. My father's solicitor.

He finds *me*.

†

Never judge a book by its cover.

It's a cliché I live by.

At the moment I'm trying very hard not to peg E.B. Watson as a wealthy, brainy snob based on his snooty suit, professor specs, and conservative hairstyle.

Meanwhile, he picked me out of a crowd at first glance. Apparently, my casual attire—jeans, red chucks, a superhero tee, and a green cargo jacket—screams *kiddie author*!

"I recognize you from the publicity photo in the back of your books," Watson explains as if reading my mind.

His British accent, if not his reserved air, is to-die-for.

"You've read my stories?" I'm shocked. Penelope's wacky adventures are geared toward pre-teens. Watson looks thirty-something and decidedly intellectual. The kind of reader who favors non-fiction and biographies.

"I choose to keep abreast of my daughter's interests. Mimi is a fan of your work."

I feel a rush of glee and then shame. Even though I haven't had a new release this year, I have a healthy backlist and a collection of foreign sales. I don't get out much, but I do keep up with emails and social media. I have a decent fan base.

Impressionable minors.

And here I am. Standing, no, swaying, three-sheets-to-the-wind.

Crud.

Watson, a good-looking, average-built, perfectly coiffed, perfectly suited man (Can you say metrosexual?) retains a respectable distance. Although, he does squint through his thick black-framed glasses for a keener look. "Are you quite well, Miss Albright?"

I imagine my appearance. Bloodshot eyes, sluggish movements, clammy skin. I'm grateful I chased that wine with three breath mints and a stick of spearmint gum before deplaning. "I'm not fond of flying," I say, while shoving on a pair of purple-tinted shades.

"Airsick?"

"And jet-lagged." I prefer small lies to the truth in this instance. I don't want him, or any young fans, to mistake me for a drunk. And I certainly have no intention of sharing my worries.

Or discussing my *Misfortune*.

He relieves me of my sizable suitcase, and then peers around my back. "Have you no other luggage?"

"Just my laptop," I say, indicating the padded backpack slung over my shoulder.

"May I?"

"I'm good. Thanks." Even though all of my stories and ideas are backed up on hard drives, flash drives, and cloud storage, I'm funny about entrusting my laptop to anyone but *moi*.

He doesn't look offended as much as puzzled.

"What?"

"Pardon the generalization, but I've never known a woman to travel so light."

"You'd be surprised at how much that suitcase can hold. It's one of those expandable jobs—a late night purchase from a shopping network. Plus," I say with a shrug, "I'm not what you'd call a Fashionista. I'm all about comfort. Jeans and tees. Sundresses. Boots and sneakers. Sweats and underwear. Mix and match essentials, toiletries, makeup, and I'm good to go."

Watson blinks and I blush. Self-conscious, I ramble on. About nightwear and deodorant, no less. I wince and stop. "Sorry. TMI."

"TMI?"

"Too much information."

The epitome of good manners, Watson smiles. "Your candor is refreshing, Miss Albright." He cocks his head. "Shall we go? The sooner I deliver you to Blackmoor, the sooner you can convalesce."

His casual tone and easy manner put me at ease. Either he's very sweet or very slick. My bull-hooey detector isn't nearly as honed as my *Scrambler*. "How long is the drive?"

"Blackmoor Manor is located in the county of Kent, on the fringes of Canterbury. Most of our drive will be on a major motorway. As long as there are no traffic delays, we'll arrive in less than two hours."

It's hard not to fixate on Blackmoor's proximity to Canterbury Cathedral and all the ghosts no doubt haunting its historical realm. Instead, I focus on the impending ride.

Two hours.

Plenty of time to grill my driver about his client, my father, Dominic Sinclair. My financial woes have taken a temporary backseat to my intense curiosity about my twice-dead parent. Given recent developments, I question anything relayed to me by Liza. I'm focused on the information supplied by Mr. Watson. Dominic Sinclair was British, wealthy, and worked for Immigration. Or at least he used to.

Dominic Sinclair is dead.

Again.

A hundred questions swirl in my head. Now I'm dizzy in addition to queasy. On second thought, maybe it's best to delay interrogating Watson until I'm one-hundred-percent sober. What if I slur my speech? What if he tells me something important and I forget?

Now that my feet are on the ground, I wish I wasn't as

high as a kite. Wiping sweat from my brow, I follow metro-man toward an exit. I keep expecting him to make a wise crack about my flamingo pink suitcase or my flower-power backpack.

He doesn't.

Nor does he comment on my colorful attire.

That said, I do turn other heads. Normally I cringe at unwanted attention, but frankly, on this new day of my already quirky existence, I'm too tired and tipsy to care. Instead, I nab my phone and fire off a quick message to Julia—ARRIVED SAFE IN LONDON. MORE LATER.—while matching Watson's brisk stride.

Given England's reputation for dismal weather, I brace for rain as we step outside.

No drizzle, but it is grey and bleak.

I shiver, blaming my sudden chill on the crisp wind rather than an ominous portent.

Just because I'm in a foreign land and climbing into a car with a stranger... Just because Penelope warned of a monster on the loose... Just because I'm completely and utterly vulnerable...that doesn't mean I'm in danger.

I hope.

Tamping down my liquored-up imagination, I inhale half a granola bar while Watson loads my luggage, and then me, into his little black car. Which, on second look, sort of, no, *definitely* resembles a miniature, boxy hearse.

THREE

A Mortifying Meltdown

THE THING about Penelope is that I never know when she's going to show up or how long she's going to stay. Sometimes she visits me in my dreams. Sometimes she's just a voice in my head and sometimes I can imagine her in such detail, she seems very real indeed. As a kid I saw her all the time. Liza, who couldn't see the bubbly little blond girl at all, *ever*, told anyone who ever caught me talking to thin air, that Penny was my imaginary friend. Since we moved around a lot and since I was homeschooled and somewhat shy, I never made tight or lasting friends. Most folks knew that and nodded in sympathy.

When I got old enough to equate that sympathetic look with *"Poor thing"* or *"Weird kid"* I stopped talking to Penny in public. When Liza told me I was too old to have an imaginary friend, I convinced myself that Penny was my muse. I was a writer, after all, and all of my stories revolved around Penny. So the muse thing made sense. In fact, it's pretty normal for an artist to have a muse. Dante had Beatrice. Rosetti had Elizabeth Siddel. Beatrix Potter had the wildlife of the Scottish Highlands. Desperate to be normal, I welcomed Penelope Pringle, The Muse, as a permanent fixture in my life.

I'm used to Penny popping in sporadically and without bidding. So I can't say why I'm startled when she swoops down from the murky sky to pedal alongside Watson's car. Even though her winged-bicycle is steam-powered, she still has to pedal. Something about firebox fanning and piston and cylinder thingamabobs.

She's pedaling fast and furious to keep pace. How fast are we traveling? Sixty? Seventy miles per hour? I had no idea the flycycle was capable of such speed. And I'm pretty sure her goggles and top hat don't count as protective headgear.

Not safe, I think hazily.

"Don't wake up," she says.

Am I dreaming? I squint through the window. Her sidekick, Balderdash (a cocky Jack Russell terrier with an adventurous streak and the gift of speech) sits, as always, in the cushioned metal basket fitted to the flycycle's handlebars. He, too, wears goggles, and he, too, looks at me and speaks. "Don't listen."

At that precise and unfortunate moment I regain consciousness, although I can't say I'm clearheaded. My ears ring with a cacophony of voices. Hundreds of voices. Maybe thousands. All talking at once. All crowding my brain.

The emotions are crushing.

Agitation. Sorrow. Fear.

Random phrases break free of the monstrous white noise.

Threats. Regrets. Pleas for help.

"Block the voices!" Penny yells just as her steam engine sputters and she and Balderdash lag behind.

I clap my hands over my ears. I *Scramble*.

"Miss Albright—"

Not listening. Not listening. La, la, la.

"What is it? What's wrong?"

This voice is clear. This voice is close.

Mr. Watson.

I'd be embarrassed if I wasn't so freaked. I struggle to orient myself.

In England. In car. Watson driving.

I survey the landscape. Not a building or cemetery in sight, just rolling green hills and pockets of forests. "Was there a battle here?"

"When?"

"Ever?"

"Many a battle has been fought upon English soil. Could you narrow it down to a century?"

"It doesn't matter. Just step on the gas. Please." *Get me out of here.*

The stylish solicitor casts me a dubious glance. Either he's concerned for me or scared of me.

He floors his shiny black sedan.

The voices rage on, although I feel a shift in emotions. I hear laughter. And music. *That's a first.* Some sort of trick to get me to lower my defenses?

I dig into my backpack and rip open a twin pack of cupcakes. I shove one in my mouth, desperate for energy, not caring that I look like a crazed, starved pig. I've never employed the *Scrambler* more. "God, I could use a cup of coffee."

Watson flexes his fingers on the wheel as he races and bumps along the narrow road. "We'll brew a pot first thing."

"Is Blackmoor close?"

"Dead ahead."

"Your choice of words is unnerving."

"Apologies, Miss Albright." He glances over. "Why?"

"Never mind." I'm too busy *Scrambling*, too entranced by the vista—dead ahead. My pulse quickens. Blackmoor Manor is larger than I imagined. We're still a fair distance away, yet I can make out its grandeur. A sprawling, three-story stone monstrosity with manicured lawns and a large pond. It reminds me of Pemberley, Mr. Darcy's estate in Jane Austin's *Pride and Prejudice.* Or rather Pemberley in any one of the screenplay adaptations. I've seen them all.

"How many rooms, Mr. Watson?"

"Please, call me E.B. Or Eb, if you wish. Short for Ebenezer," he explains.

I blink. "Your parents named you Ebenezer?"

"I only confess as such to friends and, excuse me for saying so, but you look like you could use one. A friend, that is."

He has no idea. I blush and look away. "Eb. Got it. But only if you call me Zoe." No one, aside from the cop who pulled me over three months ago for driving too slow and extremely polite children, call me Miss Albright. "So," I say, swinging the conversation back to the mansion. "How many rooms?"

"Hard to say... Zoe. Blackmoor was originally built in the 14th century. As with most English estates and castles, there were additions and renovations throughout the centuries. Presently, two of the wings are closed off. However, the

Entrance Hall leads to vast living and entertaining quarters. The Drawing Room, Dining Room, Stag Parlour, Library, Stone Parlour, and Long Gallery. And that is only the first floor."

I gawk. "How am I going to keep all those rooms clean?" It's an inane concern since I'll probably sell the place, but any conversation between Watson and myself is better than listening in on a dead zone.

"Blackmoor Manor is always spotless."

"Did my father have a housekeeping staff?" I think about it. "He must have. He was rich, right? He could afford it." I flash on my dwindling bank account and lack of new sales. "I can't afford a staff, Mr.... Eb. Not even a lone housekeeper."

"Blackmoor Manor is self-sufficient."

"What does that mean?"

"It means it's always spotless."

"I don't understand."

"No one does."

I look over. His gaze is fixed on the road. On Blackmoor. His fingers flex on the steering wheel. He's nervous. Is it me? Of course, it's me. I just devoured a chocolate cupcake—pure sugar—and popped two pills dry. They were vitamins, but he doesn't know that. My hands, I realize, are trembling.

Great. He probably thinks I'm a druggie. I envision him raiding his daughter's bookshelves and purging her Penelope Pringle collection. I want to explain. I can't. Just as the voices fade to a manageable hum, I spy something that chills my blood. Blackmoor looms just ahead and so do several stone monuments.

"Is that a cemetery?" I squeak.

"Part of the estate." Watson's looking more unraveled by

the moment.

"Don't go near it!"

"But the main drive passes—"

"Take a detour! A shortcut! The long way around!" I screech. "Evade. Evade!"

"Bloody hell." He peels to the right, arcing away from an obvious dead zone.

It doesn't help.

The grounds are alive with the sound of...*life*.

They must not know they're dead.

Another ghostly trap? I can't make sense of it. Then again my senses are clouded with mini-bottles of wine and a jet-lagged *Scrambler*.

Young people. Old people. All conversing. Some arguing. Some laughing. Some...plotting?

"As long as he's chained, I am free to conquer..."

They're everywhere. I can't see them, but I hear. And *feel*.

Danger.

Death.

"You're no match for me, Enabler."

That one feels personal. What the—

"Block the voices!" comes a familiar voice. I look out the rear window and see Penelope and Balderdash gaining speed. "Blackmoor!" Penny screams over the audible chaos. "Get inside, Z!"

"Inside," I groan to Watson. "Get me inside."

By the time he skids to a stop in front of the main house, I'm doubled over, my hands clamped to my ears, my body trembling with paralyzing fear of the unknown.

I feel ill. Faint. "Need *Energy X*," I whisper as the world goes black.

FOUR

A Blessing and a Curse

I'M DRIFTING.

Weightless, carefree, surrounded by darkness.

Serenity.

Am I dead? Dreaming? The silence stretches on.

Bliss.

Floating on air, high above the chaos.

No one can touch me here.

Safe.

No voices. No worries.

My skin prickles with...*something.*

Alarm? Excitement?

I sense a ripple of discontent. A presence. I frown at the intrusion.

Who are you?

He skirts the edges of my consciousness.

Powerful. Fierce. Curious.

He lurks in the shadows.

Tall. Dark. Dangerous.

Him.

My body burns with a disconcerting mix of lust and longing. Sin and sorrow. The serenity I felt a blip ago shatters. "Go away."

"You're awake."

I jerk upright, the quiet tainted, my senses reeling.

I blink at my surroundings. Some sort of sitting room. Antique furnishings. Lush. Tasteful.

Blackmoor?

"Awake," he says, "but confused."

Lungs tight, heart pounding, I focus on the man walking toward me. Not dark and dangerous, but polished and mild. "Mr. Watson."

"Eb," he insists. "You gave me a fright, Miss Albright."

"Zoe."

"Feeling better, Zoe?"

"Feeling weird." I massage my chest and struggle to acclimate.

"Maybe this will help." He presents a silver serving tray and a dainty porcelain tea set. "No energy drinks," he says, eying me warily, "but you also mentioned coffee."

"Coffee. Great." Embarrassed, I glance away and shrug out of my jacket.

Watson thinks I'm nuts. I don't blame him. Earlier, I had some sort of telepathic meltdown. Then I talked in my sleep. Now I'm disoriented. Something isn't right.

Then it hits me.

"Do you hear that?" I ask in an awed whisper.

He sets the tray on a lace covered table. "What?"

"Nothing."

"But you—"

"Silence. Total, blessed silence. No voices. No humming!"

At the very least, there's always been a low-level hum. Even when I'm not *Scrambling*. Come to think of it, I'm not sure I've ever experienced true silence.

Until now.

"Zoe, I—"

"Shh!" I catapult off of the chaise lounge and sail out of the cozy parlor and into a spacious foyer. I note the massive front door and think about the voices outside—the chaos still fresh in my mind.

I steer clear of the mayhem and sweep into one breath-taking room after another. Decorated and furnished in styles ranging from Victorian to Elizabethan, Blackmoor Manor looks like a freaking museum. Perfectly arranged. Perfectly spotless.

Perfectly quiet.

Silence.

A gleeful bubble wells inside my trembling body then two seconds later bursts free! By the time the bespectacled solicitor joins me, I'm whirling in a circle, arms stretched wide and giggling like a little kid.

Pure joy. Pure peace.

"Sorry to interrupt, but I need to go," Watson says, standing all stiff and proper on the threshold of...whatever room this is.

I stop mid-spin and catch my breath. Grinning like an idiot, I wheeze, "I'm not crazy."

"Of course not." He doesn't look convinced. "Just overly

tired perhaps. Jet-lagged," he offers. "What with the long flight, the time difference, it's no wonder you're ..." He grapples for a polite word.

I supply one of Penelope's. "Discombobulated?"

"Mimi adores that word." He checks his watch. "I really must leave. Mimi's with a nanny and—"

"I understand." A devoted dad. That's nice. Admirable and endearing. Envy seeps into my joyful bubble. Must be nice to have a doting father. "Your wife and daughter are lucky."

"Yes, well," he clears his throat. "Are you going to be all right? Here? Alone?"

"I'm good with alone." *Liar.* I miss Penny. The *old* Penny.

"The nearest town is a goodly distance."

"I'm used to wide open spaces." *Truth.* I've lived in the boonies most of my life.

He nods. "Then I'll leave you to explore your new home. If you have any questions—"

"I do. Mostly about my father," I blurt. "As I said on our initial call, I never knew him. I don't understand..." I gesture to my surroundings, "...this."

"We can speak at length tomorrow, after you're settled and rested."

As much as I want to grill Watson tonight, it's obvious he's in a rush and I refuse to intrude on his family time. "I'd like that." I think about the wacky ride from Heathrow to Blackmoor. "About what happened. In the car."

"We'll blame it on...discombobulation."

I smile. "You're not as stuffy as you look, Watson." *Eb,* I decide, doesn't fit.

"Thank you. I think." He moves closer, reaches in his inner suit pocket and passes me a small leather wallet.

"What's in it?"

"A key card that allows you access to the manor via any one of the exterior doors. This same card activates and disables the security system. Also enclosed is a debit card. In your name," he adds. "It's associated with your trust fund."

"What trust fund?"

"A gift from your father."

"He left me this manor *and* money?"

"Quite a bit of money. That's not to say you shouldn't live within a budget. We can discuss particulars when we next meet."

I'm too stunned to respond. Dominic Sinclair willed me a country estate and a trust fund, and most welcome of all, blessed silence. A generous miracle man? A manipulative jerk with an agenda? It's all I can do not to tie Watson in a chair until he tells me everything he knows about my mysterious father!

"One more thing," he says. "There's a car parked in the modified carriage house. Feel free to use it when the need arises. You'll find the keys and a map of the area in a marked envelope on the desk in the library."

"The library?" Of all the rooms in this place, he picked the one I hoped to avoid.

"Since you're a writer, I assumed you'd establish the library as your workstation. In addition, it's a lovely spot to read. I think you'll find Blackmoor's literary collection impressive."

"No doubt."

If I can help it, I won't be laying a hand on one single novel. Books, physical not digital, make my skin itch from the inside out. After several tests by several different doctors, my bizarre allergic reaction was diagnosed as psychosomatic. Maybe so—although I can't imagine why—but I refuse to visit another shrink. Like I want someone poking around inside my head and discovering my *Misfortune*. *"It's worse than we thought. She's also schizophrenic."*

Watson clears his throat and I realize I'm zoning. "Until tomorrow," he says with a nod.

"I'll walk you to the door," I say out of politeness. I honestly don't want to get within three-feet of whatever lurks on the other side.

"No need. I know the way."

"Don't I need to use my key to deactivate the security system?"

"I've been entrusted with a key as well. Don't hesitate to ring me if you require assistance in any and all matters," he says with a wave. "You have my number."

I slide the wallet into my back pocket and listen to his polished oxfords clicking across the shiny marble floor, listen for the door to open then shut.

And then…I bask in the silence.

Yes, I'm jet-lagged. Yes, I'm hung-over and shaken from that eerie encounter with the voices. But I'm too hopped up on silence to sleep.

I'll explore another floor of the manor. Choose a bedroom. Unpack. Maybe fire up my laptop and try to write. I realize then that I haven't heard from Penelope since she ordered me inside Blackmoor. "Penny?"

Silence.

As much as I miss my muse, the old cheerful, optimistic Penelope, I cherish the soul-soothing quiet.

Please don't let this be a dream.

I'll ponder the phenomenon later. Right now I want to savor the serenity and explore my father's home. Except for the library. I won't cross that threshold until I absolutely have to. There are plenty of other rooms to see, including those in the two closed wings.

The enormity of Blackmoor boggles my mind. Did my father really live in this massive museum-like manor? Alone? Did he purchase the 19th century paintings and furnishings or did they come with the property? Speaking of the property... Did he buy or inherit? Who is Dominic Sinclair and who were his ancestors?

"Who am I?"

My whispered query bounces off the rich colored walls and cool marbled floor.

Never have I been so curious, so anxious.

If I search Blackmoor, will I find personal belongings of my father? Books, journals, letters, photo albums? Something that tells of his past? Of Victoria? *Of me?*

Heart cramped, fists clenched, I breathe deep, hoping to catch his scent. Tobacco, liquor, cologne...

But all I smell is the familiar, soothing aroma of strong black java.

Remembering the pot of coffee graciously brewed by Watson, I head back to the parlor. Lightheaded and weirdly disconnected, I float across the threshold, toward the fragrant coffee...and stop cold at the sight of an imposing figure.

He's standing at the window and peering out at the immaculate lawn.

My skin prickles and my heart skips. "Who are you?"

He turns a fraction of an inch, his head angled as though puzzled by the question. "You can see me, madam?"

His voice is deep, seductive, and heavily accented. British, like Penelope and Watson. "Of course, I can see you," I say, cursing the hitch in my voice. "You're standing right in front of me." Actually, he's standing on the far side of the room, in the shadows.

He moves into a path of muted sunlight.

Handsome. Carnal.

The man oozes a lethal sensuality that pulverizes my wits. His age is hard to peg. Twenties? Thirties? He looks...worldly. Or maybe world weary. Dark eyes that have seen too much, a chiseled jaw that hasn't seen a razor in days, and longish, black hair that looks perpetually windblown.

His aura—if you believe in that sort of thing—is potent.

"Remarkable," he says as I continue to stare.

You can say that again. This guy is a piece of work. Pinstriped trousers, a crisp white shirt, a crimson vest, and a black knee-length coat. He looks like he stepped out of a movie-adaption of a novel by Charles Dickens or Oscar Wilde. A Victorian rake head to toe. Except...instead of shallow charm, I sense deep conviction.

And a familiar bone-deep loneliness that seizes my lungs.

I stare. I think. *I shiver.*

This guy gives off the same imposing and sexy vibe as the mysterious man who invaded my recent dream. An assassin who kicked vampyric jackalope ass and then seduced me into bed. A dream prompted by Penny.

Am I hallucinating? Is he a figment of my inebriated fancy? A concocted presence like Penelope and Balderdash?

Unsure what to make of my circumstance, I keep things light. "Okay. I'll bite. What's your name? Algernon Moncrieff? Lord Arthur Goring? Sir Robert Chilturn?" A sucker for period films, how like me to conjure one of Wilde's rogues as my Dream Man.

"Gabriel Bennett."

"Never heard of you."

"You wound me, madam," he mocks. "And your name?"

"Zoe Albright."

Real or imagined, I don't like the way he's looking at me. All predatory-like. I don't like the way my body's responding —accelerated pulse, fluttery stomach—or the erotic desires he inspires. Yes, he's gorgeous, but far too intense.

Then again... Maybe I'm misinterpreting my reaction. Maybe this surge of adrenaline is a biochemical reaction in response to potential danger.

What's it gonna be, Zoe? Fight or flight?

FIVE

Flirting with Tall, Dark & Deadly

I DIDN'T FLY across the ocean, braving a gazillion dead zones, to get bullied by a delusional hunk.

I squeeze the back of a nearby chair. I can wing it at him if I have to. At the very least, I can use it as a barrier. "Now that we've been properly introduced, Mr. Bennett, please leave. You're disturbing my peace."

He doesn't budge. Just stares.

At *me*.

His blatant appreciation of my 'assets' is unsettling and, dang it all, flattering. What the blazes is wrong with me? "It'll never work. Us," I clarify when he raises a brow. "One of us isn't real."

His gaze burns a path from my long red braids to the funky red sneakers. "What are you?" he asks.

"A writer. What are you, Mr. Bennett?" *Aside from rude?*

"A warrior."

I blink. I ponder. "As in soldier?"

"As in assassin. *Character Assassin*, to be precise."

Oooo-kay.

Considering I associate the word *assassin* with the man in my dream, I'm pretty sure my jet-lagged, wine-buzzed imagination is at the heart of this bizarre conversation. You don't just casually announce to a stranger that you're some sort of killer.

"Oh, wait," I say with a smirk. "I get it. *Character Assassin.* Clever turn of phrase for someone who annihilates reputations for a living."

"Literal title for someone who eliminates dangerous players for the greater good."

"Dressed like that?" A snarky response, but, *come on.*

I glance over my shoulder half-expecting to see Penny laughing deliriously. *"Gotcha!"* But she's not there. I'm totally alone. Except for Mr. Tall, Dark, and Deadly. I frown at the man. Real or imagined, he's working my last nerve. "Is this some sort of lame joke?"

"I never jest, Miss Albright. Lame or otherwise." He hitches back his coat, pours coffee then picks up the sugar bowl and tongs. "One lump or two?"

My brain struggles to make sense of this totally weird encounter. An enigmatic Victorian *Character Assassin* serving me coffee from a flowery china set. "This has *got* to be a dream."

Will I wake up on the chaise lounge? In Watson's car? The airport? Maybe I haven't landed yet. Maybe the plane crashed. Maybe I'm dead!

Chest tight, I gulp air.

"You are not dreaming," he says. "Breathe, Miss Albright. One lump or two?"

I pinch myself. "Ow." Not dead. Not dreaming. Which means he's not my Dream Man, but a real man. A real man who's dressed like a rakish version of Sherlock Holmes.

I suck in a calming breath and note he's patiently awaiting my decision on sugar cubes. "Three," I say. The sweeter, the better. I don't know what I'm dealing with. If I need to defend myself against a nut-ball intruder, I need all the energy I can muster.

"Who are you?" I ask, striking a confident stance.

"I believe we covered that."

"Gabriel Bennett. Right. But what are you? Really. The groundskeeper? A delivery man? If I'm not dreaming, why are you dressed like that and what are you doing in my house? Wait. Are you one of those period re-enactors? Do you work here in some capacity? Give tours of the manor or something?"

It makes sense. He blends in with the décor. He certainly possesses the grace and arrogance of an aristocrat. Maybe he's portraying the 19th century owner of Blackmoor. Only, wouldn't Watson have mentioned if the manor doubles as a tourist attraction?

Instead of answering any one of my questions, he asks one of his own. "Won't you sit down?"

I don't want to sit, but I want that coffee. *Caffeine. Sugar. Energy.* I perch on the edge of the plush velvet chaise.

Bennett passes me the cup and saucer then sits across from me in the matching wing chair.

I sip.

He stares.

I have the insane urge to unbraid my hair and fluff it. Instead, I clear my throat then chug more java.

His gaze lingers on my breasts—typical—before shifting to my face. "What do you mean, *your* house?" he asks.

"I mean I own it."

"You purchased the manor from Dominic Sinclair?"

"I inherited it."

He angles his head.

"He died and willed this place to me," I clarify.

His expression is enigmatic, but I sense shock and, even more so, a weariness that's downright crushing.

Wow.

When I learned of my father's death, the second time, all I felt was confusion.

"How?"

"What?"

"How did he die?"

"I…I don't know."

"You don't know."

A statement, not a question. And condescending to boot. "I wasn't told." *I didn't ask.*

Gabriel Bennett is a wrecking ball of pent up fury. If I thought that anger was directed at me, I'd sprint for the front door and risk a dead zone.

Morbid fascination keeps me rooted.

"Did you know Dominic?" I ask.

"Yes."

"Yes!" One step closer to enlightenment! I resist pumping my fist in the air, but can't smother the face-splitting smile. That is, until Bennett raises a judgmental brow. I'm not mourning my father's death, but apparently he is.

I sober and blush. "I mean…sorry for your loss. Were you friends? Neighbors? Employer/employee?"

Bennett leans forward and braces his forearms on his knees. His dark gaze burns into mine. "Who are you to Sinclair?"

My patience wanes. "His daughter."

"Impossible."

"Listen—"

"Dominic Sinclair had one daughter and she expired shortly after birth."

"Expired?"

"Died."

"Passed on. Kicked the bucket. I get it. Expired just sounds so…" *Cold.* "Archaic."

He says nothing more, leaving me to dwell on his former statement. So I was declared falsely dead, too? Or maybe I had a sister. Or a half-sister. Which would be exciting if she hadn't *expired.*

"Listen, Mr. Bennett, I'm a little confused about my past, but as you can see I'm very much alive."

Again with the staring. His gaze travels the length of me, burning through my clothes, searing my flesh, *scorching my soul.*

I flinch.

"Enough about me," I say, cursing the squishy, fluttery feeling in my stomach. Being attracted to a rude, possibly dangerous, nut-job is warped.

Craving something safe and familiar, I sip coffee, savor the taste, the buzz. "What else do you know about my father?"

"That he loved unwisely."

I clang my cup to my saucer. "Are you referring to my

mother?" I know little about Victoria other than she forfeited her life while trying to save haunted souls, but surely that marks her as a brave, compassionate being. My temper burns in her defense. "Was that a slight?"

"An observation."

"Well, observe this." I bolt to my feet. "Me showing you the door." I've had enough of Gabriel Bennett (whoever he is) and his cryptic, agitating doubletalk.

"Was your mother extraordinarily gifted?"

He could mean anything. A brilliant mathematician. A virtuoso pianist. But I sense he knows the truth, although I've never considered her gift extraordinary. Blindsided, I crumple in my seat.

"I see the resemblance now. Your coloring and build. Your aura. I can't believe my eyes and yet I sense the truth." He drops his gorgeous face into his hands. "Bollocks."

My stomach coils with dread and, dang it all, lust. This man stokes primitive desires that make me blush. I've never experienced such an intense attraction.

Intriguing. Unsettling. Intimidating.

He pushes out of the chair and whirls toward the massive fireplace. With his back to me now, he braces his hands on the mantle and growls. "What the devil did you do, Sinclair?"

A hundred questions crowd my tongue. I ask one. "How do you know my father?"

"We're in the same business."

"Immigration?"

He barks a humorless laugh. "Is that what you were told?"

"Yes." Another lie?

He pushes off of the fireplace, turns and drags a hand over his face. "You don't know, do you?"

Nervous now, I stand and cross my arms. "Know what?"

"What you are."

"I told you. I'm a writer."

"A writer." His lip twitches. "Ironic, considering your true purpose."

Purpose? As in destiny? I think about how Victoria used her gift and how she died. Not that I know specifics because, according to Liza, they're too horrific to speak of, but I sure as sunshine don't want to follow in her footsteps!

Desperate to fuel my *Scrambler*, I grab my purse and dig out a protein bar.

Bennett moves in. "Do you hear disembodied voices, Miss Albright?"

I choke on a mouthful of processed oats and honey. He knows my secret. It scares the bejeebers out of me. "Get out of this house, Mr. Bennett."

"My most fervent wish, Miss Albright. But impossible. As to those voices, I'm particularly interested in the conversations surrounding this manor. What did you hear, precisely?"

"Okay, then. I'll leave." I spin on my rubber heels and stalk into the foyer while digging out my key card. I deactivate the security alarm, open the door...and freeze.

Voices.

Music.

Chaos.

Panicked, I deploy the *Scrambler*, but I'm exhausted.

"Five more weeks, Professor."

"Make it three."

I slam shut the door—heart pounding, sweat pouring.

"What did they say, Miss Albright?"

Wishing I'd never left dull-as-dirt Wyoming, I turn and

face my enigmatic visitor. I size up his Victorian get-up, remember everything he said, and fight like the dickens to resist his magnetic pull. "Who *are* you?" I demand.

He doesn't answer.

"Get out!"

"I cannot."

Jet-lagged, hungover, discombobulated, and confused, I rush him...and fall right through him. He looks so intimidating, so...solid. Yet I slide though him like a spoon through *Jell-O*.

Disbelieving, I spring to my feet, snag the nearest weapon and wing the decorative vase at his stoic, absurdly attractive face.

The vase sails through flesh and bone and shatters against the wall.

Shell-shocked, I stumble back. If I stare really, really hard...I can see *through* him.

Gabriel Bennett isn't my Dream Man.

He isn't a real man.

He's my worst nightmare.

SIX

Curiouser and Curiouser

THREE THINGS REGISTER as I stir from a dreamless sleep.

Head hurts.

Stomach hurts.

Taste in mouth—disgusting.

I wake up disoriented.

In bed.

Not my bed, I think hazily as I squint at the ceiling. Not my ceiling. This ceiling is high and decorated with angels, no cupids. And clouds. A mural?

Beautiful.

I experience a moment of utter tranquility...followed by a whoosh of panic.

Where am I?

My bleary gaze bounces over cornflower blue walls, brass sconces, exquisite oak furnishings and a gilded mirror.

19th century splendor.

Blackmoor.

"Sin and sorrow."

Heart racing, I bolt upright expecting to see Gabriel Bennett hovering bedside or levitating near the window. He isn't.

I whip my gaze to the door, expecting him to walk through solid wood. He doesn't.

I don't see or sense Mr. Tall, Dark, and Ghostly. I don't hear creaking or howling or moaning or rattling chains. I flash on a scene from *A Christmas Carol*, the 1951 version starring Alastair Sims (the best Scrooge ever), where he attributed his hallucination to "a bit of undigested beef."

I didn't eat any meat.

Just tons of crap loaded with sugar.

I breathe deep and listen hard.

No muttered curses or cryptic musings. Just a soft steady ticking to my right.

A vintage clock sits on the nightstand alongside an old fashioned oil lamp. Both are embellished with red garden roses against a muted green and bronze background. Very Victorian. Very pretty. Elegant and no doubt expensive.

Slowly, carefully, I pull the clock closer and squint at the roman numerals and old-fashioned hands.

Eight-o-five.

No digital reference to indicate A.M. or P.M. but, considering the sunbeams slanting through the parted velvet drapes, it's morning. I arrived at Blackmoor around noon, so...what? I slept half the day and all through the night? The last thing I remember is throwing a vase through Bennett.

Strike that.

The last thing I remember is declaring Bennett a ghost. Did I faint? Did he attack? Or maybe I ran, slipped, and knocked myself out. How did I end up in this room? In this bed?

I close my eyes and rub my throbbing temples trying to ease the pain, trying to jog memories. Mini wine bottles dance behind my swollen lids. I had too much to drink and, aside from snacks, too little to eat. Exhausted, inebriated, and shocked by a confrontation with a ghost.

Unless I dreamed that last part.

Maybe Watson carried me straight from his car to this room. Maybe that bizarre episode with Gabriel Bennett, *Character Assassin*, was a product of my addled subconscious. I wouldn't put it past my imagination. After all, I whipped up an embellished world for Penelope where bicycles fly and dogs talk. I'm more than capable of conjuring a sexy gentleman...ghost... assassin. *Whatever.*

Breathing easier, I continue to rationalize as I knock aside multiple pillows and throw off the lavish bed covers. I'm still wearing my jeans and tee but someone pulled off my shoes.

I see my backpack and suitcase sitting alongside a beautiful chest. Someone, not me, carried them in here. Someone tucked me into this mammoth dreamy soft bed. Bennett has no substance. His arms would have whooshed right through me. Watson, though mild-mannered, is all man. He could've easily carried me—in his arms, over his shoulder.

I cringe at the thought. I'm normally quite hardy, yet I blacked out in the solicitor's presence, what? Three times? If I imagined Bennett, did I imagine the voices?

I'm beginning to question everything that happened between Heathrow and Blackmoor.

I swing out of bed and wince.

My head aches, my stomach rolls, and the room sways. I'm torn between finding a toilet to hug and crawling back into bed. Instead, I stumble to my backpack and locate my cell phone. The quickest, surest way to solve this puzzle is to call Ebenezer Watson.

Although that will entail admitting a lapse of memory and broaching the subject of ghosts. I don't want the man to think I'm a loon, although maybe it's too late for that.

I thumb on my cell. Charged battery, but no signal. "No need to panic, Z." It's not like I'm cut off from the world. If I don't get a signal in another section of the house there's always the landline. *If* there's a landline.

Out of sorts, I loosen my braids while contemplating my next move. I want to brush my teeth. I want to shower and change my clothes. I want to brew a pot of coffee and to eat something more substantial than a cream-filled cupcake. But more than anything, I want to know if Gabriel Bennett is a real threat or a product of my imagination.

Scavenging through the pockets of my bag, I pop two aspirin, a multivitamin and a ginseng supplement. In lieu of toothpaste, I fold a stick of gum into my yucky tasting mouth. Stale wine, assorted snacks, and morning breath.

Gross.

I purposely avoid my reflection as I sail past the humongous wall mirror. Bemoaning my sorry appearance would be a waste of time and energy. I have a mystery to solve.

Pulling on my warm purple hoodie, I leave the bedroom, not knowing whether to turn left or right. *Left.* I hurry down the hall, braced to run into or through Bennett. I don't.

Seconds later, I see the staircase leading down. I guessed

well.

I pad down the stairs, senses alert. Half a dozen paintings snag my eye, but not my attention. I have plenty of time to study and explore the contents of Blackmoor. Just now I'm keen on one particular vase.

After what seems an eternity (Who needs an expensive elliptical machine when you can jog up and down this endless stairway?), I breach the last carpeted step, taking care not to slip on the marbled floor in my stocking feet. I don't see anyone. I don't hear anyone.

Or anything.

Silence.

At least I didn't dream that part.

Even though I'm anxious about whatever happened last night, I can't ignore the blissful effect of pure quiet.

I could stay here forever.

Unless, of course, Blackmoor is haunted.

I tread carefully, mindful of shards of porcelain. That vase exploded into a gazillion pieces.

Only there are no shards.

There's no mess whatsoever.

I swivel and see the vase I'd thrown, not shattered on the floor, but sitting intact on a high round table.

I'm simultaneously perplexed and relieved. More a work of art than a vessel for flowers, that vase is quite beautiful— blue porcelain accented with an intricate bird and wreath design and gilded handles. Probably worth a fortune. Nice to know I didn't destroy an antique, but at the same time... I could swear I hurled it at the dark spirit's gorgeous face.

Not that I'm fixated on Bennett's good looks.

Anxious, I whiz into the parlor. I look to the window, the

fireplace, the wing chair. No nutball. No ghost.

I inspect the lace-covered table. No coffee pot or silver tray. Did Watson return it to the kitchen? Did he carry it in here at all?

I check my cell. Still no signal. More confused by the second, I move room to room, holding my phone in front of me like a divining rod. Searching… searching.

More antiques, more paintings, more silence. I barely notice. My attention is on my cell and the non-existent bars.

That is until I enter a sun-drenched room bursting with exotic plants and ferns. I can't help but gawk. A glass room framed with dark brown beams. The style—gothic. The effect —breathtaking. In my research for *The Secret Life of Penelope Pringle*, I read about the popularity of conservatories in Victorian times. Standing in this airy room, soaking in the sun and warmth and gazing out at the beautiful landscape, I understand the appeal.

The sparse, functional furnishings are of equal interest. A writing desk with a view and a chaise lounge made for musing. I imagine relaxing against the cobalt upholstery and gazing out at the verdant grounds waiting for inspiration.

With no effort at all, I imagine Penelope and Balderdash zig-zagging through the maze of manicured hedges on her flycycle. Oh, yes. I can have fun with that scenario. Can Penny? Or will she rain on my parade with talk of monsters and murder?

I tuck away my whimsical idea as if somehow guarding it from Penny's dark influence. Not that I've heard a peep from her since yesterday when she ordered me inside Blackmoor. That in itself is strange. As if she knew I'd find refuge from the voices within these walls. How could she know that?

"The plot thickens."

I marvel at the questions and intrigue vexing my mind. Issues regarding my father, Bennett, Blackmoor, and the malevolent voice outside who seems to bear me a personal grudge.

Curiouser and curiouser.

For surely I feel like Alice in some sort of warped Wonderland. If my idea for Penny's next adventure crashes and burns, maybe I can outline a mystery.

Or a romance.

My cheeks heat as I recall the erotic sensations inspired by Gabriel Bennett—who's either a ghost or a creation of my subconscious. Am I so desperate for a romantic hook-up?

Shoving aside thoughts of my non-existent love life, I move deeper into the conservatory, toward the far end of the room. The generous panes offer an expansive view of the front lawn. Vibrant wildflowers pop against the vivid shorn grass and surround the sculpted fountain. The same fountain Bennett had been peering at from the parlor window. Beyond that is a rippling pond.

I flash on a heart-tripping scene from the several different movie renditions of *Pride and Prejudice*. I squint at the distant pond, willing Mr. Bennett to emerge from the water, breeches and shirt wet and plastered to his chiseled form, ala Mr. Darcy.

He doesn't.

No matter how hard I imagine.

"Miss Albright."

I gasp and choke on my gum. "Mr..." *cough, hack*, "Watson."

The soft-footed solicitor rushes forward and whacks me on the back.

The minty glob shoots out of my mouth and into a potted plant.

"Are you all right?" he asks, blue eyes wide behind his black-framed glasses.

Hand pressed over my pounding heart, I let out a mortified laugh. "You scared me."

"Forgive me. I knocked on the front door, but when you didn't answer..."

He looks me over then looks away. Is he embarrassed because of my rumpled appearance? Or because he walked in uninvited? Of course, it could be because he saw me spit a wad of gum into a fancy urn-like pot of a delicate flowering plant.

He clears his throat, steps back and straightens his perfectly straight tie. "I tried ringing last night," he says, "and then again this morning. Your mobile kept rolling over to voice mail. I was concerned."

"I didn't hear you knock. Sorry. I guess I was..." Daydreaming about a wet and wild gentleman. "...preoccupied. As for my cell, I don't get a signal in this house. I—"

My phone blips, pegging me a liar. I glance at the screen—two missed calls from Watson, one text from Julia: HAVE FUN! Four bars, full signal. "Oh." I crook a sheepish smile. "Must be this room. All the windows."

I tuck my phone in my hoodie's pocket. "I'm sorry I worried you, Mr. Watson."

His own smile is fleeting. "I'm happy you are up and about and in good humor. You were under the weather yesterday and, even to someone of fit mind and body, Blackmoor can be...intimidating."

SEVEN

Color Me Gobsmacked

NOTHING JAZZES me more than a good story and Watson knows a doozy.

Burning with curiosity, I invite him to sit.

He goes for the desk chair. I take the chaise. Perched on the edge, I clasp my hands in my lap to keep from wringing them. "When you say Blackmoor is intimidating, how so?"

"The manor is quite large and old and...odd."

As in haunted?

I don't want to admit yet that I had a supernatural experience last night with a dude in Victorian clothing. I've spent the bulk of my life hiding the fact that I hear dead people. Now I'm *seeing* them? Confessing opens me up to ridicule, or worse, curiosity. I don't want to be questioned about my *gift* or pressed into exploring it or coerced into using it for profit or greater good. I break into a clammy sweat just thinking about the career and demise of my clairaudient mother.

"Zoe?"

"Sorry. Go on."

"I'm not sure I should."

Is he worried I'll flip out if he reveals a shocking truth about Blackmoor? Considering my meltdown yesterday and my wrecked look today (something he's been too polite to mention), I wouldn't be surprised.

Remembering how Watson previously admired my candor, I smooth my rumpled t-shirt, zip my hoodie, and meet his troubled gaze. "In spite of my appearance, I assure you I'm of sound and stable mind. Yesterday you said you'd tell me everything you know about my father. Let's start with where he lived. What—and please be frank—is odd about Blackmoor?"

"Frankly speaking," Watson says, "Mr. Sinclair didn't live here."

"But—"

"Blackmoor Manor is...*was* in his name and, as I understand it, he did spend time here, but it wasn't his primary residence. He maintained a flat in London."

"So I won't find any of his personal property here?"

"Probably not."

"Oh." I hoped to learn something about my father through his belongings. His preferences. His hobbies. Any letters or photos. I assumed they'd be here, in his house—*my* house. "But he did purchase some of these furnishings and art, right? Obviously he had a weakness for antiques and Pre-Raphaelite paintings."

"Actually," Watson explains, "everything in Blackmoor

Manor was either inherited or purchased by Lady Charlotte Moore."

The name means nothing to me and yet I flush. "Was she his wife? Girlfriend?"

"She was the former owner of Blackmoor. Lady Moore vanished in 1899 along with her lover, Gabriel Bennett."

Color me gobsmacked. "Go on."

"According to local legend, the ill-fated couple haunts Blackmoor although no one has ever seen them." He angles his head. "Have you?"

Is he poking fun? Or, like Bennett, does he have knowledge regarding my *Misfortune*? "Why would you ask me that?"

"Forgive me, but you look as though you had a restless night."

"I slept," I say a little too sharply. "In fact, I was so exhausted I fell asleep in my clothes."

I wait for him to say something like, "*I know. I tucked you into bed.*" He says nothing of the kind and instinctively I know my encounter with Gabriel Bennett was the real deal. The only thing I don't know is how the dead lover of Lady Charlotte Moore transported me upstairs.

I shake off an eerie vision of my body floating up the stairs via an invisible force.

I blow out a breath and temper my imagination.

"Why didn't you tell me about this yesterday?"

"Because you were...*discombobulated* and I didn't want to scare you."

"So you left me alone in a haunted manor with no warning?"

"If Moore and Bennett truly linger within these walls, they are as reclusive in death as they were in life."

I almost snort. *Reclusive, my eye.* Gabriel Bennett was in my face soon after I entered Blackmoor. I can't account for Lady Moore, nor do I want to. One specter is bad enough.

Deep in thought, I drum my fingers on my knee. "If no one has ever seen the ghosts of Lady Moore and Mr. Bennett, how did Blackmoor earn its reputation?"

"Ah. Well, the rooms are always in order. No dust. No wear. Everything in its place. Always." One eyebrow shoots above his glasses. "Haven't you noticed?"

"I broke a vase last night," I blurt without offering how.

"And today it's intact?"

I nod. "I thought maybe I imagined, um, dropping it. Or perhaps the housekeeper replaced it with a similar one." Yeah. That sounds reasonable.

"As I said yesterday, there is no need for a housekeeping staff at Blackmoor. Which room did you sleep in?"

Further proof that he didn't carry me, or my luggage, upstairs. "The room with the cupids on the ceiling."

"Interesting choice."

Only I didn't choose.

"Did you make your bed this morning?"

"No, I..."

"Follow me."

Speechless, I do. Out of the conservatory, up the stairs, down the hall, into the room I slept in.

I gawk at a perfectly made bed. The satiny covers are smooth and flowing. The pillows fluffed and perfectly arranged.

"Lady Moore," says Watson, "was what you Americans call 'a neat freak'. She employed a small but exceedingly efficient domestic staff. Everything is as it was on her last day here. No matter what you move, shuffle, shift, crack or break... As soon as you turn your back it is replaced or repaired. The window panes always sparkle and there is never a speck of dust."

"Amazing."

"Quite." He sighs and tugs at the hem of his fashionable suit jacket. "What I wouldn't give to live in a house that is forever clean and tidy."

Is that a slight against his wife's housekeeping? Or maybe his home is hopelessly cluttered with Mimi's books and toys. I'd lay money this man spoils his daughter rotten. I don't know why I find that endearing. I'm not big on spoiled kids.

"I know it's hard to believe—"

"I've experienced stranger things." Feeling lightheaded, I move toward my backpack in search of a granola bar. "Wait a minute."

My backpack. My suitcase. Both are ultra-modern in design and screamingly out of place in this 19th century room. "You said everything is forever as it was the day Lady Moore vanished. You said the moment you turn your back—*poof*—anything out of sort disappears or rights itself. If that's so, why is my luggage still here?"

"I don't know."

"Also, if my father didn't live here, how is it burglars haven't broken in and filched the valuables out of this place? Surely any highly skilled thief could breach the alarm system."

"Surely not. It is an intricate system. And, even if they did, the intrusion would be thwarted within minutes."

"By local police?"

"By an elite protection squad. They monitor Blackmoor's security system, among other things."

Having recently watched a high-tech caper flick, I eye the

room for CCTV cameras or laser detectors. Not that they'd be on prime display. "State of the art security system, huh? So the manor isn't *exactly* as it was in 1899."

"There have been a few successful alterations. Modern plumbing. Electricity. Wireless Internet."

So I could've switched my phone to Wi-Fi instead of counting on cell service. Something to note for the future. "Okay then," I say. "Explain this. If Blackmoor Manor is supposedly haunted, if there's a local legend about Lady Charlotte Moore and her lover and a manor that remains perpetually almost entirely as it was in 1899…where are the curiosity seekers? The ghost hunters? Documentaries and reality shows are aplenty and I'm a TV junkie. I've never heard of this place or its supernatural quirks."

"As I said, Blackmoor is a protected private estate, and Mr. Sinclair neither exploited nor flamed the legend," Watson says reasonably.

Just then his phone chimes. He excuses himself and five seconds later, excuses himself again. "I'm sorry for rushing out, especially after barging in, but Mimi suffers from anxiety attacks and she needs me."

"Of course. Absolutely." I rush after him, out of the room, down the hall and the exceedingly long stairway. What kind of kid—what is she? Eight? Nine?—has anxiety attacks? And why?

"I'll be in touch," he says.

"Okay," I say, although I really want to tackle him and ask a bazillion questions about my dad.

I've never had a father-figure in my life. I wonder if Mimi knows how incredibly lucky she is?

I'm standing at the base of the grand stairway, sorry Watson left so soon, but happy he saw himself out.

I'm still smarting from yesterday's encounter with the voices that lurk outside. I need to analyze and formulate a plan to bypass that dead zone, but for now, I'm focused on the dilemma within.

Feeling shaky, I sit on the bottom step, hoping to gather my thoughts. I can handle the bit about Blackmoor being self-sufficient. I'll just think of the manor as enchanted instead of cursed. Never having to worry about household chores is pretty cool and a petty relief.

What I can't wrap my mind around is Gabriel Bennett.

He died in 1899, yet he told me he knows and worked with my dad. How's that possible?

Unless...

Did Dominic Sinclair possess some sort of psychic ability? Like Victoria, did he use his supernatural skills to help the police solve murders? Did he try to help Bennett crossover? Is that why Bennett 'knew' him? Did Dominic successfully help Lady Moore find peace and that's why I haven't seen her? Because she already crossed to the other side?

My mind reels with a thousand questions, questions only Bennett can answer. What if last night was a one-night affair? What if he never materializes again? Or what if he shows, but dances around my inquiries, turning the spotlight back on me?

"You don't know what you are."

My blood burns just thinking about that condescending Victorian bully. Other parts heat as well, but I'm trying very hard to ignore the fact that I'm physically attracted (and that's putting it lightly) to a mean spirit (literally).

More disconcerting than his sensual hold on me is the way he unleashed my temper. I was downright rude to the man. Hostile even. I'm not confrontational by nature. I prefer avoidance or denial. Better to bury my feelings than to hurt someone else's. Better to skirt trouble than tempt it. I'm not a coward, but I'm definitely a pacifist. That explains why, over the years, I refrained from pushing Liza to discuss Victoria and Dominic. She became testy at the mere mention of my parents which in turn made my stomach churn.

I doubt Gabriel Bennett ever feels distraught, although frustration and anger are definitely in his emotional repertoire. My stomach knots in anticipation of a showdown with the unpredictable and potent ghost. A self-proclaimed assassin. What if I make him angry? What if he loses his temper? Is he as dangerous in death as he was in life? I think about Victoria and her too-awful-to-talk-about demise.

I drop my head into my hands and blow out a tense breath. "Just don't make him mad," I tell myself. "Be friendly."

You can catch more flies with honey and all that.

I don't want to alienate Bennett. I want to pick his brain. I don't know how, but he has knowledge of my father. He knows something of Victoria and intimated he knows things about me. Plus, I don't know how long I'll be here and, according to him, he isn't going anywhere, *can't* go anywhere. I need to know what to expect. Does he only haunt certain rooms? At certain times? On certain days? Or is he everywhere 24/7?

I look down at my stocking feet and baggy hoodie, consider my lack of makeup and energy. No way, no how am I going to face that man, that ghost, without feeling my most confident. I need to shower and change.

I need to eat. I need coffee. Four cups at least.

I need to fuel my *Scrambler* even though I'm pretty sure it's useless where Bennett's concerned. Still, it makes me feel better to be armed in some fashion. This is new and risky territory. Conversing with a ghost. Unfortunately, it has to be done.

"As soon as I'm refreshed," I think aloud as I rise to my feet, "we're going to have a talk, Gabriel Bennett."

"Why wait, Zoe Albright?"

EIGHT

A Freak-Fest Hook-Up

SHOCKED TO HEAR HIS VOICE, any voice, I squeal and spin.

Bennett's leaning insolently against the doorframe of the parlor. He takes my breath away, and not wholly because he surprised me. He is as I remember him, only *more*. More handsome. More carnal. More solid.

"How long have you been standing there?" I snap. *So much for friendly.*

"Why didn't you tell Watson about our encounter?"

"And have him think I'm crazy? Or worse, psychic?" I stop myself, realizing he made the conversation about me. Irritated, I shift the focus. "You eavesdropped?"

"I listened and learned from a strategic vantage point."

"Let me guess. A secret panel or passage. A place like this

probably has oodles of them. Is that why no one ever sees you? Because you hide and lurk within the walls?"

"I do not lurk. Not typically anyway. I was standing in the foyer when your Mr. Watson entered. He walked right past me and was oblivious to my presence. No one has seen me for more than a century, Miss Albright. Aside from you."

"Lucky me."

"You have no idea."

If he didn't look so somber, I'd suspect he was flirting. "So you hid behind a panel or portrait or whatever so *I* wouldn't see you. Did you enjoy spying on me?"

"You are more at ease with the dandy solicitor than you are with me. Listening in gave me an opportunity to better assess your character."

"And?"

"Your curiosity outshines your apprehension. There is hope."

"Gee, thanks." His arrogance gripes my butt. "Are you always this miserable? Wait. What am I saying? Of course you're miserable. You're dead."

"I'm not dead."

"You vanished in 1899. How old were you?"

"Difficult to say."

Obstinate. "I'm guessing early thirties—give or take ten years. If you're not dead then, given the present year, that would make you..."

"Over a century and a half. Give or take a decade."

"Right." I crook a kind and tolerant smile. At least I hope it looks kind. "Of course, you know that's impossible."

"Nothing is impossible. If I believed that I would've given up hope long ago of escaping this hell."

"You're not in Hell, Mr. Bennett. Or Heaven." I speak from years of research. "You're in what some would call Purgatory."

"I'm in a bewitched dimension, Miss Albright. Wholly alive and of sound mind and body."

I sigh. "Great. Dead *and* delusional." I whirl away, and then whirl back. "Wait. I've got it. You're one of those."

He lifts an inquisitive brow. Is he mocking me or is he truly perplexed? Since I'm trying to forge a peaceful relationship, I give him the benefit of the doubt and go with the latter.

"A confused soul," I say. "Someone who was blindsided by a quick and untimely death. You're unaware of your fate and therefore chained to earth. Unable to cross over and—"

"I am painfully aware of my fate, Miss Albright. If anyone is blind to their situation, it is you."

Something in his expression, in his posture, sends shivers down my spine. He doesn't look delusional. He looks confident and determined and very much alive. Unlike yesterday, no matter how hard I stare, I can't see through him. "You look different."

"I feel different."

That's worrisome. "Can you elaborate?"

"Not at the moment."

As with our previous conversation, he's talking in circles. My patience is slipping. I hug myself and focus hard. I will not attack. I will not flee. I need answers.

I shift in the tense silence. For someone who's spent a lifetime blocking the voices of the dead, I want Bennett to spill his guts. "I wish… Can we start over? I'm sorry I threw that vase at you. I'm not a violent person, but you scared me and I was discombobulated."

"Discombobulated."

"Shaken. Upset. Confused."

He looks me up and down, shakes his head in disgust then pushes off the wall.

I gape as he strolls past me. "Where are you going?"

"To try to make sense of this damnable mess."

"What mess?"

"You, Miss Albright."

The insult cuts like a knife. For a moment I stand there and bleed. I've spent my entire life keeping my phobias and quirks in check. I developed the *Scrambler*. I reasoned my imaginary friend into a muse. I channeled my bizarre imaginings into my writing and sold my first book at the age of fifteen. Contrary to his opinion, I'm enterprising and strong.

"You don't know anything about me!" I rail to his back.

"I know far more than you are willing or able to comprehend."

He keeps walking and I blow a gasket. I race forward and, forgetting he's an apparition, I grab his arm.

For a moment I feel the soft wool of his frock coat, followed by the cool crisp linen of his shirtsleeve. Then—*Oh, God*—I feel the hot skin of his rock-hard bicep.

I stare, horrified, as my hand disappears inside him— muscle, bone. Something slimy. Blood? Ectoplasm? Dark emotions erupt within me. Foreign emotions, sensations, and thoughts. *His thoughts.*

"What have you done, Dom?"

I recoil just as Bennett turns. His disconcerting gaze flickers with surprise then urgency. He moves toward me and I stumble backwards, my stocking feet slipping on the marble floor.

"What are you?" I rasp, staring at my trembling hand, marveling that it's intact and devoid of Bennett's innards.

"I am a *Warrior*. A *Character Assassin*. And you, Miss Albright, are an untapped *Enabler*."

I've heard that word before. Outside. *"You're no match for me, Enabler."*

I don't want to go out there, but I need to escape. Scared spitless by whatever just happened between me and Bennett, I dash for the front door.

"Don't do it," he warns. "You're not trained. Zoe!"

I burst outside, running like the Devil's on my heels, straight into my personal Hell. A chaotic storm of disembodied voices. Hundreds. Thousands. After being shielded in absolute silence for more than a day, the noise level cripples my senses.

I clap my hands to my ears.

I try to *Scramble* and fail.

No energy.

No power.

The pain is excruciating. I'm no longer running, but dropping to my knees. Weighted down and weirdly unbalanced.

My vision blurs.

Colors.

Shadows.

Ghosts.

I cry out—a choked, desperate plea. Fear of the unknown rips through me, consumes me.

Then I sense him.

Dark. Dangerous.

Bennett the *Warrior*.

I'm shockingly and vividly aware of his strength, his courage, his confusion.

"Listen to me, Zoe. Focus on my words. Not theirs."

I can't see him, but I feel him.

And hear him.

Colorful shadows ripple before me as the thunderous white noise of a dead zone rages on.

"Not ghosts," he says. *"Not all of them. And none of them can harm you. Not here. Not now. I won't let them."*

"Oh, God," I choke out. "You're inside me!"

"We are one."

"How?"

"I don't know."

"You said you couldn't leave Blackmoor."

"I could not. I suspect this is the work of Dominic and Wiz."

"What?"

"Magic."

I sense his excitement. His relief. His eagerness to explore the grounds and beyond. A fierce polar opposite to my own emotions.

I eye Blackmoor.

Sanctuary.

"No," Bennett says as if reading my thoughts.

I almost laugh. Of course, he's reading my thoughts. He's inside my frickin' head! "Need silence! Can't think. Can't breathe."

"Deflect all voices but mine."

"Can't." Drawing on Bennett's herculean strength, I push to my feet. Ironically, his courage gives me the nerve to defy him. I focus on Blackmoor and run.

"Dammit, woman!"

I burst through the door, slip and slide and crash to the floor. Strength and courage whoosh out of me as Bennett is thrown from my body, like a driver from a wrecked car.

Exhausted and traumatized, I curl into a ball and absorb the medicinal silence. I watch as Bennett stands and stalks to the door, throwing it wide…only to hit an invisible barrier.

Without a word, he closes the door then slumps to the floor, his back to the wall. His frustration and disappointment are palpable. The first time he's been free of this place in more than a century and I forced him back into prison.

"I'm sorry." I truly am.

"I cannot decide," he says while loosening his cravat, "if you are a blessing or a curse."

I don't want to ask. I'm scared to ask. But everything changed the moment I received that letter from Watson. My life as I knew it was pulled out from under me, and in order to get back to a comfortable place I have to shed my safe cocoon.

"Can you enlighten me?" I rasp. "Regarding my situation, that is?"

"Partially. Although I doubt you will believe me. The extent to which you have been sheltered, Miss Albright, is both impressive and infuriating."

Tears burn my eyes. "My life feels like one big fat lie."

"Your life, as you know it, *is* a lie."

The concept sickens me, but instead of curling into a tighter ball, I force myself to unfurl. Propped against the wall, I glare at the self-professed century-old warrior. "Should I be afraid of you?"

"If you're smart, you'll trust me. You're not here by

happenstance, Miss Albright. You need a protector. And, even more so, a teacher."

I'm struggling to absorb his words, his meaning, his intent. My brain can't process all that happened in the last few minutes, let alone hours. Just now I'm spinning on Liza's reluctance to speak of my parents in any sort of detail. *Ever.* And her rabid compulsion to convince me dead people don't talk.

"Outside," I say while massaging my temples. "What did you mean when you said, 'not all ghosts'?"

"I meant that you're sensitive to disembodied voices beyond those trapped in ghostly limbo. You're attuned to literary characters from an alternate universe, Miss Albright. A place called *Fictopia.*"

I blink. I stare.

Most people would laugh or roll their eyes. Me? I take Bennett at his word. Not because he looks and sounds earnest or because of my wicked-awesome imagination, but because I'm reeling from our freak-fest hook-up. The moment he entered my body and invaded my thoughts, any sense of the ordinary flew out the window.

I breathe...and go with the nonsensical flow.

"Characters," I repeat in a hyper-sensitized daze. "From *Fictopia.*"

"Known, by those of us who are aware of their existence, as *FICs.* F-I-C-S," he spells out while watching me hard.

I wet my lips and study him back. "So, you literally assassinate characters."

"Only the lethal ones. And only when they go rogue."

Crazy talk. And yet... My imagination sparks as do memories of Penelope's recent rants about doom and gore—

vampires, werewolves, mad scientists... KILL THE MONSTER BEFORE HE KILLS YOU!

I plunge my hands deep into the pockets of my hoodie to conceal their trembling then hike my chin. "I need fuel—food and caffeine," I say with all the bravado I can muster. "And then, Mr. Bennett, I want the truth. About everything."

NINE

Dirty Deeds and Baffles

SINCE THE KITCHEN is one of the many rooms I've yet to visit, Bennett leads the way. Even though he's indulging my needs, I sense his impatience. His pace is brisk, his silence unnerving.

What is he thinking? Planning?

I know one thing for certain. He's desperate to escape this house.

I note every painting and furnishing along our route. I memorize my way, wondering how it feels to be imprisoned within this mammoth residence day after year after decade. I don't understand the particulars of Bennett's isolation, but I empathize. I'm still adjusting to the absence of Liza and the defection of Penelope.

"You must miss her terribly," I blurt to Bennett's broad

back. "Your mistress," I add when he doesn't respond. "Lady Charlotte Moore."

"We were never lovers."

"But Watson said—"

"Physical relations between an *Enabler* and *Warrior* are forbidden."

"Lady Moore was an *Enabler*?"

"My *Enabler*."

I flush at his possessive tone. "Are you sure you didn't love her?"

More silence. Tense silence.

Touchy subject.

Got it.

But still I wonder. About her. About them. About this manor's supernatural idiosyncrasies and my ability to fuse with Bennett.

I'm dizzy with questions and musings. Amazing that food is even on my radar, although food has always been my comfort, my go-to when things get crazy. For all of the whacked things that have happened in my life, nothing compares to 'becoming one' with another being.

Wary of touching him, I trail a safe distance behind, reflecting on the bits he's shared so far. My brain bounces to connect the dots without specifics on Charlotte Moore.

Where is she? I want to ask and instead go with "So what's an *Enabler*? Aside from someone who hears voices."

"Psychically gifted, a trained *Enabler* can distinguish between ghosts and *FICs*. They are invaluable to mankind, 'enabling' *Warriors*, the physical assassins, to do their jobs."

"To kill?"

"To *Erase*."

Sugar coating the term doesn't make the act more appealing. Every fiber of my being recoils and yet I want, *need* to know more.

Get the facts and make sense of them later, I tell myself. *If there's any sense to be made.*

I think about my mother's *Misfortune*. "Was Victoria an *Enabler*?"

"One of the best, according to your father."

"Dominic. Was he—"

"A *Character Assassin*. A lethal *Warrior* and special recruit. Like me." He glances over his shoulder. "*You* are an anomaly."

A pretty word for freak or monster.

My heart pumps and not wholly because it feels like we've walked the length of a football field. I know I'm peculiar. I've always known. But now I worry about the gravity of my quirks.

"Wait a minute. You said it's forbidden for an *Enabler* and *Warrior* to, you know, have sex. Together."

He spares me a look, with an arched eyebrow to boot. "Obviously they broke the rule."

"Is there some sort of penalty for that?"

"Separation and relocation. Although in the unique case of Dom and *Vikki*—as he called her—the stakes were higher. Dom sent Vikki away, hoping to keep her condition and the baby a secret. After losing the child, I was certain Vikki would return. She and Dom were a remarkable team and he was miserable without her. Now I know why he lied about your fate and why his lover stayed away. To protect you."

"From who?"

"From those who would seek to exploit you."

Don't listen to the voices!

I shiver at the thought of a bunch of crusading *Character Assassins* exploiting my *Misfortune*. I can't imagine killing anything or anyone. Not even a monster.

I shake off a chill and focus on gathering more facts.

"I still don't understand how you knew my parents. You said you worked with my father. How? You're chained to this house. Stuck in a bewitched dimension. No one aside from me has seen you in more than a hundred years."

"You've been listening. I'm impressed. Mind your step." Bennett slips through a panel and into a narrow hall.

"So how—"

"In due course, Miss Albright. There's only so much you can absorb in one day."

"Are you suggesting I'm dimwitted on top of a damnable mess?"

"I'm suggesting there's a crisis afoot and there are more important things for you to digest other than how I knew Dom."

Noting his somber expression, I'm reminded that he was wounded by the news of my father's death. His sadness implies they were friends. Or at least friendly. Although I can't fathom how. And that Dominic must have been a stand-up guy even though he was an absentee father.

I chew on that thought while Bennett moves toward a staircase and, soon after, I focus on navigating steep, narrow steps rather than twisted relationships.

Also, I'm feeling the weakening effects of a sugar-low.

Right now I'm all about food.

Since Blackmoor's 19th century layout is intact, I'm not surprised that the kitchen is located below stairs in the servant's quarters. I just wish it wasn't so flipping far from the central living area. As someone who depends on snacks and drink throughout the day, I'm not looking forward to walking a mile every time I need a fix.

Winded and anxious to continue our discussion, I step around Bennett in search of edible fortification. Aside from a few contemporary modifications, the massive room looks similar to the kitchen featured in *Downton Abbey*. I easily imagine an invisible cook staff whipping up an exquisite meal. Too bad the magical aspects of Blackmoor only extend to 'clean-up'.

"What are you looking for?" Bennett calls as I scour the shelves of a walk-in pantry.

"Sweets. You know. Cupcakes, candy, donuts. If we're going back outside—"

"We are."

"Sweets are essential. I need a mega sugar rush in order to *Scramble* effectively. And caffeine. Do me a favor and look in the fridge or ice box, whatever you call it. An energy drink works best, but I'll settle for any kind of soda."

I marvel at the pantry's stocked shelves, but curse the lack of confections. I fairly wilt at the sight of a box of shortbread cookies. "Mr. Watson must be health nut. Poor Mimi. Did you find any soda?"

I peek out and find him backing away from the fridge with a double-decker pie and a container of milk.

"Excellent! Except for the milk." I toss the box of cookies on a table and check the fridge myself. Water, juice, and toward the very back, some bottles of some 'fizzy' something. "Score!"

When I turn around, I see a table set for one, and Bennett

lazing against a cast iron cook stove with his arms crossed over his chest.

"You're not joining me?" I ask out of politeness.

"Explain *Scramble*."

I blink, remembering now that I blurted my coping mechanism. It's been a closely guarded secret for all of my life. *My big-fat-lie-of-a-life.*

Since Bennett already knows about my clairaudient curse, I guess it doesn't matter if I tell him about my wacky, home-made antidote. Besides, if I'm forthcoming about intimate details, maybe he'll return the favor.

"It's something I do," I say as I plop on a stool and open my drink. "A skill I tripped upon as a kid. I can't block the voices, but when I'm super revved on sugar, caffeine, and adrenaline, I can garble them."

I brace for a mocking response, instead Bennett studies me with pointed interest.

Cheeks flushing, I nab a knife and cut into the pie. "What the… Where are the apples? The cherries? The anything that resembles fruit or meringue or, heck, chocolate pudding?"

"It's a meat pie. A pork pie. One cannot exist on sweets alone, Miss Albright."

Exasperated, I take a healthy swig of soda, wincing at the metallic taste and then noting the label. "Seriously?"

"Problem?"

"I can't fuel my *Scrambler* with minced meat and diet caffeine-free soda! I can't…"

I shut my trap. He's right. I need something substantial in my stomach. Something that will soak up whatever's left of that nasty wine. Something sensible, as Liza would say. Also… I sound like a whiney kid. I want Bennett to take me seriously.

I am not a damnable mess.

"Never mind. Ignore me. No. Don't ignore me. Join me. Please. Are you sure you're not hungry? Can you eat real food? How does this bewitched dimension thing work anyway? Why can I see you when others can't? Why can't you leave? You talk. I'll eat. Tell me everything. I'm especially curious about my father and mother. And *Fictopia*. I'm all ears," I say as he sits across the table from me.

"You can't absorb the enormity of the truth in one sitting."

"Try me." I realize suddenly that I'm not only hungry for food and information, I'm starving for conversation.

"We're wasting time."

"What's the hurry?"

"I've been chained to Blackmoor for more than a century."

"So we've established. And I'm your ticket out?"

"Dom wouldn't have brought you here, he wouldn't have risked exposing you unless… The situation must be dire. Time is of the essence, Miss Albright. I need to speak with people in the know and those people are in London."

"That's two hours from here."

"Only two?"

"Oh, right. The last time you traveled from here to there it was probably by horse and buggy. A lot has changed over the last century and a half."

"I'm not ignorant of technological advances. I simply haven't experienced them. Now if you've had your fill—"

"I haven't." I tense. I evade. "I told you, if you expect me to endure those voices, I need fuel. *Lots* of fuel."

"I have an alternate solution to your *Scrambler*."

"A secret stash of cake?"

"*Baffles.*" He dips into his coat pocket and then shows me his stash.

A pair of gold, jewel-encrusted baubles glitter in his palm. The backsides are spool-shaped and tipped with some sort of padding. "Earplugs?"

"Of a sort. Especially designed to baffle the voices of *FICs.*"

"Do they work on ghosts, too?"

"Blackmoor is insulated with the same medium."

And within every room, every wall of this house is true, blessed silence.

To think I can walk outside wearing these *Baffles* and go anywhere...*anywhere*...without risking an audible onslaught of tortured souls!

I look to the kitchen's archway and beyond, noting dust motes dancing on shafts of sunlight. I shove cookies in my pocket and nod toward the hall. "Where's that door lead?"

"Outside. It's a delivery entrance."

"Outside, huh?" What are the chances that the dead zone stretches to the backside of the manor?

Inspired to find out, I wipe my hands with the cloth napkin then swipe the *Baffles*, flushing from the brief, hot touch of Bennett's skin. "Let's try these puppies out."

TEN

The Quirks of Melding

MY HEART'S KICKING.

I'm nervous about what lurks outside.

I'm anxious to test the *Baffles*.

And Bennett is touching me.

Not in a kinky or intimate way. He simply grasped my shoulder and stopped me from opening the door. It's not as if he pulled me into his arms. So why am I all weak in the knees?

"Allow me to try first," he says, while pulling me aside. "Since your arrival, my presence, as you noted, has altered. What if our melding weakened the spell that restricts my personal boundaries? Perhaps I can leave of my own accord."

His posture is relaxed as is his expression, and yet I sense his desperation. *Please let the caged man free*. I smile. "Fingers crossed."

I watch as he shrugs out of his long coat. His white shirt

stretches over his wide shoulders and his trousers cling to his admirable backside. I swallow an appreciative sigh and curse myself pathetic.

After handing me his coat, Beckett reaches for the doorknob.

"Wait!" I slide my key card through the security gadget fitted on the wall. "Okay," I say as I scurry back. "Go on."

He pulls the door inward.

I feel a rush of cool air and see a sunlit garden beyond, but all I *hear* is Bennett's measured breathing.

He steps forward, slams into an invisible barrier then stumbles back.

He tries to exit the house again, never making it over the threshold. "Bugger."

I don't know what to say, so I stay mum.

Grim-faced, he slips back into his coat. "Your turn, Miss Albright."

Here's hoping my experiment is more successful than Bennett's. Handling the jeweled *Baffles* like a national treasure, I fit one inside my ear. "Where did you get these anyway?"

"I had them especially made for Charlotte."

I'm curious to know more about the *Baffles*—what they're made of, how they work—but I'm *dying* to know more about Charlotte. I meet Bennett's dark, troubled gaze. "You must have been very fond of her."

His silence says it all.

Shifting closer, he places the remaining *Baffle* in my left ear.

My lobe, along with other places, tingles. Which is totally inappropriate given he's got it bad for another woman. Also, he's more than a century older than me. *Plus*, he's not even all that nice.

"Are you up to the challenge?" he says with a nod to the door.

I shrug off his disconcerting touch, along with my warped attraction. "I can already tell they're not working. I heard your every word perfectly."

"As it should be." He nudges me toward the threshold. "Take it slow. Head first. Tell me what you hear."

Stomach knotted, I hold tight to the doorjamb and lean forward just enough so that my head breaches the outside world.

I smile. "Chirping birds. The whir of a breeze. Rustling brush and trees."

"No voices?"

"Only yours."

"Excellent. Now step outdoors and take a turn about the kitchen gardens."

"Maybe this isn't a dead zone. The voices were out front."

"They are all around us, Miss Albright. Blackmoor sits due center of a fractured border. On my mark. Three… Two…"

I feel a nudge and I'm suddenly and fully out of the house. I marvel in the silence, moving forward only to have someone —Bennett?—slam into me. The force of the hit sends me sprawling. "Get off me!"

I try to shove off the dead weight. Only he's not on top of me. He's *inside* me. *Again*. "For cryin' out—!"

"*Calm yourself. Breathe. Do not run for the house. Grow a backbone, Miss Albright.*"

"Shove it where the sun don't shine, Mr. Bennett." I push to my feet, sway. "My balance is off."

"I feel it as well. Perhaps if we give ourselves a moment to acclimate."

"Perhaps? You've never done this before? This melding thing?"

"I have not."

"Not even with Charlotte?"

"Definitely not with Charlotte."

"Swell." Searching for my/our center, I bend my knees ever so slightly. "I feel like I put on two-hundred pounds."

"I feel like the weight of the world is off my shoulders. Free of Blackmoor."

"Free of Blackmoor, but fused to *me*."

"Yes, but of course."

"Of course, what?" It occurs to me that if anyone walks by they'll see a crazy woman talking to herself. Luckily, we're in the middle of nowhere.

I laugh. I gasp. I clap a hand over my mouth, but I can't stifle my amusement. "Why am I laughing?" I ask with a frown. "This isn't funny!"

"But it is clever. Well done, Wiz."

"That's the second time you've mentioned this Wiz guy. Who is he?"

"A business associate."

"Of my father's?"

"Of every Warrior in the field. Wiz is practiced in the arts of magic and blessed with supernatural abilities allowing him to cast charms and spells of an extraordinary nature."

"Ah." I roll my eyes. "Wiz. *Wizard*. I should have known."

"According to Dom, over the decades, there have been multiple attempts to break the curse that chains me to Blackmoor. This time around, it appears Wiz explored a new option, casting a powerful

Binding Spell and chaining me to you. *Now I go wherever you go and you, Miss Albright, are going to London."*

I learn quickly that Bennett can't make me act against my will, even though he's stronger in body and mind. 'Melding' is awkward and creepy, but at least I'm not a slave to this man's whims.

The more he pushes me toward the carriage house, the more I falter. I/we have taken two tumbles so far. I'm fighting him with all my might.

"Give it up, Bennett. I told you, I'm not traveling anywhere until I shower and change my clothes."

"Your priorities are abysmal, Miss Albright."

"I don't have to explain myself to you."

"No, you don't. From my vantage point, you're an open book. You're a social misfit. Unwanted attention makes you twitchy. You're afraid people will think you're crazy if they see you talking to yourself. Yes, well, there is that. For what it's worth, you don't need to express yourself aloud, Miss Albright. I am privy to your thoughts."

I force us to a standstill. I mentally pry, listening in on Bennett's subconscious, hoping to invade his privacy the way he's invading mine. Listening for details regarding Charlotte or Dominic. Anything beyond what he's openly sharing.

Silence.

"Why can't I hear your thoughts the way you hear mine?"

"I suppose that is because I am inside of you and not the other way around. If you want further clarification, I suggest you/we ask Wiz. The sooner we get to London, the sooner we'll have answers."

Bristling, I glance toward Blackmoor. "The keys to the car are inside."

I tense with his frustration.

"What did you think was in that carriage house, Mr. Bennett? A horse?"

"As stated before I am aware of modern technology. I'm simply unaccustomed to using it."

"Yeah, well, you need keys to operate a car," I say while lumbering toward the manor. I've yet to adjust to our combined and opposite gaits. "Well, not all cars," I add. "Not these days. But Watson definitely mentioned keys when he told me about the car in the carriage house. They're in the library along with a map of the area. Print maps are archaic, but who knows? Maybe it's relevant since Blackmoor's sort of stuck in the past. Like you."

"You're allergic to books?"

"Not all books. Just..." I shove my fists in my hoodie pocket, mortified that I'm angry enough to punch something. I'm not a violent person. But apparently, Bennett is. "Hijacking my body is one thing," I snap, "but I'd appreciate it if you'd stay out of my subconscious. Prying into my thoughts and memories is rude."

"Point taken."

I slide the security card through the alarm gadget, push inside and fall face first as Bennett ejects from my body with a force that tips my balance.

"With practice," Bennett says as he rolls to his feet, "perhaps we'll learn to disengage with more finesse."

"Speaking of," I say while gingerly prying the *Baffles* from my ears, "when we leave again, can you try not to slam into me with the force of a charging bull?"

"By all means, Miss Albright. Now that I know the drill, when next we fuse, I'll slide inside you with the utmost care."

I blink. I blush. "You get the keys and map. I'll shower and change."

※

There is no shower. Only a tub. A glorious pink porcelain, claw-footed tub. Oh, how I long to soak away my troubles in the sudsy warm bath.

Instead, I speed-bathe and try not to read into Bennett's mention of drilling and fusing and 'sliding inside'. I don't think he was flirting. Especially since he thinks I'm a damnable mess. And an *anomaly*, to boot. Then again, I've never been good at reading men's sexual signals. Unless they're overt—obviously. Yet another personal defect resulting from a sheltered rearing.

"Let it go, Z, and get a move on."

Right. Like I need to complicate my already bizarre life by crushing on a 19th century assassin of literary monsters.

"No one would believe this, but me. And Penny."

I haven't seen or heard from my muse since Watson first carried me into Blackmoor. Then again she hasn't been on my mind. Instead of obsessing on my rebellious, imaginary friend, I'm preoccupied with a cursed killer.

From the frying pan into the fire.

Wistful for the devil I know, I glance up at a small curtained window, hoping I'll spy Penelope and Balderdash flying by.

I don't.

Focusing on my immediate agenda, I rinse off, towel dry,

and spritz on piña colada body spray. Since Bennett and I are embarking on a business meeting, of sorts, I guess, I opt for a flowery mid-thigh dress with a flouncy skirt, combat boots, and a denim jacket. I fluff my long red curls and apply a swish of mascara and lip balm.

I'm soapy-fresh, primped, and ready in less than twenty minutes.

My record-breaking transformation is lost on Bennett. He's waiting at the bottom of the stairs, examining the car keys and looking annoyed. "What took you so long?"

"Were you this curt with Charlotte?"

"You are not Charlotte."

Ouch.

"*Baffles*," he orders while striding to the door.

I loop my messenger bag over my shoulder then insert the miracle earplugs.

Bennett passes me the keys and map then leans in to adjust the left *Baffle*. "You smell fruity."

"Well, if the scent fits," I half joke.

"It's nice."

Was that a compliment? Instead of thanking him, I tug at his cravat—an intricate archaic tie that must take an hour to knot. "When we get to London, you're going to stick out like, well, Dickens in *Futurama*."

"No one's going to see me."

Right. The melding thing. "Let's do this."

Emboldened by the silencing *Baffles*, I disarm the security system, open the door, and hover on the threshold. If there's *FIC* or ghostly activity, I'm deaf to the chaos. Nor do I see any eerie shadows or rippling colors.

Huh.

I forgot about that one and only visual experience. Or maybe I suppressed it. I have more than enough weirdness to contend with. Conditioned by Liza, I reason away what was probably a figment of my overtaxed senses.

Relaxed and curious, I step outside.

A gentle breeze ruffles my dress and cools my bare legs. The sun warms my face. And Bennett…

Bennett is inside me.

I flush with his vibrant alpha presence. "I barely felt a thing!"

"Words I hoped to never hear from a woman."

"Was that… Are you…?" *Flirting?*

"Merely an observation."

"Oh." I'm embarrassed and disappointed—the latter being ridiculous because this/us/we couldn't have sex if we wanted to. I mentally list the reasons while cutting across a beautiful flower garden in order to get to the carriage house soonest. I sidestep yellow tulips as another thought occurs. "You're not listening in, are you?"

"That, Miss Albright, is something I'm trying to master."

I flush from head to toe, substituting lustful thoughts with the lyrics of a sugary pop song. I reach for the sliding carriage door and tug.

It's stuck.

As I try again, I feel a burst of strength. Bennett's strength.

"Wow," I say as the door flings wide. "*That* was exhilarating."

I breathe in the musty smell of a barn, a smell I know well considering my rural upbringing. I see stalls where horses used to shelter. Two different horse carriages—both antiques. And a shiny, sporty car—very red and very expensive.

"Was this my father's?"

"It's a company vehicle. Dom's favorite. I'm eager to give her a go."

"You know how to drive?"

"No. But you do. Don't you?"

"Sure. Although I've never been behind the wheel of sports car. Looks fast."

"According to Dom, it is fast. Although we'll never get to London at the pace we're going."

His references to having conversations with my father are making me crazy. How did that work? Did they have a telepathic connection? Was Dominic multi-skilled? Was he clairaudient like me? Like Victoria?

"In due course, Miss Albright."

It occurs to me that Bennett is as evasive about my parents as Liza.

Gritting my teeth, I unlock and swing open the driver's door. Or rather what should be the driver's door. "Oh, no."

"What now?"

"The steering wheel's on the wrong side. I forgot. In America it's on the left. Here it's on the right."

"A minor recalculation of what you already know."

"A major recalculation. It changes everything!"

"I fail to see how."

"And that's not the worst of it. It's a stick!"

"What?"

I point. "That thing there. It's a stick shift. A manual. I only know how to drive an automatic."

My leg moves—under Bennett's steam—and suddenly I'm climbing in. "What are you doing?"

"*Relying on your experience and Dom's reports, and giving it a go. If you lack the nerve, Miss Albright, borrow some of mine.*"

Fear rockets through my blood as I imagine smashing into another car when we shift into the wrong gear or step on the wrong pedal. As is, I'm the worst of drivers on the best of days. Adrenaline gives me the upper hand, allowing me to push out of the two-seater.

"*Bloody hell. If you are of Dom's loins, I have yet to see it.*"

Ignoring his insult, I pluck my phone from my bag.

"*What are you doing?*"

"Calling Watson. If you don't mind, I'd rather get to London in one piece, or two, as the case may be."

"*I stand corrected. You do favor Dom. You're obstinate. Fair warning. We're going to clash, Miss Albright.*"

"Bring it on, Mr. Bennett."

ELEVEN

When Things Go from Bad to Worse

"HONESTLY, this is above and beyond, Mr. Watson. All I need is a lift to the train station."

"No bother at all. I have business in Kensington. I'll happily drop you at…"

"The Museum of Miraculous Inventions," I say after a prompt from Bennett. It's the first thing he's uttered since Watson's arrival.

While waiting for our ride, Bennett yakked plenty in my inner ear. A rundown of what not to share with the solicitor (primarily anything having to do with our meeting and melding) as well as a crash course in *FIC* awareness. Not that I retained much of the latter.

I hate to admit it, but Bennett was right to question how much I can absorb in one day pertaining to family secrets and otherworldly details.

Yes, I have a stellar imagination. Yes, I've spent a lifetime engaging with a pretend friend and her talking dog. And yes, I garble the voices of the dead with a caffeinated, sugar-fueled coping mechanism. But no matter how open I am to fantastical deeds, wrapping my head around a Binding Spell and sharing my body with a man (not in a way I ever dreamed of, by the way) is mind-blowing.

And in some ways, more exhausting than *Scrambling*.

It's all I can do to walk with my usual bounce, instead of Bennett's purposeful stride. Also he keeps pulling down the hem of my dress as if I'm showing too much leg, which I'm not. Between that, and Bennett's continual attempts to twist my wild hair into a prudish knot, I'm increasingly agitated. Or maybe that's Bennett. The longer he's inside me, the more our characteristics blur.

Right now I/we can't take our eyes off of Watson as he manipulates his car—which also has a stick shift. I didn't notice yesterday, but I'm noticing now.

Bennett's fascinated.

"Don't worry," Watson says as he rolls down the lane, "I'll bypass the cemetery."

I blink. I cringe. I don't know which is worse. That Watson witnessed yesterday's meltdown. Or that Bennett's reliving the mortifying episode via my memory.

"Actually," I say, looking straight at the dead zone, "do me a favor and drive right by it."

"Are you certain?"

No. "Yes." What better way to test the *Baffles?* Sure, they blocked the voices populating the grounds right outside the manor. But a graveyard?

"You doubt me, Miss Albright?"

I bite my tongue and brace as the car speeds past listing gravestones and sculptured monuments.

Silence.

Either every soul successfully crossed over or these *Baffles* are ironclad resistant to ghostly woes. "Amazing."

"You're welcome."

"What's amazing?"

I jerk my attention back to Watson. "Oh. The countryside. The forests and meadows. Lovely. I didn't notice yesterday. I was pretty out of it. Jet-lag and all."

"It was misty and foggy, too. Unlike today," Watson says while sliding on his sunglasses.

Ever courteous, he refrains from mentioning my embarrassing meltdown. I appreciate that. He's tolerant and kind. Traits I admire.

"I don't trust him," Bennett says, *"and neither should you."*

I swallow a snarky comeback and think it instead. *You're just jealous because I like Watson. I admire his kindness. I can't say the same about you.*

"I do not want or need your admiration, Miss Albright. Only your allegiance."

I ponder his choice of words. I also wonder how I'm going to manage the next two hours. Sustaining a coherent conversation with Watson won't be easy if Bennett keeps blabbing in my head.

"So," Watson says in the wake of my awkward silence, "out of all of the museums in London, what draws you to the Museum of Miraculous Innovations? Or as avid patrons call it, MOMI."

"Research," I say, sticking to the script Bennett laid out earlier. "I'm working on a writing project and—"

"Ah, but of course. Given the steampunk aspects of Penelope's adventures, naturally you'd be interested in the future as imagined by writers, artists, and innovators of the past. Ray guns, robots, and rocket ships. If I may, I highly suggest the Jules Verne exhibit. There are stunning models of his imaginative transports. For instance in *Twenty Thousand Leagues Under the Sea…*"

"Ask him about the pedals. The process."

I'm thrown for a moment, thinking Bennett's curious about Verne's fantastical submarine. But then I realize he's referring to Watson's conventional car. His desire to learn how to drive is fierce and impossible to ignore.

"While we're on the subject of mindboggling transportation," I say to Watson, "I'd love to take advantage of the car in the carriage house, but, as I mentioned, I don't know how to drive a manual."

"It would be my pleasure to offer instruction. Perhaps I could pop over in the morning…"

"Now."

"That would be great," I say with a smile, even though I'm churning with Bennett's impatience. "But maybe you could give me a preview. Just, you know, an overview of the process. The basics."

"Certainly," he says with a befuddled expression.

He's probably wondering why I'm asking for a driving lesson instead of asking about my father. To his knowledge, it's just the two of us in this car, a perfect time to grill him on whatever he knows about Dominic Sinclair. I agree, but Bennett is beyond distracting. He's determined to learn how to drive and he's dividing, no, *hijacking* my focus.

"Observe, listen, and learn," Bennett says.

I bend to his wishes—dang him—straining against the seat belt for a better look at Watson's hands and feet, as well as the dash, stick, and pedals.

Before I know it, I'm absorbed in the highly capable solicitor's step-by-step instructions and deft coordination as he pushes the clutch and maneuvers the stick simultaneously. My fascination soon matches Bennett's. Either that or his eagerness overwhelmed my reservations. All I know is that I'm on pins and needles and chomping at the bit to 'give it a go'.

Several miles down the road and well into the demonstration, Watson says, "Believe it or not, before long it's second nature. You'll have the swing of it in no time."

"I have it now."

I blink. Did I just say that?

"Pull over. Let me try."

I definitely said *that*.

Watson's looking at me like I'm nuts. I hate that look. But instead of retreating into my shell, I push.

"Seriously, Watson. You're a great teacher and I'm a quick learner. I can't explain, but everything you said, everything I saw, clicked."

Not for me, surely. But definitely for Bennett. In this instance, in our melded state, that's the clincher. His confidence is practically shooting out of my ears like sunshine.

"One typically practices this sort of thing in an abandoned lot," Watson says as he eases to the side of the narrow country road.

"There isn't a car in sight," I say, while unbuckling. "Don't worry. I'll take it slow."

I push outside and swap places with Watson, stunned by the purpose and anticipation zinging through my blood.

"I've got this, Miss Albright," Bennett assures me as I/he/we settle into the driver's seat.

I bristle because I'm part of this, too. He needs my body to... "Push the clutch all the way down," I say while taking action. "Engage the brake. Turn the key."

Watson is sitting to my left, offering calm instruction.

Bennett's quiet but focused and fueling my efforts.

In a blip, I'm shifting from first gear to second—feeling the clutch engage, hearing the engine rev.

"That was impressively seamless," Watson says. "But..."

His voice fades as I accelerate, feeding off of the rush of being in control, of driving aggressively and joyfully for the first time in my life.

I feel the touch of Watson's hand. "Be careful."

And the force of Bennett's will. *"Be fearless."*

No one has ever encouraged me to walk on the wild side. Those who shaped me emphasized the importance of keeping my head down and my weirdness under wraps. As a result, I haven't experienced many exhilarating thrills. My big-fat-lie-of-a-life is also a big-butt-boring-life.

"Not anymore," says Bennett.

Buoyed by his confidence and grinning like a loon, I navigate the deserted roadway like a *NASCAR* superstar. The countryside blurs as I focus on an open stretch. I shift into third, ready to take on the world when out of nowhere...I spy a flock of ambling sheep!

Bennett swerves!

I brake!

And the car spins...

"I say, that was astonishing."

"You mean harrowing." My heart's pounding against my chest like a battering ram and I'm pretty sure, given my death grip, Watson will have to pry my fingers from the steering wheel.

Glancing over, I see that he looks as rattled as I feel. His sunglasses are askew and his brow's shiny with sweat.

Although my pulse is racing, blood drained from my face when we went into that terrifying 360 spin.

The car stalled along with my stoked courage. That said, we're still on the road and facing the right way. No one is hurt, including the sheep.

"If you hadn't panicked, we would have sailed past those animals without incident," Bennett says. *"That's why I swerved. Why the devil did you brake?"*

"I was blindsided by a memory from last year," I snap. "I was driving on a backroad. A deer dashed in front of me and I clipped it. I wasn't even going all that fast and it was awful. Just awful. When I saw those sheep…"

"You don't have to explain your reaction to me," Watson says while straightening his crooked shades. "I would have braked as well, although I can't swear I would have managed that spin as expertly as you did."

That wasn't me. That was Bennett. The *Warrior*. The alpha. The dark and dangerous force who shanghaied mild and wary me.

And just like that, I'm spitting mad at him for pushing me beyond my comfort zone. I bang my forehead on the steering wheel hoping he can *feel* it. "Get out."

"If only."

"As you wish," says Watson.

"Not you," I say as the smartly-suited man opens his door. "I mean. Yes. Please. Let's switch places."

"And just when it was getting interesting."

Whatever kick I got out of our exhilarating joy ride has been replaced with fury because of my reckless behavior. Because of Bennett's influence.

I allowed him to cloud my judgement. Instead of taking it slow, I pushed my/our luck. Yes, in the end Bennett regained control and managed the spin. But what if we'd flipped instead? I could have maimed or killed Watson, myself, and those sheep!

I'm seething.

"Are you all right," Watson asks as he rounds the car. "You've gone quite red in the face."

"Delayed reaction to the scare. Give me a sec. I feel a little dizzy."

I hurry away and into a field. With my back to Watson, I give Bennett hell. *"You* are a horrible influence."

"I'm the best thing that's ever happened to you. But now is not the time to discuss it."

"Now is never the time to discuss anything. Not with Liza. Not with Watson. Not with you! I'm tired of being put off or hushed up and if I hear 'in due course' one more time, I'll blow a gasket!"

"Is that somehow different to what you're doing now?"

Punching the air, I squash a frustrated scream.

"Calm yourself, Miss Albright, and think. I may have pushed you into taking the wheel, but once we conquered the challenge, you

relished the thrill. You shifted into third, not me. You were in control. Until you panicked."

I blink. I breathe. I curse him for being right.

"Had you not doubted yourself, and me, we'd still be on our way, making haste instead of wasting time."

I want to argue, but I can't. "The sooner we hit the road," I snap, "the sooner we'll get to London."

I turn on my heel, careful not to trample a patch of wild-flowers as I stalk towards the car. For the first time since melding, I'm not at odds with Bennett's earnest stride.

I sense a flicker of amusement—not mine—and a hint of a smile—also not mine. Gabriel Bennett is smiling.

Hard to imagine.

I don't even care that it's at my expense. I wish I could see it.

"In due course, Miss Albright."

Fortunately, I spend the rest of the journey in the passenger seat. And, even better, Watson is happy to answer my questions regarding my father. *Un*fortunately, he doesn't know very much.

According to the chatty solicitor, Dominic enlisted his services only two months prior.

They corresponded mostly by emails or text or phone. They only met in person once—when Dominic visited Watson's office in Canterbury to sign legal documents. That's also when he entrusted Watson with a key to a security box that stored related items such as the security key cards to Blackmoor and the debit card for me.

When I push him on Dominic's occupation, he sticks with the immigration story.

"All I know," Watson says, "is what he told me. He *told* me he worked for an elite security company that monitors and neutralizes threats to our borders. He didn't elaborate, but it sounded like an outfit that deals with illegal aliens and/or potential terrorists."

Or as described by Bennett, a *Character Assassin* who *erases* invading rogue *FICs* from an alternate universe. Which sort of translates to illegal alien, not that I intend to share any of this with Watson.

"When informed of Mr. Sinclair's death," he goes on, "I was told details are classified. I assume he died in the line of duty."

Like Victoria.

"You mentioned he has an apartment in the city," I say.

"Had."

"Do you know what happened to his belongings?"

"Confiscated by the security company he worked for. If I were you, Zoe, I wouldn't pry into your father's life. He was an imposing figure and, given his profession, he no doubt tangled with nefarious sorts."

Bennett grunts. It's the first sound he's made in miles. His/my eyes have been glued on the motorway absorbing every facet of my/our surroundings.

Paved roads, overpasses, lampposts, massive billboards, tunnels with electric lighting, shopping complexes, endless housing, and, as we near our destination, sky scrapers.

His first look at the outside world in more than a century. Instead of being overwhelmed, all I sense is Bennett's wonder.

Suddenly, Watson switches from talking about someone

he doesn't know well, to a place he apparently knows like the back of his hand.

London.

As we close in on the heart of the city, Bennett vibrates with interest.

"Are you cold?" Watson asks me. "You're trembling."

"Nervous excitement," I answer for me and my other half. For my part, I've never been to London or any other major city for that matter. Growing up, we moved around a lot but Liza always kept us to the remote edges of the smallest of towns. I've always equated isolation with serenity. The lower the population, the fewer assured dead zones.

Bennett hasn't seen this city since 1899. I wonder if he recognizes much at all.

I wonder what he's thinking.

Meanwhile, Watson's maneuvering bumper-to- bumper cars and the famous red double-decker buses. Watching him manipulate the clutch and stick in stop-and-go traffic gives me second thoughts regarding the joy of driving a manual, but Watson seems unperturbed as he embraces the role of tour guide.

"We're coming up on Westminster Bridge," he says, and then nods to his right. "*That* spectacular creation is the London Eye, Europe's tallest Ferris wheel and one of our most popular modern attractions."

Bennett's sense of awe rivals my own. And that's saying something.

"When we cross the river to the west side, on the left you'll see three of our oldest and most visited sites. Parliament, Big Ben, and Westminster Abby."

"A welcome sight," says Bennett as his mood turns wistful.

"Normally I'd urge you to put this area at the top of your sightseeing list, but given the news reports of late, I'm wary. In fact, I advise you to refrain from walking alone anywhere along the Thames and especially after dark."

Ice trickles down my spine even as Bennett burns with curiosity. "Can you elaborate?" I ask.

"Not much. The police are withholding details. Grisly affair," he says while braking for a mix of tourists and businessmen. "Far and away from any Penelope Pringle kerfuffle, I can tell you that."

Penny's recent gruesome ramblings roar in my brain and suddenly I'm envisioning every pedestrian as a potential victim. Not wanting to hear, but needing to know, I say, "The gist of it will do."

"We need to talk," says Bennett.

"Recently," says Watson, "the city's been plagued with random violent attacks on unescorted women. Due to the sinister nature of the crimes, the media labeled the unknown assailant: *The Thames River Monster.*"

TWELVE

Wicked Deeds and Primitive Reads

WHAT ARE the chances that Penny's 'monster' is the Thames River Monster?

I ponder that farfetched scenario as Watson navigates traffic in order to deliver me (and Bennett) to MOMI. He points out historical and cultural highlights as we pass through Trafalgar Square, Leicester Square, and onward to Bloomsbury.

"Although The Museum of Miraculous Innovations is fascinating," Watson says, "Bloomsbury is most famous for the British Museum—a veritable treasure trove for any lover of history, art, and culture. I highly recommend a visit and, as it happens, it's just across from MOMI. As for shopping…"

Watson's attempt to distract me from his (and Penny's) warning of a 'madman on the loose' is futile.

By the time he pulls to the curb, announcing, "This is it,"

I'm ready to jump out of my skin and leave my body to Bennett.

I'm not built for this, I think.

"You're not trained for this," Bennett corrects. *"But you will be."*

"That," Watson says while pointing to an enormous neoclassical structure surrounded by a majestic wrought iron gate, "is the British Museum. And that," he adds, nodding to a far less impressive brick building across the street, "is MOMI."

"I'm sure I'll enjoy them both," I blurt while anxiously unbuckling my seat belt.

"Are you sure you don't want me to pick you up later?" asks Watson.

"Positive. I don't know how long I'll be. I might even loop back to the theater district, catch a play, feed my creative muse," I say in a forced cheery voice. "Maybe I'll book a hotel for the night and sightsee tomorrow. You pointed out several fascinating attractions. As long as I'm here, right?"

I have no intention of doing any of those things, but Bennett is urging me to ditch Watson pronto and for an extended period. I don't feel great about that. Watson's my lifeline to normalcy. But honestly, I don't know what's in store for me next and it doesn't seem fair to drag the father of a young child into this crazy mess.

"I promise I'll be careful," I say, hoping to ease his mind. "Either way, I plan on taking the train back to Canterbury. If I run into trouble, I'll call."

He smiles at that. "Good to know. And good luck with your research. Mimi's anxious for Penelope's next adventure. As am I."

"That makes three of us. Four if you count my editor."

Pushing out of the car, I barely manage to wave goodbye before Bennett propels me down the sidewalk. My gaze ping-pongs between the museums and the multitudes of global visitors passing through their doors.

Bennett was right. The extent of my sheltered upbringing is shocking.

Midway across the stone courtyard leading to the main entrance of MOMI, Bennett looks over my shoulder. I sense his relief. *"He's gone."* And irritation. *"I'm surprised the doting solicitor didn't insist on seeing you safely inside."*

"I think it's sweet that he cares. I—" I nearly take a header when Bennett-the-body-invader reverses our course without warning. "What are you doing? I thought—"

"According to Dom, due to renovations and increased patronage, accessing HQ during the museum's operational hours is no longer advisable. Nor is it even possible without specific identification."

"But if we're not going inside—"

"We're going inside. But not through a conventional door."

Before I know it, we cross Great Russell Street and hurry south. "I'm totally confused."

I'm also talking to myself. Or so it appears to fellow pedestrians. I know those looks. I hate those looks. I force us to a stop at the corner in order to rummage through my bag. I nab my phone, fighting my own body (thanks to Bennett) to hold my ground while looping a wireless headset over my right ear.

"Miss Albright—"

"I can't insert the earbud because of the *Baffle*. But it doesn't matter. It's just for show. Now people will think I'm speaking with someone on my phone instead of talking to myself."

"Or you could converse mentally as I suggested before."

"That doesn't come naturally for some reason. I've always talked out loud to Penny."

"Ah, yes. Penelope Pringle. About her…"

Someone shoves me—*hard*—and snatches my phone.

"Hey!" I bolt after the thief, nab him by the shirt, and yank him to a stop.

He pivots with a wild swing and…

I punch him! Hard enough to send him *flying*!

He lands flat on his back, dazed and bleeding from his nose, my phone spinning on the sidewalk several inches from his limp hand.

"Holy *shite*," someone shouts. "Did you see that?"

"That bird clocked a mugger."

"And he's twice her size."

A woman gives me the thumbs up.

I blink. I cringe. As a crowd gathers, I retrieve my phone and fight the urge to puke.

"Are you all right?" some guy asks.

I nod, but I'm lying. I'm not all right. I'm sickened by my violent behavior, even though you could call it self-defense. The thief swung first. Only it wasn't me who chased the creep and landed that powerful, knuckle-smarting punch.

It was Bennett.

The mugger stirs, but the onlookers deter him while hailing a cop.

Backtracking, I duck into a coffee shop, wanting to disappear, needing a jolt of something familiar because I swear I feel myself, my essence, slipping away.

"You took control," I snap at Bennett while massaging my stinging knuckles. "*Complete* control."

"*I acted appropriately.*"

"Not for me! I don't hurt people! I don't kill people!"

"Are you all right, Miss?"

I blink through tears at a wary barista. She thinks I'm talking to myself. She's worried I'm nuts. Just like when I was little. *Poor thing. Weird kid.* But Liza isn't here to make excuses for my odd behavior. And no doubt she's happier for it. She hasn't bothered to check in on me once since flying off to Tahiti with her new husband.

It's just me.

And Gabriel Bennett—the new voice in my head.

Not trusting myself to answer the barista, I skip the coffee and make a hasty exit. My heart's pumping. Or maybe it's Bennett's. I don't know anymore.

"I'm afraid you're going to make me do something I can't live with."

"*Then I suggest we visit Wiz as quickly as possible.*"

<hr />

I pull myself together and rely on Bennett's strength. Mine is definitely waning. "I'm not hungry," I say as we hit the next block, "probably because *you're* not hungry. But whatever small part of me that's still *me* is having a sugar-low."

"*Have a sweet, Miss Albright. I'm guessing you have a supply.*"

"Oh, right." I dig through my bag and manage to inhale two crème-filled oatmeal cookies by the time we stop at a store mid-block. The museums are a short block behind us.

This storefront, unlike the garish red souvenir shop beside

it, is painted a deep, respectable blue with gold and ivory accents. I look up at the signage.

Quimby: Antiquarian Bookseller
Specializing in 18th & 19th Century Literature

"Oh, no," I say with a mouth full of cookie.

"Not to worry. Unlike you, I am not allergic to books. And it would seem that I am dominating this melding."

"Like I need a reminder."

He/we push through the ivory door. The wood creaks and a bell tinkles. I'm immediately assaulted by the sight and smell of stacks and stacks and shelf after shelf of really old books.

"May I help you?" asks a scratchy male voice.

A rail of an ancient man, no taller than my five-foot-two, is balancing on a ladder and shelving a massive book that looks twice his weight.

Prompted by Bennett I say, "Wicked deeds and primitive reads."

"110?"

"3722"

I assume we're talking code. I don't know what any of that means, but stick man, with his bluish, thinning hair and thick-lensed glasses, points down a dimly lit hall, saying softly, "Reading Room B."

I feel his eyes on me/us as I/we move deeper into the musty smelling shop.

Three doors down—Reading Room B. "Have you been here before?" I whisper as we move inside and lock the door.

"No. But Dom described Quimby's in detail."

I assume we're going to search for some secret something in one of the several books stacked on the lone table of the tiny room. Instead, we study the square panels of the wooden walls and the antique brass lighting sconces.

"I guess my father gave you that entry code, too?"

"Should I ever need it, yes."

"So what does it mean?"

"Ah. There." We're looking at a particular lighting fixture.

It's a reach for me, but he/we stretch up and tilt the base to the right, then tap the panel beneath it. A slim section of the wall swings open. We slip through to the other side, and then close the panel behind us.

"A secret passage. I should have known."

Without hesitation, we climb down steep, winding stairs, and then navigate a dimly lit corridor. It's tight, cold, and creepy. If it were just me, I'd be skittish. But, mostly right now, I'm Bennett.

Nerves of steel.

Still... "About that code," I say, wanting to break the eerie silence as we press onward. "Given the whole *Character Assassin* and rogue *FIC* thing, I sort of get the 'wicked deeds and primitive reads' reference. But what do the numbers stand for? 110?"

"A nod to the Dewey Decimal System."

I think. I frown. "The numbers on nonfiction books at a library?"

"Don't tell me you don't know what they stand for."

"Why would I know? I told you. I don't do libraries."

He grunts. *"A writer who doesn't read."*

"I read plenty. I just don't do print books and brick and mortar libraries. Remind me to tell you about eBooks some time. Digital reads."

"Dom already did."

"Sounds like my father spent a lot of time hanging out at Blackmoor and talking to thin air. Because he couldn't see you, right?"

"Right."

I wait for him to elaborate.

He doesn't.

Meanwhile we're still walking and even though I've seen several recesses and side tunnels, Bennett seems sure of this path. I wonder how much farther we have to go and how deep we're under the ground. "Is it me or are the walls closing in?"

"It's you."

"I'm guessing these are catacombs? I researched them once for a story. Any one of these alcoves could be crammed with rotting coffins, or stacks of skulls, or, cripes, long-toothed, fang-toothed rats. I'm not fond of any of those things."

"Those things are the least of your worries."

I blink. I shudder. Harnessing my imagination, I pluck my phone from my bag and focus again on the code. No signal. "Darn. I wanted to *Google* the Dewy Decimal system."

"Explain Google."

"It's a search engine. A way of looking up things on the Internet."

"The electronic encyclopedia."

"Let me guess. You learned about the Internet from Dominic."

"110 represents books pertaining to metaphysics."

I ponder. I guess. "As in otherworldly? Supernatural?"

"Precisely."

"And what about that second code? 3722. What does that stand for?"

"Think Alexander Graham Bell."

Still holding my phone, I thumb my dial pad. The numbers —and the little letters next to them—glow with potential answers. While staring at my screen, I bang my shoulder on a jutting stone. "Ow."

"Watch where we're going."

I glance up just as the corridor widens, then splits into three different directions. We veer to the left and come to a door. An arched metal door with a bunch of symbols engraved in the wall, sort of like caveman hieroglyphics.

"Headquarters," Bennett says as I tap a sequence of symbols per his bidding. *"Salvation,"* he adds as the latch trips open and we escape inside a massive room.

I breathe easier in the spacious expanse, but Bennett's exhilaration warps into confusion as we note the empty shelves and barren work stations. *"What the..."*

He/we move quickly into an adjoining room, colliding with a young man toting an armful of books.

Startled, the young dude with the man-bun drops his burgeoning load while fumbling for something at his hip.

In a flash, I'm staring down the green glowing barrel of a really weird and scary gun.

Before Bennett throws a punch, I blurt my father's name. "Sinclair! I'm a friend of Dominic Sinclair! Well, more of an acquaintance. I'm a psychic in need of a job. He said I'd find one here."

Man-Bun Book-Boy narrows his eyes. "When did he tell you that?"

"A while back," I lie. "He even trained me," I add for good measure. "A little anyway. I wasn't sure this was for me, but now I am."

"He must've seen something special in you if he supplied you with directions and codes."

"He has three seconds to divert that damned Neutralizer," says Bennett.

"He told me to ask for Wiz," I blurt.

"Ryker isn't here." Seemingly appeased that I'm friend, not foe, he holsters his sci-fi-ish revolver. "I'm Odion. ESCA's newest recruit."

Esca.

I ponder the word as well as his accent. British with a hint of Middle Eastern? His seductive dark eyes flicker with intelligence, not malice. The man and his weapon don't add up. With his long, dark hair twisted into a top knot, Odion looks like an exotic geek, not a lethal killer. "You're an assassin?"

"Indirectly. I'm the brains behind the *Warrior*," he says with a proud sniff. "The resident *Scholar*."

As if I should be impressed by the title. "Ah." I say, scrambling to peek at my phone's dial pad while he collects the mess of books from the floor.

3-E

7-S

2-C

2-A

ESCA!

"The Elite Society of Character Assassins," Bennett supplies. *"3722."*

"And you are?" Odion asks.

"Oh, sorry. I'm Zoe," I say while pocketing my phone.

"Hi, Zoe. I'm Odion."

"So you said." I realize he's dawdling with the books and checking out my legs. I don't care. But Bennett does. I clutch Odion's shoulder, not of my own volition, and pull him to his feet.

"Well, Zoe," he says while meeting my gaze. "You're either absurdly brave or certifiable."

I stare. I frown. "Why would you say that?"

"Didn't Sinclair tell you? *Enablers* are a hunted breed."

THIRTEEN

The Monster Within

BEFORE YESTERDAY, I'd never heard of an *Enabler*. Not in the sense that Bennett, and now Odion (the gun-toting *Scholar*), use the word.

An unusually gifted psychic.

Like Victoria. Like Charlotte. And according to Bennett, like me. Clairaudient sensitives trained to enable *Warriors* to track and erase their fictional quarry.

And now, in addition to having a second person declaring our existence, I've learned we're also being hunted!

The shock of this revelation reverberates twofold throughout my body.

News to me. News to Bennett.

For a moment, we grapple with the notion in silence.

Personally, I'm absorbing the confirmation that there is truth in Bennett's otherworldly ramblings.

Enabler, Warrior, Wizard, Scholar. Character Assassins.

Odion, who appears solid and very much human, is dressed in contemporary clothing—cargo pants, wrinkled tee, and trekking boots. Man-bun aside, he looks like a brainiac college student (except for the steampunk-ish gun holstered low on his hip) and he's talking the same farfetched talk as Bennett.

He also knew my father.

My head is spinning.

Bennett prompts my questions. "What do you mean a hunted breed?"

Odion, who's now packing book after book into a bronze chest on wheels, spares me a pitying glance. "This isn't a conversation I'd normally have with an outsider, but since you're here, and more so since you're vulnerable, I suppose I can make an exception.

"*Enablers* have been mysteriously dropping dead for weeks," he says while shifting to an antique shelving unit to collect more antiquated books. "I say mysteriously because we have yet to determine who or what, specifically, has been killing them. What we do know is that, for the first time in centuries, ESCA is ill prepared for a war on reality. Without an *Enabler* a *Warrior* is handicapped when it comes to hunting dangerous *FICs*." He casts me a squinty look. "I assume Sinclair briefed you on the basics."

"*Fictopia*. Alternate universe. Rogue *FICs*. Fractured borders. Got it. Go on." I'm impressed that I absorbed and retained so much considering everything I've been through today. Then again Bennett's inside me, feeding me words, controlling my actions.

Like now.

Instead of allowing me to pace off my increasing and excessive aggressiveness (*his* aggressiveness), he's got me rooted, arms crossed, and watching Odion's every move and expression.

"Surviving *Enablers*, trained veterans of ESCA," he clarifies, "are in protective custody. Most *Warriors* have gone underground. The loss of Dominic Sinclair was a vital blow. As a result ESCA shut down. Temporarily. We hope. As for the presiding *Wizard*, he relocated to an undisclosed location in an attempt to resurrect the society. Ryker is unattainable," Odion says. "Even to me."

That last part hits me hardest. "But he's my only hope!"

"Wiz?" Closing the lid on a second storage chest, Odion eyes me warily. Again. "Why?"

"Say no more, Miss Albright."

But… "We need him to break the spell!"

"What spell? And what '*we*'?" Odion doesn't wait for me to answer. He sounds and looks as anxious as I feel. He's pushing those rolling chests into what looks like an elevator.

He's abandoning headquarters like the others, I realize, but not without a massive collection of hardcover books. Are they priceless collectibles? The last of their kind? Wouldn't it be easier to house all of the stories and/or information on a hard drive or up in the Cloud? Is ESCA an archaic society mired in archaic ways? And what did he mean by 'a war on reality'?

My anxiety wrestles with Bennett's might. He's commanding my body, my movements, but he can't shut me up. When Odion returns for the final chest, I seize my last chance, desperate to break the Binding Spell. "I say 'we' because I'm not alone. I'm possessed by the spirit of Gabriel Bennett."

"*The* Gabriel Bennett? Of Blackmoor?" He grunts, looking at me now in that way I hate most. Like I'm batty. "If that's true," Odion says, "then *you* can take on this monster." Reaching into the chest, he tosses me a binder. "ESCA's got bigger problems."

His words are reminiscent of Penny's recent warning. "*Bigger fish to fry. Like a heinous mad scientist intent on global domination!*"

Crap.

"*Shite.*"

Meanwhile, Odion jams the chest into the already crammed elevator, not giving me a second look as the doors shut and he and his treasured library disappear.

I blink. I panic. I want to chase him but we don't. "Why are we letting him escape instead of picking his brain? He's our only tie to Wiz. Maybe if I tell him who I really am—"

"*I don't trust him.*"

"But he's a member of your elite team."

"*He had no knowledge of the spell that binds us. If Wiz didn't trust him enough to—*"

"Maybe Wiz was already in seclusion when he pulled this magical stunt. Or maybe we're barking up the wrong tree. Maybe someone else cast the spell."

"*Or maybe Wiz saw fit to keep your existence under wraps.*"

I feel Bennett's impatience and also his desire to parcel his knowledge. He's only divulging bits of what he knows or suspects so as not to overwhelm me. I can't *hear* his thoughts, but I *feel* his emotions. He's concerned. About me.

"*I told you. You need a protector and a teacher, Miss Albright. You're ignorant of your heritage, untrained and vulnerable, and a bloody infuriating pacifist. Of course, I'm concerned.*"

His harsh assessment stings, but I'm too flustered to retaliate. I'm standing in a deserted underground headquarters of some otherworldly society, arguing with a voice in my head. I'm desperate for a case of cupcakes and a pot of coffee. I'm dying to *Scramble*, to garble Bennett's voice. I'm itching to call Liza, who probably won't answer.

"On Dom's last visit to Blackmoor he warned there's a traitor in our midst. I do not entrust your wellbeing to anyone I am personally unacquainted with."

"Because I'm an *Enabler?*"

"Because you are Dom and Vikki's daughter."

"An anomaly," I say, repeating his observation from earlier today. "A freak. A monster."

"Unique," he amends.

Prodded by Bennett, I move to a table and dump the contents of the binder—a skinny old book and several newspaper clippings. My palms itch just thinking about touching and turning those pages.

"Mind over matter, Miss Albright."

Before I can argue, we/I open the book to the title page. *"The Strange Case of Dr. Jekyll and Mr. Hyde,"* I say. "A classic."

"You've read it?"

"No. But I'm familiar with the story. Everyone knows the concept of Jekyll and Hyde. Dueling personalities within the same body. The inner struggle of good versus evil. Over the years, this story's been adapted for film and stage dozens of times. A good man ingests an experimental serum and morphs into a violent monster who maims and kills and… "

I trail off as Bennett leafs through the newspaper articles— all dated within this last month. I say *Bennett* because I'm not interested in reading the gruesome details connected to head-lines like…

BRUTAL MAULING BY HEARTLESS MONSTER!

Or…

THAMES RIVER MONSTER STRIKES AGAIN!

Regardless, I skim the accounts against my will, cringing at the brutality and outcomes of four separate attacks on three women and one teen girl.

"Watson was right. Details are scant regarding the assailant. And yet Odion suspects Jekyll and Hyde."

"The Dr. Jekyll and Mr. Hyde? As written by…" I glance at the book's spine. "… Robert Louis Stephenson? You realize this story was published back in…" I skim the title page.

"1886," Bennett says.

"Jekyll and Hyde are a product of the author's imagination."

"A fictional character who, thanks to mankind's rabid fascination, thrives in Fictopia. Or at least he…they did until recently. If Odion is right, Jekyll and Hyde breached a border between fiction and fact and are now terrorizing the Real World. Specifically modern day London."

"You're kidding, right?"

"As I said before, Miss Albright, I never jest."

I feel a surge of rage and purpose—Bennett's purpose—and suddenly I'm jamming the book and clippings into my messenger bag while heading back toward the catacomb entrance. "Where are we going?"

"You heard Odion. Surviving Enablers *are in protective custody and most* Warriors *have gone underground. The Elite Society of Character Assassins, a security team sworn to protect mankind from rogue FICs, is crippled. Someone has to track and erase the Thames*

River Monster and those someones, by process of elimination, Miss Albright, are you and me."

"I don't know how to track and I refuse to kill—"

"Erase."

"—anyone. Not even a psychotic doctor who succumbs to dark impulses and violent behavior."

"Not even to save a fellow human being? A woman? A child? An innocent man?"

"That's not fair."

"No. That's life. Your life as it was meant to be lived."

I can feel my reservations buckling under Bennett's resolve. My pacifist nature losing to his warrior ways. I have to admit the notion of eradicating evil, of protecting the innocent, is empowering. Like a soldier or a super hero. But I know me. *Me.* Zoe Albright—creator and writer of whimsical kids books. If I physically kill someone—*anyone*—I won't be able to live with myself.

Unless I don't know myself at all.

I certainly never knew my parents or of their commitment to ESCA. If I'm a product of an *Enabler* and a *Warrior,* does that amplify my *Misfortune*? In addition to hearing voices, do I possess a killer instinct? A suppressed dark side?

Less than an hour ago, I grabbed and punched a mugger without hesitation. Yes, Bennett fueled my actions, but in that blurred moment of righting a wrong, of stopping a crime, I freely indulged a violent impulse. I didn't feel bad until after.

Panicked now, I freeze us in our tracks. "What if you're my Hyde? My monster within? What if I end up embracing the notion of killing for the greater good and morph into a heartless assassin?"

"I am not heartless, Miss Albright. Nor am I your monster within."

"Then get out. Find another way to break the Binding Spell. You said it yourself. I'm untrained and vulnerable. Rectify that and we'll stand a greater chance of tracking and thwarting a villainous *FIC*. Otherwise," I say while digging through my purse for a weapon, "I'll fight you with every ounce of my bloody, infuriating pacifist soul."

Armed with a chocolate bar, I fuel my *Scrambler*, one ravenous sweet bite at a time. As I chew, Bennett reflects. I sense his frustration, but also a blip of respect.

Seizing a chance to brainstorm, I prompt alternate scenarios like I used to do with Penny. "So Wiz is unattainable," I say. "There has to be another way to break this Binding Spell. For you and I to operate individually outside of Blackmoor Manor. Use your imagination, Mr. Bennett. Think outside of the box."

I'm desperate. I'm hopeful. I'm trusting my gut and his otherworldly experiences.

My heart sings when I feel a physical and emotional shift via Bennett. As I/we turn and stride down an unfamiliar-to-me hall.

"Here's hoping they left behind a small portion of ESCA's vast collection," Bennett says as we open a door marked: SCIENTIFIC AND SUPERNATURAL ARTIFACTS

Stepping inside a cavernous room the size of a small warehouse, I sense his relief and excitement when spying random objects displayed and/or stored in various sections. Gizmos and gadgets of assorted sizes—from electronic devices to weapons to modes of transportation. Some archaic. Some futuristic. Many, like Odion's brass-studded, green-glowing Neutralizer, have a steampunk edge.

"I feel like a sci-fi geek in the midst of a ginormous Comic Con." I'm in awe, overwhelmed, and curious to explore every awesome-sauce artifact.

Surprisingly, Bennett breezes by everything—even a badass weapons display. Urging us deeper into the room, he/I/we finally stop in front of a vehicle straight out of an H.G. Wells movie. Or, more accurately, a classic Wells' novel. I'd know this contraption anywhere.

"Thinking outside of the box," Bennett says as my pulse jumps to hyper drive. *"Or in the words of H.G. Wells, 'Changing the shape of the future.'"*

Before I know it, we're sliding into a red upholstered driver's throne and turning a bunch of dials. I'm torn between fear and euphoria as we grasp a crystal-knobbed lever that will (theoretically) set us on a path to the future or past. "Seriously?"

"If you can drive a stick shift, Miss Albright," he says as the engine whirs, *"you can handle a time machine."*

FOURTEEN

What the Dickens?

I'M FLOATING, no, falling.

Falling for my dream man. No, the man in my dream.

The man holding me, kissing me, coaxing me.

"Stay with me, Zoe."

I know that voice, miss that voice.

Don't go, Gabriel.

Abandoned. Lost. Floating. Falling.

Flying?

Muddled thoughts.

Sore thoughts. *No.* Sore head.

Did we wreck?

Damaged and delusional.

Dazed and dreaming.

I'm dreaming.

Bennett?

Two things register as I slowly stir to life.

Voice croaky.

Ceiling cracked.

Or maybe I mean my head. Cracked like an egg. Or is that *fried* like an egg? Maybe I mean my brain. Fried. Fritzed.

Forehead.

I'm grasping for words, clawing through fog.

Brain fog!

I feel disconnected or disassembled or...

Disoriented. That's the word.

I stare at the ceiling, that white cracked ceiling.

Where am I?

"Where are we?"

Bennett's silence is baffling.

Baffles.

Maybe they're blocking his voice. I reach for the magical earplugs. They're gone! Did I lose them? Did he take them?

Sluggish and sweaty, I kick off a pile of blankets. I'm still wearing my sundress, but my feet are bare. My body's achy and stiff and my head is throbbing. I palm my forehead and wince. "What the..." *Where did I get this big honking goose-egg? How...*

My brain explodes with a fractured memory.

Me and Bennett—*as one*—seated in the time machine. Spinning dials. Pulling levers... My upper body flailing as the machine bucked and shimmied with groaning ferocity. Lurching forward and...

I must have banged my head. I don't recall. As hard as I try, I can't remember anything between then and now.

I blink. I breathe. I try to calm the panicky notion that

something went terribly wrong. "Did the conk to my head knock you unconscious, too?"

No response.

"Gabriel?" I hate that I feel abandoned or is it anxious? No, *adrift*. That's the word.

Spooked, I push into a sitting position and hug my knees to my chest. On top of everything else, I'm nauseous. Puke green and dizzy.

"Get a grip, Z."

Swallowing bile, I absorb my surroundings and struggle for clarity. One thing's certain. I'm no longer in the cavernous room of SCIENTIFIC AND SUPERNATURAL ARTIFACTS.

Instead of sitting in the time machine, I'm hunkered on a lumpy mattress of a four-poster bed. Instead of retrofuturistic gadgets and gizmos, this small room is stuffed with a massive armoire, a washstand, a vanity, a burgeoning bookcase, and an old fashioned writing table.

The striped wallpaper and the flourish border are hideously busy. Worse, they clash with the flowered drapes hanging from the window across the room. The décor screams Victorian, much like the contents of Blackmoor Manor, only much more modest. And instead of spacious, this bedroom is downright claustrophobic.

It also lacks the magical sound-proofing of Blackmoor.

I don't hear voices, but there's buzzing in my ears. The low-level hum that used to be my normal before I experienced the wonder of true silence.

It's unnerving. Sort of like when Bennett first entered my body.

Bennett.

I slap my cheeks in an effort to rouse my sleeping half.

"Wake up, Gabriel! I need you." I'm desperate for a familiar face, presence, partner, whatever.

This time his lack of response startles me into action.

Heart thudding, I swing out of bed, my bare feet sinking into a coarse, floral carpet. I'm dizzy and weak. No, not weak. *Light on my feet.* "Like I've shed a hundred pounds."

That's when I get it. Bennett's not unconscious. He's out-of-reach, out-of-body. Out of *my* body! It's just me in here. I don't hear him or sense him, nor do I feel any one of his volatile, annoying, or bolstering emotions.

On the surface, this is good news. We're no longer melded. Except...if he's not inside me, where is he? He's sure as sunshine not in this room. Trust me, I'm looking hard.

I glance at the closed door. Is he just on the other side, in the next room or the one beyond? Or was he sucked back into that bewitched dimension, back to Blackmoor? Was I rescued by a fellow member of ESCA? Or taken hostage by whoever's hunting *Enablers*?

I tell myself to buck up, think smart or at least more clearly before walking out that door.

My gaze shifts to the parted curtains and a wash of daylight muted by a filmy pane. One look and I'll know where I am. In the city? In the country? In my present? In his past? In an apocalyptic future?

Punchy and curious, I step toward that lone window... and topple to my hands and knees.

Woozy from a conk on the head.

Off balance due to operating under my own steam.

Bennett was part of me for several hours. When he left my body, he robbed me of his strength and stamina. His aggression and purpose.

In my frail, shaken state, I'm suddenly and keenly aware of my extreme wariness. Of my impulse to hide from what scares me, instead of annihilating those fears and sampling a more normal existence.

Maybe Bennett was right when he called me a damnable mess. I spent most of my life appeasing my aunt, my guardian, my one and only family. I suppressed my oddities as best I could and accepted our reclusive lifestyle, per Liza's design.

But even as an adult, even after I moved out of my aunt's house, I chose to live in an isolated cabin instead of braving society in order to broaden my experiences and relationships.

I chose an imaginary friend over real friends. Celibacy over intimacy. What does that say about me?

Maybe Julia was right, too. Maybe I am agoraphobic. "And worse. A coward."

Disgusted by the notion, I take Bennett's advice and *grow a backbone*. I reach up and grab the bed's footer and pull myself upright. Ignoring my churning stomach, I square my shoulders and lumber toward that window. I steel my spine and squint through the grimy pane.

I blink. I gasp. My lungs seize even as my eyes widen in wonder.

I'm definitely in a city. A very *old* city. Where the buildings are mostly brick and no more than five stories high. Where the sky is hazed with soot and smoke and the roads are cluttered with horse-drawn carriages.

Charles Dickens's London.

Gabriel Bennett's London.

I'm an uber-fan of period movies based on classic novels. I gobble up historical romance, fantasy, and mystery cable series like candy. Medieval, Regency, Victorian... I geek out over them all, but my heart belongs to Penelope's era. I know the 19th century when I see it and I'm looking at it *now*! I just wish I had a clearer view. The sooty grime on the outer windowpane is maddening.

Even so, I press my nose to the glass, devouring every murky detail. I'm riveted.

I'm a couple of stories high and gawking at the hustle and bustle of a lively shop-lined street.

Costermongers hawking wares from donkey carts—flowers, fruits, vegetables, fish.

Sidewalks lined with gas streetlamps and populated by fashionable pedestrians. Women wearing decorative bonnets and long gowns with puffy sleeves and fitted waists. Men sporting dark trousers and overcoats, top hats and walking sticks.

The laborers on the corners and street—the newsboys, the peddlers, the sweepers, and wagon drivers—are wearing more serviceable attire.

And that's when I spot her.

A bright patch of red and yellow in a sea of brown. An animated young girl arguing with an old man who's selling apples. At least I think it's her. It *has* to be her! She's not wearing her crimson top hat with the exaggerated yellow bow, but she is wearing a crimson gown and her plentiful blonde ringlets are as familiar to me as my own red curls! I gasp as a dog pops its head out of her basket to steal an apple. *Balderdash!*

How did they get here? Or...maybe they came with me? Since they're fueled by my imagination that would make sense. Only that vendor's arguing with Penelope which means he can see her, too!

"Unless I'm hallucinating."

Anxious to find out, I try to open the window, and fail. It's flipping *jammed*!

I slap the filthy pane. "Penny!"

Oblivious to my presence, she continues on her way.

In the opposite direction!

"No, no, no." Desperate to catch her, I spin and run. Pumped on adrenaline, I yank open the door…

And slam into grotesque fanged monster.

FIFTEEN

A Terrifying Prospect

THE MONSTER—A troll? A hunchback?—yelps.

I bounce off his squishy gut, his high-pitched squeal vexing my senses as I stumble back and fall on my butt.

Shouldn't a monster growl or roar?

And then his fangs drop near my feet.

Fake fangs. Like the kind you buy in the horror section of a costume shop.

What the freak?

Still rattled from the fright and collision, I blink up and see that I not only knocked the creature's teeth out, I broke his bulbous nose. It's barely hanging from...another nose, a slender, turned-up nose.

"Gadzooks, you scared the dickens out me," he, no, *she* says. Although dressed in trousers and a mannish shirt, the creature's voice is decidedly feminine. Her accent: British.

She offers me a deformed hand up. "Are you hurt?"

I stare at that hand. Meaty and gnarled. Jaundiced and hairy.

"Oh, right." She flicks her wrists and both hands go flying. Fake like the fangs. "I was working when I heard a banging commotion and your distressed cry. I rushed to your aide and, well, you know the rest."

She's still offering me a hand up, albeit a hairless, dainty hand. This time I take it, allowing her to help me to my feet. I hate that I'm still weak and off balance and therefore vulnerable. I'm also at a loss for words.

"Gabriel warned me that you might be out of sorts when you regained consciousness."

"You know Mr. Bennett?" I croak.

"We've worked together for years," she says while peeling off layers of ugly. A rubbery bulbous nose, bushy caterpillar eyebrows, and a hideous wig of choppy, wolf-man-like hair, hit the floor one-by-one alongside the yellowed fangs.

Stripped of the grotesque accessories, I'm staring at a young woman with delicate facial features, amber eyes, brown skin, and dark auburn hair twisted into a messy, low bun. She's lovely in a wholly natural and exotic way. No wonder Bennett's enamored.

Sideswiped by a pang of jealously, I flush while assuming the obvious. "So you're Lady Moore?"

"Charlotte? Good heavens, no. She wouldn't be caught dead in a costume like this." Mumbling beneath her breath, she untucks her oversized shirt and yanks out a lumpy pillow. AKA: the squishy gut. Lovely *and* slender, she tosses the pillow on the bed and gives me a slow once-over. "I'm Henrietta Hathaway."

"Zoe Albright."

"I know. Gabriel told me all about you. Well, not *all*. Actually, he barely shared a thing. You're an untrained *Enabler* from the future and you traveled here, with him, in a time machine. H.G. Wells would be ecstatic to know that there is a working model of the contraption he inspired in his serial novella. Alas, he must never know. No one," she says in a grave tone, "aside from the core of ESCA can know."

Hands on hips, she finishes her appraisal of me with a raised brow. "Given my extraordinarily inquisitive mind, I'm terribly curious about what it's like in your time—whatever time that is. Gabriel did not offer the year. For instance, do all women dress in this shocking manner whilst in public? Short hemlines? Exposed legs? Or is this confined to American fashion? I assume you're American, given your accent. No, no. Don't tell me. I've been instructed not to pry. The less I know, I was told, the safer you'll be. Although I must say, your state of undress is highly inappropriate for 1898. I'm not sure how long you'll be here, but for today, at least, you can borrow from my wardrobe. Don't move. I'll return shortly."

She whirls and leaves me alone and dizzy from her breathless ramble.

Out of everything Henrietta Hathaway spewed, my brain is stuck on the year. Confirmation that we time traveled. And what's more, that we landed in the past, one year before Gabriel Bennett and Lady Charlotte Moore vanished. Which means his *Enabler*, the woman he refuses to talk about, but so obviously cares for, is alive and presumably well.

Did he abandon me and run straight to her? I hate that I care. I barely know Gabriel Bennett and what I know of him isn't all that likable. The intense attraction, on my part, is purely physical. He's hot. End of story.

Speaking of stories...I rush back to the grimy pane and search the street for my muse.

Just as I feared, Penelope and Balderdash are gone.

"That's if they were ever here."

That sighting could have been wishful thinking. For a moment, I'd felt less alone.

Looking down on the buttoned-up Victorians and feeling even more like a-fish-out-of-water than I usually do, I thank my lucky stars that I ran into Miss Hathaway. Otherwise, I would have burst outside and into the conservative masses, barefoot and indecently exposed.

"Is that why you kept tugging down the hem of my skirt," I ask Bennett—not that he's here to answer. "Because you thought my bare legs were immodest? Are you that old-fashioned?" Considering the scene below, I snort. "Yeah, I guess you are."

Feeling half-naked now, I nab my denim jacket from a peg on the wall and pull it on. Spying my socks and boots, I collapse on a cushioned stool and tug those on as well.

My fingers tremble as I tie the laces. I'm weak and dizzy.

And growing angrier by the moment.

Obviously, Bennett and I are no longer melded and since he had a conversation with Miss Hathaway, he wasn't immediately sucked back to Blackmoor. Also, it is now one year before he was 'cursed' into that bewitched dimension. Therefore, he's of free-will and could be anywhere.

One thing is certain. He's not here with me.

He left me unconscious and in the care of an associate. A

chatty young woman whose 'work' involves masquerading as a frightening freak.

Speak of the devil...

Miss Hathaway breezes back into the room, wearing an ankle-length, yellow-and-red checkered gown while carrying bountiful clothing and pointy-toed boots. "I couldn't decide between the sage green and the peacock blue. Both are decent day gowns, albeit not of the latest fashion. I'll leave the choice to you. I've also included appropriate shoes and fresh unmentionables. The lavatory is—"

"Where is he?" My question sounds more frantic than miffed. More worried than curious. "Is he okay?" I realize, belatedly, that Bennett could also be suffering with time travel jet-lag.

"Gabriel?" She rolls her eyes while dumping her bounty on the bed. "He's a *Warrior*. A special recruit. He is always fine. He's at headquarters consulting with Wiz regarding your dilemma."

"Ryker?"

"Who? Oh. Is that the *Wizard* of your time? No, no, don't tell me. No, I am referring to the present *Wizard*, Archimedes."

My head is spinning and throbbing. "How long was I out? Unconscious, I mean." I touch my goose egg, wondering if it's black and blue.

Miss Hathaway watches my every move. *Intently*. I feel like a rare bug under a microscope—an oddity under scrutiny.

"Several hours," she says.

"Hours?" No wonder I'm wonky.

"You must be famished. Gabriel said you would be. He also mentioned your fondness for sweets and coffee. I hope that Apple Charlotte and a pot of tea will suffice. I also have bread, cheese, and cold meats at the ready. One cannot sustain mental and physical alertness on sweets alone. And you, Miss Albright, need all the energy you can muster. Training is exhausting under the best of circumstances. Yours are not the best of circumstances."

"Training?"

"We'll begin after, or perhaps during, your revitalizing meal. Oh! I almost forgot." She pulls an envelope from her pocket. "Gabriel instructed me to give this to you should you rouse before he returned. I'm only a little late."

A note from Bennett? "Thanks. And thank you for the clothes. I'll change and join you shortly." *Please go so I can read this in private.*

She lingers for an awkward moment. Clearly, she's hoping I'll share the contents of the letter. When I don't, she sighs. "The lavatory is one door away. I'll be waiting downstairs in the dining room. This is a small terraced house owned by my father, Professor Reginald Hathaway." She points to a framed photograph on the wall. "Unfortunately, you won't have the pleasure of his company as he's on an extended expedition."

I squint at the yellowed photo of a white man with a bushy dark moustache. He looks like someone out of an old desert adventure movie. Light-colored suit, pith helmet, a leather satchel looped over his shoulder. The only thing missing is a camel.

"He met my mother, who's no longer with us, whilst on an excursion in the West Indies," Henrietta says.

Perplexed by her defiant tone, I meet her frosty gaze. It's as if she's daring me to criticize her parents' interracial relationship. Or maybe she expects me to snub her now that I know she's biracial? It would never occur to me to do either. Instead I say, "So he's an explorer? A scientist?"

"A man of astonishing intellect with an insatiable thirst for adventure," she says with a proud sniff.

"I'd love to hear about him sometime." Meanwhile, Bennett's letter is burning a hole in my hand.

Taking the hint, my host gestures beyond the threshold. "We employ a lone housemaid who has a chip on her shoulder and a narrow list of services. Hence the clutter and dust. Don't expect me to apologize."

I blink. I stare. I'm thrilled when she leaves the room.

Ripping open the envelope, I unfold Bennett's note. His penmanship, like his searing alpha aura, is remarkable.

Dear Miss Albright,

If you are reading this then you are revived for which I am relieved. It also means that you have met Henri. I ask that you follow her instruction. Observe, listen, and learn. It is vital that you understand the history of the Elite Society of Character Assassins and our eternal purpose. Keeping your heritage secret is equally vital. I implore you. Do not reveal the names of your parents to Henri or anyone else. Your very existence, and perhaps the wellbeing of mankind, rests upon your discretion.

Sincerely,
  Gabriel Bennett

SIXTEEN

The Game is On

GABRIEL BENNETT, I've decided, is a donkey's patootie.

First he abandoned me in freaking 1898—more than a century and a half before I was even a gleam in the eye of she-who-shall-not-be-named.

Then he wrote me a letter suggesting dire consequences should I divulge certain information. Seriously? If I mention my parents' names, I may never be born? *What the freak?* And what's that deal about the wellbeing of mankind? How is that my responsibility? No pressure there!

I obsess on this while racing to the lavatory, aka bathroom, to take care of necessities. At least the plumbing in this modest home is modern enough to have a flushing toilet via a dangling chain. Saved from having to use a chamber pot or outhouse. "Yes!"

There's a bathtub, too, but who has time for that? *Henri's* waiting with a meal and a lesson on the history of ESCA. I'm hungry *and* curious. A sponge bath will do. A speedy one at that.

And all the while, I fume.

How could Bennett leave before I regained consciousness? After all I did for him. *Like lending him my body!*

Minutes later, I'm back in the claustrophobic bedroom, sidestepping portions of Henri's discarded monster bits and attacking the clothes she piled on the bed.

Unmentionables is Victorian speak for underwear. I sift through assorted silk and cotton, trying to remember the appropriate names—corset, chemise, knickers, petticoat. All white. All sensible—as in *super unsexy*.

Except for maybe the corset.

Although… Once fastened and laced, the heavily boned contraption is tiny—as in size sub-zero. *That's the point*, I remind myself. In this era, hourglass figures are fashionable. The smaller the waist, the better.

Um. No.

There's an Apple Charlotte waiting for me—whatever that is—and I intend to gorge. Without the *Baffles*, I'll need to *Scramble* before venturing outdoors. That requires mega sweets and caffeine. Restrictive undies are out.

Even without the corset, I marvel that Victorian women wear so many layers underneath their cumbersome gowns. No thanks. I'm already sweating given the contents of Bennett's letter.

Your very existence, and perhaps the wellbeing of mankind, rests upon your discretion.

My stomach cramps with dread as I step into the A-line skirt of the silky green gown.

Maybe Henri's history lecture will give me insight into the nature of Bennett's ominous warning. Of course, Bennett could shed light, too.

"If he was here."

I know he's with the *Wizard*, discussing possible solutions to our spellbound dilemma, but he should've included me in that brainstorming session. After all, it's me that Bennett's fused to in the 21st century. Speaking of…

How much time lapsed during our time travel jaunt? How long have we been gone? What if we're stuck in the past for weeks? Or *forever*? How will Liza feel if she never sees or hears from me again? Will she mourn my absence? *Or welcome it?* The biggest headache in her life *gone*. Free to live her life as she chooses without having to feel even a little responsible for the wellbeing of her sister's freaky daughter.

Now, in addition to obsessing over Bennett's absence, I'm spinning on my complicated relationship with the woman who raised me. Yes, we clashed, but she's family. The only family I have. The only one who didn't abandon me or die on me.

Liza isn't the perfect parent figure, but at least she put me first.

Unlike *Dom* and *Vikki*.

My thoughts and emotions are volatile and I'm struggling with the bazillion hooks and eyes of the matching bodice. At least the closures are in the front, but *jeez*. I'll never take zippers for granted again.

"Is everything all right in there?" Henri asks through the door.

"Peachy!" I snap. "I mean, I'm good. I'm fine. Be there in a jiff. Thank you."

"Very well. I'll be waiting downstairs in the dining room."

Which, in my frustrated state, sounds like: *Get the lead out, Miss Albright.*

Challenge accepted. The game is on. A game initiated by Bennett.

Observe, listen, and learn.

I bristle. I frown. "I'll show you, *Gabriel*."

I hide his letter in my messenger bag, in between the yellowed pages of *The Strange Case of Dr. Jekyll and Mr. Hyde*. I try not to think about the Thames River Monster and the evil, disgusting crimes he's committing in my time.

"*You can stop it,*" I imagine Penelope saying. If she was here, really here, I'd ask how. It's as if she had insight into this *FIC* stuff months ago. How's that possible? She's a figment of my imagination. A powerful imagination, but still. If *I* didn't know about 'monsters on the loose', how could she?

Irritated, I snag an elastic band from a zippered pocket and twist my long curls into what I hope is an acceptable period bun.

Next, cosmetics. I skip lip balm and mascara, but use my concealer and powder to camouflage the yellowish knot on my forehead. I step back from the vanity mirror, tripping on the skirt's train as I vie for a fuller view.

I blink. I marvel.

My green eyes, red hair, and milky complexion pop against the sage green gown with the bold yellow trim. Given the demure neckline, long sleeves, and floor-length skirt, I thought I'd look conservative and boring.

I don't.

Not to be shallow, but I look, well, *pretty*. Even with the goose-egg. Almost elegant, albeit it in a vibrant, offbeat way.

"Huh."

How do I stack up to Lady Charlotte Moore, I wonder? Will I compare in Bennett's eyes? I hate that I care.

Returning the makeup to my bag, I ignore my stash of emergency snacks. Who knows when I'll need to fuel my *Scrambler* on the fly?

I snag my phone and tap the screen.

Dead.

Even if I could charge it, there are no cell towers in 1898. No mobile calls or texting or Internet or social media. On top of that, television has yet to be invented. No cartoons or movies. No cable news or mini-series. No computers, no tablets, no digital playlists.

The extent of my primitive surroundings hits hard.

Vowing to embrace the adventure, I hide my bag under the bed, square my puffy-sleeved shoulders, and switch to a positive mindset. Instead of dreading whatever training Henrietta Hathaway has in mind, I'll pick her brain and use that knowledge to my advantage.

I am not a damnable mess.

I am resourceful, dammit.

⸝

A British terrace house is sort of like an American townhouse. Two-stories, compact, and connected to an identical property. Finding my way from the upstairs bedroom to the downstairs dining room is easy. Unfamiliar territory, yes, but no chance of getting lost.

Unlike with my creepy trek through the dark and dank

catacombs in order to reach, what turned out to be, the abandoned headquarters of ESCA.

"It could have been worse. There could've been rats."

I shudder and focus on my present innocuous journey. Under different circumstances, I'd take it slower and snoop along the way. I mean this isn't a museum. It's an honest-to-gosh 19th century home. In terms of research for my Victorian based writing, this is gold. However, I'm not on a leisurely field trip. I'm on a mission. To find out as much as I can about Gabriel Bennett and the *Elite Society of Character Assassins*.

That said, I can't help but notice an overabundance of books. I'm careful not to touch them. They're stacked and scattered on almost every surface of every room. Even the hallway floor. Undoubtedly, Henri's aforementioned clutter.

By the time I reach my destination, I've also formed a conclusion.

Hovering on the threshold, I'm trembling with impatience and contemplating etiquette. My host isn't seated at the dining table. She's curled on a sofa at the opposite end of the room with her nose in, you guessed it, a book, and she's seemingly oblivious to my presence.

Should I clear my throat? Rap on the doorjamb? Is it a breach of good manners to enter uninvited? Victorians are prim and persnickety and have a bazillion rules on proper societal behavior. I haven't even mastered social propriety in my own time.

"You're ESCA's *Scholar*," I blurt. So much for a polite greeting.

Henri lowers the book, puffing with pride as she springs to her feet. "Gabriel bragged about me?"

"No. That is, he didn't mention the names of any of his

associates." Aside from my father—a taboo subject and an alliance that I still don't understand.

"Oh. Then I assume you met my future counterpart."

Odion. "I did. He—"

"*He*? ESCA recruited a man to... No, no. Don't tell me. A man as *Scholar*. In the future, no less." She grunts. "So much for progress."

A Victorian feminist. Interesting. And a *Character Assassin* to boot. I hurry to the sofa before she directs me to the table. I sit without invitation. "So, what does a *Scholar* do?" I ask. I want to start my training *now*. "I mean aside from collecting and reading a lot of books."

Instead of sinking gently onto the sofa (like Victorian women do in the movies), Henri plops. Sitting scant inches from me, she widens her eyes. "Gabriel wasn't exaggerating. You *are* oblivious."

My face burns. My blood boils. *Gabriel's* slurs are endless and maddening.

"And I often speak without thinking. I didn't mean that as an insult," she says, "just an observation. We tend to speak bluntly in ESCA."

"I've noticed." Although calling Bennett blunt is an understatement.

"Wouldn't you prefer to eat before delving into specifics?"

"I can't believe I'm saying this, but, no. Henri... May I call you Henri? No, surely that's improper. Miss Hathaway then? If you don't mind, Miss Hathaway, I'd like an immediate course in whatever you can teach me about ESCA and all those involved. My world has been turned upside down and I want to right it. Knowledge is power.

"Bennett," I plow on, "Mr. Bennett, only shared bits and

pieces about ESCA and *Fictopia*, refusing to answer many of my questions because he said I could only absorb so much in a day. But that was yesterday. Or maybe the day before. Or the day before that. I have no sense of time.

"All I know is that when Gabriel Bennett and I next meet, I want to be fully armed, or at least better armed to deal with my circumstance. Not to mention Bennett. He's tightlipped, arrogant, and infuriating. I'm not oblivious, I'm sheltered. I'm also socially awkward which explains my rambling. And sweating." I dab my clammy upper lip. "I'm not used to speaking frankly. I was warned and taught years ago to put a lid on my weirdness. But since you deal in weird... What I mean is..."

She stares. She blinks.

I struggle for coherency.

"I know what you mean," she finally says. "And by all means call me, Henri. You won my regard with 'knowledge is power'. Knowledge is what makes me invaluable to ESCA. As for Gabriel..." She inclines her head and lowers her voice. "He is everything you mentioned... and worse."

SEVENTEEN

ESCA 101

AS A WRITER, I end a lot of chapters with cliffhangers. *"Leave the reader wanting more,"* Julia always says. I never realized how irritating a cliffhanger could be until Henri delivered me a doozy in person.

"As for Gabriel, he is everything you mentioned... and worse."

Then she abandoned the sofa and left me hanging!

On pins and needles, I watch as she obsesses over the dining table, rearranging place settings—once, twice. As if she's uncertain of the proper placement of utensils. As if I care!

"What do you mean *worse?*"

"Don't worry," she says. "The good outweighs the bad. Most importantly, Gabriel is devoted, fearless, and essential."

I bristle. "He's a killer."

"A *Warrior*. Our best, save for one."

I wait for her to elaborate. She doesn't.

Seriously?

Instead, she motions me to join her. "I'm not used to entertaining. Just remember, I promised fortifying, not fancy."

She sounds a little defensive. Or is it awkward? I put myself in her boots and instantly empathize. I've never hosted dinner for a stranger. I've never prepared a meal for anyone other than myself and Liza. Is Henrietta Hathaway socially impaired like me? Is she an outcast in a rigidly moral era? Is she worried about etiquette in her time versus etiquette in mine? Is she self-conscious about the meal? About her home? Yes, it's small, modest, and cluttered, but no more so than my cabin.

Moving toward my host and her table, I absorb details that I missed when I first rushed in. Based on the furnishings and the setup, I'm guessing this room doubles as a dining and sitting area. All of the wood is dark and the fabrics—the curtains, the table linen, and the upholstery—are deep ruby red. There's a fireplace with a mirror hanging above it and a sideboard crowded with knick-knacks, assorted china, and what I assume is dessert.

Henri's gone above and beyond to accommodate me. The clothes, the food, the dessert. *"Gabriel said you'd be famished."*

"I can't have you fainting in the middle of my lesson," she says. "Trust me, I'd take offense. As would Gabriel. We can talk and eat at the same time."

No way, no how am I going to refuse her hospitality a second time. Besides, now that I'm actually looking at the platters of cold meats and cheeses, my stomach's rumbling in earnest. "Sounds good to me," I say with a smile. "Looks good, too."

Visibly relaxing, Henri invites me to sit as she pours our tea. "You did well, by the way. Dressing yourself, I mean. You look smashing, almost as if you belong in this time."

"Almost?"

"You skipped the corset."

"You can tell?"

"I can. How radical of you. And the boots."

"Yours were too small," I say. "I opted for mine. I didn't think anyone would notice them given the long hem of the skirt."

"I noticed. They're not too awful, I suppose. Just inelegant. Boyish."

"Anything else?"

"I have questions," she says as we fill our plates. "But I'm not allowed to ask."

"Bennett instructed me to guard my words as well."

"Irritating, that."

"Yup."

We smile across the table at one another and I suddenly feel as though I'm sharing a meal with a friend. It's a foreign feeling, one I intend to hold close for as long as I can.

"So about my otherworldly studies," I prompt.

"Starting with your first inquiry," Henri says. "The definition of a *Scholar.*"

She tears off a hunk of crusty bread then launches into her lesson with verve. "There are four positions within ESCA. *Wizard, Scholar, Warrior* and *Enabler.* The *Scholar* is a learned individual of superior intellect who reads and studies works of fiction, specifically those with memorable characters written by revered authors. The *Scholar* is the brains of ESCA."

She pauses as if waiting for me to applaud her 'superior intellect'. Odion possessed the same whiff of arrogance. "Impressive," I say and I mean it. Something tells me that Henri worked hard to win this position. In addition, her social skills suck almost as bad as mine, at least by Victorian standards. There's nothing prim or proper about the young woman who's presently stuffing food in her mouth. How in the world does she navigate strict codes of behavior when in public?

She's fascinating.

"Through our studies," Henri says around a mouthful of chicken, "we learn every detail available about the rogue *FIC*, then enlighten society members as to the character's background, habits, strengths, flaws, etc. I often go a step further, masquerading as the fiend as a way of delving deeper into his or her psyche."

"Is that why you were dressed like a troll?"

"Not a troll. *Mr. Hyde.*" She flashes the book she'd been reading on the sofa. "I was trying to emulate Robert Louis Stevenson's Hyde as described within this novella. Gabriel mentioned your problem in the future. The possibility that this character has breached a border and gone rogue."

"I just don't understand how a made-up character—"

"By the time I get through with you, you'll not only understand, you'll believe." She pauses, moving to the sideboard and returning with the Apple Charlotte, a molded dessert that looks to-die-for.

I replenish our tea as she slices into the gooey concoction. Caffeine and sweets. I don't know which jazzes me more. The prospect of fueling my *Scrambler*? Or the infectious enthusiasm of Henrietta Hathaway?

"It started in 1836," she says as I take my first bite of crumble and apples, "four centuries after Guttenberg developed the modern printing press, and precisely one month after a seemingly unstoppable mystery man started killing off those who challenged his claim of Tintegel, the rumored location of Camelot.

"The founding *Wizard* of ESCA, who at the time was working independently as a consultant to the British Prime Minister," she goes on, "suspected that a literary character, *Mordred*—the notorious traitor of the Arthurian legend—had somehow slipped over the border from a fictional world into the Real World. That theory was confirmed and dealt with single-handedly by the *Wizard*. But then a second case emerged less than a year later involving Mary Shelly's *Dr. Frankenstein* and his monstrous creation."

Something in Henri's tone and expression ices my spine. "Frankenstein? Seriously?"

"A chilling episode and one I'll gladly recount at a later date. For now, let's focus on the founding *Wizard's* analysis of the crisis after an in depth interrogation of Dr. Frankenstein."

Suffice it to say… I. Am. Riveted.

Gaze intense, Henri plows on. "In his report to the PM, the *Wizard* concluded that wildly popular literature spawns characters who live and breathe within an alternate universe dubbed *Fictopia*—a universe fueled by man's imagination. Most *FICs*, according to Dr. Frankenstein, are blissfully content or blindingly absorbed in their penned destinies and therefore live out their stories again and again with no thought or wish to break free of their existing plots."

"But then there are the malignant, discontented few," I pipe in. A prior lecture from Bennett explodes in my mind. It sounded like gobbledygook at the time. In one ear and out the other. Or so I thought.

"Diabolical masterminds," I rush on. "Monstrous creatures and tortured souls who, after learning of the existence of the Real World, look for ways to crossover in order to take control of their destinies. To rewrite their tale, so to speak. Gabriel told me."

While waiting for Watson to arrive and to drive us into London, Bennett gave me an earful about *FICs* and how to deal, or rather how *not* to deal with them. At the time, I was reeling from our first and second melding and overwhelmed with otherworldly information.

"You can only absorb so much in one day."

Apparently I absorbed more than we both thought possible.

"I'm only now remembering parts of that discussion," I explain to Henri. "Information overload."

"Perhaps we should break for a while."

"No, no. I'm good." I'm anxious to understand my circumstance in full. I'm also gaining insight into what made my mother and father tick. Getting to know them, even by the nature of their work, helps to appease my rabid curiosity and to soothe a new sense of loss.

"What else did Gabriel reveal?" Henri asks while serving a second slice of dessert.

"He said something about an escalation over the years of villainous *FICs* breaching fractured borders and wreaking heinous havoc. He also mentioned that, due to their supernatural abilities and/or evil masterminds—compliments of their author—rogue *FICs* are essentially impervious to mortal law enforcement."

"Pity that," Henri says, "but true. After the third breach, it was apparent that new measures were in order and that the *Wizard* needed help. Extraordinary help. Which is why the Prime Minster ultimately instructed him to create and organize a secret and highly selective enforcement squad—*The Elite Society of Character Assassins.*"

"Fascinating."

"Quite. I assume," she says in hushed tone, "given what little I know of your plight, that ESCA is still functioning in the future and that *Fictopia* thrives. Since we are talking decades or perhaps centuries ahead, then that means there are countless more stories in your time and countless more *FICs*. Stories that have been published the longest have even more readers, and therefore the featured characters are even more powerful. Hence, the Mr. Hyde of your time could well be a warped or intensified version of the Mr. Hyde of now."

I blink. I cringe. A warped and intensified version of a deranged, violent abomination? "They call him the Thames River Monster," I blurt.

"Interesting."

"I probably shouldn't have told you that."

"Probably not." She looks up from her empty plate and smiles. "It will be our secret."

I can't help but smile back. For the second time I'm struck by the notion that I've made an honest-to-gosh living, breathing *real* friend. Unlike Penelope. Unless...

My head spins at the mere thought. What if Penelope isn't an imaginary friend turned muse? What if she's a *FIC*? A discontented secondary character that slipped over the border to become the star of her own show?

I think of all our brainstorming sessions. The way she

fanned my imagination, causing me to feature her as the main character in all of my books!

Considering everything Henri relayed to me, given my ancestry, and since Penny keeps lecturing me on monsters and mad scientists, maybe 'my muse' found a way to bounce between two worlds. I mean, hello. I time traveled! *Anything* is possible.

"I can't wrap my brain around it," I mutter. "If it's true, what does it mean?"

"The sooner you accept the nonsensical," Henri says, "the easier your training will be." She scrunches her brow. "What are you referring to specifically? What can't you believe?"

I ache to pour my heart out, to share everything about my life as I know it and everything as revealed by Bennett. About my parents, my upbringing, my *Misfortune*, and my muse. Something tells me Henrietta Hathaway, *Scholar* and *Character Assassin*, would have some insight or advice pertaining to my dilemma. But that would mean revealing facts about the future, which could be dangerous. No. There's only one person I can safely speak with and that person's not here.

"Don't be offended, but I better button my lips before I do major damage. Do you have any idea of when Gabriel will return?"

"Truthfully, I expected him before now."

We sit silent for a moment, both struggling with what we can and can't say.

Henri perks up first. "I can ring headquarters and inquire."

"You can?" I rack my brain trying to recall the year telephones were invented or at least in commercial use. Liza must have covered that at some point in my homeschooling.

Henri pops up and takes off.

Startled, I follow, tripping over the hem of my gown twice in my hurry.

By the time I join her in the den, living room, parlor, whatever, she's got her hands on a super old-fashioned phone. I've seen pictures, but nothing like it in person until now. It looks downright bizarre.

"It's called a Candlestick Telephone," she says in answer to my gawking. "Do they have modes of communication like this in your time? No, no. Don't tell me," she says. "Even though I'm dying to know."

I think about my touch-pad cell phone hidden upstairs. Making calls is just one of its many functions and it literally fits in my palm. Henri's Candlestick Telephone is, well, the size of a fat candlestick *and* it has two parts. A tall wooden stick with a mouthpiece and a rotary dial, plus an earpiece attached by a cord. Oh. And the whole thing's wired to the wall. Archaic, but it's something. A way to connect.

With Bennett.

It's all I can do not to grab the thing out of her hands. Instead, I eavesdrop on a one-sided micro-short conversation that seems to start with Wiz and end with Bennett.

Henri hangs up, with a sigh and frown.

"Well?" I nudge. "What did he say?"

"That due to an unforeseen complication, his meeting with Wiz has only begun. He told me to educate you regarding Dr. Jekyll and Mr. Hyde. And he said to tell *you* to stay put and heed his warning. He also said to tell you that Bloomsbury is a mine field of dead zones. Whatever that means."

I'm burning mad. He's doing it again. Bullying. Controlling. Manipulating. "You're not the boss of me," I grumble under my breath. Incensed, I meet Henri's gaze. "It means he's trying to scare me into staying inside. It's why he took the *Baffles*, but, ha, thanks to you, I can *Scramble*."

"What is... No, no. Don't tell me. Bloody hell."

Revved on several cups of strong, sweetened tea and two fat slices of Apple Charlotte, I hike my skirt and jog up and down the stairs to kick my coping mechanism into high gear. From the look on her face, Henri thinks I'm screwy. Then again, she's quirky, too. Who dresses in costume to mind-meld with evil characters?

An unconventional, imaginative woman of superior intellect (if she does say so herself), that's who.

"How far away are we from headquarters?" I ask while pivoting to make a second run.

"Only a couple of blocks."

"Perfect."

"What are you doing?" she asks as the annoying hum in my ears decreases by half.

"Giving Bennett the finger."

EIGHTEEN

Defying Gabriel Bennett

"GABRIEL WILL KILL ME."

"No, he won't." I smirk. I smile. "You're not a rogue *FIC*."

Henri grunts then alerts me of an oncoming carriage as we cross the mucky street. "Be that as it may," she says as we quicken our pace, "this is a monumental breach of trust. He specifically instructed me to keep you inside."

"Under house arrest?"

"Out of sight and trouble."

"I'm as good as invisible in this black overcoat and drab bonnet. Plus, I'm keeping my head down and voice low."

A difficult task considering the intensity of my curiosity. The sights, sounds, and smells of Victorian London, while ordinary to Henri, are extraordinary to me. It's like I'm on another planet or a movie set. Everything is surreal. And yet so similar to the world I created for Penelope Pringle—minus the sooty fog and stench of sewage.

"No one is paying me any mind," I assure her as we step onto a crowded sidewalk. Resisting the urge to hold my nose, I scan the immediate area in search of Penny and Balderdash. This morning's sighting—at least I think I know what I saw—is bugging me, along with the notion that they might be *FICs*.

Let it go, Z. Focus!

"We've only just crossed the street," Henri says. "We have two blocks to go. Anything could happen between here and there and that one thing could alter history. Why, oh, why did I allow you to talk me into this?"

"Because you know I'm right about wanting a say in whatever plan Gabriel is concocting with...Archimedes."

I started to say Wiz, but, Henri cautioned me against using language pertaining to ESCA and *Fictopia* when in public. She cautioned and lectured me about a lot of things. Unwittingly, she gave me the courage to defy Bennett and to brave ancient dead zones in order to shape my own fate.

Armed with otherworldly knowledge and with my *Scrambler* charged, this is the closest I've ever felt to normal. Sure, the history of ESCA and the existence of *Fictopia* is straight out of a sci-fi/fantasy book or movie, but when explained by Henri, the absurd seems plausible. She's not only informed, but persuasive.

Plus, I traveled back in time, which blows the door off of *impossible*.

Appealing to Henri's ego, I pat the gloved hand that's anchored to my arm. "I have complete faith in your ability to keep me and the future safe for the short time it will take us to walk to the museum."

"Be that as it may," Henri says with a haughty hike of her chin, "Gabriel will be displeased and that's putting it lightly."

"*Gabriel* has been displeased with me since the moment we met. Trust me, I can take his guff. Besides if he was so worried about me, he should have stayed with me instead of pawning me off on you. Considering he took advantage of my body..." I falter. I blush. "Never mind."

Henri stops abruptly and, since she's got a death grip on my arm, so do I.

"I *knew* there was something between you two."

"I didn't mean...Wait. What do *you* mean?"

"The kiss."

"What kiss?" And then I remember. A fuzzy memory. The feel of his lips. The sound of his voice. *"Stay with me, Zoe."*

I press my fingers to my knotted forehead. "I thought I was dreaming."

"No doubt. Do you know how many women have tried to win the affection of Gabriel Bennett?"

I blink. I snort. "We barely know each other. Plus, we don't get along. At. All. You're mistaking concern for affection. I bumped my head. I was unconscious and... He thinks I'm a piece of fluff, Henri. A clueless, infuriating pacifist."

"All I know is what I witnessed. Twice."

"Twice?" We're clogging pedestrian traffic and drawing attention with our middle-of-the-sidewalk discussion. Noting the shop behind us, I tug Henri toward *Mrs. Kipling's Millinery.*

"Pretend like we're admiring bonnets." With our backs to those passing, I press my companion for details. "What did you witness? Exactly?"

Focused on the window display of several ridiculously excessive hats, Henri shrugs. "I was in the artifacts room, looking for a particular pirate's sword, when I heard an explosion. I rushed toward the sound and was shocked by what I saw."

"The time machine?"

"You and Gabriel locked in a lovers' embrace."

Her scandalized expression causes my cheeks to heat. The last I recall, I/he/the-melded-we were seated in the driver's throne—as one. Bennett was inside me. "That can't be right, Henri."

"You were sitting on Gabriel's lap. His arms were locked around you and he was whispering in your ear. It was shockingly intimate."

"We must have separated the moment we arrived," I muse aloud.

"I know what I saw. You could not have been closer."

I ache to differ, but I don't.

I don't know if Bennett told her about the Binding Spell and his letter instructed me to keep my lips zipped regarding my heritage. I don't want to open a can of worms that will lead us to how I got to Blackmoor in the first place.

"Catching Gabriel in a suspect moment was embarrassing, but also confusing," she says in a near whisper. "I thought he was in Paris. With Charlotte. That's when he explained that I was seeing a version of his future self. That he traveled back in time with you and that the stakes are high on multiple levels. When I asked who you were to him, he answered, '*My prodigy*'."

"*You're not here by happenstance, Miss Albright*," I remember Bennett saying. "*You need a protector. And, even more so, a teacher.*"

More than ever I'm anxious to see him. How can he exist

'twice' in one lifetime? Will he look different? Act different? Does the version of him that's in Paris with Charlotte sense that something is amiss? Does *that* Gabriel Bennett feel conflicted or confused?

"Since keeping your presence secret was paramount," Henri rushes on, "and since you were obviously unwell, we bundled you in blankets, explained to the coach driver that you were my ailing cousin, and then transported you to my home. Gabriel instructed me to care for you and to educate you regarding ESCA, should the chance arise.

"Before he left to track down Archimedes, I walked into the bedroom and caught him kissing your forehead. Another intimacy although he brushed it off. His feelings must be intense if he took advantage of you, Zoe. Gabriel is a lot of things, but he is not a lecher. It is not within his character."

She sounds incensed. On whose behalf, I'm not sure. "Oh, Henri. I didn't mean it like that. When I said Gabriel took advantage of my body, it wasn't intimate, although yeah, it was, but not in the way you're thinking. I'll explain later, if I can. Just put that lecher thought out of your head."

The same way I'm trying to block the vision of a very real and virile Bennett in a romantic city with his cherished Charlotte.

⚑

The present (past?) Museum of Miraculous Inventions looks almost exactly as it did (does?) in the 21st century. From the outside anyway. Instead of taking me through a labyrinth of underground tunnels, Henri walks me through the front doors of the brown brick building.

My heart's pounding.

How will Bennett look when I see him? Other worldly? Wholly human? The thought of going weak in the knees when I see him is maddening. My goal is to impress him with my newfound knowledge and comprehension. To prove that I am not a damnable mess, but a work in progress. And, dare I hope, an equal to him in might, if not purpose.

Lost in my thoughts, I'm oblivious to MOMI's exhibits. If not for Henri's guidance, I would've clipped the wing of an intricate flying contraption.

"Gadzooks, Zoe. Destroying a speculative modernized model of one of Leonardo da Vinci's ornithopters, or any other exhibit, will make us the center of attention. Watch your step."

"Sorry."

"Did Da Vinci have it close?" she asks out of the side of her mouth. "In the future, do people fly through the air like birds?"

Would she be shocked if I told her I flew across the ocean along with a hundred other passengers on a humongous seventy-five ton airliner? Probably not. Henrietta Hathaway is well acquainted with fantastical events. Still…

"I'll take your silence as a yes." She sighs while finessing a locked door. "Oh, to know the wonders of the future."

"Modern innovations don't compare with the revelations of an alternate universe where literary characters live and breathe and, upon occasion, break free of their established plots." Fascinated by the concept, I tamp down my imagination while following her down a steep, winding stairwell. "Although on second thought, I suppose it boils down to perspective. Our 'normals' are not the same, Henri."

On that note, we hit the bottom step and what looks like an endless hallway. "If we see anyone, other than Gabriel and Wiz," she says while unlocking the third door on the right, "let me do the talking."

I'm vaguely aware of my surroundings as Henri whisks me through another door and into a cavernous underground room. So this is what headquarters looked like before ESCA abandoned it in my time. A cross between a library, a museum, and a police squad.

She knocks on yet another door—a door marked: THE QUEST ROOM

"Come in."

We barge into a dark paneled room crowded with floor-to-ceiling bookshelves, an old-fashioned slate blackboard, a massive round table, and two exceedingly larger-than-life men. One of them being Bennett.

Sin and sorrow.

My breath stalls at the sight of him. Handsome, carnal, and vibrating with harnessed savagery. The aggressive quality that had caused pacifist me to face-punch a thief.

His disapproving gaze bounces from Henri to me. *Oomph.* A punch in the gut. And a definite blow to my knees.

Both men stand. I don't know if it's out of respect or means of intimidation.

Bolstering my spine, I ignore Bennett completely. Pulling off my bonnet and gloves, I focus on the older, white-bearded gentleman standing on the far side of the elaborately carved table.

"Archimedes, I presume. Otherwise known as Wiz. A wise, clever individual practiced in the arts of magic and blessed with supernatural abilities allowing you to cast charms and spells."

"Miss Albright," he returns. "A clairaudient from the future. More lion than lamb, as I was led to believe," he says with a side glance to Bennett. "And perhaps more learned."

My eye twitches with annoyance, solely directed at the man who'd once been inside my head. "I might have been *clueless* before, but let me assure you that is no longer the case."

Smiling, Archimedes settles in his chair and spreads his long-fingered hands wide. "Do tell."

Glaring, Bennett perches on the edge of the table, arms crossed.

Henri gives a supportive nod as if saying, *'Do me proud.'*

Determined to wipe that smirk off of Bennett's face, I focus and spew. "The *Wizard* is the supernatural force of the *Elite Society of Character Assassins*. Utilizing the information provided by the *Scholar*," I say with a nod toward Henri, "the *Wizard* conjures an enchanted *WOD*—weapon of destruction —designed to destroy the specified rogue *FIC*.

"Which brings us to the *Warrior*." I move toe-to- toe with Bennett and stare up into his dark, stormy eyes. I think about what Henri witnessed—the embrace, the kiss—and marvel that she mistook his actions as affectionate. I don't spy a flicker of fondness in his regard, only irritation. I hate that I'm disappointed.

"Mr. Bennett," I continue on, "is one of six *Warriors* in this time—albeit it, one of two special recruits. All *Warriors* possess a noble heart, immense courage, and great strength. They are skilled and experienced enforcers with one purpose: To slay evil *FICs*, therefore, protecting the Real World from the worst creations of mortal man's imagination. The *Warrior* is the brawn of ESCA."

"Henri taught you well," Archimedes says, sounding appropriately impressed.

Bennett says nothing, but if looks could kill, I'd be as dead as a canceled sitcom.

Fury sparks beneath my calm and confident demeanor. Fury, and blast it all, lust. Hot? Gabriel Bennett is smoking.

"Which brings us to me," I say while backing away from the man and peeling off my suffocating overcoat. "An *Enabler*, albeit a work in progress."

I drape the coat over a chair and strike a defiant stance, hands on hips. "A person with telepathic abilities. Extraordinarily gifted individuals can be trained to weed through the thoughts of the living or dead, zoning in on *FICs*. *Enablers* work in tandem with *Warriors*. Locking in on the thoughts of *FICs*, they alert the *Warrior* of the *FIC's* whereabouts or intentions, enabling the *Warrior* to achieve his end. Sensitive to the 'voices' of the dead or imagined, the *Enabler* is the heart of ESCA."

I'm surprised by the vehemence in my voice and the passion welling within. Because of Henri's insight, I'm thinking of Victoria Albright in a new and positive way. I'm beginning to understand why my mother was so dedicated to her work and why she cautioned me against listening to the voices.

She didn't want me to follow in her footsteps. She wanted to protect me.

Yet here I am.

Defiant, I poke Bennett in his chest, instantly and keenly aware that my finger did not penetrate his body. He's solid as a flipping rock and wholly separate of me. "I'm all you've got in the future, buster, which makes us a team. Which means I should be in on whatever plan you're concocting with Wiz."

"I agree," says Henri.

Archimedes nods.

"Excuse us," says Bennett without looking at either one of his associates.

At once his strong hand is at the small of back and he's propelling me out of the office.

I don't think to fight him. My thoughts are muddled. By his touch. By his aura.

He wings me around a corner, pressing me into a tight crevice in between two towering bookcases.

My back is plastered to the wall and his body is plastered against me.

My heart is in my throat, on my sleeve. Somewhere. It's beating so hard, surely it's on the verge bursting through my chest.

While my thoughts and emotions are flailing, Bennett pushes rogue curls from my face, examines my goose-egg and then meets my gaze.

Is he relieved to see me up and about? Impressed by all the knowledge I absorbed? Is he going to praise me? Curse me? *Kiss me?*

My breath stalls as the heat of his breath scorches my neck, my ear.

"Tell me, Miss Albright. What part of 'stay put' did you not understand?"

NINETEEN

Mess with Me, I Mess with You

I DON'T HAVE a lot of experience with men. I don't have a lot of experience with people, period. But I know when I'm being messed with. And I know I don't like it.

Even so, I'm torn between '_screw you_' and '_do me_'.

I'm trapped between a brick wall and Bennett's menacing body. His sexy, menacing body. My brain glitches with fifty shades of naughty. Being dominated by this man, in a racy sense, would be thrilling...if he hadn't insulted my intelligence.

Heart pounding, I harness my warped libido and shove. "Back off."

Unfortunately, my voice sounds more breathless than bristly.

Crap. _Crap_! I'm conflicted and sending mixed signals.

Touching him was stupid. Yes, I shoved, but he didn't

budge and now I'm gripping those broad shoulders as if to say *'don't go'*.

The panic and longing I felt when I woke up and realized he was no longer with me is back and dueling with the relief and adrenaline rush of being reunited. Not as *one*. Not as woman and ghost or *Enabler* and *Warrior*. But as woman and man.

Whether I like it or not—and I don't—I'm physically, insanely, attracted to Gabriel Bennett. I'm dying to kiss him stupid. In the words of Henri, *Gadzooks*.

Bennett instantly shifts, distancing himself as if reading my mind. Apparently, we don't need to be melded for him to know my thoughts. That or my body language is telling.

As is his.

I've been dropped like the proverbial hot potato.

It's mortifying. I'm paralyzed with embarrassment and reliving every clumsy exchange I ever had with a guy. None compare to this epic fumble.

"It will pass," he says.

"My annoyance?"

"The attraction."

I flash on what Henri saw and assumed. "You're attracted to me?"

"*You* are attracted to me."

My jaw drops. "Of all the arrogant..."

"Not arrogance. Experience."

"Oh, right." I cross my arms and smirk. "Women frequently throw themselves at your feet. Henri told me. So, naturally you assume *every* woman wants to climb into your bed."

"Not every woman." He eyes my Victorian transformation head-to-toe, a slow appraisal that heats my blood in more ways than one. "Lest, you forget, Miss Albright, I was inside you."

Trust me. I remember every irritating and awkward moment. "Meaning?"

"I was privy to your thoughts, random memories, and a fantasy or two. As someone who has never been seduced, you are easily smitten."

"*Smitten?*"

"As you said when we first met, it'll never work. Us," he clarifies. "Shall I list the reasons?"

"You're insufferable."

"That's not one of them."

I ball my fists and rage within.

"What else did you and Henri discuss aside from my reputed antics with the fairer sex?" He looks to make sure we're still alone. We are. Regardless he lowers his voice. "Did you bemoan your *Misfortune*? Boast of your inheritance? Ponder our melding? Perhaps you enlightened Henri regarding your Penelope Pringle character. Something you and I have yet to discuss."

I hug myself to keep from socking him. "I didn't tell her about any of those things you sanctimonious jerk. In your letter you implied that I could seriously muck up the future by mentioning my parents. Everything you just stated leads back to them! Like I'd risk erasing my existence or eviscerating mankind."

"I also told you not to leave Henri's house. Yet here you are." He drags a hand through his mussed hair. "Why in the devil did you risk your safety and tempt fate?"

"To have a *voice* in my fate! You dragged me back centuries—"

"You told me to think outside of the box. I transported us to a year before I was cursed so that you and I can operate independently. So I can train you for what lies ahead." He moves in and grasps my shoulders. "You are unprepared, Zoe. And worse—vulnerable."

Rarely has he called me by my first name. It throws me for a loop. Or maybe I'm rattled by his touch. Sure as sunshine, I'm jittery about my role in a faceoff with an evil *FIC*. However, I'm no longer oblivious or in denial.

"I'm a WIP." I duck his touch and slip past him, needing air, needing distance. "A work in progress," I explain. "Henri gave me a crash course in the history and purpose of ESCA. I swallowed the tale hook, line, and sinker." I point toward where Archimedes and Henri are waiting. "Weren't you listening back there?"

"I heard. It's a start."

I frown. I seethe.

The corner of his mouth twitches. "A good start."

My bones liquefy. "Is that a smile?"

"Absolutely not."

The air sizzles between us, around us. It's mesmerizing.

And short lived.

Henri rounds the corner, dousing the heat with her presence and huff. "*There* you are! What are you…" Her gaze bounces between us. "No, no. Don't tell me. And what I already know, I'll forget. Your secret is safe with me."

"There is no secret," Bennett and I say in tandem.

"If anyone can read between the lines," says Henri. "It's me. Just stuff it and get back in the Quest Room. Archimedes has a proposition."

"Let's start with what we know."

Archimedes is all business. And by that I mean he's dressed in a conservative black suit, not a flowing purple robe and pointy hat like some Merlin-esque wizard. Sure, he has a white moustache and beard and a wooden pointer that looks a heck of a lot like a wand, but that's where stereotypical comparisons end. Between the wire-rimmed spectacles perched on the end of his beak-like nose and his stuffy attire, he looks more like a professor than a sorcerer.

Like students in a quirky classroom, Bennett, Henri, and I are seated at the round table and paying close attention to the man with some answers. Or at least a 'proposition'.

He taps the pointer to the slate board where he listed several facts in white chalk.

- *Gabriel cursed and chained.*
- *Miss Albright untrained and at risk.*
- *FIC Uprising/ESCA Underground*
- *Binding Spell*
- *Counter Spell*

He elaborates on each circumstance without relaying specifics. *Undisclosed date. Undisclosed person/persons.*

Obviously, Bennett only shared essential information in order to safeguard the future.

"The greatest challenge will be to train Miss Albright and

also to counter a future spell without altering the course of history in a negative or chaotic way." Archimedes eyeballs Bennett. "A disruption in a chain of events from now until whenever you and Miss Albright first meet could be disastrous."

"I'm aware," Bennett says with a withering look to me and Henri.

"We made it a point not to engage with anyone between my house and Headquarters," says Henri. "And we didn't."

"What if someone had engaged with *you*?" asks Bennett. "What of happenstance?"

"Yes, what of it?" I ask, wanting to take the heat off of Henri. "What if another *Character Assassin* walks in on this meeting? Or what if you run into a friend on the street? Everyone thinks you're in Paris with Charlotte."

"I *am* in Paris with Charlotte," says Bennett. "The Victorian me, that is."

"How does that work?" Henri asks. "What if Victorian Gabriel returns from France early and runs into you—his future self?"

"That could create a new timeline," says Archimedes, "and/or an alternate universe. We could ruminate on the laws of physics and time travel paradoxes for hours."

"I won't meet myself," says Bennett. "I'm in Paris for the next six weeks."

"With Charlotte," I say.

Henri kicks me under the table.

What? Do I sound jealous? I *am* jealous. Every time her name is mentioned, Bennett tenses. Why? So much has happened over the past few days. So much has been said. Even so, Bennett's relationship with Lady Charlotte Moore and whatever happens to her in 1899 is shrouded in mystery.

"Be that as it may, Gabriel," Archimedes says, "Miss Albright is correct. Crossing paths with anyone who knows you is risky. I need time to research the Binding Spell you mentioned as well as a counter spell. It could take days."

"What if we hunker down at Henri's house?" I feel as comfortable with her as I did with Mr. Watson. She's far more offbeat, but equally grounding in moments of bizarre. "Could I complete my training there?"

"You and I need to work as a team," says Bennett. "Near dead zones and fractured borders."

"But not here in London," says Archimedes. "Hence my proposition. A report came in. Rumblings of a beast up north terrorizing locals. The accounts could be exaggerated."

"Or rooted in fiction," says Henri.

Bennett leans in. "Where in the north?"

"A small village in Nottinghamshire." Archimedes lifts a brow. "Do you know this case?"

"I do."

"And the outcome?"

"Yes."

"*FIC* infiltration?" asks Henri.

"Yes."

"Can you give me a hint so I can start researching the character?" she asks.

"No, he cannot," says Archimedes. "Do you think you and Miss Albright can train without engaging with the not-to-be-named *FIC*?" he asks Bennett.

"Knowing what I know, I think so. As long as Miss Albright follows my explicit directions."

I bristle at yet another reference to my leaving Henri's house against his bidding, but I let the grievance slide. Bickering with the man in front of his associates, who by extension are now *my* associates, strikes me as unprofessional.

My associates.

It hits me hard that after twenty-one years of virtual solitude, I'm interacting somewhat normally with three grown and complex adults. Not over the phone or Internet, but in person. And what's more, there's no need to hide or deny my *Misfortune*.

"Are you all right?"

I realize that Henri's squeezing my hand. The touch of a concerned friend. I swallow an emotional lump. "Couldn't be better."

Bennett shoots me a quizzical look, and then turns back to Archimedes. "We'll travel north by train first thing in the morning. We'll need aliases, identification, appropriate clothing."

"Since you're traveling together and without a chaperone," says Henri, "you have two choices. Pose as brother and sister or husband and wife."

I shoot her a look. *What the…*

What? she silently shoots back, making me realize her suggestion was purely logical. Still.

"Given Miss Albright's American accent and her unfamiliarity with our customs and era, posing as man and wife is the wisest option," Archimedes says reasonably.

Great. *Not.*

"Agreed," says Bennett, although clearly, at least to me, he's not happy about it.

"It may require random shows of affection," Archimedes says to me. "Will that offend your proprieties?"

As someone who comes from a decade where people frequently indulge in casual hook-ups, not that I'm an expert, I'm hugely amused that Wiz is concerned I'll be offended by handholding or a peck on the lips. Then it occurs to me that it also means sleeping in the same room and maybe even the same bed with Bennett.

My imagination soars. My stomach flutters. A flurry of fantasies crash and burn when I realize there's optimal opportunity for me to make a fool of myself.

Henri kicks me under the table.

Bennett raises a brow.

I'm staring. At him.

And everyone's aware.

I clear my throat and bolster my shoulders. "I have no problem with that scenario." Rising to the challenge, I take warped pleasure in the notion of pushing Bennett out of his comfort zone. For once in our short and combative association, maybe I'll have the upper hand. "I've spent years mastering the art of pretending."

"That, Miss Albright," Bennett says with a parting shot, "was child's play."

TWENTY

A Shocking Revelation

OCTOBER, 12th, 1898

Dear Journal:

I can't believe I used to think of myself and my life as weird.

Hearing dead people talk, nurturing a lifelong relationship with an imaginary friend and growing up in near seclusion seems ridiculously tame compared to everything I've experienced in the last few days or weeks or however long it's been since I first laid eyes on Gabriel Bennett.

In that short, chaotic time we occupied one body, MY body, time-traveled back to 1898, and now we're on our way to a remote village to connect telepathically with a 'beast' who's terrorizing, and possibly killing, the locals. A literary character who escaped from an alternate universe known to the privileged few, which now includes me, as Fictopia.

Now THAT'S weird.

Last night, while I lay in Henri's guest bed (alone), I waffled between fretting about a FIC confrontation and dreaming about a FIC confrontation. Scenarios ranged between terrifying and horrific.

I also fretted and dreamed about Gabriel Bennett. Every scenario was sexual.

My obsession with him is growing and that, even more than a lack of restful sleep, is cramping my mood.

I regret being short with Henri this morning as she laced me into a rib-crushing, waist-cinching corset and then transformed me, layer by layer, into Mrs. Emma Knightley. American wife and personal assistant to a London based writer, Mr. William Knightley.

Why ~~Bennett~~ Mr. Knightley gets to portray the writer instead of me (because, hello, I AM a writer) was puzzling until Henri explained that, given the era, it was a more believable dynamic. She has a special knack for making sense out of the nonsensical.

She also has a way with creating illusions.

By the time she was done with me, I looked every inch a Victorian lady from an elaborate up-do hairstyle right down to my new pointy-toed button boots. The burgundy traveling dress is lovely, but suffocating. She said I'd get used to it.

When I told her the corset was squeezing the breath out of me, she said I'd get used to that, too.

Three hours later and I'm still not used to it, but I have to admit I appreciated my reflection in the mirror. And I sure as sunshine didn't mind Bennett's double-take when he got his first look at his faux bride.

Not that he paid me a compliment.

Nor did I comment on his brow-raising transformation.

Instead of looking this side of elegant, he looked/looks this side of eccentric. Sort of like Robert Downey Jr's version of Sherlock Holmes. Adorably scruffy. Boldly romantic. He even adopted a pair of tinted wire-rimmed shades that he swapped for clear-lensed spectacles once we boarded the train.

Who knew glasses could look so sexy on a man?

But I digress.

The point is I'm worried I bit off more than I can chew. What if I freak out when I hear or see that monster? What if I misstep and blow our guise as husband and wife?

Whatever bravado I enjoyed yesterday is slipping away with every clackety-clack of iron wheels on iron rails.

The good news is, this morning I woke up with a new story idea for Penelope. I borrowed this blank journal from Henri (although she dubbed it a gift), intending to draft a synopsis. Instead, I'm freewriting about what's foremost in my mind.

Bennett and monsters.

Oh, well. At least I'm writing.

More later,

Zoe Mrs. Knightley

I close the journal, and then tuck it inside my messenger

bag which I hid inside a more period-accurate tapestry carpetbag.

I fidget. I frown. I silently curse the boned corset that's got a vise grip on my torso. I'm *this* close to asking Bennett to turn his back so I can rid myself of the contraption. We're alone in a private compartment. I could quickly swap the corset for my bra and *breathe*!

But somehow that feels like giving up. It's way too early in the game for that.

Instead, I sit straighter, hoping impeccable posture will ease my discomfort.

Bennett, on the other hand, is slouching on the cushioned bench across from me and deeply engrossed in reading the latest articles (old news to him?) in the *Daily Telegraph*. I hate that he looks so comfortable and relaxed.

I hate that I love looking at him.

"You've been abnormally quiet this morning," he says without taking his eyes off of the newspaper.

"You're not exactly chatty yourself."

"I have a lot on my mind."

"Same here, Spanky."

"Your word choice at times..." Sighing, he lowers the paper, adjusts his specs, and squeezes the bridge of his nose. "Do try to think like a Victorian and, when in public, think hard before you speak lest you draw undo attention to yourself. I *know* you don't like that."

How like Bennett to throw something in my face that he learned while inside my head! Talk about an invasion of privacy.

For a moment, I seethe, wading through my angry thoughts, *thinking before speaking.*

I hear the steam engine chugging, the metal wheels clacking, and the sound of my heart *thudding* in my ears.

I settle on brutal honesty. Bennett's preferred mode of communication.

"Speaking of thinking before opening your mouth, you'd do well to take your own advice, *sir*."

"Meaning?"

"Meaning, more often than not you're downright snippy with me."

"Snippy?"

"Rude. Mean. Condescending. Take your pick. It's hurtful and annoying. Insensitive and thoughtless."

He sets aside the paper and studies me hard.

"We're supposed to be happily married," I rush on. "When in public, at least *try* to like me."

"I do like you."

I blink. I flush. I spin the new wedding band on my finger around and around, certain I misheard.

"Your life, as you've always known it, has been upended. Over the last week, you've experienced multiple, fantastical situations and events and instead of shutting down, you've stepped up. You have deep reservations about *enabling* me or any *Warrior* to erase a dangerous *FIC*, yet here you are."

I blink. Again. I feel like an idiot. A speechless idiot. It almost sounds like Bennett admires me. From damnable mess to a woman with promise?

"I take back my former declaration," he says. "You do possess traces of your father's qualities."

I don't know if I should feel proud, but I do. Mention of my father shifts my focus and emotions. "Should I feel good about that? Was he a good man?"

"Are you familiar with knightly virtues?"

"You mean like chivalry?"

"Extreme gallantry toward women." He nods. "But that is only a portion of a knight's code of conduct."

I'm on pins and needles. Breathless with anticipation. Have we finally reached the point when Bennett's willing to talk about Dominic at length? "I'd *Google* the list of virtues if I could," I say, "but obviously I can't." *Please fill me in.*

"Mercy toward the oppressed. Honor. Sacrifice. Courage. Faithfulness. There are more virtues and Dom owns them all."

Present tense. Has Bennett not yet come to terms with my father's death? "Sounds like he was the best of the best."

As soon as the words are out of my mouth, I shiver with a memory. Something Henri said while speaking of Bennett and his skill as a *Warrior.* "Our best, save for one."

A chill ices my spine even as my body burns. My mind explodes with snippets revealed by Bennett in our initial conversations.

He was in the same business as my dad.

He *knew* my dad.

Knew of his relationship with my mom. Knew about my conception. Knew that the sporty red car in the carriage house was Dominic's favorite company vehicle. And yet…

"No one has seen me for more than a century, Miss Albright. Aside from you."

My hands tremble and tingle. Sweat rolls down my back.

"You said my dad must have conspired with Wiz to bind me to you. That he wouldn't have willed me the manor and risked exposing me to those who would take advantage of me unless circumstances were dire."

My imagination is screaming scenarios. My head hurts. My chest hurts. *Can't breathe.*

"Miss Albright—"

"You said you worked with Dominic Sinclair and intimated that he trusts you to protect me," I rasp between pained gasps. "You were friends and associates yet you were invisible to him at Blackmoor, in my time, locked in a bewitched dimension for more than a hundred years!"

I think about how Bennett told me not to speak of my parents or to make any mention of Dominic when speaking to Henri or Archimedes and how neither one of them referred to any other *Character Assassin* by name.

It can't be true, and yet I've recently learned *anything* is possible.

"Is Dominic one of the *Warriors* of *this* time? Does he exist *now* in 1898?"

For once Bennett doesn't hedge. "Yes."

He shifts to sit beside me. His arm is around me, I think, holding me upright. I'm not sure. I'm tingly to the point of numb and I'm seeing double.

"And yet he lived and loved and sired a child in the 21st century? How is that possible?" My imagination ticks through a list of credible and incredible explanations. I go with the obvious. "Was he somehow...*immortal?*"

"Yes."

And with that, my brain and body collapse.

TWENTY-ONE

The Ramifications of Truth

"COME BACK TO ME, ZOE."

A jolt to my heart.

His voice resonates deep within, coaxing me out of a fuzzy stupor.

I open my eyes and lock gazes with Tall, Dark, and Deadly. I catch a flicker of the affection Henri swore she witnessed twice. "Am I dreaming?"

"Not at the moment."

That affection is muted now and replaced with concern. He's sitting beside me, hovering. Cradling the back of my neck and pressing a cool cloth to my brow. "How do you feel?"

"Confused." I'm flat on my back, stretched out on the cushioned bench. "What happened?"

"You fainted."

"From shock?" How embarrassing.

"I believe there was more to it than that. I took liberties. Forgive me."

Standing, he averts his gaze and drags a hand through his hair. "More than one woman has swooned as a result of a too tightly laced corset."

I realize suddenly that the pressure I'd suffered all morning is gone. Removing the cloth from my forehead, I push to my elbows and note my shirtwaist is gaping. Looking down, I see that I'm still wearing the protective corset cover, but the corset beneath has been unlaced. At least partially.

"Henri is a stickler for details," he says with his back to me. "No need to suffer for beauty or fashion, Miss Albright. I'll step into the hall so you can rid yourself fully of that torture device."

He leaves before I can respond.

Even though I'm woozy, I spring into action. The sooner I swap the corset for my bra and make myself decent, the sooner we can resume our conversation.

Peeling off layers, I revisit our last exchange and the stunning revelation.

Dominic Sinclair was Immortal.

It's ridiculous and impossible, but then so is most everything I've heard or witnessed lately. What's taxing my brain most is a paradox.

If Dominic Sinclair was immortal, how can he be dead?

Watson didn't mince words in the letter he sent me. And although he didn't share details pertaining to the manner of death, in subsequent discussions, he maintained that Dominic died and left me an enormous inheritance.

My brain races as I struggle to keep my balance on the

rocking train while worming out of the corset Bennett loosened. I'm too jacked up on the immortal thing to dwell on anything sexy. Otherwise I'd be all over the thought of the gorgeous *Warrior* undressing me.

I roll and stuff the demon undergarment into my carpetbag, marveling that Dominic Sinclair, the father I never knew, is alive and *somewhere* in this century. This decade. This *year*! The knowledge is bittersweet. As much as I want to meet him, I know I can't. Or at least, I shouldn't.

I can think of at least two sci-fi movies where the time traveler meets a version of himself or a family member and, as a result, mucks up his own future.

I'm mucked up enough, thank you very much.

And then there's the possibility that my selfish actions could have a harmful effect on mankind overall. I have Bennett to thank for planting that seed in my brain.

Even so, I can't help imagining ways I can maybe *see* Dominic without interacting. Or maybe interact without revealing my identity.

"Get a grip, Z."

Trembling with frustration, I redirect my focus to my state of undress. Yes, Henri's a stickler, but she rightly pegged my lacy bra as anachronistic. Better to go without. Better to stick with Henri's original layers minus the corset.

I'm already wearing the sleeveless chemise. It's sort of like a tank undershirt and soft against my skin. I top that with the corset cover—also soft. It reminds me of a frilly vest with ribbons and buttons and lace. Slender fitting, but comfortable.

Two layers of cotton fabric between my breasts and the velvet shirtwaist, which is also formfitting. "Good enough." *I hope.*

I rush to the door, pull it open, and fairly plow into Bennett who's waiting in the narrow hall.

"Mr. Knightley," I say, in case anyone's within earshot.

"Mrs. Knightley."

I yank him inside before he has a chance to say another word. "We need to talk."

"I'll tell you what I can."

"I don't like the sound of that. It implies you're not going to be wholly forthcoming. And if you say there's only so much I can absorb in a day, my head will explode."

"Then I'll say nothing of the kind. What I will say," he continues while we sink onto opposing benches, "is that certain information is highly classified."

"I'll take what I can get." *For now.* I'm not happy. I want...I *deserve* full disclosure. This is my father, my life, but at least Bennett's willing to tell me *something* about the man who sired me.

Unlike Liza.

I shrug off a pang of resentment and blurt out the questions crowding my mind. "Was Dominic a victim of a curse or a spell? Did he make a bargain with the devil? Drink an ancient elixir that gave him eternal life? Was he bitten by a vampire? *Was* he a vampire?"

"You left out the possibility that he's an Olympian God."

I blink. "Was... *Is* he?"

"No. Nor is he a vampire."

Bennett isn't smiling, but it feels like he's laughing at me. "I happen to watch a lot of TV and movies," I say. "Not that you know what those are."

"I know what they are. The people who visited Blackmoor over the last century and a half couldn't see or hear me, but I could see and hear them. I listened and learned. It kept me sane."

For a moment I'm reminded of our time within the manor. Bennett had vibrated with intense negative emotions. Frustration, loneliness, anger. I sense none of that now. Of course, *now* he's not trapped inside a bewitched dimension. He's not chained to Blackmoor or even to me. He's a free man in his own time. An era where he thrives as one of ESCA's greatest *Warriors*.

Alongside his beloved Charlotte.

Instead of feeling jealous or envious of Bennett's feelings for Lady Moore, I'm suddenly and fiercely sad.

"It must pain you," I say. "Knowing we have to go back to the future at some point. Knowing you can't stay and reclaim the life and people you loved and revise your destinies. I mean, you know Charlotte disappears in 1899, the same year you're cursed into that bewitched dimension. That's only a year or less from now. You could do or say something to change all that."

"But I won't."

"Because it would alter the future for everyone else?"

He doesn't answer. He doesn't have to. Of course, that's his concern. Who would want to risk instigating a ripple effect that could rewrite history for the worse?

"Dom favored television and film as well. He quoted from them as often as he quoted from books. Perhaps you'll recognize one of his favorites." Bennett leans forward, forearms on his knees, eyes on me. *"The needs of the many outweigh the needs of the few."*

"Dr. Spock's last words in one of the old *Star Trek* movies." Riveted, I search Bennett's intense gaze. "To which Captain

Kirk responded, '*Or the one.*'"

He doesn't flinch, but I sense his misery all the same.

I don't want to ask, but I have to know. "What happens to Charlotte?"

"She's killed by the *FIC* who damns me."

A kick to my gut and conscience. It doesn't matter that his tone and expression are flat, a world of ache and fury knock me for a loop.

I'm sick. I'm speechless. And in befuddled awe of Gabriel Bennett.

What kind of restraint and conviction does it take to sacrifice a loved one as well as your own happiness and freedom in order to protect people you don't even know?

"How do you bear it?" I rasp.

"By focusing on the hand fate dealt me. You."

My mind whirls, replaying bits of things he's shared, piecing together fragments, brainstorming scenarios. "You're sacrificing Lady Moore to protect me?"

He doesn't answer and I know it's true. Or at least partially true.

"I'm gonna throw up."

"What?"

I stand. I sway. I clasp my stomach while bolting for the door. "The bathroom. Lavatory. Whatever."

I push into the hallway before he can stop me, but he's instantly beside me, turning and guiding me in the opposite direction.

"This way," he says, his arm firm about my waist. "Breathe, Mrs. Knightley."

I don't respond. I can't respond. I'm swallowing the bitter taste of bile.

Through welling tears, I see someone approach. A man in uniform. A porter? A conductor? "Is everything all right?" he asks.

"My wife is ill," Bennett says as we reach the lavatory and he finesses me inside. "We'll be fine."

I shut the door between us and barely make it to the commode before hurling.

Soon after, my stomach clenches with dry heaves. Trussed up in that stupid corset, I barely ate breakfast, thinking I was *this* close to popping the laces. I guess that's a good thing, considering. Still.

Tears roll as I force myself to relax. To *breathe*.

I'm consumed with the thought that, if it weren't for me, maybe, just maybe Bennett would do something to alert his past self of what's to come. That he'd find a way to circumvent Charlotte's impending murder. Yes, I know we all die at some point. Even Dominic, who's supposedly immortal, eventually ceases to be. What I can't stomach is the notion that someone must die so that I can live.

And that's *exactly* what Bennett implied.

A soft rap on the door prompts me to the wash basin. Miraculously, I think before speaking, replacing 'in a sec' with, "One moment."

I cup water in my hands and sip, rinsing away the gross taste of vomit. Then I splash my clammy, tear-streaked face. In doing so, my trembling fingers brush the *Baffles* nestled tightly in my ears. *Baffles* made for Charlotte. Bennett returned them to me this morning. Are they water proof? Not knowing, I panic a little, prying them out and drying them off.

That's when I hear her.

Sobbing. Begging.

"Don't! Please. I won't tell. I won't tell. Have mercy..."

I'm alone. I can see I'm alone. Only I'm not. My mind screams, *Dead zone!* A memory warns, *Don't listen!*

The *Baffles* are clenched in my fist. Frozen in horror, I fall back against the wall, her fearful pleading ringing in my ears. On instinct, I *Scramble*. And fail.

I listen.

I scream.

TWENTY-TWO

A Creature is Born

BENNETT BUSTS INTO THE LAVATORY. "What the devil?"

He grabs me by the waist and pulls me to my feet.

I didn't realize I'd slumped to the floor. Or that I'd covered my ears with my fists.

My heart pounds as her voice goes on and on, begging someone to let her go, promising not to tell. Her manic pleading digresses from whimpering to wheezing and then…

Silence.

A deafening silence thick with confusion, fear, and regret.

And then back to the same manic pleading.

I'm mesmerized. Horrified.

Pressing me against the wall with his lower body, Bennett pries my fists from my ears and then the *Baffles* from my right hand. "Bloody hell." He wraps something around my palm and squeezes. "Tell me what you hear."

I see his lips moving, his voice a whisper compared to hers.

"Don't crumble on me now," he says close to my ear. "Tell me what you hear, Zoe."

"A woman," I manage. "Crying, begging."

"What's going on?" Another voice breaks through my daze. "Is your wife in need of a physician?"

"No," Bennett snaps over his shoulder. "Thank you, but, no. Allow us a moment, please."

Bennett focuses back on me. Cradling my face, he forces me to meet his gaze. His reassuring gaze. "What is she saying? Sharing? Listen. Really listen," he says in a calm, assured tone. "Steel your heart, open your mind, and determine her dilemma. No need to be frightened. I'm here."

My racing pulse slows by half as I embrace and absorb Bennett's strong presence.

"She's like a broken record, repeating the same things over and over. There's a man. He touched her, took her. Forcibly. She's ashamed and scared. Petrified. She promises not to tell —*Don't hurt me!* She's wheezing now, gasping, choking. Then silence."

I've got a death-grip on Bennett's arms and a vise around my heart. "I think he strangled her. Raped and strangled her."

He nods. "Let her know you hear her. That she's not alone. She's reliving a moment of terror again and again. Break the cycle."

I close my eyes. I steel my heart and open my mind. "I hear you. I'm with you. Don't be afraid. I...I want to help."

Holding me steady, Bennett looks back to the uniformed

man crowding up the doorjamb. "Did someone suffer a violent death in this lavatory?"

"A couple of years ago," I hear him say as I mumble reassurances to a tortured soul. "A young woman was assaulted and…"

"Murdered?"

"Strangled. Like your wife said. But… How does she know? It was hushed up. Bad press for the railway. Who is she talking to? Is she bonkers?"

"Psychic," Bennett clarifies.

"Abigail," I say as the woman shares her name. "I'm speaking with Abigail." I'm stunned that I managed to distract her from her dying moments. That she somehow hears me as clearly as I hear her. "She's worried about her son."

"Was she traveling with a boy?" Bennett asks the man.

"I'm not supposed to talk about this."

"I'll make it worth your while."

I divide my focus between the conversation I'm having with Abigail and the one Bennett's having with train man. Surprisingly, it's not so hard. Then again, I spent years managing conversations with Liza while Penny blabbed in my ear.

"Yes," the man says in a low voice. "There was a lad. His grandmother, the woman's mum, took him in. As I understand it, the railroad paid her a pretty pence for emotional compensation. He's well cared for. If that helps," he adds while taking a wad of bills from Bennett.

"Was the assailant captured?" Bennett asks.

"And prosecuted."

"Imprisoned?"

"Hanged."

I flinch. I nod. "Good news," I tell Abigail. "No one else is at risk and your son is living with your mom, your *mum*. They are well. No need to worry. No need to be scared."

"You can leave now," Bennett says to the man.

"If you're a pair of charlatans…" he warns. "If you think you can shake down the railway—"

"Sod off." Bennett shuts the door in his face, locking us away in the cramped, smelly lavatory.

With Abigail.

He's still holding me and I'm still talking.

To a ghost.

I assure her that the attack wasn't her fault. That justice was served. That her son is well and loved. "No regrets," I say. "No guilt. Let go and move on, Abigail. Move toward the light."

"*Papa*," she says.

"Your papa? Where? Can you see him? Do you see the light?" Is her father dead? My heart pumps. "Loved ones await on the other side. Go to them, Abigail. Go with peace. They're waiting."

She says something I don't catch. I listen hard but all I hear is the clacking of the train and a dim hum. That familiar hum. But no distinct voices. I shiver in the peaceful near silence. Free of pain. Free of Abigail.

I don't know how I know for sure, but I do. "She's gone."

I drop my forehead to Bennett's chest as he strokes my back, soothing me, warming me. "I don't hear her anymore," I say. "I don't sense her. I think she crossed over. I think she's at peace."

Bennett squeezes my shoulders then finesses me into the hall. "You're a natural, Mrs. Knightley."

I suck in the fresh air, or at least it seems fresh compared to the pungent smells of the lavatory.

I lean into Bennett for strength as he escorts me back to our private compartment. My legs are shaky and my emotions are wrecked.

"I read about it a lot," I rasp. "Psychics who communicate with the dead," I clarify. "It's what my mother did. At least, after I was born. She worked with the police to solve murders. She helped tortured spirits cross over. I always thought it was an awful job. She was always so anxious. But maybe it wasn't because of what she did, because this wasn't so awful."

As we move into our compartment, new tears well, blurring my vision as Bennett eases me onto the plush seating.

"Don't get me wrong. Experiencing Abigail's horror scared the crap out of me and I'll probably have nightmares," I say, "but helping her to let go was... It was a good thing."

"A noble deed."

Bennett stoops in front of me and inspects my right hand. I see now that he'd wrapped a white handkerchief around my palm. It's stained with blood. *My blood.*

I must have squeezed the *Baffles* so hard, the jewels punctured my skin. I didn't feel a thing at the time. And now, I'm too jacked up on adrenaline and racing thoughts to feel any pain.

As Bennett tends to the wound, I let my tearful musings fly.

"Maybe Victoria was anxious because she couldn't be with Dominic," I reason. "Because she was in hiding. Or rather, she was hiding *me*. Protecting me from those who would take advantage of me if they knew I existed. Because I'm... I'm an *anomaly*. That's what you called me, right? Because I'm the product of an *Enabler* and a *Warrior*. A mortal and immortal. Unique, but how so?"

"I don't know the answer to that. Not yet."

"I must possess some untapped gift or unrefined talent. A quality or skill that would be valuable to…who? ESCA? The government? Evil *FICs*? Something in addition to or beyond my *Misfortune*. My clairaudience," I clarify. "Because every *Enabler* possesses some telepathic power, right?"

"This is so."

He's watching me now. Watching me puzzle through whatever he's wary of sharing.

I swipe tears from my cheeks and sniff back snot. "Did I inherit Dominic's immortality? Is that even possible? Will I stop aging at some point? Am I immune to lethal injuries and disease?"

"Why don't we come back to this later? You're exhausted."

"No, I… What aren't you telling me? Is this the classified part?"

"Not officially, no. In fact, to my knowledge, this is unexplored territory. "

He hands me a clean hankie. He must have a small supply of them. An essential, I suppose since disposable tissues have yet to be invented.

I take it and blow my nose. Loudly. I must look awful. I don't cry often but when I do, it's ugly.

I keep waiting for Bennett to tell me to suck it up or grow a backbone. Snarky tough guy. That's his style. Instead, he's walking on eggshells.

"Whatever you know, whatever you're keeping from me must be pretty honking huge. Are you worried I won't believe you? Or that I'll freak out? Or fall apart?

"Think about all I've been through the last several days," I plow on. "Okay, I didn't always keep my cool and I sort of melted down with the ghost thing. But that's always been my biggest fear—listening in on a dead zone—and I faced it. With your help. I thank you for that. I'm grateful even, because I think I finally understand something about Victoria. You can't possibly know how much that means to me. And, yes, the part about Dominic being immortal is freaky, but at least I know something honest and real about him.

"What's driving me insane is learning about their lives in dribs and drabs and not understanding why *my existence, and perhaps the wellbeing of mankind, rests upon my discretion.* I hate that you wrote that in that letter to me. But now it's stuck in my brain and I just want to know. I'm asking you straight out, Gabriel. What is it about my parentage that makes me so special in your eyes?"

He doesn't blink. "You're one of a kind."

"Gee, thanks, but—"

"An offspring of an earthborn and *FIC.*"

TWENTY-THREE

Kissing and Kaleidoscopes

I CAN'T STOP LAUGHING.

It's a bizarre reaction to Bennett's shocking and sober revelation, and quite possibly a sign that I finally snapped.

"I know, I know. You're not kidding," I rasp even as I double over with sidesplitting laughter. "Just…" *gasp, snort*, "… give me a sec."

My brain short circuits for several lovely moments as I give in and give over to the absurdity of my existence.

I'm no ordinary freak. I'm the mother of all freaks! The offspring of an earthborn and *FIC*. I freaking *excel* at freakdom!

Winded and dizzy, I force myself upright, swiping tears of delirium from my cheeks as the giggles and snorts subside.

In contrast to my lingering bemusement, Bennett's as solemn as a gravestone.

I get it. Who lapses into snorting laughter on the heels of sobbing their eyes out? I'm a little out of control and all over the map, but can he blame me? Seriously? First the ghost confrontation, now this?

"Don't worry. I didn't flip my lid. I just... I don't know. It's just so...bananas. I mean you're suggesting I'm a byproduct of two universes. Half earthborn, half *FIC*. Half real, half imagined."

I rub my aching ribs while holding Bennett's gaze. As ludicrous as the notion is, he's totally deadpan.

Logic says his declaration can't be true. Then again, I've been at odds with logic since I was four and my dead mother spoke to me from her casket. What's one more kink in my already twisted life?

Sighing, I raise a brow. "Are you sure about this?"

"I'm certain Dom was born of a writer's musings and thrived—once upon a time—in *Fictopia*. I'm certain, by way of Dom, that Victoria entered the Real World as all earthborn, newborns do. A conventional being aside from her clairaudient gift."

"So if Dominic and Victoria are truly my birth parents, I'm..."

"Unique."

"Bi-universal." I bang the back of my noggin against the wall, pounding my origins into my brain. Henri has nothing on me. At least both of her parents are plain ol' humans. "I don't think there's such a word, by the way. But it's more telling than *unique* and far less creepy than *alien species*."

At long last, Bennett smiles. A real smile.

Too bad I'm too distracted to enjoy it. "I'm glad you find

this funny." Even though I was laughing my butt off five seconds ago, his sudden good humor grates.

He crosses his arms and angles his head. "On the contrary. Your ethnicity is perplexing and a possible dilemma. I am amused, however, that you consider the notion *creepy*. That suggests you are frightfully strange. Or somehow terrifying. Trust me, Miss Albright. You are neither."

"Says the man who assassinates fictional monsters. Trust *me*, creepy is a matter of perspective."

As Bennett considers the notion, I offer more evidence.

"Liza, my aunt, the woman who raised me, was totally spooked the first time I told her I heard disembodied voices. So much so, she rushed me to a shrink. And then there are the people who caught me having conversations with Penelope— a girl they couldn't see or hear. Unlike me.

"I've been called everything from delusional to weird, Mr. Bennett. What would those same people call me if they learned my father is a fictional character? A figment of a writer's imagination? A being from an alternate universe?" I frown. I groan. "For as long as I can remember," I say with another head thunk, "all I ever wanted was to be normal."

"Maybe you are. Maybe everything that causes you to feel abnormal is perfectly normal for someone of…Bi-universal descent."

I perk up at that. It's an interesting spin. A positive spin. A spin I can—

The train jerks. *Hard.*

I lurch forward and topple partially on the floor, partially in Bennett's lap.

Screeching wheels and a blaring whistle scream trouble.

We're braking at an alarming rate.

My adrenaline spikes as I brace for disaster.

Morbid thoughts fly.

At least I'll die happy.

Bennett's protective embrace is intoxicating. And short lived.

As the train slows to full stop, he finesses me from an undignified sprawl and places me firmly beside him. "Are you all right?"

I nod. "Just startled."

After a bolstering, *platonic* squeeze, he presses the *Baffles* into my unwounded hand, and then moves to the window. After peering outside, he swaps his clear specs for tinted shades, and then unlatches the outer door of our compartment. "Stay put."

"Wait!"

But he jumps to the ground.

The door slams behind him, prompting me out of my seat.

I look out the window and see him striding through a thin veil of fog. Moving toward the front of the train and into the unknown without hesitation.

Up ahead, the railway gently arcs to the right, giving me a limited view of the engine and the next two cars.

Nothing looks amiss from what I can tell. Still, more people, make that *men*, pour out of the train. I hear movement in the hallway as well. Perhaps other women who were told to *stay put*? I could stick my head out and ask any one of them if they know what's going on. Instead, I'm compelled to follow Bennett. We're supposed to be a team.

All I know is that something feels off. My senses are buzzing and a creepy, yes, *creepy*, hum is intensifying. It's coming from the countryside, wafting in through the open window along with a chilly breeze.

The miraculous, silencing *Baffles* are burning a hole in my hand, but instead of inserting them in my ears, I hide them in my carpetbag for safekeeping. As if by protecting them from damage or loss, I'm protecting Charlotte as well.

On instinct, I nab a tucked away pastry (compliments of Henri) and scarf it down while pulling on my coat. Not much in the way of *Scrambling* fuel, but better than nothing. Besides, I don't want to garble or block the voices completely. The incident with Abigail taught me that I can manage my anxiety and channel my *Misfortune* for some sort of good, rather than cowering and hiding in ignorance and fear.

As long as Bennett talks me through it.

Again, the thought occurs that we're a team. That he needs me as much as I need him. At least, it does my pride good to think so.

My determination swells as I hop from the train and spring into action.

Unfortunately, learning that I'm half-FIC doesn't awaken any dormant super powers. I slog my way over uneven terrain like any ol' human. It's a sloshy trek through glistening knee-high grass. Soggy earth sucks at my boot heels, compliments of recent rain, and yet I press on.

That is, until I get stuck.

"Crap."

Bent over and struggling to pull my right boot out of ankle deep mud, I wrestle with distractions. Wet weeds slapping at my cheeks. Burning coal stinking up my nose. And most disconcerting, the vexing assault on my ears. Distant voices of the men congregating around the steam engine and the garbled hum wafting from the misty woodland beyond.

In the sensory chaos, someone nabs my arm.

I yelp. I straighten. I frown. I snap. "Don't sneak up on me like that!"

"I didn't sneak, but that's beside the point." Bennett glares. "Had you followed my advice—"

"You mean *order?*"

"—you would not be in this predicament." He reaches down and, with one quick tug at my calf, yanks my foot from the muck.

Unbalanced, I fall against him. In contrast to the toxic train odors, Bennett smells yummy.

But that's beside the point.

I push away from him, straighten my spine, and swipe annoying, loose curls from my face. "So what's going on?"

"Not this train. That's for certain. The tracks are mangled."

"Mangled?"

"Destroyed."

He goes from looking over my shoulder to pulling me in for a kiss.

What the—

My brain glitches as his mouth moves over mine. As he palms the small of my back, the back of my neck.

As kisses go, it's tame. Not even any tongue. And yet I'm nearly blinded by a jolt of white hot passion.

Bliss.

Color me dazed and disappointed when he eases away to focus on someone else.

"Ah, Mr. Appleton," he says with a sheepish smile.

Gabriel Bennett? Sheepish?

"Mr. Knightley. Forgive the intrusion."

I turn and blink at a short, stout man dressed in a uniform similar to the train dude who witnessed my ghostly encounter. Clearly, Mr. Appleton deems our kiss indiscreet. Like Bennett, he looks embarrassed. Only for real.

As for me, I'm struggling to get my head out of the clouds. Discombobulation by chaste kiss. How pathetic am I?

"My wife was distressed when I explained we're stuck in the middle of nowhere for who knows how long," Bennett explains.

Distressed?

"I was assuring her that she is safe with me." He squeezes my hand. "Always."

So the kiss was a ruse. Period. A show of affection to sell us as man and wife. I want to sock him. Instead, I put my arms around him and cling. I'm American. Even in Victorian times, we're known for being brazen, right?

"My husband would have you believe I am delicate, Mr... Appleton, is it?" I smile. "In truth, we are recently wed and can't keep our hands to ourselves."

Appleton turns a brighter shade of red while Bennett gives me a subtle, warning squeeze.

"Yes, well," Appleton stammers while tugging at his collar, "I was instructed to direct you back on board. It's not safe out here for women folk." His wary gaze darts toward the woods. "Or anyone, for that matter."

"And why is that?" I ask, keeping my tone light even as my spine ices.

"The engineer swore he saw a large creature on the tracks," says Bennett.

"More like a beast," says Appleton. "He sounded the

warning whistle, hoping to scare it away, only it held its ground. Lumbered off just before collision. On its two hind legs!"

"Maybe it was a bear," I say reasonably. Meanwhile, I'm imagining a cross between Bigfoot and the Abominable Snowman.

"No bear in these parts, miss. Plus, it was strong enough to mangle iron."

"*If* it mangled the rail," says Bennett. "You don't know that for sure. The engineer confessed that his vision was obscured by fog."

"He only said that to squash panic among passengers. Not that you're hearing this from me," says Appleton while urging us back toward our car, "but there have been rumors just north of here—"

"I'm aware," says Bennett. "In fact, that's why we're traveling to the village of Wembly. As a fan of urban legends and a writer of fantasy, I'm intrigued by the recent accounts of a hairy menace. Mrs. Knightley is a crackerjack assistant in terms of research and documentation." He looks down at me through those tinted specs and winks. "We're a team in more ways than one."

He sounds like a total dweeb. Apparently he's an ace actor in addition to a deadly assassin, because he's unbelievably believable as a fantasy geek and writerly nerd.

As it happens I come by those traits naturally.

I smile at Appleton and let my inner geek fly. "We thought we'd combine Mr. Knightley's present writing project with our honeymoon," I say with a girlish giggle. "I hope I can stand the excitement."

Appleton coughs into his hand. "Yes, well…"

"How far is Wembly from here?" Bennett asks.

The trainman offers a lay of the land, but I'm distracted, by the garbled voices coming from the woods behind us.

Only they're not so garbled now.

The sugar from the pastry must be waning. Plus, I'm not jacked on adrenaline. I'm oddly calm in my ruse as Mrs. Knightley and that calm allows me to tune in, instead of tuning out.

"Something about the joyous sounds pains him," I say while falling back and turning toward the voices.

And colors.

I see them now dancing among the mist. Colorful, swirling shadows. Punctuated by a rush of emotions. Vivid emotions. None of them mine.

I'm mesmerized.

I've seen this before. Felt this before.

On the grounds of Blackmoor.

Somewhere behind me, I hear Bennett dismissing Appleton, telling him to go on without us, and Appleton muttering something about wacky writers while tramping away.

I feel, more than hear, Bennett closing the distance between us. He's standing beside me now, looking toward my source of fascination, but not seeing. "What is it, Zoe?"

The more I relax, the more I see. It's like peering into another world through a souped-up kaleidoscope. "A fractured border."

TWENTY-FOUR

Slap me Speechless

I'VE NEVER BEEN one for leaping into the unknown or taking scary chances. So no one is more surprised than me when I move closer to the alternate universe where the father I never knew and can never know once thrived.

Bennett nabs my hand and yanks me back. "What the devil are you doing?"

"Getting a closer look."

"Look?" he asks incredulously. "You can *see* the border?"

"It's right there." I tug my hand from his tightening grip and point at a massive gnarled oak less than twenty feet ahead. "To the right of that tree. A veil of rippling, bursting colors and shapes. Kind of like a cross between a kaleidoscope and the Northern Lights. You know, Aurora Borealis?"

He stares into the woods without a flicker of wonder.

I'm stunned. "You don't see it? How can you not see it?"

"To my knowledge no one has ever *seen* a fractured border," Bennett says. "Not from this side."

"But...you said Blackmoor sits due center of a fractured border. How could you know that unless—"

"Charlotte. She could...*can* hear *FIC* activity. Multiple stories playing out. Hundreds of characters conversing. Never ending audible chaos in a concentrated area. She thought she was going insane until...."

He trails off, shoves a hand through his hair, and then looks behind us. "Crew and passengers are still congregating near the engine. I don't want to draw attention to this area. Let's go."

But I'm already drifting closer to the magical *chaos*. "I can see people. Characters, I guess. They look like psychedelic cartoons from this side, but if I can cross over or at least peek my head in—"

"Why the hell would you do that?" he snaps while thwarting my advance a second time.

"To see and hear more clearly?"

I hate that I'm trembling, but his anger is unnerving. And perplexing.

I tear my gaze from the border and focus on Bennett. Gone is the façade of a geeky fantasy writer. He's all *Warrior*. A dark and deadly *Character Assassin*.

I'm not afraid of him, but I am wary. "If there truly is a *FIC* uprising—"

"The conspiracy and uprising take place in the 21st century. This is 1898."

"I know. I..." I palm my forehead. I don't want to admit that I'm confused, but clearly—or not so clearly —I am.

"The voices," I say. "I can't make out every word, but they *are* conspiring. A young prince and a band of followers."

I look back to the rippling colors. Driven by curiosity, I embrace a fantastical mindset as my eyes adjust to the visual brainteaser. "They're in a…castle? It's medieval looking. Wood rafters, stone walls. Long tables set with plates and pitchers."

"Extraordinary."

"Hay-oh…"

"Heorot. It's a mead hall. The royal residence of Hrothgar, a legendary Danish King of the 6th century. The young prince is Beowulf and they're conspiring to kill Grendel."

I glance from one puzzle to another, gaping at Bennett as though he spoke in a foreign language.

"*Grendel,*" he repeats. "A giant troll-like monster motivated by isolation and a grim hatred of men. A demon who's provoked by the 'joyous sounds' emanating nightly from Hrothgar's mead-hall. A savage creature that devours…" Bennett looks at me in disgust. "You don't know the story."

As if that's a crime.

"Yet you're ready to 'cross over' or 'peek in' on a tale that's been horrifying readers for centuries? *You* who lived in fear of dead zones for your scant twenty-one years?"

No one, hello, *no one* provokes me like Gabriel Bennett. "Why are you being so obnoxious? Wasn't it you who told me to be fearless? Who encouraged me to walk on the wild side?"

"That pertained to driving a bloody car not joy-riding in *Fictopia.*"

"*Joy*-riding?"

"We're done here."

And with that he hauls me off my feet and into his arms. I'm stunned. I'm seething. "What the—"

207

"Since eyes are upon us, *Mrs. Knightley*," he says while carrying me back to the train, "I suggest you play the part of a smitten wife. An *injured* smitten wife."

I see now that the passengers who had disembarked are now re-boarding. Several are looking our way.

I'm a curiosity, I realize. One, because I'm the sole woman on the grounds. Two, because Bennett and I were lingering near the woods instead of the engine. No doubt they're wondering what we were up to.

Unwittingly, I've made us a source of gossip.

Right now I'm too peeved to care.

Bennett brought me north to train as an *Enabler* and yet when I make a breakthrough, he shuts me down. Not only that, I realize while glancing back to the trees, he somehow obstructed my ability to see the border.

The rippling, colorful veil is gone. Or at least no longer visible.

It's like having a part of me ripped away.

"Ho, there," someone calls. "Is everything ducky?"

I put a lid on my boiling fury as a suited man trots closer.

"May I be of assistance?" he asks.

Bennett pauses mid-stride. "Kind of you, but I can manage. My wife stepped in a hole and twisted her ankle."

"Clumsy of me," I manage in a meek voice. Meanwhile, I'm mad as a hornet.

"Shall I inquire about a physician?" asks the do-gooder. "Perhaps there is one on board."

Bennett looks down at me with a doting expression. "What say you, my love?'

Oh, how I wish he could read my mind. I have plenty to say and it doesn't involve a doctor. Although Bennett might need one later, considering I'm dying to lash out in more ways than one.

Instead, I smile—at Bennett and then the do-gooder. "It's not as bad as it looks. My husband is overprotective."

"Can you blame me?" Bennett asks the man while giving me an endearing—*Ha!*—squeeze.

The man smiles. "Indeed not."

Being presented and perceived as a 'pretty, helpless female' only worsens my mood.

"This is our compartment," Bennett says. "If you wouldn't mind opening the door?"

"My pleasure." Do-gooder complies, adding, "For what it's worth, we've been told that, due to the extensive damage to the rails, we'll be reversing course shortly. Backtracking to the nearest station in order to make alternate traveling plans. Can't imagine what happened."

"Appreciate the update," Bennett says while lifting me inside and swiftly following, "and the help. Good day, sir," he says with a smile while shutting the door in Do-gooder's face.

As soon as Bennett faces me, I sock him.

Pent up fury packs a powerful punch. At least, I thought it was powerful.

Bennett didn't flinch.

Maybe I should have aimed at his jaw instead of his shoulder. That I hit him at all is disconcerting. I'm not a violent person. At least, I didn't used to be.

And just like that, I'm filled with shame. "I—"

"If you're going to apologize, Miss Albright, at least do so for the correct infraction."

I flush a shade hotter. "And that would be?"

"Ignoring my instruction. The next time I tell you to back

away from a situation, do so without question. Your life and the welfare of countless others could well depend on it."

"Stop doing that!" I explode. "Stop making me feel responsible for the *wellbeing of mankind!*"

"What if you *peeked* over the border only to get sucked into *Fictopia*? Or dragged in?"

I blink. I swallow. I confess my imaginings were whimsical more than wary. "Well, it's not like I'd be alone," I reason. "You would follow me, right?"

"And then two of us would be trapped within a story not of our own making."

"We'd simply learn from the experience and cross back to reality."

"There's nothing simple about it."

"How did Dominic cross over?" I've been wondering about that along with a hundred other things. "How did he get from *Fictopia* to the Real World? What's *his* story? What happened when he left that story? To his character, I mean? And what did that mean to the existing plot? I don't understand—"

"Neither do I."

Slap me speechless.

And here I thought Bennett had all, or at least, most of the answers. Yes, he's been evasive on several fronts, but I don't sense he's dodging now. He's not stonewalling.

He's frustrated.

And furious.

He's also gathering our luggage.

"What are you doing?"

"We're not going back to the last station. We're going forward."

"On foot?"

He wrenches open the door, tosses our two bags to the ground, then jumps out and hands me down. "Keep up and stay close."

Toting both bags, he stalks toward the mangled part of the tracks just as the steam engine chugs in reverse.

My heart hammers and my feet sprout wings as I race-walk to keep pace with Bennett. "Where—"

"I want to introduce you to someone," he says while striding into the mist.

"Who?"

"Grendel."

TWENTY-FIVE

A Titanic Blunder

OCTOBER 12th, 1898 (Entry #2)

Dear Journal:

My brain hurts.

Also, I'm woefully out of sorts.

Bennett and I have barely spoken to one another for... well, it's been quite a while. I'm not wearing a watch and I don't see a clock in this room he rented for us. I'm not sure of the time. I only know that he left me to freshen up and change my clothes while he walked into the village to snoop around.

As it happens, we were only a couple of miles from Wembly when the train was forced to reverse course. And it was an even shorter walk to the Thistle Inn and its attached pub, a quaint establishment on the outskirts of the village.

Bennett had gotten directions from Mr. Appleton during the moment I'd been distracted by 'voices' via the fractured border. Not that Bennett told me we were heading to the inn when we set off on foot. He TOLD me he was going to introduce me to Grendel. The monster who 'maybe' vandalized the rail tracks. The monster who 'might' be terrorizing locals.

So I spent the entire walk tense and dreading a face-to-face run in with my first rogue FIC.

Thankfully, it was not to be. Instead my 'introduction' to Grendel, according to Bennett, would come later this evening and from a distance. It would have been nice if he'd clarified that right off the bat. But like I said, we're hardly speaking.

For the most part, Gabriel Bennett has been a bristly, infuriating man from the moment I met him. But ever since my sighting of the fractured border and my attempt to peek into Fictopia, he's been obnoxiously bad tempered. Not that I've been a picnic, but at least I know my reasons for being a moody spaz.

It's only been a few hours since I last jotted my thoughts in this journal and yet I've experienced several shocking episodes.

I withstood a horrific encounter with a ghost and eased that tortured soul's distress enough to help her cross over. (Thanks to Bennett's support and guidance.)

I saw a fractured border and could make out enough of the characters, visually and audibly, to pinpoint a story in progress on the other side. In an alternate universe! (Although, to be fair, it was Bennett who actually cited the tale.)

Both of these fantastical instances wowed me, to say the least. But it was another instance that blew me away and left me floundering.

Learning the truth about my ethnicity.

Although I've acknowledged that I'm Bi-universal—half earthborn and half FIC—I have yet to wrap my brain around the concept of being partially real and partially imagined. I don't look or feel differently than I did before Bennett dropped that bombshell. But I AM different. One-of-a-kind, according to Bennett, although I'd like to believe he's wrong about that. It's an incredibly lonely notion.

As someone who's lived a mostly solitary life, I'm only now realizing how very isolated I was before arriving at Blackmoor Manor. Yes, my life was less complicated (although far from normal) pre-Bennett, pre-ESCA, and probably safer, but, thanks to Victoria and Liza, I was socially lame. And worse, living in fear.

If I've learned one thing during this fantastical adventure, it's that I'd rather be a Bi-universal freak than a sheltered recluse. I no longer mind being weird. My weird is actually normal within the realm of the Elite Society of Character Assassins. I don't want to lose that sense of belonging by being declared one-of-a-kind.

I really need to speak to Bennett about that.

Which entails us actually conversing.

I guess this means I need to pull on my big girl bloomers and address head on whatever went wonky between us. At least this time I 'stayed put' like he instructed. That should make him happy. That's if 'happy' is even a part of his emotional landscape. How sad if it isn't.

Speak of the devil, I think he's returning.
Be still, my pathetic nerves.

Until later,

~~Mrs. Knightley~~ Zoe Albright

My plan to engage Bennett in a private heart-to-heart goes south the moment he walks through the door.

He's crowding up our tiny lodging room with his impressive height and brawn coupled with his massive ego.

It's annoying. And distracting. I'm crushing on the man instead of addressing our issues.

"I arranged for a meal downstairs," he says. "Shall we?"

"I... Oh. Now?"

"You haven't eaten since morning and even then you ate very little, according to Henri. You must be famished."

"Yes, but..."

"I can't have you fainting in the middle of a session. Also, if you're not going to wear the *Baffles*, you should *Scramble*. Or at least have the ability to do so, should you become overwhelmed."

"I won't... Never mind." I tamp down flaring irritation. He's all business. I get it. We're on a mission. But does he have to be so bossy? And condescending? Unless this is a ploy to toughen me up. What did he say about Grendel?

A monster from a tale that's been horrifying readers for centuries.

I couldn't stomach Penelope's menacing rants about

vampires, werewolves, and mad scientists. And now I'm gearing up to face down a giant of a troll-like monster who devours...

Bennett didn't specify *what*, but I can guess given Grendel's hatred of *men*.

I suppress a shiver and press a hand to my fluttery stomach. "I guess it wouldn't hurt to fuel up. But...can you... Would you mind helping me? This bodice laces in the back, at the waist. I couldn't reach...that is..."

Without a word, he steps in behind me.

My body tingles as he manipulates and tightens the laces of what Henri described as a *hunting* suit. The skirt and bodice aren't nearly as pretty or feminine as the traveling gown I wore this morning, and yet I feel oddly sexy.

The nearness of Bennett is stimulating, *intoxicating*.

He touches my back, my waist, finessing the cinched fabric with what feels like a practiced touch.

"Get a grip," I tell myself. *"It's not like he's UN-dressing you."*

And yet I feel...*sensual euphoria.*

By the time he turns me around I'm remembering our chaste kiss and aching for more.

So much more.

His enigmatic expression intensifies my fluster.

"I..." I clear my throat and struggle for professionalism. "Do I look okay?"

"The gown suits you. Or rather it suits Emma Knightley."

"Right. Good. I guess that's good. What about my hair?" The action packed day wrecked Henri's twisty up-do. I couldn't replicate the style so I pulled back the sides and let the bulk of my curls hang loose. "It works, right?" I ask in the wake of his unnerving silence. "I mean it's sort of Victorian looking. I remember in the movie *Titanic*, Rose wore her hair... Wait. That was closer to the Edwardian period. Never mind. I... Forget it."

I'm babbling. And twisting my wedding band round and round and round.

Crap.

I straighten and ball my fists at my sides. "I'll do my best to live up to her reputation."

"Rose?"

"Charlotte."

Bennett looks down at me, all dark and stormy like.

"Henri said she's an exceptional *Enabler*. And I know you held...*hold* her in high regard. I just..." I choke back a sob that comes out of nowhere. Why did I go here? This is far and away from the heart-to-heart I had in mind. "If she has to die so that I can live, I want to do her proud. You know. As an *Enabler*."

Bennett grasps my shoulders and narrows his eyes. "Your soft heart is my greatest vexation. It is also your Achilles Heel. Mark my words, Zoe. Tracking rogue *FICs* requires focus, objectivity, and a scrap of ruthlessness. I fear your path is not as simple as Charlotte's or any other *Enabler*."

It's not what I want to hear. Not even close. But at least we're talking. And believe you me, I'm noting Bennett's every word and the underlying meaning.

Get your head out of the clouds and in the game, Miss Albright, because this is where shite gets real.

He's committed to protecting mankind, and me, from otherworldly danger and I'm acting like an enamored schoolgirl vying for her hunky teacher's affection.

Color me duly chastised.

Rejection noted and filed.

Vowing to annihilate my sexual attraction to this man if it kills me, I shrug off his touch and grab the dark jacket that matches my skirt and mood. "Ready when you are, Mr. Bennett."

TWENTY-SIX

Rising Above the Cliché

I'M IN A MOOD.

Mostly I'm angry with myself. Crushing on the handsome, older mentor is a flipping cliché. Also, who obsesses on lust when lives are at stake?

Someone who isn't truly grounded in their new reality, that's who.

Someone who isn't ready to track monsters.

Not that I'll admit that to Bennett. Right now I'm all about saving face.

So here I sit pretending to enjoy a meal with my *husband* in a secluded corner of the pub while trying my hardest not to feel like the woman scorned. If anything tops the frustration of writer's block, this is it.

"The first thing you need to master," he says softly, "is

recognizing the difference between the voices of ghosts and those of *FICs*. I explained the nuance back at Blackmoor."

"I remember. Sort of. It was part of the crash course you gave me on *FIC* awareness while we were waiting for Watson to drive us into London."

It feels like a lifetime ago.

Reminded of what I left behind—ahead?—my mind races as I pick at my roast chicken. When presented with a menu that boasted dishes like turtle soup and pigeon pie, I glommed on to the most bland of offerings. Even so, my appetite's lacking.

"I wonder if he's worried," I say. "Watson, that is. I mean we've been gone, what? Two, three days now? Did I just disappear? Or did my essence split somehow? Is there a contemporary me operating in the 21st century like there's a Victorian you vacationing here, now, in Paris? I can't believe I'm just now wondering."

And believe you me, I'm happy for the distraction.

"You've had other things on your mind," Bennett says. "*Should* have other things on your mind. Focus, Dove."

It's a dictate delivered with a smile. I take that smile and the endearment with a grain of salt. Even though we're discussing ESCA business, we're doing so in character as William and Emma Knightley. To anyone glancing our way, we're a happily married couple enjoying an intimate meal and quiet conversation.

That said, the pub is nearly deserted. The barkeep and the two men seated at the bar are clear across the room and engaged in their own conversation. The woman who served us our food and drinks retreated to the kitchen. She seemed a little on edge and warned us away from the north end of the village after dark, although she refused to elaborate beyond, *"Wounded howls and shadowy stalking."*

"I can tell the difference by the way. Between ghosts and *FICs*," I say as my mind drifts to Grendel.

"Since when?"

"Since Abigail and Beowulf. I didn't think about it at the time, but thinking back there was a definite difference. And since Beowulf *'sounded'*..." I hook my fingers in air quotes, "...a whole lot like the professor and his minion, I now know that *they* were *FICs* as well. Not ghosts. *FICs*."

Bennett abandons his half-eaten duck. "What professor? What minion?"

"Back at Blackmoor. After my first creepy encounter with you. You know, when my hand melted through your arm?"

"Go on."

"I tried to run away, but when I opened the door I was assaulted by a rush of disembodied voices. Most of them were scratchy whispers—like Abigail—but others cut through as clear as Beowulf. One said, *'Five more weeks, Professor.'* The other, the professor, I assume, answered, *'Make it three.'* I didn't tell you this?"

"You did not."

I lean forward and force a loving smile. "Your cranky *Warrior* side is showing, *dear*. You may want to lose that scowl."

He drinks deeply from his frothy ale.

"Or hide it." In kind, I sip brewed tea—my second sugar-laced cup—in order to smother a smirk. Bennett isn't as perfect at pretending as he boasted.

"What else did you hear back at Blackmoor?"

"Nothing. No, wait. That's not true. Before that. When

Watson first drove me from the airport to the manor. I woke from a deep sleep and, again, heard a barrage of voices. Only three were clear. Penelope and Balderdash and—"

"Balderdash?"

"Penelope's dog. He talks. And... I didn't know the other voice, but... Wait. Maybe... Yes, I think it was the professor!" It's all I can do to keep my voice and enthusiasm in check. "I caught two clear sentences in the chaotic audio storm. First, he said, '*As long as he's chained, I am free to conquer.*' And then a few seconds later, '*You're no match for me, Enabler.*' I didn't know what that meant. I'd never heard the word *Enabler* in that context, but it felt like a personal jab."

I take another hit of my sugary tea and then inhale the gooey cranberry sauce that came as a side with my chicken. Caffeine and sugar. It's like I'm regressing. Fueling my *Scrambler* to gear up for combat. Old habits die hard.

"*As long as he's chained,*" I repeat. "Do you think he was referring to you being imprisoned in Blackmoor? And the *Enabler* part? Was he referring to me? Only how could he know about my *Misfortune*? And how... Can he *see* over the fractured border to the other side like I can?"

"You *saw* the professor?"

If Bennett clenches his jaw any tighter, I'm worried his teeth will crack.

"No. But... When I rushed out of Blackmoor the second day, the first time we melded, I saw colors and shadows, a muted version of what I saw today in the woods. A brief glimpse at a fractured border. I didn't know what it was back at Blackmoor."

"Why didn't you tell me this before?"

"Like I said, the sighting was brief. So brief, I forgot about it until later and then I chalked it up to my imagination. If you remember, in that moment before and after we melded, I was freaked out and melting down."

Bennett pushes up the rims of his faux glasses and squeezes the bridge of his nose. "What about the next day? When we melded and crossed the grounds to the carriage house. Did you see the border then?"

"No. But... That time we melded as soon as I stepped outside. No lag time. It's different, *I'm* different when you're inside me." I blush. "I mean—"

"I know what you mean."

"Also," I rush on, "I think my ability to see the border and beyond that, into *Fictopia*, is enhanced when I'm in a Zen-like state—meaning calm and attentive. Similar to how I felt with Abigail after you told me to steel my heart and open my mind.

"When you started arguing with me and physically carried me away from the border, my adrenaline surged," I say with a burst of resentment. "My emotions exploded and the rippling kaleidoscope faded. I had a sense that the border was still there, but I couldn't see it anymore."

"Your ability to hypothesize and summarize is impressive."

"Years of musing and brainstorming with Penelope."

"Penelope Pringle. I have questions about her. And Balderdash."

"Join the club."

"Language, Mrs. Knightley."

Victorian speak. Right. "As do I. But, if you don't mind, I'd like to save that subject for a later date. I'm over my other-weirdly quota for the day and we've yet to discuss Grendel."

"If you were able to achieve that Zen-like state, as you called it, at will, and without me inside you," he says without an ounce of flirtation, "do you think you could see the fractured border and beyond into *Fictopia* from the vantage point of Blackmoor?

"I don't know. As you said, I'm only hypothesizing."

"Then let's conduct a solid case study by returning to the woods near the railway."

I blink at his sudden turnaround. "I thought you didn't want me near that border."

"I don't want you to *cross* that border," Bennett says while abandoning his seat and offering me his palm. "But I'll support a hard look. The potential payoff is worth the risk."

I shiver even as his warm hand closes around mine, even as he pulls me to my feet and against a *Warrior* body that promises keen protection. "What potential payoff?" I ask in a tight voice.

"Once we return to Blackmoor, if you can pinpoint the fractured border and effectively spy on the professor from 'this' side, maybe we can sabotage a deadly *FIC* invasion well ahead of his three week target."

Something in his tone, something dire, causes me to grab his lapels in a manner that demands bald truth. Something he's been evading all through dinner. "Who is this professor?"

Dropping his mouth close to my ear under the pretense of spousal affection, Bennett whispers, "My worst nightmare."

TWENTY-SEVEN

A Warrior's Fall from Grace

"RELAX."

"I'm trying."

"Why didn't you tell me this was your first time?"

"Because you took me by surprise and it's not something you admit in front of a stranger when your *husband* should know something this *significant* about his *wife*."

When Bennett told me he wanted to return to the fractured border, I thought we'd travel through the woods and meadow the same as we did before—on foot.

Instead, after leaving the Thistle Inn, he steered me toward a livery stable where he rented a horse named *Jack*.

I smiled and played the doting 19th century wife who, of course, would be acclimated to the most common form of transportation in an era before *automobiles* existed. I even swallowed a gasp when Bennett lifted me onto the massive black horse in a sideways fashion. As he swung easily into the saddle behind me, showing he was a confident horseman, I thought, *I can do this.*

But as he finessed Jack down the dirt lane and into a trot, my anxiety spiked, causing me to bury my face against his shoulder and to hold on—*to him*—for dear life.

"Given your American roots, I assumed you were unaccustomed to riding sidesaddle," says Bennett. "That is why I acquired one mount instead of two. However, it did not occur to me that you would be so completely lacking in equestrian skills."

"Did I make fun of you for not knowing how to drive a car?"

"I am not 'making fun,' as you say."

"Maybe not. But you're making me feel stupid. As in unworldly or uneducated. Just because I've never ridden a horse… Or read *Beowulf*…"

"*Beowulf* is an epic poem dating back to the 8th century. Since then it has been retold, translated, and adapted in multiple formats countless times. It is considered one of the most important works in Old English literature. Even in the 21st century."

"No doubt required reading in high school or college." On edge, I tighten my grip as we veer off the lane and cut toward the woods. "So once again you assumed something about me," I grit out. "For your information I didn't go to a public… learning institution. Liza tutored me at home. And I skipped college or university or whatever *you* call higher learning because I was already making a good living as a writer."

"As an authoress of books for children."

"Publishing may be a fluffy career choice compared to

Character Assassin," I say with a trace of snark, "but it's equally noble and important."

"I agree."

I loosen my hold enough to ease back and note his expression. "You do?"

"I hold writers in the highest regard, Miss Albright. As for riding, I am duly reminded of your limited life experience. Most of which you cannot be blamed for. I apologize if I offended you."

"You *do*?"

"In the future I'll try not to *assume* where you are concerned. Now...Which would you prefer first? Instruction on riding or a rundown on Grendel?"

"Given there's a *FIC* on the loose, a riding lesson, at this precise moment, seems like a waste of precious time, don't you think? I mean, you're not going to let me fall, right?"

"You have my word."

"Even so, I'd feel better holding on. To you. Purely for stability reasons," I clarify because this is so not about me wanting to cling to his hunky bad self. "If you don't mind."

By way of an answer he pulls me in snug while managing the reins with one hand.

Buoyed by Bennett's competence, I relax into Jack's gait as we hasten toward the open grasslands. I have scarier things to contemplate aside from being bucked off of spirited, yet disciplined, horse. "Why does Grendel hate men? Why is he upset by joyful sounds?"

"This tale, this *monster*, is a subject of much study and debate. Henri, or Odion, I'm sure, could relay diverse analysis. But one common notion is that Grendel is a descendent of

Cain, who by biblical accounts, was banished after committing the first sin against God."

Cain, who murdered his brother, Abel. The first two sons of Adam and Eve. Now *that* story I know.

"Like Cain," Bennett goes on, "Grendel is condemned to a life of despair in the shadows. Exiled and excluded from society, he's a lonely, angry, and vengeful creature who lashes out violently against those he deems favored by the Creator. Those who exhibit happiness—like the men in King Hrothgar's mead-hall. Men who express joy through drink and song."

"Like men in any one of Wembly's pubs?" I ask.

"Quite."

I counted at least three drinking and dining establishments. And sure, the clientele was sparse and the mood subdued at the Thistle, but it was still early. What about after dark when people socialize over several pints of ale?

"Although," adds Bennett, "so far, Grendel has been restrained. At least in comparison to the atrocities he committed in his original story. Earlier, when I spoke to random villagers under the guise of research for my book, no one admitted a close look at 'the beast'. Many have heard eerie howling. Some have felt stalked. A few, like the engineer of the train, had obstructed glimpses of what looked to be a grotesque animal. To date, one man has gone missing and one was found mutilated in a field."

I wince. "You call that restrained?"

"Yes."

I swallow hard, my gaze darting toward the leafy canopy on the perimeter of the meadow and then to the mangled railway to our left. "Do you think he's lurking nearby?"

"Do you hear him? Sense him?"

I close my eyes, steel my heart, and open my mind.

"No." All I hear is the wind rustling through the trees and a distant whirring drone. All I sense is the calming nearness of Bennett. "This is probably a dumb question," I say while squinting up at my mentor, "but does Grendel speak English or some other, you know, human language?"

"As it happens, there is a language barrier. Another source of his discontent. He can understand humans, but he himself has not mastered our words."

"So when he speaks, no one understands him," I say. "Adding to his sense of isolation."

"Don't make the mistake of feeling sorry for him, Miss Albright. He's a brutal, irredeemable killer."

I don't answer, but I am musing.

Grendel is an outcast. Lonely. Frustrated. Regardless of Bennett's warning, I empathize.

I'm deep in thought, contemplating the monster's inherited banishment, his intense suffering, and crushing solitude when a voice cuts through my daze.

"I hereby renounce sword and the shelter of the broad shield, the heavy war-board: hand-to-hand is how it will be, a life-and-death fight with the fiend."

I know that voice.

I repeat what I heard and Bennett replies, "Beowulf. His words as written by the author."

I open my eyes and, just ahead, near that massive ancient oak, I spy the rippling veil of colors. The magical kaleidoscope. "The fractured border."

Shadows and shapes.

Swirling colors and patches of disjointed scenery that slowly fall into place.

One by one by one.

Until suddenly, magically, my eyes adjust to the wonder of peeking into another universe.

I've been listening all the while. Hearing the scattered dialogue and narrative of a story already in progress.

"They look like primitive Vikings and yet they speak perfect English," I say in wonder. "Except...I'm not familiar with a lot of the words. And the sentence structure... It's weird. But I can tell you one thing," I say to Bennett. "Beowulf is a braggart."

Supremely confident. Warrior confident.

Like Bennett.

I don't know how long I've been standing here gazing over the border and into *Fictopia* and, specifically, into the tale of *Beowulf*, but I know Grendel is not the first or last of the Scandinavian hero's demonic foes.

Even though Bennett declared this artistic work an epic poem (and maybe that's why it sounds strange to my ears), it's playing before me like a movie on a rippling film screen. Albeit a movie that occasionally burps, glitches, and clouds.

In other words, it's not a perfect picture and at times the sound stinks as well. Every time I strain closer for a clearer look and listen, Bennett pulls me back.

I don't fight him. My goal is to stay relaxed. If I get riled, I'll lose sight of the border.

Instead, I parrot portions of the story so Bennett benefits from my *Misfortune.* In turn—when we leave here—I hope he can fill in the blanks because there's a heck of a lot I don't understand. Particularly regarding the layered complexities associated with Grendel.

I'm watching. I'm listening. I'm sorting through emotions, motivations, and boasts.

"Weaponless warfare?" I'm confused by Beowulf's decree.

When the monster finally bursts onto the scene—in *Fictopia*, not the Real World—I gasp and stumble back.

My heart pounds with sickening dread.

Abandoning the story narrative, I squeak, "He's gigantic and...and hideous! Pointy teeth. Dagger claws. He's...furious! And he's slogging through the moors straight for the mead-hall!"

"Look away."

I'm too riveted by the story to heed Bennett's order. Even as the visual and audio aspects blur and glitch, I stare.

"Look away, Zoe."

But it's too late.

"He's clawing through the door and ripping it from its hinges! He's... He's...scooping up a warrior and..."

I scream, my terror spiking as someone grabs me from behind. Spooked, I lash out.

Kicking! Punching!

Fighting for my life!

"Zoe! Open your eyes!"

He restrains my thrashing, pulling me tight against his body. A semblance of sanity returns as he frames my face with his hands.

Gabriel, not Grendel. Gabriel, not Grendel.

Sick to my stomach, I open my eyes and meet Bennett's gaze. "He ate him. *Ate* him! Grendel bit off that man's head, his hands, his feet!"

"Devoured him. I know."

"And some version of that monster is out here," I wave one arm wild, "in the Real World, stalking the people of Wembly! We...we...have to stop him."

"We can't interfere."

"Are you *crazy*?"

"We're here to observe. To train. We can't alter history, dammit."

"How can you be so calm? So cold?" I gawk at Gabriel Bennett, the man I lusted after, with shock and disgust. Shaking with anger and visceral fear, I glance toward the village. "I can't let them die."

With a burst of Herculean adrenaline, I break free of my mentor and run.

TWENTY-EIGHT

A Prodigy's Plan and a Fragile Truce

BENNETT SLAMS into me from behind.

We go down fast and hard, but somehow he rolls beneath me, taking the brunt of our fall as we skid through slick, weedy grass.

We've danced this dance before. On the grounds of Blackmoor. Our second jarring and awkward melding. But instead of magically fusing, we're locked in a tangle of limbs.

I'm stunned. I'm trembling.

Even before I catch my breath, he flips us again so that I'm trapped between the soggy earth and his hard body. "Get off of me!"

"Not until you come to your senses."

"Don't treat me like a child!"

"Then stop acting like one."

I glare at him. It's all I can do. I'm pinned flat under his considerable weight and he's got a stronghold on my wrists. Biting or spitting isn't my style, and since I've never kneed a man, I'd probably botch that, too. Still, I'm too angry to cry *Uncle*.

"You're crushing me," I grit out.

"Likewise."

I blink. I muse. Given his upper hand physically, he can only mean that emotionally.

"Meaning you're disappointed in my reaction to seeing a man being eaten *alive*? Well, excuse me for freaking out!" I shriek. "Unlike you, a professional *assassin*, I'm not desensitized to horrific violence!"

He holds my gaze and his tongue, causing me to take pot shots at guessing his gripe. "Or is it that you're exasperated because I'm unwilling to turn a blind eye while a monster ravages the villagers of Wembly?"

His refusal to intercede boggles my mind and hurts my soul. His continued silence grates.

"Allowing an atrocity to take place just because you're worried about *possibly* mucking up the future," I ramble on, "is…is unimaginable to me. Although, I don't know why I'm surprised by your coldhearted choice," I say on a final puff of indignation. "You're willing to let your beloved Charlotte die in order to safeguard me—a woman who's obviously a pain in your ass. Why would you bend rules for strangers?"

Bennett blinks and I flinch. His expression is flat, but, instinctively, I know my words sliced deep.

Shame tempers my fury. I've never been purposely cruel. My first impulse is to apologize, but I don't.

After an excruciating stare down, Bennett finally speaks. "Are you finished?"

"For the moment." I'm a bundle of messy thoughts and emotions. I want to cry, but I won't. I want to rail, but I don't. Knee jerk reactions don't cut it with Bennett. If I want to plead my case regarding that monster and the villagers, I need to do so rationally. I need to calm the rage and fear churning within.

As if sensing a fragile truce, Bennett shifts and pulls me up with him.

Once on my feet, I break from his grasp. His clothes, face, and hands are splattered and smeared with mud. I no doubt look the same.

"How are we going to explain our appearance to the livery guy and the staff at the inn?" An off topic question while I gather my frazzled wits.

"I doubt anyone will ask."

"Well, if they *do* ask, let's keep it simple," I say while swiping my hands down my stained skirt. "We slipped while walking."

"And rolled around in the mud on a lark?" Bennett asks with a raised brow.

"If you have a better idea—"

"As I said, I don't think they'll ask. In this day and age, it's rude to openly pry."

He passes me a pristine handkerchief (How many of these suckers does he have?) and then gathers the reins of the stallion calmly standing nearby. A gentle giant.

Unlike Grendel.

My stomach rolls in memory of the monster's barbaric crime.

Bennett approaches me with the horse in tow, and then glances over his shoulder. "Can you see the border?"

I look toward the massive oak while wiping mud from my cheek. "No. Then again I'm anything but Zen-like right now."

"Which proves your theory. That your ability to see a fractured border increases when you are calm and attentive."

"And the longer I retain focus, the better my view. Instead of a colorful cartoon, the characters gradually morphed into live action figures making them and the story more *real*. But when Grendel appeared, when my emotions spiked, what I saw and heard faded in and out and broke apart in splotches of swirling colors. More like a kaleidoscope than an animated picture."

"This was a valuable lesson learned, Miss Albright. If, as a Bi-universal being, you're capable of *seeing* fractured borders, and what's more, seeing *into Fictopia*, then what the devil else is within your power?"

⸎

We ride back to Wembly in silence.

The temperature is dipping with the sun, but my shivering is due more to dread. I keep expecting a giant troll-like monster to burst out of the woods, blood and flesh dripping from his pointy teeth and claws. That's how my imagination rolls.

Since I don't *hear* Grendel's thoughts—however indiscernible they may be—Bennett assured me the rogue *FIC* isn't close by.

During my training session back in London, Henri had also mentioned an *Enabler's* sensitivity and ability to hear the thoughts of a *FIC* circulating in the Real World.

"That's how you track them," she said. *"That's how you glean*

clues to their location. You lead your Warrior to the FIC and he engages and erases. It isn't always pretty, but luckily you don't have to watch."

"Does the Warrior always win?" I asked to which she replied, *"Eventually."*

The details of tracking and erasing didn't fully sink in until I started contemplating ways of thwarting Wembly's *beast.*

I'm tense in the saddle and my mind's racing with a solo brainstorming session. What if I'm capable of this...or that... or... The possibilities inspire a dozen plot twists in my developing story as a Bi-universal being.

Bennett, I assume, is absorbing my new found skill of border peeking as well as my unacceptable (in his mind) behavior. First I freaked out then I acted out. I don't think my reactions were childish. I think they were normal given the extreme circumstance, but whatever. He can ponder and stew until the cows come home, for all I care. Although we ended the bizarre and volatile outing on a diplomatic note, I'm still bent out of shape.

Unlike Bennett, I'm not willing to stand idly by while a monster terrorizes innocent, or even not-so-innocent, people. I certainly can't stomach the notion of Grendel mutilating or devouring someone when maybe I could have warned potential victims. Or maybe scared Grendel off? I don't know how I'd do that, but...

"If it makes you feel better," Bennett says out of the blue, "there isn't another killing for more than a week. We'll be long gone at that point."

He tightens his arms around me and I realize that I'm still

shivering. I don't know if he thinks I'm scared or cold. Either way, the gesture is kind.

It's also unsettling.

Cursing my fluttery stomach, I steel my spine and tone. "Whether we're here or not, my conscience will smart all the same." *Unlike yours*, I want to add, but I don't. That would be petty. *Childish.* I want to reason with Bennett, not alienate him.

Which spurs an idea.

I shift, risking eye contact with the perplexing *Warrior* for the first time on this return ride. "You said that, for the most part, the Grendel of the Real World has mostly only stalked. Whereas the Grendel in *Fictopia*, in the story, killed nightly for years. Why is he showing restraint here? Now?"

"There's a theory," he says while reining Jack from the woods to the road, "or at least there will be after ESCA addresses this infiltration in earnest a few weeks from now. It pertains to one of the monster's greatest frustrations."

"The language barrier?"

Bennett nods. "Henri will surmise that the essence of Grendel that peeled away and escaped into this world was the part of him that's keen to study the villagers' speech and behavior."

"Lurking and stalking to learn?"

"That is the generous assessment."

"He's desperate to connect, to communicate. No one understands him, but what if I can?"

With the outskirts of the village and the livery stable within sight, Bennett brings the horse to a full stop. "What do you mean?"

"You said *Beowulf*, the story of Beowulf and Grendel, has

been translated into many languages. Yet I tripped upon an English version from the get-go? What are the chances?"

When Bennett doesn't respond, I plow on. "What if a perk of being Bi-universal is the ability to understand a *FIC* in any language? What if every spoken word—even if it's gibberish—sounds like English to me? What if I can hear and understand and reason with Grendel? What if I can talk him into returning to *Fictopia*—"

"There's no reasoning with this monster, Miss Albright. With any monster. But especially *this* monster."

"But what if I can?"

He's staring at me so hard I swear he's looking into my soul. "You'd still be disrupting the timeline," he says. "As it played out before, the beast terrorized this area for another two weeks. What about everything that happened between now and then? And I mean *everything*."

"How many more lives does he take?"

"Two."

I muse. I nod. "Okay. How about this? What if I can make him understand that no one wants to welcome a murderer into their circle? That his chances of learning and communicating and being accepted are greater if—"

"Surely, you're not this naïve."

I'd take offense, except he almost sounds impressed.

"All I need to do is to curb his inclination to kill. To temper that urge for two weeks. Until someone else from ESCA shows up and kicks his butt back to *Fictopia*. Surely we won't be risking much by saving just *two* lives."

Grasping his forearms, I appeal to his *Warrior* logic. "If nothing else, it will be a solid case study. If I can communicate with a *FIC* who only speaks gibberish, then we've nailed down yet another one of my Bi-universal gifts."

He nudges the horse toward the stable, all the while holding my expectant gaze.

"Well?" I ask.

"I'm thinking."

Reaching our destination, he swings out of the saddle then reaches for me. He lowers me to the ground, his hands firm on my waist, his eyes riveted on my face.

Something akin to respect sparks in Bennett's gaze. "Still thinking?" I croak.

"It's been a full day, Mrs. Knightley, and as you said, you're over your other-weirdly quota. As for your plan," he says while finessing me toward the inn, "let's sleep on it. But first, let's get you out of these wet clothes."

TWENTY-NINE

Bonding with Bennett

OCTOBER 12th, 1898 (Entry #3)

Dear Journal:

I don't know what I expected, but I know what I imagined.

Bennett peeling off my damp, muddy clothes—layer-by-layer—and admiring my naked curves while, he, too, stripped bare. And then the two of us crawling into bed.

Together.

It didn't go down like that at all.

After arranging a hot bath for me, Bennett disappeared. I undressed, bathed, and changed into a nightgown and robe in private.

That was over an hour ago and he's still not back. Although I wager he didn't venture far. I don't think he trusts me not to run off in search of Grendel.

He needn't worry. A) I'm not sure I have the guts. B) I'm certain I don't have the energy.

This has been the longest and most adventurous day of my life. Flipping back and reading my two earlier entries —both from today, mind you—I'm amazed I've yet to pass out. I'm physically and mentally exhausted and my emotions have been through the wringer.

To be honest, I barely have the strength and focus to wield this fountain pen, but I'm determined to document my experiences in 1898. What if the memories are wiped away during our jaunt back to the future? I don't want to forget any of this. Not even the worst of it.

Like reliving the attack and murder of Abigail via her ghostly death loop.

Or seeing a hideous monster biting off the head and limbs of a living man. Yes, I know they were/are characters in a story, but it looked and felt real to me.

I also don't want to forget that my father, Dominic Sinclair, is a FIC and that I'm Bi-universal. I don't want to forget that, when in a calm state-of-mind, I can see fractured borders and, when focused, through the rippling veil of colors and into Fictopia.

I don't want to forget everything Henri taught me and everything Bennett shared.

I don't want to forget his kindness. Or his callousness. And I sure as sunshine, don't want to forget our chaste, yet sinfully delicious, kiss. Or how my heart bloomed and my skin tingled when he framed my face with his hands.

Although I vowed to annihilate my sexual attraction, I'm realizing that my attraction to Gabriel Bennett is not purely sexual. I wish it were as simple as that. He inspires the heady sensations that I associate with falling in love. I say 'associate with' because I've never actually been in love. Unless you count 'pretend love' like the kind I've felt for numerous fictional heroes. That's what happens when you're a recluse and obsessed with film and television.

But I digress.

I just...I don't want to forget. Because, for me, this could be as good as it gets.

Feeling grateful and melancholy,
  Zoe

⚐

I'm trapped.

Locked in a tight space, consumed with fear. *Her* fear.

And panic.

"Don't! Please. I won't tell. I won't tell. Have mercy..."

Abigail?

"Get off of her!" I scream.

But he ravages her, and laughs at me. *"You're no match for me, Enabler."*

He's strangling her, choking off her pleas, her air.

Suffocating.

Her fear. My fear.

I try prying his fingers from her neck. *Can't breathe.* "This will only isolate you more," I reason. "No one welcomes a murderer..."

Claws.

His fingernails grow into talons and his face sprouts hair.

Troll.

Grendel!

He rips off her head and…

"Zoe!"

He breaks through the wall of terror.

Powerful. Fierce.

Mentor. *Warrior.*

Bennett.

He smells like soap. Clean. *Good.*

"Open your eyes, Dove."

He gives me a hard shake, ripping me out of the monster's grip and into his arms.

Lungs burning, throat raw, I weep against his shoulder. "Abigail. Monster."

"Nightmare." Bennett smooths his hand down my back. "She's safe. You're safe."

I struggle to acclimate to his voice, his touch—to the notion that *this* is my reality.

"Dreaming."

"Not anymore," he says. "Open your eyes."

Through the blur of my tears, I see Gabriel Bennett—rumpled, but real—in our dimly lit room.

"I didn't hear you come in."

"You were out cold. I've been here for quite a while."

He's cocooning me and crowding the bed. "*Here?*"

"There." He glances across the room.

I follow his gaze. Using the sleeve of my nightgown, I wipe away tears and focus on a cushioned chair and a matching footstool. "You were sleeping sitting up?"

"I was reading."

I note the small table, a book, his fake specs, a bottle of

liquor, and a burning kerosene lamp. Reading and, perhaps, watching over me?

Slowly coming to my senses, I disentangle myself from Bennett and, leaning against the headboard, pull my knees to my chest. Hugging myself instead of him, I ask, "What were you reading?" *Please don't say my journal.*

"*The Strange Case of Dr. Jekyll and Mr. Hyde.* I remembered how you'd stowed it in your bag and..." He drags a hand through his already messy hair. "I wanted to prepare for when we're back in the future. I would have asked before invading your belongings, but..."

"You didn't want to wake me." I clear my croaky throat. "I don't remember falling asleep."

"You were exhausted."

"Aren't *you*?"

He doesn't answer, but I can tell that he is. I can see it in his bloodshot eyes. Also, I've never seen him so disheveled. He obviously bathed and changed into clean clothes, but his voluminous shirt is partially unfastened at the neck, wholly untucked from his trousers, and the sleeves are rolled midway up his forearms.

"Feeling better?" he asks, pulling my attention away from a glimpse of bare chest.

"Feeling shaky. That nightmare..." I shudder. "It seemed so real."

Bennett studies me for a moment then pushes off of the bed.

I instantly miss him.

He returns and passes me a glass of amber liquid.

"What is it?"

"Whiskey."

"I don't drink alcohol." I flash back on my trans-Atlantic wine spree. "Well, not usually."

"Think of it as a tranquilizer."

"Only if you join me." I don't know why I said that, except I'm still rattled. The closer he is, the calmer I feel.

I clasp the glass between both hands, watching as he pours himself a drink and then reaches for the chair.

"You don't have to drag that over," I say while scooting to one side of the mattress. "There's plenty of room."

He eyes my granny nightgown—so not sexy—and my bed-mussed hair.

"I'm not feeling frisky," I say. "If that's what you're worried about."

"Frisky."

"Aroused. Randy. Horny. Oh, what would you call it?" I ask while searching my brain for an archaic synonym. "Wanton?"

"I would not call it anything, Miss Albright. And no translation required."

He isn't being priggish, I tell myself, just proper. "I guess men and women don't discuss stuff like that back in your day."

"We *are* in my day and it depends." He surprises me by accepting my invitation. Settling on top of the blankets, he relaxes against the headboard and clinks his glass to mine. "Now that I've joined you…"

I lift my glass to my nose, sniff and gag. "It stinks."

"It's the peat. Strong. Smoky. Just sip." While eyeing me, he raises his glass to his lips.

Like I'll let the challenge pass. I sip, choke, and make a godawful face.

"It's an acquired taste."

"It's gross." But I take another sip. It's a slow burn—over my tongue, down my throat—that catches fire in the pit of my stomach. "So what did you learn?" I rasp over a cough. "About Jekyll and Hyde?"

"Let's talk about something other than monsters. For now."

"Like what?"

"Tell me about Penelope Pringle."

"Before or after she turned dark on me?" Hearing the bitterness in my voice, I take another sip of the high-octane liquor. I don't want to feel angry or sad. Or frustrated and scared. Numb would be nice.

"What about from the beginning?"

"You asked for it." In a burst of energy I didn't know I possessed, I revisit my youth and the imaginary friend who eventually morphed into my muse.

Bennett listens with obvious interest as I remember aloud how Penny kept me company and inspired my creativity. How she never judged my quirks or denied my *Misfortune*.

Unlike Liza.

And just like that, my mind jumps tracks.

"I wonder if Liza knew that Dominic was from an alternate universe. It's possible that Victoria confided in her sister, right?" I muse and drink more whiskey, forgetting for the moment that I don't like the taste.

"Possible," Bennett says. "Unless Vikki was as adamant as Dom about keeping your ethnicity under wraps."

"I'll have to ask her—Liza, that is. If we ever speak again."

"You're not on good terms?"

"Awkward terms." Feeling overheated, I shove my hair off of my face and scrunch my brow. "I always assumed Liza resented being my sole caretaker because it meant giving up her freedom. Also, I think, strike that, I *know* she finds my crooks, I mean, *quirks* exhausting.

"But what if?" I ponder, my fuzzy brain stuck on that one scenario. "What if she knew I wasn't wholly human? You know, like her. Maybe that's why she couldn't fully accept me as her own or…or for who I am. Zoe Albright: Alien Freak. I guess I'm lucky she didn't pawn me off on a circus."

Frowning, Bennett takes my almost empty glass from my hand. "She mistreated you?"

"No. Never. She was overprotective, manipu…" My tongue struggles with the word. "Ma-nip-u-la-tive, and frost…*frust*ratingly secretive about my parents, but she was never abusive."

"She knew about your clairaudience?"

I snort. "She hired a shrink, you know, a head doctor, to convince me dead people don't talk. I learned early on to manage my *Misfortune* on my own."

"To *Scramble*."

I nod. "And to keep any random and unfortunate dead zone incidents to myself."

Running out of steam, I shift and roll onto my side, pillowing my hands beneath my cheek. "And then there's Penny," I say on a sigh. "Liza hated Penelope, not that she could hear or see her, because when I was very young, I'd chat with Penny any and everywhere—even in public."

"But to Liza and everyone else, it looked like you were talking to yourself."

I wink and touch my nose, missing the tip as intended and glancing off a nostril. "Spot on." Him, not me. "That's why

Liza kept moving us from town to town. To circumvent gossip. About me. The crazy kid who hears voices."

"Or maybe she moved you around to make you harder to find."

"By those who would take advantage of my Bi-universal gifts?"

Bennett touches the end of his nose—*spot on.*

"Something to ponder when my thought process clears. I miss her, by the way. Penny," I clarify on a yawn. "And Balderdash," I add with a smile. "So much so, that I thought I saw them back in London. Your London. From Henri's second story window."

Bennett looks down at me with a raised brow. "Is that so?"

"Wishful thinking, I guess. But enough about me." My tongue feels thick, my eyelids heavy. "Tell me about you. Where were you born? What did you do before you joined ESCA?"

"I'm not nearly as interesting as you."

"I don't believe it."

He smooths my hair from my face. "How about if I tell you about your father?"

"Finally." Half asleep and lulled by Bennett's comforting presence, I cuddle closer and close my eyes. "I'm all ears."

THIRTY

The Calm Before the Hunt

I WAKE WITH A START.

And a honking big headache.

I lie still, very still, palming my forehead and staring up at an unfamiliar ceiling.

Where am I?

I think hard, pushing my throbbing brain well beyond its comfort zone. Slammed by a barrage of memories, I wince and groan.

Ghost encounter. Border encounter.

Bennett encounter!

Oh. My. *Gawd.* "I slept with Gabriel Bennett."

I bolt upright, looking around the tiny rented room. I'm relieved I'm alone, relieved he didn't hear me. I sounded like a smitten groupie. Not that we shared any sexy time. I'd remember that, wouldn't I? It's not like I had that much to drink. Just a few sips of whiskey.

Strong? How about toxic?

After the plane incident and this incident, it's obvious I'm one of those people with zero tolerance for alcohol.

Mortified, I push out of bed and stumble to a corner table and the provided chamber set. The beautiful porcelain basin and matching large-mouth pitcher contain water for sponge bathing. Also there are towels and a cup for teeth brushing.

Henri supplied me with tooth powder and a primitive-to-me toothbrush. I make quick use of them—*scrub, rinse, spit.* The powder tastes nasty, but not as nasty as stale, smoky whiskey.

Glancing in a small mirror I see that my long curls are a wild mess. Taming them with my fingers, I hurry to my messenger bag and start rooting. The Jekyll and Hyde novella. My dead phone. Assorted cosmetics. Assorted snacks. *Gum.*

I pop a minty stick and chew, a welcome palate cleanser after the chalky tooth powder. Then I dig my journal and pen out of my carpet bag and plop at the writing desk. I don't know where Bennett is or how long he'll be gone. I'm in a hurry to record whatever memories I have of our late night discussion.

As I recall, I did most the talking, except toward the end. Bennett shared details about his relationship with my father. I open the journal and tap the pen to the page.

I think. I write.

October 13th, 1898 (Entry #4—Day 2 in Wembly)
Dear Journal:

Yesterday, as you know, was jam packed with other-weirdly encounters. Those encounters prompted a terrifying nightmare. Thank goodness, Bennett came to the rescue. Otherwise, I might've had a heart attack and died in my sleep.

He could've told me to buck up—it was just a dream. But instead, he distracted me with drink and conversation. In bed. Unfortunately, we were both fully clothed and stayed that way. Although, I did get a peek at his bare chest which was, of course, spectacular.

But I digress.

Even though I was a lot tired and a little drunk (apparently I'm vulnerable to whiskey), I learned a few things last night.

NOTE: Gabriel Bennett is a good listener. I went on and on about Penelope. About my publishing career and writer's block. About my troubled relationship with Liza. And about my Misfortune. Instead, of dismissing any one of my quirks or experiences as crazy-talk (like Liza) or blaming it on my wild imagination (like Liza), Bennett accepted everything I said as plausible truth.

NOTE: Dominic Sinclair was Gabriel Bennett's mentor. Bennett joined ESCA a year after my father, and my father—who excels as a Warrior—took Bennett (who used to be a cocky mercenary with sketchy morals) under his wing.

Since Bennett is pretty darn cocky now (by my standards) I can't imagine what he was like before. At any rate, they eventually shifted from mentor/prodigy to devoted friends. Also, he didn't out and out say it, but it's pretty clear Bennett worships the ground Dominic walks on. No wonder he was so upset when I informed him of my father's death.

NOTE: Although Bennett didn't tell me how, Dominic was the one who learned that Bennett had been cursed to a bewitched dimension and trapped within Blackmoor Manor. At first Dominic and Archimedes, the presiding Wizard, worked hard to break the spell. But they failed time and again and over the years those within ESCA started doubting Dominic's story. It's not like anyone, including Dominic, could see or hear Bennett. But Dominic never gave up. Decades passed and...

I stare down at the written page and my stalled pen. "Decades passed and what?"

For a moment I worry that I'm paralyzed with writer's block. Except I'm not making this stuff up. It's fuzzy, but I remember Bennett lying on his back, one arm around me, allowing me to snuggle close instead of pushing me away. I can hear his voice, full of respect as he spoke about my father until...

"Decades passed and..." I groan. "I fell asleep. Crap."

Someone knocks on the door.

"One minute, please!" I shove the journal and pen back in my carpet bag and pull on my robe. Cinching the sash tight around my waist and cursing my pounding temples, I paste on a smile and crack open the door. "Oh. Hi." My heart thuds at the sight of him.

"No, 'who is it' before opening the door?" Bennett raises a condemning brow. "What am I going to do with you, Mrs. Knightley?"

I can think of a thing or twelve. "Sorry. My bad. That wasn't very safety conscious. I was…" I flutter my hand in the air. "…distracted."

The other brow hikes. "My bad?"

"Right. Victorian speak. My mistake." Eyeing the tray in his hands, the covered plates and the silver pot, I breathe deep. Coffee. Sausage? *Heaven.* "Is that breakfast?"

"It is."

Stomach grumbling, I open the door wide. "I think I love you." I blink. I flush. "I mean—"

"I know what you mean." He sets the tray on a table. "Thought we'd take our meal in private."

He sounds and looks all business. Dressed in the eccentric style of William Knightley, including the oval specs, he holds the chair while I take my seat.

"Thanks," I say, trying not to fret about my appearance. At least *his* rumpled look is on purpose. "Seems like forever since I've had coffee," I say, while pouring us each a cup.

"Thought you might prefer it to tea this morning."

There's no censure in his tone, still, I fidget. "I don't have much of a head for alcohol, but at least I didn't have any more nightmares. Thank you for that and…" I fish for a polite way of saying it. "…for keeping me company."

"Thank you for the restful night's sleep. Had you not invited me, I would have stretched out on the floor. Not nearly as comfortable."

I didn't expect him to be so forthright about us sharing a bed. Are we in new territory after last night? Is Bennett loosening up?

"I'm not used to sleeping with anyone," I say as he adds sugar lumps to my java. "I didn't hog the bed, did I? Or touch you inappropriately somehow?" I roll my eyes. "Sorry. I just... whiskey clouded my memory. Who knows what it did to my judgment?"

"Are you concerned that I took advantage of you?"

"The other way around, actually."

His lip crooks with the hint of a smile. "You were the perfect lady."

"Too bad. I mean, *phew*, that's a relief." I bite into a greasy link of sausage. *Yum.* "One more thing about last night. I think I fell asleep during one of your stories about Dominic."

"What's the last thing you remember?"

I tell him and he says, "There wasn't much more to it. Just that Dom never gave up on his belief that I was indeed there, somewhere, within Blackmoor. Over the decades, he continued to visit, although not with any regularity. Mostly when he needed to escape the chaos or tedium of being an immortal *Warrior*."

Immortal. My brain's still struggling with that whammy.

"Sometimes he'd stay for an hour," Bennett goes on. "Other times for days. He'd update me on matters pertaining to ESCA and to the world in general. Sometimes he blew off steam. Sometimes he pondered a case. Upon rare occasion, he contemplated his personal life."

"That's how you learned about Victoria, my mother." I'm gobbling up his memories as fast as my sausage, eggs, and beans. Bennett doesn't know it, or maybe he does, but he's filling an emptiness that's pained me for years.

"Mostly he spoke of Vikki in a professional sense. Of all the *Enablers* he partnered with over the years, she was by far the most gifted."

My chest swells with pride.

"He brought her to Blackmoor twice. For the serenity—as you call it—but also, given her extraordinary clairaudience, he was curious as to if she could hear me."

"Could she?"

"No. But she *sensed* something, someone, an entity. It was enough to reinforce Dom's belief that I was alive and trapped within."

Riveted, I shake my head. "I can't believe I fell asleep for even a portion of that enlightening report."

Bennett eyes me while slathering marmalade on toast. "I was longwinded last night."

"No, you weren't. You didn't have anyone to talk to for over a hundred years. Well, you could talk, but no one could hear you."

"You could."

I blink. I muse. *Because I'm Bi-universal?*

He passes me that slice of sweetened toast and refreshes my coffee. *Sugar and caffeine.*

"You're fueling my *Scrambler.*"

"I slept on it," he says. "Your plan. I want to know if you can understand Grendel."

THIRTY-ONE

Tracking a Monster

WHEN I WAS a kid and Liza wanted alone time to do whatever, she'd plop me in front of the television and gift me with snacks and the remote. She knew I'd stay riveted on the sofa for an extended period of time, sometimes for hours.

Sucked into one fantasy world after another, I was easily entertained by made-up characters manufactured by someone other than me. Meaning make-believe company other than Penelope.

As someone who disapproved of my frequent chats with my imaginary friend, Liza welcomed my fascination with the likes of *Cinderella*, *The Powerpuff Girls* and, later, contemporary heroines like *Bridget Jones* and *Mia Thermopolis* and historical favorites like *Elizabeth Bennet* and *Emma Woodhouse*.

Drama, comedy, historical, fantasy. You name a genre, I watch it. With one grand exception.

Horror.

Oh, sure. I've seen snippets of monster flicks—*Dr. Jekyll and Mr. Hyde*, for instance. *Alien. The Shining.* But only while flipping through channels and I never, *ever* linger.

As a rule, I avoid scary and slasher productions. I don't get a kick out of jump scares. I don't want to be horrified, psychologically disturbed, or creeped out of my gourd. I have never understood why someone would willingly (and sometimes *gleefully*) watch an evil entity maim and murder—even if it's only pretend.

My aversion to blood and gore is epic. I even cover my eyes during the battle scenes of some of my most beloved historical films. In light of that, it's amazing that I didn't look away when Grendel grabbed and devoured that poor soldier.

But that was *Fictopia*, not film.

I don't know why it would be different and maybe it's not. Maybe it just took me by surprise. I do know that it left me raw and dreading a repeat performance.

Even though I'm presently preoccupied with my fraidy-cat tendencies and zip tolerance for brutality, I don't share any of these musings with Bennett. He's already worried about my soft heart. When it comes to otherworldly encounters, he's seen me freak out on several occasions. When I punched the dude who stole my phone, I felt sick and made no bones about my disgust. Granted, Bennett prompted my aggression. Still. I'm not comfortable with violence.

Or malevolent forces.

I do think Bennett was impressed when I broke away from him yesterday, intent on saving the village from Grendel even without his help. But I think he suspects, as I do, that my incensed attempt was a knee-jerk compulsion.

Now, as we make our way toward a small church at the north end of Wembly, I'm pretending I have nerves of steel and courage out the wazoo. I'm telling myself that if *Sarah Connor*, a timid waitress–in–distress, could overcome her monumental fear to fight in order to crush a 'terminating' cyborg, then Zoe Albright, storybook writer, can suck it up and 'listen' to a man-eating monster.

According to Bennett that's *all* I'm supposed to do. *Listen.*

His dictate was clear. And frustrating. *"We have two goals this morning. Period."*

To explore my ability to 'track' a *FIC* via my *Misfortune*. And to learn if I can understand a monster's gibberish.

Considering my intense dislike of terrifying circumstances, I should be happy that he nixed my plan to try to reason with Grendel. But I'm not. And even though I'm supposed to follow his instruction without question, I can't. "I wish you'd reconsider—"

"No."

Forgetting for the moment that we're in public and that we're supposed to be a happily married couple out for a pleasant stroll, I glare up at Bennett. "I should have equal say in this mission. We're partners. *Enabler* and *Warrior.*"

"Prodigy and mentor," he counters. Steering me off the cobbled walkway and into the verdant, overgrown churchyard, Bennett nods toward a secluded stone bench.

Taking his cue, I settle on the cold hard slab. Noting my surroundings, I'm intensely grateful that I buckled under his persistence and, before leaving the inn, inserted Charlotte's *Baffles.* He'd pointed out the wisdom in blocking distracting voices should we pass through a dead zone. Yes, I can mute them by *Scrambling*, but that would tax my energy. *Baffles* are self-sustaining and infallible.

Good thing.

We're presently sitting smack in the middle of the parish's cemetery.

I take great pains not to fixate on the weathered gravestones or to exhibit anxiety. I mean, *come on*. A graveyard? Is he purposely testing my nerve? My resolve? I stare him down and raise one brow as if to say, *"Really?"*

He ignores my mental snark. "Before we proceed, *Mrs. Knightley*, I want your word that you'll respect my parameters."

"Your restrictions limit this mission to a half-assed assessment of my Bi-universal gifts, *Mr. Knightley*."

Even though my voice is whisper-soft, I'm keenly aware of my crude language. I should have said *half-hearted* or *half-baked*, and, normally, I would have. But, this moment, I'm a jacked-up, kick-ass *Sarah Conner* (fragile-waitress-turned-hardened-warrior) wannabe. Or rather, *have-to-be*. The normal *me* wouldn't be in my muddy tracking boots right now for all the coffee in Brazil.

Keeping up pretenses, Bennett adjusts his geek-sexy spectacles and crooks a semi-adoring smile. "Dom entrusted me with your safety. Your life."

"You don't know that for sure."

"But I know him. And, to a lesser degree, I know you. Subjecting you to a showdown with Grendel is risky on multiple levels."

"What if I promise not to get too close?" I fidget under his uncompromising expression and struggle not to sound miffed or whiny. "It's not enough to know if I can understand his gibberish, I need to know if I can connect and make a difference."

Suddenly I'm not thinking about *Sarah Conner* at all. I'm thinking about my mother. "Victoria used her superb clairaudience for good," I reason. "After ESCA, she worked with the police to solve murder cases and she enabled ghosts to crossover. Okay, she suffered a horrific death in the line of duty, but *she* wasn't half-FIC."

"What kind of horrific death?" Bennett asks. "How so and by whose hand?"

"I don't know details. Liza would never say. And since you don't know, I guess Dominic was also tightlipped on the subject."

"Or perhaps he was unaware of the particulars."

"Maybe. But that's not the point. The point *is*," I say, not wanting to get sidetracked, "maybe I'm more Dominic's daughter, than Victoria's. Maybe, when facing a *FIC* in the flesh, meaning the Real World, I'll surprise both of us and prove myself to be a *Warrior*. Or…" I shiver at the thought of it, "…immortal."

Bennett studies me a long moment, long enough to make me squirm. "Interesting," he concedes. "But this is not the time or place to test that theory. Are you familiar with the saying: Take only memories. Leave only footprints?"

"Not really. But I assume you're referencing the time travel paradox and revisiting your aversion to disrupting events as they originally went down. You're refusing to allow me to save two lives on the chance it *may* alter the future for the worst."

Repeating a tipsy gesture I made the night before, Bennett touches his finger to the tip of his nose.

Spot on.

I want to punch him.

Luckily, for him, he's saved by the bell. *Church bells.*

I glance ahead and see a bridal party and guests—dressed in their Victorian best—pouring out of the quaint stone church. Joyful sounds abound, filling me with expectation and dread. And, surprisingly, the thrill of the hunt.

Bennett stands and reaches for my hand. "Come on."

My senses fire up and sizzle as he wings me around the backside of the church.

As to the parameters of this mission, I didn't change his mind with calm logic. But I also didn't promise to play by his rules.

§

Bennett removes his glasses and tucks them in a pocket. I do the same with my *Baffles.*

Ready for action.

Sounds sexy, right? We're even dressed in black like a couple of super spies. But instead of utilizing high-tech equipment to survey the situation, we're hiding in the bushes like a couple of Peeping Toms, watching and listening to the festivities from afar.

After leaving the church, the bridal party took a short carriage ride to a small, but lovely country home. According to Bennett, in this age most weddings take place early in the day and are followed by a breakfast reception. It's closer to lunchtime, but food is food, I guess, and, as far as I'm concerned, there is no wrong time for cake.

Since the sky is grey and splotchy with ominous clouds,

the reception is inside which makes it difficult to see anything or anyone in detail. But we can see activity compliments of several windows and, since it's unseasonably warm and many of those windows are open, we can hear the bride and groom and their guests rejoicing.

"The music is unusual," Bennett says close to my ear. "Dancing is typically saved for elaborate evening affairs."

I want to ask if there was anyone before Charlotte? If he's ever been married? Or if he knows how to dance? Striving to be professional, I keep those questions, and a dozen more, to myself. But it reminds me of how little I know about Gabriel Bennett's personal life.

Stifling my curiosity, I focus hard on the house and the lively celebration of love.

Chatter, laughter, music.

Camaraderie.

Something Grendel has never experienced. The insult that stokes his envy and ire.

Suppressing a shiver, I cast Bennett a glance. "Are you *sure* he's not going to storm that house the way I saw him attack the *Fictopian* mead-hall? I'm braced for just about anything, but that doesn't include a bridal party massacre."

"He doesn't attack the reception, but the merriment does rile his temper. There were…will be reports of eerie howling and destruction."

"Like what he did to the railway tracks?"

"Something like that."

"Around here?"

"Close enough for us to track him on foot." He focuses back on the house. "Since our objective depends on your comprehension and tracking skills, I'll leave it at that."

I wish his confidence and calm was infectious. I'm pretending to be badass. Gabriel Bennett *is* badass.

As instructed by Henri, I hitch up my hunting skirt in a manner that allows me to run with greater ease. As I'm fiddling with the fasteners, a howl rips through the air and knocks me off balance.

Bennett steadies me, studies me. His expression is telling.

"You heard it, too," I say.

A pained roar follows. It saws through my bones like a rusty knife. *Raw. Savage.* My stomach churns with curdled sausage and eggs.

"He's close," I say. "Close enough that we both hear his howls. But how do I hear his *thoughts*?"

"Remember your training," Bennett says without moving a muscle.

I dig deep, replaying Henri and Bennett's lectures and Bennett's advice. I steel my heart and open my mind.

I'm instantly and viciously blindsided by a wall of deafening, *terrifying* noise.

Even though my pulse is galloping, I refrain from *Scrambling*.

I listen. *I hear.*

Stilted English among the raging gibberish.

"I understand him," I say in a rush. "Not fluently. But intermittently."

I've got a death grip on Bennett's arm. With every word that resonates, my nails dig deeper.

Bennett doesn't flinch.

"He's angry. He's hurt. Confused and wailing. *Why? Why don't they inblob...involve...include me?*"

My mind gridlocks as I struggle to make sense out of

Grendel's chaotic thought-stream. A mish-mosh of legible English and guttural animal cries. More than tangled words, there's a scramble of emotions.

"Sheep. Men. Hate. Crush." I spew a string of Grendel's disjointed laments and take off at a dead run west.

We passed a fenced meadow on our way from church to house. Grazing sheep. Freaking innocent, fluffy *sheep!*

My feet have wings, or so it seems. I backtrack, zig-zagging through trees and brush, and before I know it, I'm there. Bennett's there. He raced alongside me, but now he drags me to a stop.

"Close enough," he says, hauling me into the shadows of the woods.

Just beyond, in the vast rolling meadow, Grendel is raging through the fencing. With swipes of his massive claws, wood splinters and stones fly.

He's as hideous as the Grendel I saw in *Fictopia.*

A giant abomination.

And only slightly less terrifying.

"We're done here," Bennett says as the beast stomps toward the flock of panicked sheep.

Shaking with fury and fear, I interpret Grendel's manic roars. *"You hurt me, I hurt you!"*

He's exacting his rage on the bride's father's property. Fences destroyed with angry stomps and wild swipes. Sheep mutilated…

"Stop!" I scream.

Bennett clamps his hand over my mouth.

I bite and kick. I push.

Blinded by rage, I run into the chaos.

Shepherd dogs yap at the monster's feet. Protecting the herd. Protecting the innocent.

"Leave them be!" I shout. Chest heaving, lungs burning, I confront the gruesome monster with all of the righteousness in my soul.

The rogue *FIC* ignores me, squashing the life out of a helpless animal and mangling my sensitive heart.

I want to puke, but I don't.

Fury overwhelms. Overtakes. I imagine several nasty fates for the ruthless beast!

Suddenly, *wondrously*, Penelope bursts out of the black clouds, pedaling her flycycle with the might of a mother-flipping-super-hero! Her crimson hat and the yellow sash popping bright in dismal skies.

Grendel bats at the air, as if swiping at a pesky fly.

That *pest* is Penelope and Balderdash. They're zooming about his head, around and around, distracting him from the sheep and dogs.

From me.

The monster clips the flycycle's wheel and Balderdash freefalls from the attached basket.

Heart in throat, I slide through the slick grass, catching the pup and holding tight. "Gotcha!"

"Bitch!" the monster wails.

"Friend!" I retaliate, meaning *I understand*. Meaning, *I'm not the enemy*. "I feel and hear your pain!"

And with that, he scoops me, and Balderdash, into his massive, blood-dripping claws.

THIRTY-TWO

Tempting Fate

DROWNING IN BLOOD.

Choking on rot.

I swim toward the light, toward his voice.

Head hurts.

Heart hurts.

I break through the stinking darkness...

And gag.

The stench in my nose, on *me*, is revolting.

Bleary-eyed and disoriented, I roll to my hands and knees and hurl my breakfast.

On the last heave, my vision clears enough to note the blood and puss-like slime on my hands and sleeves and, even though I thought my stomach was empty, I puke some more.

Depleted, exhausted, I crumple into a sitting position, desperate for one of Bennett's hankies.

Bennett.

He crouches in front of me, prompting a scream that sticks in my aching throat.

Soaked in blood and splattered with gory bits, he looks like he's been through hell and back. He stinks worse than me —like rotting flesh and sewage. And his blazing eyes telegraph a fury that knots my already frazzled nerves.

"What the devil did you do to me?" he snaps.

I blink. "What?" My mind races and skids to my last memory of him. He was holding me back, silencing my screams. "I was desperate to stop Grendel. To save the animals. I bit your hand. I...I kicked your shins. I don't remember..."

"You shoved me with a force that sent me flying two stories high and several meters away."

"That's not possible."

"Trust me. I didn't imagine it."

"But *I* did." I flush with the prompted memory. "I was angry. Furious and panicked. While struggling to escape your grip, I imagined knocking you to kingdom come."

Bennett absorbs my recollection, frowns. "Thankfully, you fell short of your mark."

"I don't understand. I don't have that kind of physical strength." I can't wrap my brain around his claim, but why would he lie? I study his bloody appearance with a terrifying thought. "Did...did I do that to you?"

"You did some damage. But this," he says while flicking hairy gore from his coat, "is Grendel."

My brain glitches as I survey my surroundings. No monster. No sheep. No dogs. No meadow. Also missing: Penelope and Balderdash. I'm alone with Bennett, sitting on soggy ground beneath the shelter of trees. Beyond his shoulder is a large pond or a small lake.

I palm my forehead, grappling with a sketchy memory. "Where are we?"

"In hiding, for the moment."

"How did we get here?"

"I carried you."

"The last thing I remember is being swooped up by Grendel."

"Which wouldn't have happened if you hadn't knocked me so bloody far away. By the time I got back to the meadow, you were in the beast's face."

"I was trying to reason with him."

"And how did that go for you?"

His razor-sharp snark cuts deep. Hurt and annoyed, I push back. "I had to do *something* to save those poor animals, because *you* sure as sunshine bailed."

"What is it with you and sheep?"

I gape, perplexed by the question, before remembering that I caused us to spin out in Watson's car by braking for a fleecy herd crossing the road.

"You, Miss Albright, are a menace. A miracle and a menace." Bennett pushes to his feet and offers me a hand up. "We can't go back into the village looking like this. Come."

I'm stuck on his conflicting assessment of me and momentarily speechless. Even though his palm is smeared with blood and goo, I grasp it and blindly follow his lead while sorting through my disjointed memories.

"I can't recall anything beyond the terror of being swooped up by those huge, foul talons. Did I pass out from the shock?"

"I charged Grendel at that precise moment, causing him to drop you. You didn't pass out, you were knocked unconscious."

"You went one-on-one with that gigantic monster?"

"You gave me no choice."

I flash back on Grendel's destructive and deadly antics. How could an ordinary man survive such powerful violence? I glance up at Bennett and quickly acknowledge that he is far from ordinary. He's a *Warrior* and, perhaps, something more.

He pulls me to a stop at the edge of the lake and then breaks away to pull off his boots.

"What are you doing?"

"Getting rid of the stink and stain of an *erased FIC*."

"You assassinated Grendel?" I'm stunned. "How? I don't recall Archimedes arming you with a 'weapon of-destruction.'"

"No WOD. Our instruction was to observe, not to interact."

The condemnation in his tone is clear. He's mad. At me. I get it, but I don't regret intervening. Ultimately, my actions spared the lives of more than a few animals plus the lives of two unknown-to-me villagers. I don't feel bad about that and I'm pretty sure I'd do it again.

"If you didn't have a weapon," I ask as Bennett wades into the water fully clothed sans shoes, "how in the world did you kill that thing?"

"The same way Beowulf killed it," he answers, and then dives into the depths of the murky lake.

I don't know how long I stood at the lake's edge contemplating my first character assassination. Even though I'd been unconscious for the actual erasure, I absolutely did my part as an *Enabler*.

I honed in on a rogue *FIC's* thoughts and led a *Warrior* to his location.

I don't know how Beowulf killed Grendel. And it's obvious Bennett expects me to read the story in order to find out. I could ask Henri, but I won't. I can't tell her anything about this.

I shiver as alternate consequences to my actions begin to sink in. I disrupted the timeline. Because of me, Bennett *erased* Grendel, kicking his hairy, evil ass back to *Fictopia* two weeks ahead of schedule. Did I alter the future in a negative way?

Bennett's wondering the same thing. That's why he's so fired up. That coupled with the fact that I put myself in danger. If he hadn't burst onto the scene at that exact moment, Grendel might have squashed me and Balderdash like he squashed the sheep.

Balderdash.

Did Bennett see the goggle-wearing terrier? Did he see Penelope on her flycycle? He didn't mention them, but what if? *What if?* I'm jazzed by the possibility that someone other than me saw my muse. Although, *wait,* Grendel saw them! He sure as heck swatted at something!

Pulse racing, I plop down, unlace and pry off my boots. The process practically rubs my nose in the slimed, reeking fabric of my hunting suit. Gagging, I push to my stocking feet and slosh into the lake.

I gasp, surprised by the chilly temperature, but not daunted. Like Bennett, once thigh-high, I dive in, going under to rinse the 'stink and stain' from my hair, skin, and clothes. I swim toward where I last saw the infuriated *Warrior*, but when I break the surface, he's gone.

Treading water, I paddle around and look toward the shore.

He's walking out of the lake, clothes drenched and plastered to his body. As he shoves wet hair from his face, I'm visualizing the scene in *Pride and Prejudice* when hunk-a-licious Mr. Darcy emerges from the pond. Although it feels like a lifetime ago, just days ago, I peered at a pond back at Blackmoor, fantasizing about a like performance starring Gabriel Bennett.

The real show is mesmerizing.

Yes, he's incredibly attractive, but in this moment my feelings run far deeper than shallow appreciation for a handsome face and hot physique. I'm overcome with bone deep affection for a man who defied his fervent code regarding timelines in order to rescue me from a monster.

I didn't even thank him.

Profound change washes over me as I swim back to shore. I've experienced a lot of crazy stuff in my life, and especially these last few days, but the altercation with Grendel and the fallout with Bennett have shaken and altered my sense of self. I can't put my feelings into precise words yet, but I am very aware of a major shift within.

Pushing aside thoughts of Penelope and Balderdash and a dozen other questions, I slosh out of the water and go toe-to-toe with Bennett.

"I know you hold my father and your friendship in high regard. I know you believe he entrusted you to protect me. I also know you went against your better judgement and disrupted a timeline to save my life. I don't take that lightly. I really don't."

Balling my fists at my sides so as not to hug him, I grace him instead with a sincere smile. "Thank you, Gabriel."

Thunder rumbles in his silence, warning of a torrential storm.

I hold my breath as he pushes my wet, matted hair from my face, as he studies me hard.

I'm vividly aware that the electricity crackling between us is of a sensual nature as opposed to the charged weather.

It's exhilarating.

"You were a sight to behold, Dove. Watching you challenge fate and a monster was almost worth the risk."

And with that, he finesses me to his side and into a run.

THIRTY-THREE

A State of Undress and the Perfect Storm

THE CLOUDS BURST and pour rain.

Lucky that.

It saves me and Bennett from having to explain our drowned rat appearance when we return to the Thistle Inn. What follows is a low-key, rushed departure based on an only slightly tainted truth.

Mr. Knightley has urgent business south.

Bennett's mania to get us the hell out of Wembly and back to London is compounded by his fierce determination to get us back to the future *pronto*.

His reluctance to pause long enough for us to change into dry clothes or to define his sense of urgency amplifies my stress.

Unfortunately, the carriage ride to the nearest train station is slowed by muddy roads and crappy weather. And since we have to share the cab with another traveler, I'm not free to ask Bennett any one of a bazillion questions pinging around my brain. The more I muse, the greater my frustration.

By the time we board a train, I'm chilled to the bone and chomping at the bit. I'm desperate for private time and a candid exchange. I manage to play my part as the demure Mrs. Knightley until the moment my *husband* ushers me and our luggage into a private compartment.

As soon as he shuts the door, I spew questions and concerns, punctuated with a sneeze.

Instead of remarking on any one of my issues or even offering a polite 'bless you', he frowns and spouts an order. "Change out of those wet clothes. I'll return momentarily."

He leaves.

I gawk. "Seriously?"

Wired to the max, I pull down the window blinds and then wiggle out of my jacket and skirt. Because I've grown accustomed to the 19th century fastenings, I shed several damp layers, including *unmentionables*, lickety split.

Rather than going commando, I slip into my bikini panties and lacey bra. Since we're preparing to travel back to the 21st century, no need to obsess on being one-hundred percent Victorian, right? But even as I welcome the comfortable fit of contemporary underwear, I don't entirely connect with the old me.

My mind and heart are struggling with passion and purpose as I stretch and grow into new skin.

But one thing's for sure.

My days as a social misfit and reclusive writer are over.

I yank out my two-piece traveling gown from the day before and get distracted when my journal tumbles to the floor. Snatching it up, I nab my fountain pen, perch on the cushioned seat, and organize my hot mess musings into a streamlined list. Everything I want to discuss with Bennett.

NOTE: My Bi-universal gifts. Seeing fractured borders. Witnessing tales in progress in Fictopia. Understanding any FIC language. Superhuman strength? How did I push Bennett such a great height and distance? WHAT'S MY STORY?

NOTE: Bennett's Warrior skills. How did he survive the fall he described? How did he best a monster? Why did Henri call him a 'special recruit'? WHAT'S YOUR STORY?

NOTE: Penelope and Balderdash. Did Bennett see them? Or did I imagine them? WHAT'S THEIR STORY?

NOTE: The attraction. Enabler and Warrior. Prodigy and Mentor. Zoe and Gabriel. WHAT'S OUR STORY?

I pause, reflecting on our lakeside showdown when the air crackled between and around us. I felt that same charge when we faced off back at ESCA headquarters. Bennett can deny it until the cows come home, but I know it in my heart of hearts. The sexual attraction is mutual.

There's also a level of undeclared affection. I've felt it in his touch. Heard it in his tone. Rare, but memorable moments.

Plus, Henri swore she witnessed two 'shockingly intimate' incidents (Bennett holding me in his arms and whispering in my ear. Bennett leaning over me in bed and kissing my forehead.), lending credence to my theory.

Unfortunately, I was unconscious and have no memory of those accounts. But I can easily imagine.

"So what if he *is* attracted to me?" His heart is with Charlotte and his mind is focused on averting a dangerous *FIC* infiltration. "Which is where *my* focus should be."

Rising above my lovesick contemplation, I put my pen back to pad, and jot more notes.

I'm scribbling madly when I hear a knock. "Come in," I say, while finishing off a concern about the time machine and the reliability of its calendar device.

I mean, seriously, what if there's a malfunction and we end up in 1950 or 5019? Or…

NOTE: What if we end up exactly where we took off but something is drastically, dreadfully different because I disrupted the timeline?

"This is a sight to behold as well," Bennett says, "although I shouldn't be seeing it."

Startled by his voice, I glance up and meet his gaze. A hot gaze fixed on scantily clad me. A day ago he would've looked away or turned his back. This moment, his appraisal is unflinching.

Simultaneously rattled and aroused, I state the obvious. "You're staring."

"Curious attire, Miss Albright."

"Modern unmentionables. Bra and panties, to be precise."

He gestures to the open journal resting on my bare thighs. "Do you always write in a state of undress?"

"Almost never, but I have a lot on my mind."

Like the sexual tension snapping between us like a freaking live wire.

I sidestep the subject.

For now.

"Sorry for the shock." I set aside the book and pen and snatch up the bottom half of the burgundy gown. "I was in the midst of changing my clothes and got distracted. It's not that big of a deal, by the way, you seeing me like this. In my time, a lot of girls show more skin than this on the beach."

I'm actually, *painfully*, self-conscious of my semi-naked state, but only because I'm stoked by his blatant appreciation of the female form. *My* form.

Stepping into the voluminous skirt, I struggle to keep my balance as the train picks up speed. "Just saying, people aren't as uptight in my time. If we're heading back to the future and continuing with this mentor/prodigy thing, we'll be spending a lot of time together. Best not to get hung up on the small stuff."

"Interesting attitude," he says while shrugging out of his own wet coat.

"Where did you go anyway?" I ask while pulling on my coordinating shirtwaist.

"The dining car. Hot tea and soup will be delivered shortly. Can't have you coming down with a cold."

"That was thoughtful," I say while finessing hooks and eyes and ribbons and whatnot. "Thank you."

Fully clothed now and moderately balanced, I turn and catch Bennett rooting through his bag for a dry shirt.

I blink. I stare. The man is nude from the waist up. Since his back is to me, I openly admire his wide shoulders and tapered waist. His sculpted muscles roll with his efforts, intensifying my carnal appreciation.

But then my ogling takes a backseat to a perplexing observance.

Closing the short distance between us, I place my palms on his shoulders and smooth them down his back. His *flawless* back. "Where are the scars?"

He turns and gently nabs my hands, preventing me from exploring his bare chest as well.

Transfixed, I scan his chiseled torso, his shoulders and arms. "A couple of hours ago, you battled a gigantic beast with razor-sharp claws. Plus, by your account, you suffered damage from a massive fall caused by me. You were bloodied and battered and yet there's no evidence of injury. *Ever.* No scars of any kind. You tangle with monstrous *FICs* for a living, Gabriel. Are you telling me not even one ever got the best of you?"

He studies me for a moment and I instantly know there's a story. I also suspect he won't share it.

As proof, he repeats my advice. "Best not to get hung up on the small stuff, Dove."

That's the third time—yes, I remember every instance—he's called me *Dove*. Not sure how I feel about that particular nickname, especially since he believes my gentle heart and pacifist nature are liabilities. Still, each time he refers to me as such, I mentally sigh like a silly, smitten girl. I hate that I love the sensation.

Maintaining eye contact a spine-tingling second longer, he squeezes my hands then breaks contact and pulls on his shirt. "Now tell me," he says with a nod to my journal. "What else is on your mind?"

Kissing, I want to say, but I don't.

Making a graceful retreat, I take a seat, leaving him to tuck in his shirt while I refer to my bulleted notes. Since he doesn't want to talk about what makes him 'special' and I don't want to talk about 'the attraction' (clearly, he's still in denial), that leaves two immediate hot topics.

I start with my Bi-universal skills, listing what we know I'm capable of thus far, and ending with the outstanding mystery. "It's not that I don't believe you, but I don't remember pushing you with a force that sent you, in your words, *flying two stories high and several meters away*. And I certainly didn't witness it."

"But you did imagine it."

"Yes, but..."

"Your focus was on Grendel and the sheep. Otherwise, I might well have ended up in kingdom come." Bennett sits across from me and drags a hand through his damp hair. "I have a theory."

"I'm all ears."

"I think your most powerful, and potentially genius, ability is your imagination."

I absorb the notion with a scrunched brow. "You think by simply imagining something, I can make it real?"

"I don't think it's simple at all. Instead of exploring and mastering a raw talent peculiar to your *FIC* blood, you've spent a lifetime containing your imagination to a narrow margin—Penelope Pringle and her antics. At this point, I think there needs to be a perfect storm of mindset, desire, and emotions in order for you to bring an imagining to life."

I don't know which is louder to my ears, the clacking of iron wheels on tracks or the beating of my heart.

"In the moment that you pushed me away with super-human force," Bennett says, "you were in a frenzied mindset and experiencing multiple intense emotions."

"I was terrified of Grendel," I say while reliving the moment, "but even more horrified that he was slaughtering sheep and that the Shepard dogs were next. I was furious with you for not stopping him and for holding me back. I was desperate to escape you and to save the animals."

"Mindset, emotions, and desire. And given that perfect storm, your imagination manifested into a miraculous blow that knocked me out of your way and then some."

"I'm so sorry. I don't… It's not in my nature to hurt someone."

"I know. But it is in your nature to protect."

An empowering notion that inspires noble purpose. Something to absorb and analyze at a later time.

"But instantaneous superhuman strength?" I race through a lifetime of memories. "I've never experienced a like phenomenon."

"Before this, you've never been in a harrowing situation where someone's life depended on your actions, right? Victoria, and then Liza, made sure that you had limited interactions with outside forces. As I said before, the extent to which you have been sheltered is astonishing."

Trembling with emotions, I twist my wedding band round and round, rooting myself as my thoughts take flight.

"In the midst of facing Grendel," I say, "I felt outraged by his cruelty. I imagined several nasty fates for that monster, but they were muddled and overshadowed by the realization that I was out of my league. I thought, *I need help*, and I imagined Penelope riding to my rescue."

I lock gazes with Bennett and ask what I've been dying to know. "Did you see her?"

"Yes."

My pulse skips and sputters.

"Breathe, Miss Albright."

"I'm breathing, I breathing. I'm just…" I blink back tears. "I'm confused. Are you sure?"

He describes Penny's clothing and flycycle in detail. He relays how she circled Grendel's head, distracting him from the sheep, and how Balderdash fell out of the basket, exactly as I remember it.

"Nice catch, by the way," he adds.

I want to cry, but I don't. I do, however, scoot to the edge of my seat. "No one, aside from me, has ever seen Penelope or Balderdash. Not Liza. Not the head doctors. Not any one of the random people who caught me talking to 'my friend'. Why couldn't they see her?"

"Just a hunch," Bennett says, "but wasn't Penelope your *only* friend?"

I'm saddened and embarrassed by the truth of that. I swallow hard and nod.

"I suspect, subconsciously, you didn't want to share her."

His reasoning makes simple sense. "But this time," I say, latching onto to his theory, "was different. In that showdown with Grendel, while I was whipped up and determined to save those animals, Penelope and Balderdash came alive. For real."

"As soon as you were knocked unconscious," Bennett adds, "they disappeared."

"Which left you to fight the monster on your own."

He doesn't reply, but I can see his wheels turning as fast as mine.

"Liza used to say 'It's just your imagination.' All those years, all those times, she was right." In a heartbeat, I'm reevaluating our relationship. "I need to speak with her. As soon as we get back I…"

I trail off, concerned by Bennett's dark expression.

"You need to brace yourself," he says. "I have no idea how *much* we disrupted the timeline."

"What do you mean? I…" I brainstorm, frowning at a worst case scenario. "In 1898 as it originally played out, who *erased* Grendel?"

"Dominic Sinclair."

THIRTY-FOUR

A Killer Kiss and an Unexpected Twist

THE ACRID FACTORY smoke and pungent, bountiful horse poop stinking up Victorian London is nothing compared to the foul, reeking stench of a soulless monster. I breathe deep, thankful to be alive. Grateful for all I've learned.

"Mind your step," Bennett says as he grasps my elbow and whisks me across Great Russell Street. What he's really saying is, *don't slip*. I know now that what I thought was *mud* is mostly mashed dung from the city's thousands and thousands of work horses.

As disgusting as it is, I walk right through it.

I'm memorizing every aspect of this time, this city. Bennett's city. Dominic's city. Charles Dickens and H.G. Wells's city. I want to sear the sights, sounds, and, yes, smells, into my brain. I don't want to forget any detail of this miraculous adventure, and that includes the harrowing parts.

My only regret is not meeting my father. I know that option was never on the table, but as long as we're here at least there is a possibility of a chance encounter.

If Bennett has his way, we'll be back in the time machine and en route to the future within the hour.

After arriving at the train station, he hired a courier to transport our Victorian luggage to Henri's home. All I kept was what I came with, my messenger bag—packed with my contemporary belongings, including my sundress and denim jacket. Oh, plus the journal Henri gave me.

Even though we're dressed in the full guise of Mr. and Mrs. Knightley, Bennett whisks me toward a back entrance of MOMI. "I don't want to risk being recognized. Remember, the Victorian me is in Paris."

With Charlotte.

I'm immediately heartsick with the thought of her impending doom. And the reminder that Bennett feels the necessity to sacrifice her life in order to protect mine.

Heavy with guilt, I force my thoughts to someone else.

"I hope Henri's here," I say as we navigate a narrow stairwell. "I'd like to say goodbye." *We could have been friends.*

My throat tightens as I reflect on our short time together. I'll never forget slamming into what I thought was a grotesque fanged monster. In hindsight, Henri's costume was somewhat comical. Although, I do admire her devotion to picking a villain's brain by stepping into his shoes, so to speak. I wonder if she's ever studied Grendel. I wonder if she thinks there's even the slightest possibility of tempering his rage.

I'm almost certain I saw a flicker of surprise in his bulging eyes when I announced myself as *friend.* I know he understood me. Did he realize I could understand *him*? If given longer, could I have reasoned with him? Or, given another second, would he have bitten off my head?

I shudder at the thought.

Bennett pulls me along a cramped hallway that I don't recognize. "If we're lucky, we'll find Wiz alone. If so, let me do the talking."

I give him a quick snarky salute, projecting a calm, good-humored mood. In reality, I'm a tangle of emotions.

Brushing aside cobwebs with only an ounce of disgust, I lower my voice to a whisper. "What if Archimedes hasn't figured out a counter spell yet? What if we're still melded when we arrive in the 21st century?"

"Then we'll have to think quick and creatively on our collective feet."

"I just... I don't understand the rush. What's done is done and if Archimedes needs another day—"

"The longer we stay, the greater the risk of *inadvertently*," he says with a glance toward me, "altering another chain of events."

I blink. I flush. "Are you talking about me? Are you worried I'll imagine something and—"

"My gut is telling me to leave. *Now*. The last time I ignored my instincts there were grave consequences. I'm not making that mistake again."

"Are you talking about Charlotte?"

He doesn't answer and my own gut sinks. So he blames himself for her death?

The hall is so narrow that I'm forced to walk behind, instead of beside, Bennett. He's holding my hand though, and tugging me through the dimly lit corridor.

His touch, his grasp, his acute sense of alarm is electrifying.

"What if we don't make it back?" I blurt as my thoughts take an ominous turn. "What if the time machine malfunctions? What if we blow up or land in prehistoric times or a dystopian future?"

"Dark imaginings aren't helpful, Miss Albright."

"But it could happen, right?"

"Anything's possible."

He stops, causing me to bump into his back. "Sorry," I say.

It's all I can do not to lean into him, to delight in the feel of Bennett-the-wholly-solid-and free-man for what could be the last time. If Archimedes doesn't come through with a counter spell, Bennett will revert to the limited existence of someone trapped in another dimension.

I squash that depressing thought before it takes full flight. Dark imaginings are worse than useless. In my peculiar case, they can be dangerous. "Where are we?" I ask as Bennett feels along the wall.

"A back entrance to the Quest Room."

I squint up at a panel of symbols—much like the panel I saw when we entered HQ from the catacombs beneath contemporary London.

Bennett punches a sequential code. A small stone slides open, revealing a peep hole. He takes a gander then shuts the stone. "Good news. Wiz is inside and he's alone. Whether he has the counter spell, or not, we'll leave as soon as I can report my transgression."

"You mean *our* transgression. I was in on that erroneous erasure. I initiated the face off with Grendel, remember?"

"Vividly," he says with a conflicted smile, reminding me that he found at least some part of my madness admirable.

That smile and his begrudging respect stokes a suppressed craving.

"Wait," I whisper as he starts to tap out another code. I reach up and grasp his hand, demanding his full attention. "I'm not imagining anything bad, I swear. Nothing specific, that is, but, if something bad *does* happen during the time-hop, I prefer to bite the dust with one less regret. Please don't take this personally."

Consumed with longing, I reach up and palm the sides of his achingly handsome face. My heart rockets to my throat as his gaze turns dark. Before I lose my nerve, I pull him down and into a kiss—nothing chaste about it.

As he welcomes my tongue and allows me to indulge, a fluttery ache works its way from my heart, to my stomach, and beyond. Startled, by the sheer sensual wonder, I ease back, dazed and breathless.

"If you're going to tempt fate, Miss Albright," he says in a throaty rasp, "make it count."

With flawless finesse, he pulls me into his arms and shatters my senses with a heady, possessive, deep and deadly kiss.

I'm a goner.

The 'L' word floats through my fuzzy mind.

The ache below intensifies even as he eases away.

"Don't take this personally, Dove, but end of story."

Not in my book.

I swallow a sigh. I smile. "Glad we cleared the air. No regrets." Faking a casual attitude with every liquefied bone in my body, I motion for him to continue with the entry code.

A second later, the wall slides open and we slip into the Quest Room.

I don't dare look at Bennett, fearing my heart is in my eyes. I'm amazed my noodly legs are even working.

Archimedes looks up from a gigantic, thick book. "You're back early."

"I messed up," I croak.

"We messed up," Bennett says.

"You interfered." Archimedes pinches his beaky nose. "How bad is it?"

"Premature assassination."

"How premature?"

"Two weeks. And it shouldn't have been me. It should have been Dom."

"And that's potentially significant?" the *Wizard* asks with a glance at me.

"Yes," Bennett answers.

Archimedes marks a page in his book before closing it. "Tell me what you can without telling me too much."

While I'm grappling with what or what not to share, Bennett takes the lead. "The rogue *FIC* was Grendel."

"Beowulf's Grendel?" Still focused on me, Archimedes crooks a bushy brow. "And you tracked it?"

Bennett intercedes. "As I stated before, her gift is extraordinary. Can you at least assign Dom to the Wembly area during that time frame?" he rushes on. "Concoct a mission that causes him to be in the right place at the right time even though Grendel is long gone. If you can line things up—"

"Maybe he'll come back," I blurt out. "Grendel, that is. When you erase a rogue *FIC* from the Real World, he still exists in *Fictopia*, in his story, right? Maybe that part of his essence, the part that's desperate to connect with mankind, will peel off and cross the fractured border a second time. Maybe within the next few days. Not that I wish more terror and killing upon the people or sheep of Wembly, but it would enable events to unfold as they did in the natural march of time."

"It's possible," says Archimedes.

"But not probable," says Bennett. "Secondary infiltrations are rare."

"I'm siding with possible," I say. "And even if Grendel doesn't return, there's also the chance that our meddling doesn't muck up anything of great consequence. That the timeline plays out differently, but not catastrophically for key players."

"Also possible." Archimedes studies me hard. "Exploring scenarios comes naturally for you, Miss Albright."

"It's the storyteller in me. I brainstorm a lot."

"You're a writer?" He turns to Bennett. "Interesting twist."

"One of several," says Bennett while tossing me a look that suggests I zip my lips. Or at least mind my words. "Speaking of twists, did you have any luck with a counter spell pertaining to my curse?" he asks Wiz.

Archimedes thumps a hand to his book—a Book of Spells, I'm guessing. "No. But I may be on to something that will alter the future *Wizard's* binding spell."

"If it means Gabriel won't have to inhabit my body in order to function outside of Blackmoor Manor," I say, "we'll take it!" So much for zipped lips.

"What are the particulars?" asks Bennett.

"I'm not sure yet."

"When…" Bennett trails off at the sound of voices coming from the hall beyond the main door of the Quest Room.

The words are muffled but a deep, distinct laugh causes Bennett and Archimedes to stiffen.

"Bollocks," says Bennett.

I tense. "What's wrong?"

"An unexpected twist," says Archimedes. "Take her out the back way," he says to Bennett, who's already half carrying me to the secret sliding wall.

"You won't see us again, Wiz."

"Understood."

Bennett whisks me into the back hallway.

The wall slides shut, but not before I hear Archimedes greeting his unexpected visitor.

"Dominic. I say, old boy, what the devil?"

THIRTY-FIVE

Spellbound

I'M SHOCKED SPEECHLESS. But only for a few deafening heartbeats.

"Go back," I rasp as Bennett steals me away from my father. I'm choked up and close to hyperventilating. "I just... I want to see him. Let me look through that peep hole. We—"

"Can't risk it."

"I won't say a word. I..." I squirm and pry at his hands. "Put me down, Gabriel. Please! I—"

He cuts me off with a quick, hard squeeze. "Stop thinking with your emotions. Stop talking. And, for the sake of mankind, don't imagine."

His dire warning slaps me sane.

Mindset, emotions, desire.

I'm whipped up and desperate to see the father I never

knew. To hear his voice. To feel his touch. A kind word or a caring hug. I'd settle for a teasing wink, for cripes sake!

The perfect storm.

Aware that I could inadvertently spark a catastrophe with a rogue imagining, I go limp with defeat.

Bennett tightens his hold in a comforting manner that misses its mark.

"I hate this. I hate you." Bitterness and grief are a potent, painful mix and I'm wallowing.

Next thing I know, we're clear of the stuffy hall and navigating an area that's crammed with eclectic gadgets.

Scientific and Supernatural Artifacts

Through a haze of angry tears, I spy the giant brass disc, the dials, levers, and cylinders, and the plush red throne of the time machine.

Bennett slides into the driver's seat, pulling me with him and onto on his lap.

All the wonder and trepidation I felt the first time we climbed aboard the retrofuturistic vehicle are decimated by the crushing disappointment of being robbed of a glimpse of my father. A *FIC* who gave up the earthborn he loved to protect the daughter-that-shouldn't-be. The man who willed me a home and a protector. When we return to the future, Dominic Sinclair will be dead.

Unless Bennett altered his fate with the premature assassination of Grendel.

I cling to the possibility while breathing deep and quieting my frenzied thoughts and emotions. With ferocious effort, I temper two of the three storm factors while Bennett spins dials and revs the machine.

It's a tight fit, putting me in even closer proximity to the dash I bonked my head on the last time we lurched into motion.

Apparently Bennett notices as well. "Spin around and face me," he orders as the vehicle shimmies and whirs.

It means hiking up my long skirt and straddling his lap. It means facing him, which I do, but I refuse to look him in the eyes. It would only stoke the resentment I'm working hard to snuff.

"Hold tight," he says close to my ear.

My last look at ESCA HQ 1898 is a nauseating, dizzying blur.

One second, we're surrounded by a cyclone of colors and snippets of scenes—people blurring by in evolving fashion from prim to flapper to bohemian to disco—as we fast-forward through the decades.

Mesmerizing.

Next thing I know, I'm discombobulated and hugging the back of the driver's throne, instead of the driver.

What the...

Where's Bennett?

Squashing a wave of panic and nausea, I palm my throbbing head and squint at my surroundings. ESCA HQ. The room of *Scientific and Supernatural Artifacts* specifically. Although, I'm not sure of the year. Gadgets and gizmos of the steampunk ilk are timeless.

Woozy, I feel my way around until I'm facing the control dash of the time machine.

I blink, bringing a dial into focus. I gawk at the day, month, and year.

I don't remember passing out, but I must have. Either that or we time traveled almost two centuries in the blink of an eye.

"Are you all right?"

I jerk toward the sound of Bennett's scratchy voice. He's sitting a few feet away, legs sprawled and back against the wall. He looks as dazed as I feel.

"Did you get thrown from the machine?" I ask.

"Something slammed into me." He drops his head into his hands. "Bloody hell."

I, too, feel like I've been hit by a truck. Certain I'll crumple if I try to stand, I voice my concern from where I'm sitting. "Are you hurt?"

"Either you're talking to yourself," another man interrupts, "or the spell worked."

Holding onto the dash so as not to tumble out of my seat, I turn toward a stranger's voice. But instead of an honest-to-gosh person, I'm staring at a televised presence on a ginormous flat screen.

I'm only seeing him from the chest up, as if he's sitting at a desk. He's surrounded by stacks of books. An older, dark-skinned man with close-cropped, salt-and-pepper hair and a neatly trimmed goatee. He's wearing an army-green tee and looking back at me with an intensity that makes me shiver.

"Zoe Albright," the man says. "You bear a keen resemblance to your mother."

Rattled, I glance around looking for a hidden or mounted camera. How can he—whoever he is—see me?

"HQ is fitted with a state-of-the-art surveillance system," he says as if reading my mind. "Much like Blackmoor. Since I was expecting you, but *couldnae* be present this day or week, I prepared for this telecommunication ahead of time, yeah? Your movement triggered sensors and alerted me of your arrival."

I struggle to absorb his words and to pinpoint his accent. Scottish? Irish? My brain is mush. "But how did you know we were coming. No one knew we time traveled, except—"

"Archimedes." The man holds up a ginormous book.

I squint at the familiar green and gold spine. "Is that his Book of Spells?"

"We call it a Book of Shadows, but, yes. It contains spells, rituals, and other notable information. He documented your visit in a way that would be seen by a future *Wizard* at the appropriate time."

"So you're…" I flash back on my conversation with Odion. "…Ryker?"

"The *Wizard* of now," Bennett snaps. "Ask him about the spell."

Head spinning and annoyed by the barked order, I bark back. "Why don't you ask?"

"Because I *cannae* hear or see him," Ryker intercedes. "Him, being Gabriel Bennett, yeah?"

"Just swivel one of your secret cameras around." I point to where Bennett's slumped. "He's sitting right there."

"He's in a bewitched dimension, Miss Albright. Invisible to my eye, to the camera's eye, but apparently not to your eyes. Interesting."

On a long hard stare, I notice Bennett looks fuzzy around the edges. *Crapola*! "I don't understand," I say to Ryker.

"Before, he couldn't leave Blackmoor Manor without using my body as his vehicle."

"That was a Binding Spell. The spell I *initially* cast after Dominic informed me of your existence."

Sounding irritated now, he narrows his eyes and races on. "It was a wild card attempt to free Bennett—something my predecessors deemed impossible— by binding him to you so that he could instruct and protect you while ESCA was in crisis mode. While I thought my solution somewhat brilliant, it appears that your displeasure prompted drastic, potentially disastrous measures. Such as carjacking ESCA's time machine."

Is he reprimanding us? Seriously?

"Frankly," he plows on in a grave tone, "if you are who Dominic says you are, I think you should be underground with us, but Dom believes otherwise. Given his sacrifice, I honored his request."

"Sacrifice as in sacrificing his life? Or...as in sacrificing my safety by making you, and possibly a *Fictopian* bad egg, aware of my lineage?"

Silence and a hard stare.

"You spoke of my dad in the present tense," I push. "Before we time traveled, he was dead. Or at least that's what I was told. Did Gabriel and I alter Dominic's fate when we intervened in the past?"

"Ah, yes, the premature Grendel assassination," he says while drumming his fingers on Archimedes's book. "A dangerous intervention, but not one that altered Dom's fate as I know it."

His evasiveness is maddening. I look to Bennett who says,

"I don't know any more than you do. But I never fully accepted Dom's demise."

Buoyed by Bennett's doubts, I turn on the presiding *Wizard*. "Listen. Up until a few days ago, I was blissfully ignorant of *Fictopia*, of monstrous creations fueled by mankind's imagination, and the flipping *Character Assassins* who keep them in check. My life's been upended and I am trying very hard to adjust. The least I'm flipping owed is the flipping truth! Is Dominic Sinclair alive or dead?"

Ryker holds my gaze. "Let's just say he's on another plane, yeah?"

"As in an alternate universe? As in *Fictopia*?" I blink. I breathe. I glance at Bennett who's utterly motionless. I want to grab him by the lapels of his ancient jacket and shake him to life. Thing is, I don't have the strength. Also I'm worried he's no longer solid to my touch. It's not a theory I'm ready to test. "Are you hearing this?"

"Hearing loud and clear, Miss Albright. Ask Ryker about the damn spell."

As hard as it is to veer from the topic of my father, I take a quick detour to appease Bennett—who's yet to push to his feet. "If we're no longer under a Binding Spell, then why is Bennett here with me instead of back at Blackmoor? He was cursed to a dimension within the manor."

"Because you're under another spell—a Shadow Spell. As suggested by Archimedes. He *didnae* perfect the spell before you left, but he passed his notes onto me. I prepared and cast a modified version. When you landed in this century, you slammed right into our spell. What you're feeling is the ill effect of time travel coupled with the onset of a powerful enchantment. You'll recover soon enough and when you do—"

"Wait. Are you saying that wherever I go, Bennett goes?"

Ryker nods. "Hence the shadow reference."

"So we're still chained together?"

"But operating as separate entities." He raises an impatient brow. "It will have to do."

"But why? Why can't you just whip up a counter spell that breaks the curse? I'm already committed to partnering with Gabriel. I'm not going to turn my back on ESCA or the people at risk from rogue *FICs*. You don't have to force us to be inseparable."

"Yes, he does," says Bennett.

"Take note," Ryker says. "Bennett can still possess your body—should the need arise—but you have to invite him to take control, yeah? If you're truly Dom's daughter," he adds, "then rise to your heritage and work with Bennett to erase the Thames River Monster. Until you do, others will suffer his wrath. You'll find an electronic tablet containing directives near this monitor. The rest of ESCA, what's left of ESCA, is working to come back from the brink of extinction."

"Does that include my father?"

Instead of answering, Ryker looks over his shoulder, and then severs our connection.

"What the—" I stare at the blank screen, fuming. "Why did he cut me off? Why is he being so evasive about Dominic?"

"I'm surprised he told you as much as he did," says Bennett. "I think we can assume Dom is battling the potential invasion from within."

"Within *Fictopia*?" I flash on Grendel and at least a dozen other nasty literary villains. "Alone?"

"Most likely with an *Enabler*."

"But, you said no one, other than me, has ever seen a fractured border from this side. How did they cross into an alternate universe?"

He pushes his hair off of his exhausted face and nails me with a look that hammers my heart. "The same way Charlotte and I crossed over. Someone wrote them in."

THIRTY-SIX

A Diabolical Crime and Curse

EVERY TIME I think this adventure can't get more weird, it does.

I gawk at Bennett who's yet to recover from our spell-charged reentry into this century. Being physically tapped didn't stop him from delivering yet another otherworldly whammy.

"Someone *wrote* you and Charlotte into *Fictopia*?" I scrunch my brow. "How does that even work?"

Instead of answering, he tries to push to his feet, and fails. "Coldcocked by a damn spell."

He sounds incredulous. No doubt the slow recovery is hard on his *Warrior* pride.

"I'm shaky, too, but at least the urge to puke is passing." I test my own legs, climbing out of the time machine, while holding onto the side rail for balance. "I think I'm good."

"I'm impressed," Bennett says. "I feel like *shite*."

"I don't feel like dancing, trust me, but I can at least make it to you." With my messenger bag slung crosswise over my body, I hitch up the long hem of my skirt, determined not to trip. Dizzy and weak, I manage two steps then crumple to my hands and knees. "Crap." At least I saved myself from a face plant.

Bennett shifts to come to my aid, but I wave him off. "Stay where you are. I'm okay. I just…I need to take it slow. My head's spinning."

"Same here."

Unwilling to risk a second embarrassing tumble, I crawl to where he's sitting and collapse next to him against the wall. The three inches between us zings with our mutual frustration.

"I know," I say. "It's almost like we're back to square one." I study him and frown. "It's like the first day we met. If I look hard, you're vaguely transparent."

Which probably means if I touch him, my hand will go through him. My heart sinks. "I already miss our physical connection."

He crooks a brow. "Even though you hate me?"

In the moment that he whisked me away from my father, the fury was real. Now it's numbed by relief (Dominic's alive!) and a heavy dose of compassion for the man beside me.

"Words spoken in anger," I say. "I think you know how I really feel which makes this Shadow Spell especially sucky. You're here, but you're not."

Holding my breath, I reach for his hand, groaning when my fingers literally slide through his. Melting through Bennett's skin and bones is an eerie sensation, although I wouldn't call it gross. Getting slimed with monster puss and blood was gross. *This* is depressing.

Biting back an ugly curse, I knock my head against the wall. "I don't understand. If Ryker can link us with a powerful Shadow Spell, why can't he counter the curse that damned you to metaphysical limbo?"

"Because he doesn't know who initiated the curse nor is he aware of the specific magical elements. Charlotte didn't live to tell the tale and I couldn't communicate the facts. No one, aside from you, has seen or heard me since before that botched mission."

"But you said Dominic visited you at Blackmoor, that he shared things about ESCA and about himself on the off chance you could hear him. Obviously, *he* knew about your imprisoned fate."

"He knew about the curse, but he didn't know specifics. He learned the basics through whispers filtering out of *Fictopia*."

"All right, but *you* know who cursed you. Tell me so I can tell Ryker. Better yet, tell me everything relating to the incident."

I wait. I sigh. In Bennett's maddening silence, I glance at the darkened monitor. Ryker said I'd find a tablet containing directives on the table next to that screen. I assume his notes pertain to the Thames River Monster, but I'm also hoping they include instruction on how to report back to him. An email address? A videophone account?

One step at a time, Z.

Tackling a rogue *FIC* would be a lot less daunting with Bennett in the flesh and occupying *this* dimension, *my* dimension.

"Since we don't have the strength yet to take on Jekyll and

Hyde," I say reasonably, "let's make the most of this recovery time. I know you don't like to talk about Charlotte, but you have to move past the pain. Otherwise," I say, cheeks hot with resentment, "she died in vain."

Bennett eyes me. "That was harsh, Dove."

"I know and I'm only a little sorry. I feel partially responsible for her death." I gesture to the time machine. "You could have warned her while we were back there, but because of me, you didn't."

"Fair enough." He drags his hair off of his face and palms his temples. "One moment."

While he gathers his wits, I root in my messenger bag for a snack. Maybe a sugar rush will annihilate the lingering effects of travel lag and getting slammed with a potent spell. In addition to a chocolate bar, my fingers brush my phone.

Ridiculously happy to reconnect with modern technology, I power up. Or try to anyway. The battery's dead. "Rats." Spying an outlet, I pull a power adapter from my bag and wiggle sideways to plug it in.

"What are doing?"

"Charging my phone. Could come in handy when we leave here." I scoot back to his side. "Okay. Spill."

Looking annoyed, Bennett sits straighter against the wall as if bracing in uncomfortable territory. "June 1899. ESCA was reeling from a rash of *FIC* invasions, the most recent involving Dracula."

"*The* Dracula? Notorious vampire of Transylvania fame? "

"A particularly challenging case and one that drained our resources immensely."

"But you erased him, right?"

"Eventually, yes. But not without losses."

"Oh." A sobering reminder that not everyone working with the *Elite Society of Character Assassins* is immortal.

"We were overtaxed and exhausted," Bennett says. "Typically *FIC* invasions are few and far between. Not so that year. ESCA was concerned about the escalation and clueless as to where these rogue *FICs* were breaching universal borders, so we voted to go on the offense."

"Wait a minute. I thought you said Charlotte was aware of the fractured border running through the grounds of Blackmoor."

"She was. She heard plenty of activity coming from the other side of that border, but, at the time, it did not prove a source of entry."

"Got it. Sorry. Go on."

"Combining Henri's scholarly knowledge with Archimedes's innovative magic, and using an extensive library as our portal, Henri "wrote" a story wherein the featured characters—me and Charlotte—came alive in *Fictopia* as covert spies."

Rather than interrupting him again and voicing my wonder, I nibble at my candy bar and nod, urging him to continue. My creative writerly brain is eating up every fanciful nugget of Bennett's story.

"Our objective was to infiltrate various stories in progress throughout *Fictopia*, to observe and chronicle rogue rumblings, and to pinpoint various borders and specific, vulnerable fractures.

"We successfully floated from story to story as minor characters, never engaging—a body in the shadows, a face in a crowd. It was a tricky affair and without precedent, but Charlotte's keen tracking abilities eventually led us into a mystery horror story including a diabolical criminal similar to Professor Moriarty of Sherlock Holmes fame. Only in addition to being a ruthless intellectual, this villain is also versed in black magic."

I tense. I tingle. I'm riveted.

"His name is Professor Thornheart and although he's a brilliant character, the rest of the story—*The Case of the Rose-Colored Glasses*—was poorly written and failed to gain popularity with readers. Charlotte and I were unfamiliar with Thornheart, but *he* knew *us*."

My last bite of chocolatey sweetness turns bitter on my tongue. It's all I can do to swallow. "How?"

"His story, his 'lair' specifically, skims a fractured border, the border that runs through Blackmoor."

My heart pumps. "So you could see the Real World from the *Fictopian* side?"

"It was like looking through a warped and scratched window or a two-way mirror," Bennett says while staring into space. "Not at all like the colorful rippling veil that you described."

I sit straighter, pulse racing, brain humming. "Maybe it depends on which side of the border you're standing on. Or maybe the appearance of the fracture depends on the viewer. Eyes of the beholder and all that. Could Charlotte see the fracture from the *Fictopian* side?"

"Yes. We both saw Blackmoor and the surrounding grounds. We also heard a conversation taking place between our cook and gardener. Who knows how many times Thornheart witnessed *us* walking the grounds and talking?"

"So he could stake out the Real World and peek into your

lives, the way I watched the story of Beowulf and Grendel playing out."

"So it seems. Our confrontation was short and lacking in verbal queries or taunts. In the split second Charlotte and I realized he knew we were *Character Assassins*," says Bennett, "Thornheart attacked. He must have thought we'd been assigned to take him out. He fired a pistol aimed at me, but the bullet passed through and grazed Charlotte's shoulder."

"Oh, no." I massage my chest, trying to soothe the welling ache.

"The next part happened in a blur and haunts my days and dreams." Expression dark, he stares into space. "Fired up on fury and adrenaline, I shoved Charlotte toward the border and told her to run. We could see the fracture. I prayed she'd breach that window while I lurched at Thornheart. But dammit, she hesitated and called my name."

"She didn't want to leave you. Oh, Gabriel."

"Thornheart thrust out his left hand, pinning me to a wall with an invisible force while firing point blank at Charlotte. The bastard shot her through the heart. As I helplessly watched the light go out of her eyes, Thornheart chanted an incantation that damned me somewhere between both universes, trapped inside the walls of Charlotte's home, a house that will stand for eternity."

My heart is on the verge of imploding.

"As I felt myself dissolving from his lair and from Charlotte," Bennett says, Thornheart's last words and heinous laugh followed me into limbo. '*A mighty Warrior immobilized while I corrupt Fictopia and plot to rule Reality!*'"

I blink. I shiver. "*As long as he's chained, I'm free to conquer.*

That's what I heard when I first arrived on the grounds of Blackmoor. That was Professor Thornheart and he was referring to you. He's the one who's coordinating the *FIC* invasion. Charlotte's murderer." I blow out a breath. "Your worst nightmare."

"You have what Ryker needs," he says while shoving to his feet and shaking off his funk.

"Professor Thornheart from *The Case of the Rose-Colored Glasses*," I say while following his lead. Even though I'm still wrung out, it's more due to Bennett's sad tale. "If Ryker reads the book, will he learn whatever he needs to know about the magical elements you mentioned?"

"Yes."

"You said it's an obscure story. What if he can't find it?"

"Between him and Odion, they'll find it."

Even though he's fuzzy around the edges, even though I know I can't hug him, I move as close to Bennett as I can. "It wasn't your fault, Gabriel. You tried to save Charlotte—"

"I never should have taken her with me. An earthborn inside *Fictopia*. What the devil was I thinking?"

Heart thudding, I stare into his tormented eyes, waiting for him to confess what I've suspected for a while now. When he doesn't, I realize it's not something I really want to know. Not yet. It's too much to process, but I do ask him something else. "Why did Thornheart curse you into limbo? Why didn't he just kill you?"

"Because he didn't have the means."

"But a gun..."

Holding my gaze, Bennett says, "It will take more than that."

"Because you're immortal?"

"Not quite, but close." He reaches out, intending to brush

my hair from my face, but all I feel is a faint tickle. "Your gifts include clairaudience and a magical imagination. Mine include accelerated healing."

"Accelerated healing?" I raise a brow. "Is that even a thing? As in a 'real' thing?"

He cracks a hint of a smile that's more bolstering than ten chocolate bars. "In my world it is."

THIRTY-SEVEN

The Naked Truth

"DO YOU KNOW how to use that contraption?"

"It's a 2-in-1 laptop. Doubles as a computer with a keyboard and a tablet with a touch screen. I write all of my stories on something quite similar."

Even though Bennett's a 'shadow', I can feel him breathing down my neck. "Looks complicated," he says.

"If you can learn to drive a manual car in one lesson, you can learn your way around a computer. I'll be happy to teach you after we bust you out of that dimension."

"I admire your optimism."

"Dark imaginings aren't helpful, remember?" As the screen blinks to life, I tingle with an epiphany. "Why didn't I think of this before?" Stoked and smiling, I whirl. "Maybe I can free you from the curse with my imagination!"

"Thornheart's curse complicated by Ryker's modified

310

version of Archimedes's spell." He rubs the back of his neck. "A monumental feat for even the most seasoned practitioner. You, Miss Albright, are severely lacking in experience."

I raise a sardonic brow. "I almost knocked you to kingdom come, didn't I?"

"In the midst of a perfect storm, not by calm and calculated design."

"Well, jeez. Cynical, much? What happened to anything's possible?"

Taking a step back, he waves me on, inviting me to give it a go.

"No pressure," I mumble to myself, but then I imagine with all my heart and might.

I imagine pricking the invisible barrier between us like a bubble. I imagine shattering the walls of the bewitched dimension with a magical hammer. I imagine charging him and knocking us both clear of curses and spells.

All of those scenarios play out in my mind and yet Bennett stands before me, arms spread, waiting, and fuzzy around the edges.

I close my eyes.

Mindset, desire, and emotions.

In a herculean attempt to manifest a perfect storm, I conjure my most fervent fantasy. Remnants of a dream prompted by Penny and augmented by me. Whipped into a frenzy of longing and passion, I give my imagining voice. "One minute we're fighting side-by-side, kicking monster ass. The next we're tangled in sheets, doing the nasty and swearing allegiance."

I can see it. See him.

"Miss Albright."

Naked. Glorious. All man. My man.

"Zoe!"

Startled out of a deep state of imagining, I flush at the result. "Oh, my, God."

"Not helpful," Bennett says.

He's naked. Stark naked. And—*Holy Crow*!—SO AM I!

"Oh, my gosh. Sorry. So sorry." I spin away, showing him my backside as mortification spikes and my imaginings reverse.

"It's all right," he says with a twinge of humor in his voice. "Turn around."

Dizzy with a rush of emotions, I blink down at myself. I'm now wearing jeans, red chucks, a superhero tee, and a green cargo jacket. The clothes I wore when I first arrived at Blackmoor! I touch my face, my hair—even the style is the same, two long braids. "What the—"

Did I imagine us into the past, into Blackmoor? But, no. I'm facing Ryker's darkened flat screen and surrounded by sparse shelves of random eclectic gadgets. I'm still at HQ which—thank God—appears to be abandoned.

Bracing, I turn and face Bennett—half relieved, half sorry —that he, too, is fully clothed. Pinstriped trousers, a white shirt, a crimson vest, and a black knee-length coat. Dressed exactly as he was when we first met. A Victorian rake head-to-toe.

Head cocked, he tucks his hands in his trouser pockets. "*That* was illuminating."

"Please tell me that my mortification is worth it." I step closer, look closer. I frown. "It didn't work." My spirits dip as I reach out and melt though his arm. "It's as if we have the barest connection. Just enough to tease of your freedom."

Cheeks hot, I avert my eyes. "Sorry about the naked thing."

"Miss Albright. *Zoe.*"

I meet his dark, soulful gaze and melt in another way altogether.

"I'm no saint."

"Meaning?"

"I'm not sorry about the naked thing."

I blink and will my noodly legs steady.

"You're a striking woman and although you are very much off limits, if you persist in your flirtations, should we once again find ourselves in the same dimension, I cannot promise I won't succumb. But know this. It would complicate an already vastly complicated partnership."

Pulse racing, I swallow hard, struggling for a heartfelt reply. Instead, I give him two thumbs up. "Got it."

He gestures to the laptop. "The sooner you share pertinent information with Ryker, the better."

Better in a personal sense or a business sense? "Will do." Feeling gobsmacked and out of my league, I abandon talk of seduction and attack a login portal, hoping to gain access to Ryker.

"I wish I could ring him up via this flat screen for a two-way convo, but I don't see a way to do that. Looks like he has control and shut down the video feed on his end. If we're lucky," I say with a cringe worthy thought, "he disengaged the surveillance cams as well. Using my imagination to strip us both bare wasn't professional, to say the least."

"But it did shed light on your unique and powerful ability."

"Oh, it shed light on something, all right." Bennett's hot naked self is branded on my brain.

Focus, Z.

After five creative attempts at logging in, I remember that Ryker left directives for me *and* Bennett. This time I type in the obvious, utilizing various caps, symbols, and order. On the third try, I get it right.

USERMAME: zoe&gabriel

PASSWORD: 3722

The numerical code for *ESCA*. The code Bennett used to gain access to Quimby's reading room.

"Lazy, weak passwords," I mumble as I gain access to a 'welcome' note and two immediate files. "Says here that I should utilize the stored data to track the Thames River Monster. There's also a link to a secured email provider and info for an ESCA account."

"To be used to alert Ryker after we erase the monster," Bennett says while reading over my shoulder. "But otherwise for emergency contact only."

"Arming him with the information he needs to break Thornheart's curse," I say while speed typing, "counts as an emergency."

I relay essentials pertaining to Professor Thornheart and the curse, but then I pause. "How much should I share about Thornheart?"

"What do you mean?"

"You mentioned that Dominic warned of a potential traitor from within. Do you trust Ryker? Do I tell him that we suspect Thornheart's plotting an impending *FIC* invasion and that his point of entry could well be the fractured border on the Blackmoor estate? ESCA went underground because someone or something has been killing off *Enablers*," I say as my mind spins scenarios. "What if Thornheart arranged those killings in order to weaken ESCA, thereby increasing his odds of a successful massive infiltration?"

"You absorb information and muse like Henri," Bennett says, looking impressed. "As far as Ryker, Dom told him about you, a uniquely gifted daughter who he intentionally hid for years. He coordinated with Ryker to ensure you were protected via the Binding Spell and me."

I nod. "So we follow Dominic's lead and trust Ryker." I type. I wonder. "Is it possible for Ryker to share this information with Dominic?"

"I'm not sure."

"Could Archimedes communicate with you and Charlotte while you were in *Fictopia*? Or vice versa?"

"No. But there could be advancements that I don't know about."

I glance over my shoulder at Bennett who looks deep in thought. "Pointing Dominic directly to Thornheart would expedite his mission from within *Fictopia*," I say with welling concern. "But it would also put him and his *Enabler*, if he even has one, in the same position as you and Charlotte. Pitted against a diabolical mind with ruthless ambition. What if they suffer a similar fate?"

"Knowing Dom, he would deem the end worth the risk."

I blow out a breath. *"The needs of the many outweigh the needs of the few?"*

"If our suspicions and assumptions are correct, then Professor Thornheart has been plotting and engineering this invasion for almost two centuries." Bennett nails me with a troubling stare. "Imagine the Real World polluted with an army of heinous literary villains and their minions. On second thought, *don't* imagine. Better to channel your sunny, whimsical nature, Miss Albright."

"Positive thinking," I say with a shiver. "Happy endings. Right."

"Let Ryker and Dom worry about Thornheart. You and I are needed here in London."

"To protect innocents from the evil of Dr. Jekyll and Mr. Hyde. Right."

Adrenaline spiking, similarly to when I saw Grendel slaughtering helpless sheep, I continue typing our report. To think I suffered from writer's block for the last several months. My fingers are flying.

After a quick proof read I hit 'send'. "What if Ryker doesn't reply right away?"

"Then we carry on per his directives," Bennett says, while pointing to the file labeled: *Thames River Monster*. "At this point, any carnage inflicted on an earthborn by Jekyll and Hyde is blood on our hands."

And with that depressing thought I click open the file. Two paragraphs in, I blink. "Holy…"

"Shite."

THIRTY-EIGHT

Zoe's New Reality

"THIS CAN'T BE RIGHT." My heart pounds as I reread the opening portion of ESCA's report on the Thames River murders.

"A total of fourteen gruesome attacks and murders over the last two months," Bennett says while reading over my shoulder.

I flash back to the moment Watson first warned me about the 'Monster'. "Watson said the attacks had started *recently*. And the newspaper articles that we got from Odion were all dated within the last *month* and reported only *four* murders."

"Quite the discrepancy," Bennett says.

I pluck *The Strange Case of Dr. Jekyll and Mr. Hyde* from my messenger bag and leaf through the pages, looking for the articles. "Where are they?" I glance at Bennett. "You were reading this book in our room at the Thistle Inn." Was that last night? The night before? My concept of time is whacked. "Did you study the articles, too?"

"I did. But I placed them back inside the book when I joined you in bed."

Ah, yes. The nightmare and whiskey episode. I struggle to conjure a factual timeline. "I handled this book in the hotel room and also in the train compartment when I was going through the Victorian carpetbag."

"Maybe they fell out."

"Or maybe they no longer exist." I push out of the chair I'd pulled up to the table and rush over to the time machine. "The date you set for arrival and the one that shows here," I say while inspecting the calendar dial, "is the same date that we initially left this century."

"Meaning we were only gone for a few hours in real time," Bennett says. "But the date of the last murder in Ryker's report takes place, *took* place two days after we left."

"The timeline is off. Completely off! *Now* the murders started an entire month earlier and involved far more victims. Also, if the date of the last murder in the ESCA report is correct, then the calendar dial on the time machine glitched. What day is it really?"

I hurry back to the laptop, minimize the file and try to connect with the Internet. "I'm blocked. I have access to the private email server, but nothing more."

"Why does that matter?"

"Because I could confirm the day and year via the Internet. I could also search for the latest news here in London and globally. I could check in with Mr. Watson, with my editor, and with my aunt. How long were we gone and how else did we alter the previous timeline?"

I glance at my phone which is still charging. "We need to get out of here. I need cell phone signal."

"We're not going anywhere half-cocked, ill-informed, and unarmed. Breathe, Miss Albright, and stop thinking the worst. What happened to your irritating Pollyanna tendencies?"

"They've been polluted by Penny, you, and Grendel."

"Don't say that, Dove."

My temper flares. "Yesterday, the other day, *whenever*, you pegged my soft heart as your greatest vexation. You also called it my Achilles Heel."

"Assessments I stand by. But I'm also beginning to view your kind nature as a moral beacon. You challenge my cynical views and hardened ways. I don't like it, but I do see the value —for myself as well as other *Character Assassins*. Now sit. Let's go through the rest of the report and see what else we can learn."

I remind myself that he's my mentor, my protector, and that he has my best interest at heart. I tell myself that worrying won't change whatever alterations I initiated with the premature Grendel assassination. I sit and focus and try my best to *rise to my heritage*.

The report as provided by Ryker is extensive.

"Odion made it seem as though ESCA had only recently connected the Thames River Monster to Jekyll and Hyde," I say. "But this file says they already had a team working the case. The *Enabler* was killed and Ryker ordered the wounded *Warrior* away from London and into a safe house."

"Pulling a *Warrior* off of a case, especially when they'd documented a critical lead, demonstrates how dire circumstances are for ESCA," Bennett says.

He's referring to the part of the report that mentions *The*

London Crier. A newspaper account regarding a break-in at a scientific facility specializing in research linked to the Jekyll/Hyde Syndrome.

"A lab that's experimenting with meds to combat personality disorders," I say. "And Dr. Jekyll is breaking in to tweak or replicate the serum that unleashes his evil alter ego? It seems too obvious."

"One way to find out."

"So we go there and stake the place out. If he's there, we erase him. If he's not there, we walk the bank of the Thames until I can hear his thoughts and then we track and erase him."

Bennett points to a section of the report. "Ryker even devised the WOD."

An enchanted *Weapon of Destruction* designed to destroy the specified rogue *FIC.* "It's hidden in the Quest Room." I close out the file and shut down the device. "The sooner we do this, the better. Let's grab the WOD and roll."

Desperate to know the day and year and to touch base with Julia and Liza, I stow the slim tablet in my messenger bag and unplug my phone from the outlet.

Bennett scowls. "We need to discuss the specifics of the assassination."

"We can talk and walk."

Just then I hear a ping and Ryker appears on the flat screen. "I got your message," he says in a terse voice. He looks me over, noticing my drastic change of clothes, but not commenting. Thankfully. If my mentally engineered stripshow was caught on camera, I'd rather not know.

"Even with those specifics pertaining to the curse," he says, "devising a counter spell will take time, but I'm on it, yeah? As for Professor Thornheart, I'm on that, too. Did you read through the file, Miss Albright?"

"I did. *We* did. We're on our way to pick up the WOD and then we'll head for the facility. I know you can't promise, but I...*we* would be grateful if you could break the curse before we face the monster."

"Just remember what I said. You can invite Gabriel to inhabit your body. He'll get the job done and the citizens of London will be safe from an evil *FIC's* carnage. At least for now, yeah? Just *donnae* make it personal."

I scrunch my brow. "What?"

"We deal in professional hits, not revenge killings."

I blink. I tense. My pulse and adrenaline rev as the screen goes black.

⸸

"Slow down, Miss Albright."

"No can do." I'm race-trotting through the underground tunnels that lead back to Quimby's antiquarian book store. "Just keep directing me!"

The last time we made this trek, Bennett was inside me. In fierce control of my body, he propelled me through these dank catacombs without voicing instruction. This time he's shadowing me and I'm reliant on verbal guidance. Although I'm no longer spooked about tripping over coffins or rats or spiders, I sure as sunshine don't want to get lost. The sooner we get above ground, the sooner I can ease another fear altogether.

Before leaving ESCA HQ, Bennett directed me to collect a few gadgets. A neon glowing 'torch' to light my way, a smaller

BETH CIOTTA

version of the Neutralizer gun Odion had aimed at me, and a small case containing some sort of 'distracters'. They're all tucked into a leather backpack along with the WOD, and slung over my shoulders along with my jam-packed messenger bag. Although I'm weighted down, my red chucks are flying over uneven ground.

Fear of losing a loved one is a powerful motivator.

"A right here and up those stairs," Bennett says. He's behind me, but close on my heels. I swear I can feel him breathing down my neck as I take the narrow stairway two steps at a time.

I hit a wall—literally—at the top of the landing. Winded, I turn and face Bennett. "The reading room?"

"Yes. But make sure it's vacant before you enter."

He directs me to another one of those stone sliding peep holes. I have to stand on my tip toes to see through. A table and chairs. Shelves and books. But otherwise... "Empty," I report. "Where's the thingamajig to trip the entrance? Or is there a code?"

"You're learning, Miss Albright."

"Just tell me."

"I'm thinking."

That's when I remember he only has secondhand experience with Quimby's and the alternate underground access route to MOMI. It's a modern precautionary detour. One he learned about from Dominic.

"There." He points to a camouflaged keypad. "Try ESCA in reverse."

I punch in 2273 and the wall slides open just enough for me/us to squeeze through. Once inside I flop on the floor and dig out my phone. I hit speed dial.

Liza, Liza. Please answer. Come on, come on.

I'm greeted with a beep and an automated message. *"The number you have dialed is no longer in service."*

Stomach knotted, I quickly dial her husband only to learn... *No such number exists.*

"What the..."

Bennett crouches in front of me. "What's going on?"

I wave him off while calling Julia. On the third ring she answers. "Zoe. Honey. It's the middle of the—"

"Have you heard from Liza?"

After a tense moment of silence, she sighs. "Honey, are you high? Medicated?"

"What? No!"

"You have to come to terms with this."

"To terms with what?"

"Are you really going to make me say it?" She blows out a breath. "Liza's gone, Zoe."

"I know. She's on an extended vacation in Tahiti with her new husband."

"Sweetie, these delusional scenarios have got to end. Liza is dead. Dead and cremated. You can't wish or imagine your aunt back to life."

No, no, no. I want to scream, but I don't. I try to speak, but I can't.

"Dwelling in denial is one thing," Julia goes on, "but spinning alternate truths? Liza never married and she didn't go to Tahiti. She flew to London, something about old family business. The very first night, while walking from a restaurant back to her hotel, she was tragically murdered by a serial killer. The papers even gave him a name. The Thames River—"

"Stop!" *Oh, my God!*

"Not until you accept the awful truth."

I press my back into the wall, refusing to double over in a pathetic ugly cry. Bennett reaches for me, melting through my hand and making me feel even worse. "When? When did Liza die?" I ask, struggling to accept this horrible twist in the timeline.

"Almost two months ago. Zoe, for the love of...I flew to Wyoming to be with you when her remains were flown home. I don't mean to be cruel but, sweetie—"

"She got married eight months ago," I persist. "I've been living on my own for eight—"

"You've been on your own for two months, Zoe." She blows out a frustrated breath. "Two months. Not eight. You flew to England to get closure on your aunt's death, to explore an unexpected inheritance, and to overcome your writer's block. I thought you were on the road to recovery but now... I fought to renew your contract, but maybe it's better that I lost."

Certain my head's going to explode, I palm my forehead in a ridiculous attempt to keep my brains intact.

"Time to explore new avenues, kid. I'm sorry for the rough timing, but your sales have been slipping and... "

"I've been dropped." The sting of having my book series canceled is muted by the news of Liza's death. "I have to go." On the verge of hyperventilating, I disconnect.

"Your aunt's dead?" Bennett's stooped in front of me— within touching distance and yet untouchable. Cursed to another dimension and hovering on the fringes of my life.

My body and brain rage with the awful truth and crappy circumstances.

"Killed by the Thames River Monster. I can't believe..." I

massage my aching chest. "That's what Ryker meant when he said not to make the assassination personal."

I'm incredulous. Furious, bereft, and reeling. "Liza's blood is on my hands."

"Don't go there, Dove."

Trembling with guilt and anger, I push to my feet. "We have to go. We have to do our job."

"Not when you're in this state of mind."

I blow right through him. "I'm not willing to risk even one more attack." I hike the backpack with the WOD higher on my shoulders and exit the reading room, emotions churning. "I know what to do and I'll do it with or without you."

THIRTY-NINE

In the Name of Justice

MY THOUGHTS ARE A HOT MESS. A tangle of 'what ifs' and 'what-the-freak'.

I don't need Bennett to warn me about the danger of being distracted and yet he's doing just that as I race-walk through Quimby's.

"Erasing a *FIC*, killing anyone or anything, isn't cut and dry. Especially for you," he says. "You go out of your way not to trample flowers, for bloody sake. In addition to possessing a WOD, focus and objectivity are vital. Reign in your emotions and harness your imagination, Miss Albright. Otherwise, I will delay a confrontation until you're of sound mind."

"And how do you propose to do that?" I snap as I sidestep a cart of books and a sleeping cat. "You're a shadow. It's not like you can wrestle me to the ground or lock me in a room.

Unless I invite you to inhabit my body, you have no control over me physically."

"Ramped up emotions and a false sense of confidence are counterproductive. You can't protect the citizens of London or mankind in general if you're dead."

I freeze in my tracks and whirl. "Stop doing that. Stop marking me as some kind of Bi-universal messiah. I'm a writer, not a savior."

"You're both." He holds my angry, conflicted stare, reminding me that, even though he's trapped in another dimension, Gabriel Bennett—*Warrior*—is a force to be reckoned with.

I blow out a breath. "Listen. I get it. I'm destined for something more than a publishing career or a quiet life in seclusion. But I can't think about the bigger picture or a greater purpose right now. I'm supposed to keep my imagination in check, remember? Once we wrap this assignment, we can discuss the future. I'm not even sure of my freaking past anymore. Apparently the last few months, if not more, have been revised."

Someone coughs.

Startled out of my one-on-one with Bennett, I look behind me and see a familiar face. The short, scrawny, senior dude who'd been shelving books when I initially entered the store is now seated behind the cashier counter and regarding me with a raised brow and a cocked, balding head.

Glancing to where he's nodding, I see a woman with an armful of books walking his way and frowning in my direction.

I know that look. She thinks I'm talking to air. She thinks I'm nuts. I used to hate that freaking look. The pity. The ridicule. Now I'm indifferent. I don't even care enough to pretend I'm talking on my phone. I just turn and resume my exit, whizzing through the creaky main door and out onto the 21st century version of Great Russell Street.

Talk about culture shock.

Even though my view is muted by dense grey fog, I recognize the fashion, technology, and vehicles of my own time.

Instead of being comforted by the modern sights and sounds of the vibrant city, I'm wistful for the sense of belonging that I felt with Henri and Archimedes. Both Odion and Ryker lack the warmth of their predecessors. I shiver with the feeling of being thrown to the wolves. *Sink or swim*, I can almost hear Ryker saying. Sure, he waved a wand and partnered me with one of ESCA's greatest *Warriors*, but that *Warrior* is in metaphysical limbo.

"Can we walk to the institute?" Bennett asks while surveying the congested street.

I consult a map on my phone. "No." I peer through the haze, toward the British Museum. "There's a bunch of cabs over there. Come on."

While crossing the street, my ears buzz with a low level hum that intensifies to a muddled roar—ghostly woes from a nearby dead zone. I'm not spooked, but I am wary. Now's not the time to get waylaid by a tortured soul like Abigail. After years of avoiding ghosts, I'm not sure I'll be able to turn my back on a needy specter ever again. Best not to test that theory now.

I dig through my bag and silently celebrate the fact that Charlotte's *Baffles* still exist. They could have disappeared like the newspaper articles that used to tucked inside my

Stevenson novella. Respecting their function and her memory, I press the bejeweled earplugs into place.

Achieving audible serenity, I slide into the backseat of the lead black taxi and relay the address for the scientific facility to the smiling, young cabbie.

After commenting on the pea-soup fog and the snarled traffic, the driver engages in flirty conversation as he pulls into the bumper-to-bumper fray. Not long ago, I would've welcomed his flattering remarks, but that was before I fell hard for a *Character Assassin*, and long before I knew I was Bi-universal and potentially responsible for 'the wellbeing of mankind'.

"Tell him to sod off," says Bennett.

I temper the cabbie with kinder words then scowl at my mentor, who, I remind myself, is invisible to our driver. I don't know if Bennett's jealous or overprotective or just in need of my full attention. Dressed in an authentic period suit, he looks like the proverbial fish out of water. He *is* a fish out of water, a man out of his time, and yet he's fully in the moment.

"How is it I'm experiencing cultural shock," I grumble under my breath, "and you look so at home?"

"Because I'm focused on the now. On you and a dangerous mission. As soon as we reach the facility," he says, "invite me to meld. We'll track and erase the monster together. As one. Understood?"

I nod, but I'm only half listening. Checking the date on my phone, I see that it's three days later than indicated on the time machine. Did another 'me' exist and carry on in this century while 'I' was training in the past? Or did my contemporary self 'go missing'? My brain hurts even wondering how that works.

I check for emails and texts and voice messages. *Nothing.* It's as if my phone was wiped clean of exchanges during the time hop. I wonder what I'll find on my personal laptop? What else changed in my life aside from losing Liza and my publishing contract?

Liza.

Even though our relationship was strained, she was the woman who reared me. She was blood.

My heart aches while questions swirl like the fog. What kind of old family business brought her to London? Was it something to do with ESCA? With my inheritance? Did Dominic enter *Fictopia* before or after she was killed? Did she suffer greatly? Was her end as horrific as my mother's? Will I ever know the specifics of either woman's death?

My life as I knew it flashes before my eyes as Bennett lectures WOD protocol in my ears.

I'm remembering all of the years Liza cared for me, all of the sacrifices she made in order to give me shelter and a tailored education. All she did to keep me *safe.* Instead of dwelling on her controlling nature and our awkward kinship, I'm focused on her selfless devotion. I'm holding those memories tight and hoping they don't fade as my life detours with the altered timeline.

When the taxi stops in front of the institute, I turn away from memory lane and toward the subject at hand. I pass the cabbie my credit card, the one given to me by Watson, hoping that it works.

It does.

My inheritance, at least, is still intact.

"Not much action in these parts on a weekend," says the cabbie. "You take care now, Miss."

"Will do. Thanks." Noting the sparse traffic—vehicular *and* pedestrian—I shake off a chill. Then again, the fog is thicker here and the daylight dim. Visibility sucks. Considering what I'm about to do, I guess that's a good thing.

"Invite me inside," Bennett says as I/we push out of the taxi and onto the curb.

As soon as the taxi's taillights disappear in the mist, I slip into the shelter of an alley. I shift the *Weapon of Destruction*—an injection gun loaded with a charmed toxic serum—from the backpack to my jacket pocket for easy access. I tell myself erasing the Thames River Monster isn't revenge; it's justice.

"Miss Albright…"

I remove the *Baffles*. I listen. I track.

"I hear him." *Un-freaking-believable.* "What were the chances of an instant connection?"

Bennett's looking left and right, peering into the shadows and mist. "You're sure it's him? You didn't study the entire story."

"I *know* the story. Everyone knows the story." I shiver as the monster laughs. "*Unscientific balderdash, my arse*, he just said. He's thinking about the modified potion he just took. He's excited about the extended metamorphose."

"As Jekyll or Hyde?"

"I don't know. What does it matter. It's him!" And I'm going to stop the carnage *now*!

Heart pounding with the righteousness of a vigilante, I hurry toward the sound of the rogue *FIC's* thoughts. Extending my arms, I feel my way through the disorienting fog. "This weather is right out of a horror movie. Nice touch. *Not.*"

"Dammit, Zoe…"

"He's thinking about the man he brutally beat to death, the girl he trampled and the woman he…" I trip on something, catching myself before I fall. Hands braced on my knees, I fight the urge to puke. "He stabbed a woman to death," I say in a choked whisper, "and then he cut her heart out. I hope to God that wasn't Liza."

"In the novella, Hyde's method of killing never reached that level of barbarity," says Bennett.

"Henri warned me about character distortion. She said stories that have been published the longest have an escalated readership, and therefore the featured characters are even more powerful. She cautioned that the Mr. Hyde of my time could be a warped or intensified version of the Mr. Hyde as first written in 1886." I gasp. I straighten. "He's on the move."

Bennett reaches for me, his hand melting through my arm. "Invite me to fuse, dammit."

"I will, but not until we see him. I'm afraid once you're inside me, you'll overpower my ability to hear and track." And with that, I take off, knowing Bennett is on my heels and mad as hell.

Distracted now, I tear around the corner and slam into a sinister figure. Not a troglodyte, but a man. A man with an evil aura. "Dr. Henry Jekyll," I squeak.

In response, he grabs me by the throat.

FORTY

Dove vs. Hawk

CHOKING.

Panicking.

My toes are barely touching the ground. My back's mashed against a wall.

Frantic, I claw at my assailant's hands in an attempt to break free of a suffocating chokehold.

I flash on Abigail's gruesome strangulation. I share her visceral terror. But unlike that tortured soul, I'm not begging for my life. I can barely breathe, let alone speak. I'm in primitive survival mode—scrabbling with a vengeance.

Don't want to die a horrific death! Don't want to die AT ALL! I want to live to save innocents from monsters like you! Back off, back off, back off!

Just as my vision darkens around the edges, he lets go. My legs give way and I collapse into a wheezing, boneless puddle.

"Where's your partner, little girl?"

I gulp air, struggling to breathe, struggling to think.

My attacker crouches in front of me. His eyes are dark and wild and drilling into my soul. "*Enablers* don't work alone. That's what you are, right? I've no patience for your kind."

"Then…" *gasp, cough* "why are we having this…" *cough* "conversation?"

He laughs—a wicked, ugly sound that fouls the air. "Aren't you the cheeky one?"

Through the dazed roar in my ears, I hear another voice. "Invite me the hell inside, Zoe."

My partner. My mentor.

A Warrior.

Bennett's hovering over Jekyll (or is it Hyde?) in a menacing fashion—not that Jekyll's aware of his other-dimension presence. Once inside me, we'll attack and the 'Thames River Monster' will revert to *Fictopia*. I want that with all my angry, hurting heart, but what if this monster has information on Professor Thornheart and the impending invasion? What if he can help us?

What if?

"I expected an ugly, hairy monster. A deformed troglodyte," I croak. This man, this murderer is far from hideous looking. He's quietly handsome, well built, and dressed as a 21st century business professional. I easily see him passing as one of the facility's staff.

His lip twitches. "Look closer and you'll see the grotesque."

The fiend within the angel? "*Man is not truly one, but truly two,*" I recite from memory.

"You know my words."

"Robert Louis Stevenson's words."

"Ah. My Maker. The writer who gave me life. And penned my death," he says with a scowl. "I choose to live, little girl."

"And to kill." Fury fuels my efforts as I push to my feet. I'm not so little and I will not cower. "You murdered my aunt."

He rises along with me, towering over me by at least a foot. "Your aunt, you say? The *Enabler* who tracked me the first time?" He grunts. "She threatened my new reality. She got what she deserved. I wish I could say the same for her *Warrior*. Which prompts me to ask once again, where's your partner?"

Liza wasn't an *Enabler*. At least, not in the life I knew before the altered timeline. I tell myself that detail doesn't matter. Not at this moment. What's pertinent is that she was one of fourteen innocents murdered by this immoral deviant.

"Where is the good in you?" I ask. "The doctor who forfeited his life to put an end to the fiend who stole his conscience?"

"That version of myself acted rashly on the presumption that Hyde—*the heinous troglodyte*—would take over this body," he says while dragging a hand over his clean-shaven face, "permanently. And that I would be caught by authorities and punished for Hyde's...*my* atrocities. My thinking is no longer that rigid or pathetic. I'm thriving in the Real World and no one, especially some pathetic, vengeful *Enabler* is going to stop me."

As he spews ugly, arrogant crap, I notice changes in his appearance. The transformation from man to monster—at least visually speaking—is happening before my eyes.

He shrinks in height even as his fingers grow abnormally long. His broad shoulders hunch. His eyes sink into their sockets. His teeth yellow and morph into a fanged overbite.

And that's only the beginning.

It/he is changing into something more hideous than I would ever willingly imagine. Henri didn't come close to replicating his bizarre deformities.

Did the writers who produced multiple adaptations of Stevenson's story contribute to this severely augmented version of Hyde? Is Jekyll and Hyde's intensified darkness connected to Fan Fiction and the violent impulses of fringe Gamers?

Is this character distortion to the max?

More disturbing than the horrific changes to his body is the evil oozing from his aura and infecting the air. I cough, choking on the depravity. Why, I wonder, would any writer want to create such a vile character?

Bone-deep fear rivals morbid fascination. Both keep me rooted as he talks through the transformation. It's as if he's showing off. Or maybe he's trying to frighten me to death —*literally*. His thoughts on the good and evil within us all are chilling. Especially since his inner demon is running amok.

Transfixed and conflicted, I battle my own duality. Gentle-hearted freak vs. Bi-universal Badass. Dove vs. Hawk. How do I kill without forever tarnishing my soul?

Bennett bristles in the wake of my inaction. "You're playing with fire, Zoe. You're scatty if you think you can reason this *FIC* back into *Fictopia*."

And then I remember I want information. In his arrogance, Jekyll's assuming I'm scared stupid by his terrifying metamorphosis. Although I'm shaking in my chucks, I still have my wits and my gift. Mentally spying, I eavesdrop on the rogue *FIC's* thoughts, listening for any reference to Thornheart or the invasion as the transformation reverses and monster reverts to man.

"As you can see," Jekyll says while rolling his hunched shoulders back to normal, "I'm still experimenting. I have surrendered to the 'greed of curiosity' and accepted my 'true self.'"

"Show's over," Bennett warns me. "Invite me inside. *Now!*"

Flexing his fingers, Jekyll creeps closer. "I'll enjoy this."

I jerk the WOD from my pocket and take aim. Cursing my trembling hands, I will my voice strong. "Stay back!"

He hesitates, but laughs. "You may want to kill me, but you won't. There's not enough darkness in you, little girl."

"You're wrong!" But before I can invite Bennett to meld, Jekyll lunges, knocking the WOD from my grasp and punching me hard in the jaw.

Knocked off my feet, I crumple—ears ringing, vision blurring.

Jekyll straddles me, unleashing a barbaric rage and landing blow after blow.

I think I'm fighting back. I'm not sure. So much pain. My pain. Liza's pain. And the pain of thirteen others. On the verge of blacking out, I imagine this monster burning in hell.

The pummeling stops. Screaming ensues.

I swipe blood and tears from my mouth and eyes and squint toward the panicked roar.

Jekyll's suit is afire and he's slapping at the flames.

My conscience struggles as he drops and rolls and the fire intensifies.

Can't watch. Can't listen. And I don't have the strength to put him out of his misery. "Gabriel!" I rasp. "Join me! Help me!"

He possesses my body in a heartbeat. Strength surges through my broken self as I/he/we reach for the WOD. Braving flames, we press the gun to Jekyll's neck and inject him with the charmed serum.

The man, the monster explodes into tiny pieces of gore.

It's messy and shocking but then... Random gore morphs into scattered words. Literal words. Countless words. They float in front of my eyes and then swirl into a frenzied tornado. A flurry of visible dialogue and narrative that blows upward, taking the fog with it as the essence of a *FIC* vanishes from earthly sight.

I'm fascinated. Sickened and fascinated.

Zoe Albright: *Character Assassin.*

I don't know whether to cry or cheer.

"We'll talk about this later," Bennett says.

He's no longer my shadow. He's the *Warrior* within. Instinctually, I know if I ask him to leave, I'll die. My eyes are almost swollen shut, but I can see blood on my hands. The monster's *and* mine. I also sustained a few burns and I'm pretty sure my nose is broken along with a few other bones.

"You're in a bad way, Zoe."

"No, shit, Sherlock."

My vulgar snark surprises us both. On Bennett's steam, I make it to where I dropped the ESCA backpack and my messenger bag. "Need to let Ryker know that we erased the rogue *FIC*," I say.

"In due course," Bennett says as he/I/we dig out my phone instead of ESCA's tablet. *"This Sherlock needs your Watson."*

FORTY-ONE

The Cost of Defiance

THE DRIVE from London to Blackmoor blurs, much like the first time Watson chauffeured me from the city airport to the country manor. I'm even wearing the same clothes. Only this time I'm not jetlagged and trashed on wine. I'm monster-whipped and possessed by Bennett.

Fortunately, Watson was doing business in the city when I called him so wait time was minimal. Even so, by the time he picked me/us up near the scientific institute, the worst of my visible injuries—swollen eyes and lip, bloodied nose, singed and bruised skin—had mostly faded. With Bennett inside me, I'm not only benefitting from his strength and experience, but also from his gift of accelerated healing.

Unfortunately, my inner wounds—sprained and bruised muscles and a few broken bones—are healing at a much slower, painstaking rate. Even with Bennett absorbing the brunt of my anguish, I hurt all over. I'm also exhausted and somewhat disoriented.

Secured in the passenger seat of Watson's little black car, I'm staring distractedly at the passing countryside.

"Are you sure you don't need a doctor?" Watson asks for the second time since leaving London.

"I'm sure. I know I look bad, but I'm just achy and rattled," I lie while sliding on my purple-tinted shades.

"Considering you took a tumble down a stairway, I'm surprised you don't look worse."

I did look worse, much worse, but I keep that fact to myself and thank my lucky stars that Watson actually believes my concocted story. Even though Bennett trusts the solicitor enough to get me/us home, he's still wary of imparting the man with any information pertaining to ESCA.

"I just need some R&R," I say with a forced smile. "You know. Rest and relaxation?"

Watson smiles back in the same shaky fashion. "Understood." He focuses back on the road. "I'll have you back at Blackmoor in a jiff."

"Thanks." I turn away and slump against the window, feigning sleep. I'm not up for conversation. I'm barely up for breathing.

That said, my brain is hobbling along, trying to make sense of my new reality. Since we're still melded, Bennett has access to my thoughts and feelings. Taking advantage of something more than his medicinal powers, I mentally sort through my muddled circumstance.

"Watson thinks I spent the last three days exploring the city and conducting research for a new Penelope Pringle story." I think, while reflecting on our brief and surreal phone conversation.

"Unless you remember it differently," says Bennett, *"we'll take Watson's version of events as gospel."*

"All I remember is what I experienced in Victorian London. I documented everything in the journal Henri gave me because I worried my memories would be wiped when we returned to this century. I'm happy that's not the case. Those experiences opened my eyes to new purpose and passion, but I'm totally confused about the altered timeline. My new reality consists of losing my aunt, my publishing contract, and almost getting killed by a rogue FIC."

"You could have circumvented the latter if you'd invited me to meld when I first instructed you to do so."

I cringe at the reprimand. I know he's right. Even though I had my reasons, logical reasons (for the most part) for the delay.

"Warriors and Enablers who work as a team need to trust one another implicitly," says Bennett. *"When dealing with a rogue FIC you've defied me twice now."*

His displeasure is evident. But instead of ruffling my feathers, it fills me with dread. *"Meaning?"*

"Our relationship is severely flawed, Miss Albright."

I swallow hard. *"You mean our working relationship."*

At first he doesn't answer, which is bad enough, but then he blindsides me with questions of his own. *"Do you know how I felt watching as Grendel nearly crushed you to death? Or looking on helplessly as Hyde beat you within a breath of your life?"*

I put myself in his shoes. My pulse races and my spirits sink. *"I can imagine."*

"You do that, Dove, and don't hold back."

I hear his frustration, sense his anger. I try taking solace in knowing he deeply cares about my welfare, about me, but I can't. Even though Bennett's inside of me, I feel a rift between us that's a mile wide. *"I'm sorry."*

"So am I."

He falls silent then and, even as I feel his healing energy working its magic on my bruised and broken body, my aching heart weeps.

"Miss Albright. Zoe."

Someone squeezes my arm. I jerk awake and strike out.

"Crikey."

"Easy, Dove."

Two distinctly different male voices.

Bennett is in my head, in my body, although his presence is sluggish—like me. Watson is sitting beside me, rubbing his cheek.

I flush. "Oh, my God. Did I *hit* you?"

"My fault," says Watson, looking shell-shocked while unbuckling his seat belt. "I startled you."

Did I pass out? Fall asleep? What the hey?

"Apologies," says Watson.

"No, no. I'm the one who's sorry. I was…"

"Discombobulated?"

He smiles now and I smile back—a genuine smile. One of Penny's words and, as a huge fan of Penelope Pringle, one of his daughter's favorite words as well. "I feel rude for not asking before," I say as I gather my wits and bags. "How is Mimi?"

His smile slips as he shoves his trendy glasses up his nose

and then cuts the engine. He looks puzzled or perhaps at a loss for words.

I blink. I tense. *Please don't say you don't know who I'm talking about. Please don't let your daughter be a casualty of the altered timeline.*

"Don't borrow trouble," says Bennett while controlling my hand and pushing open the door.

I fight him to stay in the seat a moment longer, and win. *Huh.*

"Unfortunately," says Watson, "Mimi's anxiety attacks have intensified instead of lessening."

Mimi still exists. Thank goodness. Although I'm sorry for her woes. "That must be upsetting, not only for your daughter, but for you and your wife. Not to be nosey, but do you know the source of Mimi's anxiety?"

"Oh, yes," he says looking somber now. "It's the loss of her mum."

Oh, no. "I'm so sorry. I didn't know. You didn't say."

"It's still painful and not something I like to talk about. My wife perished in an automobile accident."

My heart pounds. "When?"

"Ten months ago now. Seems like yesterday. For me and obviously for Mimi."

I tell myself that this was the case even before the altered timeline and that his wife didn't die because I defied Bennett. It's selfish, but I'm already guilt ridden and it *could* be true.

"Yes, it could," Bennett says.

His voice sounds raspy to my ears and suddenly I'm filled with new alarm. Is he losing himself to me? Am I draining his resources by soaking up his restorative powers?

Hearing my thoughts, he responds, *"Just get us inside."*

Something is definitely wrong.

"Sometimes Mimi misses her mummy so much, she thinks she sees her," says Watson. "Wishful thinking, according to the child psychiatrist, and mostly I agree."

My skin prickles. Wishful thinking? As in *just her imagination*? Although the death of my mother played out differently for me, I instantly and deeply empathize with Watson's young daughter.

"But sometimes..." Watson says while gazing at Blackmoor. "Sometimes I wonder if maybe, just maybe, Alicia is watching over Mimi. That she haunts Mimi, the way Lady Charlotte Moore and Gabriel Bennett supposedly haunt Blackmoor." He laughs then. "You must think me ridiculous."

I touch his arm. "I don't. I totally don't." Shivering from Bennett's impatience, I hurry on. "I'm so sorry for your loss, Watson. And for Mimi's distress. Maybe I can visit her sometime and chat with her about Penelope." And perhaps have a chat with Alicia—if her ghostly presence is truly an issue.

Watson reverts to his lighter demeanor. "That would be lovely."

"I'll even write Mimi a special story."

"I say... That's extraordinarily kind of you, Miss Albright. *Zoe*."

"My pleasure. It's the least I can do. Thank you for the ride, Eb. I'll be in touch." I swing out of the car, swallowing a yelp of pain when I push to my feet.

Watson shouts out. "At least allow me to escort you to do the door. After all, you're still shaken."

"For bloody sake," Bennett complains.

"I'm good. Honest," I say to Watson. "And I don't want to

keep you from Mimi one second longer. Thank you again. Drive safe."

I wave while turning toward the manor. For cripes' sake, even waving hurts.

"That's because you're still healing," says Bennett. *"Apparently I can only do so much. You need to get off of your feet. You need rest. As do I."*

That last part hastens my pained steps. "You're hurting because of me. I'm so sorry."

"I'm not. But get your arse inside and out of Thornheart's view."

The fractured border.

I'm tempted to turn around, to search for the rippling veil, but that would mean defying Bennett's instruction. *Again.* I resist with all my might and, no doubt, with a little of his.

I keep walking and, with the front door in sight, I acknowledge a connected and troubling realization. "Why don't I hear voices? We drove through a dead zone. We're surrounded by a fractured border. Why..." I palm my ears. *"Baffles.* No wonder. I don't remember putting these in."

"You didn't need the distraction of otherworldly drama. You, we, needed rest. I prompted you to insert the Baffles just as you were dozing off."

And again I'm filled with concern that I've somehow put Bennett at risk.

Retrieving the key card from my messenger bag, I disengage the security sensor and open the door.

Watson beeps his farewell as he drives away. If it weren't for Bennett, I'd feel abandoned and, yes, scared. My skin crawls knowing that Professor Thornheart—the *FIC* who murdered Charlotte and cursed Bennett, the fiend who prompted Jekyll and Hyde to infiltrate reality, the mastermind behind an upcoming invasion—could be watching me from the backside of the *Fictopian* border.

Rushing inside and shutting the door, I expect Bennett to instantaneously eject from my body like he did in past meldings.

He doesn't.

"Compliments of Ryker's Shadow Spell," he reminds me. "You have to verbally evict me, but don't do it until I help you upstairs. You won't make it on your own."

Mind and body more weary by the moment, I don't argue. "Whatever it takes for both of us to recuperate," I say as we slowly ascend the massive stairway. We have a lot of work to do."

He doesn't answer.

Shifting the weight of the backpack and messenger bag to my other shoulder, I suppress my mounting dread regarding our alliance. "I know you're angry with me. I know you don't trust me. But know this Gabriel, I'm not giving up on us—professionally or personally.

"I have a lot of questions," I rush on in his maddening silence, "and some doubts and concerns. But I'm dedicated to the task of foiling Thornheart's impending invasion. Whatever it takes. You and ESCA have my allegiance."

Something he once claimed he wanted more than my admiration.

"Your allegiance," he says, "but with divided focus."

I pause on the top landing to catch my breath. "What do you mean?"

"Watson. His daughter. His wife. You spent a lifetime avoiding dead zones and now you're ready to explore your mother's moonlighting ventures?"

I bristle at his condescending tone. "The ghostly intervention with Abigail was terrifying, but it felt good to help her crossover. Also, after all we've been through over the last few days and given all I've learned, I'm not convinced that Victoria's 'horrific demise' was related to a ghost. It could have been *FIC* related. I'm hoping Dominic will have some answers for me when he gets back from *Fictopia*."

"If he gets back."

"That was harsh," I say as I/he/we resume our trek. "And pessimistic. I'm going to meet my father, one way or another. I feel it in my bones. Speaking of," I say as we breach Charlotte's bedroom. "How much longer before I'm totally healed?"

"I have no point of reference. As with many things pertaining to you, Miss Albright, this is a first. But this I know. You're operating on days of little sleep and the fall out of time travel and FIC interventions. Rest is imperative. For both of us."

Concerned for a whole lot of reasons, I crawl onto the bed and prop myself against the pillows. "Since I'll be severely weakened after you leave me, please stay inside a bit longer. After I type the report for Ryker, we'll split like a banana."

He doesn't reply, not that I expected him to. Moving as fast as I'm able, I pluck the ESCA tablet from my bag and power up. "We have wireless Internet connection up here. Bonus."

I sign on to the ESCA account and type an email to Ryker.

Mission complete. Thames River Monster erased. Just so you know, Jekyll wasn't part of Thornheart's massive invasion. He was a singular distraction prompted by Thorn-

heart. The professor's army of literary villains won't be so easy to track.

"You pried into Jekyll's thoughts," says Bennett.

"Yup," I say, fingers pecking at my less than speedy norm.

Due to my inexperience and reckless judgement, I was injured during the assassination. Bennett is helping me to mend. We are at Blackmoor recovering. Hoping to join you and ESCA soonest in order to stop Thornheart. Not to rush you, but releasing Bennett from his curse and all connected spells would be helpful.

Thanks, Zoe

I send the message and almost immediately hear a ping. "That was fast."

I click onto the Ryker's response.

Good work and good news. I'm closing in on a counter spell. Will come to you within the week. Until then, stay put.

–Wiz

"You're welcome," I say with a trace of snark. "Kind of a cold fish compared to Archimedes," I say as I power off.

"All I care about is the counter spell," Bennett says as I set

aside the tablet and stretch out on the bed. *"Free of the curse. Free of Blackmoor."*

"Free of me?" Heart heavy, I sigh and flutter my hand. "You can make like a tree and leave."

"Your juvenile word choice—"

"Get out of my body, Mr. Bennett."

"As you wish, Miss Albright."

Instead of ejecting with force, he gently peels away. With his departure comes pain. *My pain.* I blink back tears, determined to bear my injuries with dignity. I'd be dead if it weren't for Gabriel Bennett.

He's beside me now, propped on one elbow, and peering down at me. "It will pass."

I assume he's talking about physical wounds and not my aching heart. His gaze is wholly professional. He's not fully solid, but God he looks good. Knowing he can no longer read my mind, I think to myself: *You look hot even when you're wrung out. So not fair.*

And then I say aloud, "About our future, as mentor and prodigy, I mean. When you're free of the curse—"

"We have a lot to sort out. Get some sleep, Miss Albright."

"As you wish, Mr. Bennett."

FORTY-TWO

Illuminating Ruminating

I WAKE WITH A START.

Muddled thoughts. Heavy limbs.

I palm my forehead, slick with sweat, and curse a dull throb.

Where am I?

Squinting through my dazed fog, I'm greeted by angels.

Panic sparks adrenaline and—*poof*—my vision clears.

I sigh. I smile.

Not angels. *Cupids.*

I'm not dead. I'm not floating on a cloud or flirting with heavenly beings. I'm cocooned in fluffy blankets and staring up at a romantic mural.

Charlotte's ceiling. Charlotte's bed.

Anxious, I roll to my side, hoping to find Charlotte's *Warrior.*

No such luck.

Even though I'm disappointed by Bennett's absence, I take it as a good sign. He recovered enough to get up and go. He's back to his cursed self and brooding somewhere within the walls of Blackmoor.

Knowing him, he's in the library studying a copy of *The Case of the Rose-Colored Glasses,* reacquainting himself with Professor Thornheart's villainy, while awaiting the arrival of Ryker and his liberating spell.

That thought slaps me full awake.

"What time is it? What day?"

I nab my phone from the nightstand, check the time, the date. "Okay, okay. Good. That's good." I only slept through the rest of the day and night. It's scarcely dawn.

New day. New start.

I stand and stretch. I marvel.

Bennett, or rather his restorative powers, worked miracles. I walk across the beautifully decorated room—a room frozen in 19ᵗʰ century splendor—without an ounce of discomfort. No limp. No shortness of breath. No pain in my jaw.

I wave at my reflection in the mirror mounted over mahogany vanity. No ache in my wrist. Gone are the agonizing injuries of my monster mauling.

I feel fine. Great even. I look fine, too. No bruises or scratches. No swelling or burns. What's more, my broken nose healed perfectly straight.

My braids are frizzed and my clothes are rumpled, but otherwise I'm perfect. *Strike that*, I think after getting a noxious whiff of my pits. *I stink.*

My tee, I realize, is not only wrinkled, but sticking to my

skin. Did part of the healing process involve profuse night sweats?

I turn to make sure I'm still alone.

I am.

No sight or sound of Bennett.

Determined to look and feel my best before tracking him down to 'sort out' our alliance, I nab my toiletry bag and a selection of clothes from my screamingly 21st century flamingo pink suitcase. First stop: Charlotte's gloriously deep, *pink* Victorian tub.

The longer I soak in a scented warm bath, the more I absorb the crappy aspects, as well as the intriguing prospects, of my new reality. The more I compare 'what was' with 'what is' and ponder the potential magnitude of several 'what ifs', the greater my impatience.

By the time I primp my hair and makeup and pull on jeans, a black tee, and a pair of kick-ass boots, I'm ready to take on the world. More precisely, the diabolical *FIC* intent on conquering this world. But first, I have to square things with Bennett.

As anxious as I am to find him, I put on the brakes long enough to make the bed I slept in. According to Watson, Charlotte was a neat freak. Arranging the bed covers and pillows the way she preferred them and removing my clutter from her nightstand and dressing table is the least I can do. By no wishes of her own, I inherited her home as well as her *Warrior*.

After consolidating and storing my phone, journal, personal laptop, and ESCA tablet inside the society's backpack, I hide my personal luggage and dirty laundry under the dressing table.

Later, I'll do one better and move all of my stuff into a different bedroom. One I can make wholly mine. Maybe on a different floor or in the closed-off wing. Whatever room I choose, I silently vow to squash my clutter-bug tendencies.

At first, I accepted the otherworldly clean-up crew as a personal bonus. No housekeeping chores or expenses for me. *Woot!* Now it strikes me as disrespectful to rely on the magical force, enchantment, *whatever*, to keep the manor dust-free and ever-spruce. Now I can't disassociate the fantastical tidiness from Lady Charlotte Moore herself. Maybe she *is* haunting Blackmoor after all, just not in a typical ghostly sense.

On the off chance she can hear me (stranger things have happened), I belatedly introduce myself by way of a soul-baring ramble.

"Once upon a time," I say while leaving her room with my tech bag, "I led an uneventful and sequestered life. I considered my inherited clairaudience my *Misfortune*. I inhaled energy-infused food and drink, *Scrambled* to block disembodied voices, and embraced the lifestyle of a recluse rather than risking dead zones to explore and engage in reality-based relationships.

"I channeled my imagination through a pretend friend turned muse," I continue while descending the grand staircase, "and enjoyed a career as a prolific author of Penelope Pringle's whimsical adventures."

In my mind, I fast-forward over details and emotions

pertaining to my aunt and my mother and father. The truth of it all is distorted by evasion, lies, and now, an altered timeline. Something I need to come to terms with somehow, some way. As Bennett would say, *in due course.*

Stepping down from the last stair onto the gleaming, marble floor, I offer Charlotte a final glimpse of the Zoe Albright 'who was'. The social misfit and reclusive writer. A young woman who'd been sheltered and manipulated into believing she was a defective oddity and therefore unsuited for meaningful alliances.

Life before Blackmoor was not only regimented, but filled with injustice.

"Once upon a time," I rasp, "I couldn't imagine a sane man willing to engage in a relationship with a freak like me. Then I met Gabriel."

Considering our illuminating adventure thus far and the daunting journey yet ahead, I'm finally able to look beyond my girlish crush and to recognize the immense value in Bennett as mentor and protector. "I hope you don't mind, Charlotte, but I need him."

A heartfelt admission that receives no response. Not that I expected one. And with that, I slip into the one room I swore I'd never enter.

The first thing that strikes me about Blackmoor's breath-taking library is that Bennett isn't in it. *No need to linger,* I tell myself. And then I do just that.

I can see why Watson assumed I'd eagerly adopt this space as my writer's lair. It's a bibliophile's dream.

Three walls are dominated by recessed floor-to-ceiling bookcases, beautiful wooden shelves crammed with hundreds of hardcover books. A spiral staircase leads to a wood and iron balcony—easy access to the second tier of the massive literary collection.

The fourth wall, paneled in the same rosy wood as the shelves, is bisected by elaborate floor-to-ceiling windows. The view of the manicured grounds is stunning, even under dismal overcast skies.

A hanging tapestry and large Turkish carpet add warmth to the already cozy ambience along with the muted glow of period enhanced lighting.

The furniture, like everything else in the manor, is what we would now call antique, yet it looks relatively new and wonderfully inviting. As beautiful as the ornate writing desk is, I'm drawn to the plush oversized sofa with its many pillows and the coordinating octagonal library table. Spying a nearby outlet, I decide to set up shop here instead of the conservatory.

I keep expecting Bennett to float over the threshold or to emerge through a secret panel. This has got to be where he reads and researches *Fictopian* affairs. Since we need to discuss Professor Thornheart's invasion and my future with ESCA, this feels like the right place to be.

Feeling as comfortable as I can, what with Bennett being angry with me, I settle on the sofa and arrange all of my devices on the table in front of me. The longer I dwell in this room of literary wonder, the more I'm jazzed.

My fear of breaking into hives when in close proximity to physical books has, at this point, waned. I walked through Quimby's antiquarian bookstore twice. I sidestepped and stepped over piles of books in Henri's house. Not once did I experience a full blown allergy attack. Even when I handled Robert Louis Stevenson's novella, all I felt was an odd tingly itch. Nothing I can't live with.

Maybe I've outgrown the bizarre allergy or maybe as an adult I've built up immunity. Or maybe it really *was* psychosomatic, and yet another notion instilled in me by Liza—a protective measure pertaining to my *FIC* side. Who knows?

Even so, rather than skim the massive library collection for a hard copy of *Beowulf* (which could take forever), I fire up my laptop. I've been twitchy with curiosity ever since I asked Bennett how he defeated Grendel and he answered, *"The same way as Beowulf."*

Connecting with the Internet (thanks to ESCA's high tech upgrades to the manor), I conduct my research as I usually do. Digitally.

HOW DID BEOWULF KILL GRENDEL?

One tap of a key and the answer appears.

I read. I blink. I cringe. "He ripped the monster's arm off with his bare hands?"

I'm simultaneously grossed out and bowled over. Does this mean Bennett is also gifted with superhuman strength? Or maybe magic was involved? Either way, he tore off a being's arm. The viciousness of the act is troubling and yet I tell myself not to judge. After all, I set Dr. Jekyll on fire.

I'm still wrestling with that atrocity. Me, who avoids trampling wild flowers.

Once again, I glance toward the entrance and then over my shoulder. "Where are you, Gabriel?"

Uneasy now, I trade my personal laptop for ESCA's tablet. My pulse skips when I see a new message. If the time stamp is correct, it came through at two in the morning. "Crap."

Counter spell created. On my way.
   –Wiz

Smiling, I pump a fist in in the air. "Yes!"

But then I start wondering.

Where is Ryker coming from? How long is the trip? Was he already here and gone? Did he show up in the middle of the night and perform his magical woo-woo? Did he break the Shadow Spell and Thornheart's curse with one or multiple incantations? Is Bennett free of the bewitched dimension? Unchained from Blackmoor as well as me? Did he take off with Ryker, intent on rallying whoever's left of ESCA while leaving me sequestered and supposedly safe within Blackmoor?

What if, what if, *what if!*

Springing to my feet, I blow out of the library, calling his name as I race-walk through the main floor. The drawing room where we first met and argued. The foyer and conservatory where we also argued.

"Dammit, Gabriel, where are you?"

Torn between anger and panic, I head for the downstairs kitchen, grateful I memorized the route the one time we ventured there. The trek is long and freaking lonely. When Bennett led the way, we talked the whole time. Now I only have my thoughts to keep me company and they're creeping me out. Do I seriously want to go down those steep stairs, down into the bowels of the manor where something nefarious could be lurking in the pantry and waiting to gobble me up?

Um, no. Not even the promise of java and cookies can lure me below.

First, I yell down the stairwell for Bennett.

No answer.

Then I order myself to rein in my imagination before it kills me. More evidence that I need a mentor. Someone who can help me understand my Bi-universal gifts. Someone who can teach me to wield my imagination in a controlled and beneficial way instead risking the unpredictable chaos of a perfect storm.

Heart pounding, I spin and retrace my steps. If Bennett is free of the curse, maybe he's testing his freedom. Maybe he's strolling the grounds or staking out the fractured border—not that he can find it without me.

Once in the foyer, I pause at the front door. I'm not afraid to go outside. I'm not afraid of the voices. But I am worried Thornheart might see me. If Bennett is free and conducting ESCA business, the last thing I want to do is muck up his progress.

I swipe my clammy palms down my jeans and blow out a breath.

"You're an *Enabler*," I tell myself. "The Bi-universal daughter of Victoria Albright and Dominic Sinclair, two of ESCA's fiercest *Character Assassins*. You are a uniquely gifted WIP and Gabriel Bennett is your sworn mentor and protector. Wherever he is, he'll be back."

I repeat that proclamation like a mantra as I return to the library and settle on the sofa. "He'll be back."

In the meantime, distraction, *positive* distraction, is imperative. Remembering my promise to Watson, I open a new file on my laptop. As soon as I think of Mimi, a story comes to mind. It's whimsical and uplifting.

And it features Penelope Pringle and Balderdash.

FORTY-THREE

One Prodigy's Dream

"BLOODY HELL, Zoe. What have you done?"

That voice. I know that voice. Love that voice. Well, except for when he's chastising me. Bennett sounds annoyed, but *whatever*. I smile and open my eyes. "You're back."

He frowns in response. His eyes are dark and stormy, like the first time we met, and he's studying me with an intensity that makes me shiver. Although my trembling could be due to the cold. I'm freezing.

"I'm *naked!*" Mortified, I snap fully awake. "You're naked, too!" We're in bed together. *Naked together!* "What the...?"

Did I dream the bit about waking up before? About bathing and dressing and going downstairs in search of him? Has he/we been here the whole time? Only...

Where the heck is *here?*

I'm suddenly and fiercely aware of my highly quirky

surroundings. The wall treatments and furnishings resemble the Victorian decor of Henri's modest home. Except, the color scheme is off. Vivid purple and bright pink. Sunny yellow with splashes of red. "This isn't Charlotte's room."

"This isn't Blackmoor."

Gathering my dazed wits, I pull the fruity-scented blanket over my breasts and palm Bennett's sinfully handsome face. My heart hammers with joy. "You're solid. Whole. Real. Just like you were when we traveled back in time."

"Ryker showed up early this morning. He broke Thornheart's curse."

"You're free of the bewitched dimension?"

"And all associated spells. We took a short drive off of the estate in order to discuss ESCA business a safe distance away from the fractured border. One minute I was sitting in his car discussing a plan, and the next..." He gestures to me, to the bed. "What the hell?"

Discombobulated, I fall back on an overstuffed pillow and blink up at the purple ceiling. "I was sitting in the library writing a story for Mimi. It started off as a short story about Penelope and Balderdash, but then I got distracted by thoughts of you. Of you and me and how we can never be. Because, well, for all sorts of reasons according to you."

Heart in throat, I slide him a look. "I revised our circumstance and wrote us a happy ending."

"Shite."

"Crap!"

We spring out of bed as if it's on fire and our lives are at risk.

Wrapping myself in the fluffy pink blanket, I gawk as Bennett pulls on a pair of badass black leather pants.

So much for harnessing my unprofessional crush.

We hurry to a window that's shaped like a flower and marvel at a steampunk version of London. Fanciful hot-air balloons and steam-powered airships populate smog-free blue skies. Below us, the poop-free streets are crowded with mechanical horses and funky cars. It's market day and my cartoonish version of the Victorian city is bustling with colorful characters in outlandish, fantastical fashion.

"It's exactly as I imagined," I say in shocked awe. "Exactly as I typed and saved it. Penny's story. Our story."

On cue, Penelope Pringle and her pup partner sail past our third-story window on her flycycle. Wearing goggles and smiles, both she and Balderdash give me a cocky salute.

"Bloody brilliant," Bennett says as they pedal toward an airborne dog park. "You wrote us into *Fictopia*."

"Or imagined us in." So much for suppressing my Utopian nature and creative madness. "I'm so sorry."

"I'm not." Bennett puts his arm around me and pulls me close to his side. The gesture is more protective than affectionate, but I'll take it. "I don't know what you're fully capable of, Miss Albright, but we're going to find out."

"Meaning?"

"We'll find Dom and work together to squash Thornheart's plan to dominate the Real World. ESCA has never succeeded in policing fractured borders from this side. Then again," he says, while glancing down at me, "we've never had a Bi-universal colleague."

Colleague as in cohort as in associate. I flash back to 1898 while inside the Quest Room with Bennett, Archimedes, and Henri. To the first and only time I ever felt connected to kindred souls. As if I'd found my tribe. It's a treasured memory and I'm over-the-moon thrilled that Bennett didn't taint it by referring to me (as he has in the past) as a Bi-universal 'savior'. A notion that sets me apart, whereas 'colleague' suggests I'm part of a team.

Speaking of... I *may have* I wrote caricatures of Archimedes and Henri into this story. I know I definitely *thought* about it. Does that mean we'll find some version of them here in this alternate universe? For now I keep that exhilarating thought to myself.

My heart's happy dancing for all sorts of reasons, but after tangling with two other villainous *FICs*, I also have the good sense to be scared. We'll have to navigate *Fictopia*, a minefield of endless literary tales, in order to locate *The Case of the Rose-Colored Glasses*.

Passing through stories-in-progress without calling attention to ourselves or disrupting the existing plots will be a challenge. Also every story has a villain of some sort. In Penny's adventures, it's the mean-spirited Crankalopasys.

Shudder.

"Since you've been here before with Charlotte," I say, "I assume you know how to travel from one story to the next."

"I do. But be warned, Dove. Story-hopping is not for the faint of heart."

"Lucky for you *and* me, I'm ready to embrace my destiny." Absorbing the fantastical, fictional world beyond this absurdly-shaped window, I'm breathless with wonder and purpose.

The prospect of finding my father and forging a bond fills me with giddy anticipation. Joining forces to save the Real World from an apocalyptic invasion is a daunting, but motivating bonus.

I'm pumped and ready to cultivate my Bi-universal gifts.

I'm ready to slay monsters.

I'm sure as sunshine anxious to nurture my alliance with key members of the *Elite Society of Character Assassins*. Most especially with the society's two special recruits.

"You do realize that one or both of us may not make it back to the Real World," says Bennett.

"I haven't forgotten what Thornheart did to Charlotte. Or you."

"And in order to find Thornheart, in order to protect humanity," he gestures to our half-naked selves and the fairy tale outside, "we'll need to abandon our 'revised circumstance.'"

"I won't lie. That part stinks."

"Then why are you smiling?"

Holding my enigmatic *hero's* gaze, I tingle with an epiphany. "Because I'm a work-in-progress. I don't need to know every detail of the upcoming chapters of my life. The thrill is in the unexpected twists."

Ready to fly-by-the-seat-of-my-pants into a genre-bending adventure, I squeeze my mentor, my *Warrior*, my friend and partner's hand. "Because when I typed THE END, it was only the beginning."

NOTE TO READERS

Thank you for indulging my imagination and for joining me on this fantastical heartfelt adventure! Zoe, Gabriel, and *The Elite Society of Character Assassins* have been crowding up my mind for *years*. I'm so thrilled that I finally had the opportunity to bring them to life. If you enjoyed THE ASSASSIN'S PRODIGY, please consider writing a review on any relevant e-tailer or a review site (such as Goodreads). Positive reviews and word-of-mouth recommendations are gold for any author.
Your support is appreciated!

Interested in more of Zoe's extraordinary quest? Visit my website for updates regarding *The Elite Society of Character Assassins*. While there, you can also explore my other worlds. From steampunk to paranormal to contemporary romance. Something for everyone!

ACKNOWLEDGMENTS

It takes several professionals to bring a book to life. I very much appreciate the efforts of my agent, Amy Moore-Benson, as well as the opportunity to initially write this story in serial form via *Radish Fiction*. A unique and welcome experience.

My undying gratitude to Mary Stella for her eagle eye, publishing experience, and stellar copy editing. Her support and praise during the creation of Zoe's tale were invaluable!

I'm also indebted to Elle J. Rossi of *Evernight Designs*. In addition to the technical formatting of this story, she created not one, but two inspired covers for THE ASSASSIN'S PRODIGY. The serialized and novelized artwork are vastly different and equally stunning! Elle is a creative rock star of many talents, including storytelling. How lucky am I to also call her critique partner, friend, and sister?

A special shout out to my artistic soulmate, Cynthia Valero—

my champion, my friend, and a constant source of inspiration. A huge thank you to my marketing advisers: Bards of Badassery. You know who you are. (Rachel Aukes, Elle J Rossi, and Cynthia Valero) And my everlasting gratitude to my husband, Steve, for supporting my every dream!

ABOUT THE AUTHOR

Storytelling comes naturally to award-winning author Beth Ciotta. Dubbed "fun and sexy" by *Publisher's Weekly* and "delightfully imaginative" by the *Chicago Tribune*, Beth is published in contemporary, historical, steampunk, and paranormal romantic fiction, as well as speculative (genre-bending) fiction.

Beth lives in NJ with her husband, two zany dogs, and a crazy cat. A veteran professional performer, Beth now pours her artistic passion into her writing. To sign up for her newsletter and to learn more about her colorful life, visit her website at www.bethciotta.com

37724673R00224